(o A

Jack M..... ....acher, and motivational trainer, and is now a full-time writer. Eleven of his novels have been Nebula finalists. *Seeker* won the award in 2007. McDevitt lives in Georgia with his wife Maureen.

Praise for Jack McDevitt:

'You're going to love it even if you think you don't like science fiction. You might even want to drop me a thank-you note for the tip before racing out to your local bookstore to pick up the Jack McDevitt backlist'
Stephen King

'A real writer has entered our ranks, and his name is Jack McDevitt'
Michael Bishop, Nebula Award winner

'Why read Jack McDevitt? The question should be: Who among us is such a slow pony that s/he isn't reading McDevitt?'
Harlan Ellison, Hugo and Nebula Award winner

'You should definitely read Jack McDevitt'
Gregory Benford, Nebula and Campbell Award winner

'No one does it better than Jack McDevitt'
Robert J. Sawyer, Hugo, Nebula and Campbell Award winner

LC

B000 49

D1423808   LIBR.. .RIES

Jack McDevitt titles published by Headline:

The Alex Benedict Novels
A Talent For War
Polaris
Seeker
The Devil's Eye
Echo
Firebird

The Academy (Priscilla Hutchins) Novels
The Engines Of God
Deepsix
Chindi
Omega
Odyssey
Cauldron

Jack McDevitt
SEEKER

headline

Copyright © 2005 Cryptic, Inc.

The right of Jack McDevitt to be identified as the Author of the
Work has been asserted by him in accordance with the Copyright,
Designs and Patents Act 1988.

First published in Great Britain in 2013 by
HEADLINE PUBLISHING GROUP

First published in 2005 by Ace Books
A division of Penguin Group (USA) Inc.

1

Apart from any use permitted under UK copyright law, this publication may
only be reproduced, stored, or transmitted, in any form, or by
any means, with prior permission in writing of the
publishers or, in the case of reprographic production,
in accordance with the terms of licences issued by
the Copyright Licensing Agency.

All characters in this publication are fictitious and any resemblance
to real persons, living or dead, is purely coincidental.

Cataloguing in Publication Data is available from the British Library

ISBN 978 1 4722 0311 3

Typeset in Sabon LT Std by Palimpsest Book Production Limited,
Falkirk, Stirlingshire

Printed and bound in Great Britain by
Clays Ltd, St Ives plc

Headline's policy is to use papers that are natural, renewable
and recyclable products and made from wood grown in sustainable forests.
The logging and manufacturing processes are expected to conform to
the environmental regulations of
the country of origin.

HEADLINE PUBLISHING GROUP
An Hachette UK Company
338 Euston Road
London NW1 3BH

www.headline.co.uk
www.hachette.co.uk

For T.E.D. Klein and Terry Carr with my appreciation

Acknowledgments

I'm indebted to Michael Shara of the American Museum of Natural History, to David DeGraff of Alfred University, and to Walter Cuirle, for advice and technical assistance. To Jerry Oltion, for reading and commenting on an early version of the manuscript. To Ginjer Buchanan, for editorial assistance. To Ralph Vicinanza, for his continuing support. And, as always, to my wife and in-house editor, Maureen McDevitt.

Prolog

We advise that our patrons not attempt the slopes today, other than the Blue Run. A distinct danger from avalanches is still present throughout the skiing area. It would be prudent to remain in the chalet, or perhaps to consider spending the day in town.

1398, RIMWAY CALENDAR

Wescott knew he was dead. There seemed little chance for Margaret, either. Or for his daughter. He had followed the instruction and stayed inside and now he lay beneath tons of ice and rock. He could hear weeping and screams, lost in the dark around him.

He was trembling in the cold, his right arm crushed and pinned beneath a fallen timber. He could no longer feel the pain. Or the arm.

He thought of Delia. Just beginning her life and almost certainly swept away. Tears ran down his cheeks. She'd been so anxious to come.

He closed his eyes and tried to resign himself. Tried to place himself again aboard the *Falcon*, where he and Margaret had met. Those had been priceless years. He'd known the day would come when he would wish he could go back and do it all again.

1

The *Falcon*.

My God. It occurred to him that, if Margaret had not escaped the building, their discovery would die with them. Delia knew about it, but she was too young to understand.

They had told nobody! Except Mattie. Mattie knew.

He tore at the timber, tried to drag himself free. Tried to change his angle and get his feet against it. He had to survive long enough to tell them. Just in case . . .

But Margaret was not dead. Could not be dead.

Please, God.

The cries and screams around him dwindled, became occasional moanings. How long had it been? It seemed like hours since the chalet had crashed down on him. Where were the rescue workers?

He listened to his own labored breathing. The floor had shaken, had stopped, had shaken again. Then, after the shocks, when everybody in the dining room had thought maybe it was over, he'd heard the sudden roar. They'd looked at one another, some people had gotten up to run, others had sat terrified, the lights went out, and the walls had imploded. He was pretty sure the floor had collapsed and that he was trapped in a cellar. But he couldn't be certain. Not that it mattered.

He heard distant sirens. Finally.

He pushed at the timber that held his arm. He didn't feel entirely connected to his body anymore. He'd retreated into his head and looked out, not unlike a spectator hiding in a cave. Beneath him, the ground trembled again.

He wanted to believe Margaret had survived. Bubbly, immortal, farseeing Margaret, who was never, ever, taken by surprise. It didn't seem possible she could be caught in all this, swept aside in that single terrible moment. She'd gone back to their room to get a sweater. Had left just moments before it had all happened. Had gone up the staircase and vanished forever from his life.

And Delia. In the apartment. Eight years old. Sulking because he'd refused permission for her to go out on her own, I don't care if they're saying the Blue Run is safe, we'll wait until we hear everything's okay. The apartment was on the third floor, toward the front of the building. Maybe it had been spared. He prayed they were both standing out there somewhere now, in the snow, worrying about *him*.

When they'd issued the warning, they'd said the chalet was safe. Safe and solid. Stay indoors and everything will be okay. Avalanche-free zone.

In the dark, he smiled.

They'd been sitting in the dining room with their newest acquaintance, Breia Somebody-or-Other, who was from his hometown, when Margaret had gotten up, said something about now don't you two eat all the eggs I'll only be a minute, and walked off. A group of skiers stood near the front doors, ready to go out, angrily complaining about the level of caution at the chalet and how Blue Run was for beginners. Two couples sat amid potted plants enjoying a round of drinks. A heavyset man who looked like a judge was descending the staircase. A young woman in a gray-green jacket had just sat down at the piano and begun to play.

Margaret would just have had time to reach their room before the first shock came. The diners had looked around at each other, their eyes wide with surprise. Then the second jolt, and the fear in the room became palpable. There'd been no screams, as best he could remember, but people were throwing back their chairs and starting for the exits.

Breia, middle-aged, dark-haired, a teacher on vacation, had looked out the window, trying to see what was happening. His angle was bad so he couldn't see much, but his hair stood straight up when she gasped and whispered *Run* in a terrified voice. Without another sound she threw back her chair and fled.

Outside, a wall of snow appeared and bore down on them. It had been smooth, rhythmic, almost choreographed, a crystal tide flowing down the side of the mountain, engulfing trees and boulders and, finally, the heavy stone wall that marked the perimeter of the chalet's grounds. As he watched, it swept over someone.

3

Man or woman, it happened too quick to be sure. Somebody trying to run.

Wescott had sat quietly, knowing there was no place to hide. He took a sip of his coffee. It was as if time had stopped. The desk clerk, a simulation, blinked off. So did the host and one of the doormen. The skiers near the front door scattered.

Wescott held his breath. The rear and sidewalls blew into the dining room and there was a sharp pain and the sensation of falling.

Somewhere, doors slammed.

Something wet was running down his ribs. Tickling him, but he couldn't reach it.

Breia hadn't gotten out of the dining room. She was probably within a few meters. It was hard to speak. He didn't seem to have much air in his lungs. But he whispered her name.

He heard a voice, far away. *'Over here.'* But it was a male voice.

And then there were boots chunking through snow.

'See if you can get him out, Harry.'

Somebody was digging.

'Hurry.'

No answer though from Breia.

He tried to cry out, let them know where he was, but he was too weak. No need anyhow. Margaret knew he was in trouble, and she was surely out there somewhere, with the rescue workers, trying to find him.

But a deeper darkness was coming. The rubble on which he lay was fading, and he stopped caring about the secret that he and Margaret shared, stopped caring about the timber that pinned him down. Margaret was okay. Had to be.

And he slid away from his prison.

1

. . . But what provided the truest sense of the antiquity of (the Egyptian tomb) was to see graffiti scrawled on its walls by Athenian visitors, circa 200 C.E. And to know the place was as old for them, as their markings are for me.

—Wolfgang Corbin,
The Vandal and the Slavegirl, 6612 C.E.

1429, THIRTY-ONE YEARS LATER

The station was exactly where Alex said it would be, on the thirteenth moon of Gideon V, a gas giant with no special characteristics to recommend it other than that it circled a dead star rather than a sun. It was in a deteriorating orbit, and, in another hundred thousand years, according to the experts, it would slip into the clouds and vanish. In the meantime it was ours.

The station consisted of a cluster of four domes and an array of radio telescopes and sensors. Nothing fancy. Everything, the domes and the electronic gear and the surrounding rock, was a dark, patchy orange, illuminated only by the mud brown gas giant and its equally mud brown ring system. It was easy enough to see why nobody had noticed the station during several routine

5

Survey visits. Gideon V had just become only the third known outstation left by the Celians.

'Magnificent,' Alex said, standing by the viewport with his arms folded.

'The site?' I said. 'Or you?'

He smiled modestly. We both knew he wasn't good at being humble.

'Benedict strikes again,' I said. 'How did you figure it out?'

I hesitate to say Alex ever looked smug. But that day he was close. 'I am pretty good, aren't I?'

'How'd you do it?' I'd doubted him all the way, and he was enjoying his moment.

'Simple enough, Kolpath. Let me explain.'

He had done it, of course, the way he always did things. By imagination, hard work, and methodical attention to detail. He'd gone through shipping records and histories and personal memoirs and everything else he could lay hands on. He'd narrowed it down, and concluded that Gideon V was an ideal central location for the exploratory operations then being conducted by the Celians. The planet, by the way, was given the Roman numeral not because it was the fifth world in the system. It was, in fact, the only one, the others having either been swallowed whole or torn from their orbits by a passing star. It had happened a quarter million years ago, so there'd been no witnesses. But it was possible to compute from the elliptical orbit of the remaining world that there had been others. The question up for debate was their number. While most astrophysicists thought there'd been four additional worlds, some put the probable total closer to ten.

Nobody really knew. But the station, several hundred light-years from the nearest occupied world, would be a treasure trove for Rainbow Enterprises. The Celians, during their golden age, had been a romantic nation, given over to philosophy, drama, music, and exploration. They were believed to have penetrated deeper into the Aurelian Cluster than any other branch of the human family. Gideon V had been central to that effort. Alex was convinced

6

they'd pushed well beyond, into the Basin. If so, there was considerably more to be found.

Several centuries ago, the Celians had gone abruptly downhill. Civil war erupted, governments across the home world collapsed in chaos, and in the end they had to be bailed out by the other members of what was then known as the Pact. When it was over, their great days were also over. They'd lost their fire, become conservative, more interested in creature comforts than in exploration. Today, they are possibly the most regressive planetary society in the Confederacy. They are proud of their former greatness and try to wear it as a kind of aura. *This is who we are.* But in truth it's who they *were*.

We were in the *Belle-Marie*, maybe twenty thousand kilometers out from the gas giant when the domes rotated into view. Alex makes his living trading and selling artifacts, and occasionally finding lost sites himself. He's good at it, seems almost to have a telepathic sense for ruin. Mention that to him, as people occasionally do, and he smiles modestly and ascribes everything to good luck. Whatever it is, it's made Rainbow Enterprises a highly profitable operation and left me with more money to throw around than I would ever have thought possible.

The thirteenth moon was big, the third biggest among twenty-six, the biggest without an accompanying atmosphere. Consequently it had been the first place we'd looked, for those two reasons. Large moons are better for bases because they provide a reasonable level of gravity without having to generate it artificially. But you don't want one so large that it has an atmosphere. An atmosphere is always a complicating factor.

As far as we were concerned, vacuum had another advantage: It acts as a preservative. Anything left by the Celians when they closed up shop six centuries earlier was likely to be in pristine condition.

If you could have thrown sunlight on Gideon's dark rings, they would have been spectacular. They were twisted and divided into three or four distinct sections. I couldn't be sure. It depended on your angle of vision. The thirteenth moon lay just beyond the outermost ring. It moved in an orbit a few degrees above and below their plane, and the result would have been a compelling not-quite-edge-on view had there been any light to speak of. The gas giant itself, as seen from the station, never moved from its position halfway up the sky over a series of low hills. It was a dull, dark presence, not much more than simply a place where there were no stars.

I put the *Belle-Marie* in orbit and we went down in the lander.

The moon was heavily cratered in the north and along the equator, with plains in the south streaked with ridges and canyons. There were several mountain ranges, tall, skeletal peaks of pure granite. The domes were located midway between the equator and the north pole, on relatively flat ground. The antenna field was to the west. Mountains rose to the east. A tracked ground vehicle had been left in the middle of the complex.

The domes appeared to be in good condition. Alex watched them with growing satisfaction as we descended through the black sky. A half dozen moons were visible. They were pale, ghostly, barely discernible in the feeble light from the central star. Had you not known they were there, you might not have seen them.

I eased us in carefully. When we touched down I shut the engines off and brought the gravity back slowly. Alex waited impatiently while I exercised what he routinely called a surplus of feminine caution. He's always anxious to get moving – let's go, we don't have forever. He enjoys playing that role. But he doesn't like unpleasant surprises either. And that's supposed to be my job, heading them off. I broke through the bottom of a crater years ago into a sinkhole, and he still hasn't let me forget it.

Everything held. Alex gave me a big smile, well-done and all that. The talk about let's move it along got put aside while he sat looking out the viewport, savoring the moment. You go into one of these places, a site that's been empty for centuries or maybe millennia, and you never know what you might find. Some have been rigged with death traps. Floors have been known to

8

collapse and walls to give way. In one way station, air pressure built up when something malfunctioned and it all but exploded when a Survey team tried to enter.

What you always hope for, of course, is an open hatch and a map of the premises. Like they found at Lyautey.

I unbuckled and waited for Alex. Finally, he took a deep breath, released his harness, swung the chair around, climbed out of it, and pulled on his air tanks. We ran a radio check and inspected each other's suits. When he was ready I decompressed and opened the hatch.

We climbed down the ladder onto the surface. The ground was crumbly. Sand and iron chips. We saw myriad footprints and tracks from vehicles. Untouched down the centuries.

'*Last ones out, you think?*' Alex asked.

'Wouldn't be surprised,' I said. I was more interested in the view. A slice of the rings and two moons were visible just above the mountains.

'*Something wrong,*' Alex said.

'What?' The domes were dark and quiet. Nothing moved on the plain, which stretched to the southern horizon. Nothing unusual in the sky.

In the dark I couldn't see Alex's face, encased in his helmet. But he seemed to be looking at the nearest dome. No, past it at one of the other units, the northernmost, which was also the largest of the four.

There was an open door.

Well, not open in the sense that the hatch was ajar. Someone had cut into it. Had cut a large hole that we should have seen coming down if we'd been paying attention.

Alex grumbled something over the circuit about vandals and started angrily toward it. I fell in behind. 'Watch the gravity,' I said, as he stumbled but caught himself.

'*Damned thieves.*' Alex delivered a series of imprecations. '*How's this possible?*'

It was hard to believe that someone had beaten us here because

9

artifacts from Gideon V had never appeared on the market. And there was no historical record that the base had been found.

'Has to be recent,' I said.

'*You mean* yesterday?' he asked.

'Maybe they didn't know what they had. Just broke in, looked around, and left.'

'*It's possible, Chase,*' he said. '*Maybe it happened centuries ago. When people still remembered where this place was.*'

I hoped he was right.

It was usually the case that when archeologists found a ransacked site, the ransacking had been done within a few hundred years of the era during which the site had operated. After a reasonable length of time, people forget where things are. And they get permanently lost. I sometimes wonder how many ships are floating around out in the dark, having blown an engine and eventually faded from the record.

I should mention that we're not archeologists. We're strictly business types, matching collectors with merchandise, and sometimes, as now, hunting down original sources. This had looked like a gold mine moments ago. But now – Alex was holding his breath as we approached the opening.

The hatch had been cut away by a torch. It lay off to one side. And there was only the lightest coating of dust on it. '*This just happened,*' he said. I'll confess that Alex is not exactly eventempered. At home, in social circumstances, he's a model of courtesy and restraint. But in places like that lunar surface, where society is a long way off, I occasionally get to see his real feelings. He stared at the fallen door, picked up a rock, said something under his breath, and threw the rock halfway into orbit.

I stood there, a kid in the principal's office. 'Probably my fault,' I said.

The inner hatch was also down. Beyond it, the interior was dark.

He looked at me. The visor was too opaque to allow me to see his expression, but it wasn't hard to imagine. '*How do you mean?*' he asked.

'I told Windy.' Windy was Survey's public relations director, and a longtime friend.

Alex wasn't appreciably taller than I am, but he seemed to be towering over me. *'Windy wouldn't say anything.'*

'I know.'

'You told her over an open circuit.'

'Yeah.'

He sighed. *'Chase, how could you do that?'*

'I don't know.' I was trying not to whine. 'I didn't think there'd be a problem. We were talking about something else and it just came up.'

'Couldn't resist?'

'I guess not.'

He planted one boot on the hatch and shoved. It didn't budge. *'Well,'* he said, *'no help for it now.'*

I straightened my shoulders. Shoot me if it'll make you feel better. 'Won't happen again.'

'It's okay.' He was using his spilled-milk voice. *'Let's go see how much damage they did.'*

He led the way in.

The domes were connected by tunnels. Staircases led to underground spaces. These places are always ghostly, illuminated only by wrist lamps. Shadows chase themselves around the bulkheads, and there seems always to be something moving just outside the field of vision. I remember reading how Casmir Kolchevsky was attacked in a place like this by a security bot that he had inadvertently activated.

The vandals had been relentless.

We wandered through the operational sections, through a gym, through private living quarters. Through a kitchen and dining room. Everywhere we went, drawers were pulled out and their contents dumped. Cabinets were cut open, storage lockers broken apart. The place had been ransacked. There wasn't much remaining that could have been put up for sale or would have been of interest to a museum. We found ourselves treading carefully past broken glass and data disks and overturned tables. Some clothing will survive for a surprisingly long time in a vacuum. But we found only a handful of pieces, most of them victims of whatever chemicals had been in the original material. Or sufficiently mundane that nobody would have cared. It doesn't much matter where a pullover shirt has come from. Unless it's been worn by a legendary general or an immortal playwright, nobody cares. But the jumpsuits, which usually carry a shoulder patch, or a stenciled identity over a pocket, GIDEON BASE or some such thing, are worth their weight. We found only one, badly frayed. The inscription was of course in Celian characters, framing a tall, narrow peak. 'The station's emblem,' said Alex.

They'd also stripped the operations center. Electronic gear had been taken. They'd torn the panels apart to get access. Again, the objective had been to find parts marked as belonging to the base. It looked as if anything not meeting that standard had been yanked out and dropped on the deck.

Alex was in a rage by the time we were finished. All four domes, and the underground network, had been treated the same way. There'd been one exception to the general chaos. We found a common room, littered with debris. The deck was covered with projectors and readers, and data crystals that would have gone dry long before six centuries had passed. A broken pitcher and some ice lay in one corner, and a partially torn-up carpet had been dragged into another. But a small table stood in the center of the room, and a book lay open on it, arranged for the convenience of anyone seated in the lone chair.

'Well,' I said, looking down at it, 'at least it won't be a complete blowout. That thing will bring some money.'

Or maybe it wouldn't.

It was last year's edition of *The Antiquarian Guide*.

'Look as if the vandal knew we'd be here,' Alex said. 'He's saying hello.'

2

I told him he was an idiot. I explained that he was auctioning off our history, converting it to baubles and handing it over to people who had no concept who Mike Esther was. And that when he was finished, when the last crystal had been taken from the museum and sold to the jewelers, there would be nothing left of the men and women who had built our world. He smiled and shook his head and I thought for a moment that his voice caught. 'Old friend,' he said, 'they are already long gone.'

—Haras Kora,
Binacqua Chronicles, 4417 C.E.

Winetta Yashevik was the archeological liaison at Survey, and she doubled as their public relations chief. Windy was the only person to whom I'd revealed our destination, but I knew she would never have given information away to any of Alex's rivals. She was a true believer. In her view, we turned antiquities into commodities and sold them to private buyers. It was an offense against decency, and she always contrived, without saying anything directly, to make me feel that I was ethically unfit. I was, if you like, the lost sheep. The one that had been corrupted by the mendacity of the world and didn't seem able to find its way home.

It was easy enough for her to sit in judgment. She'd been born into wealth and never known what it was to go without anything. But that's another matter.

When I stopped by her office at the Survey complex, on the second floor of the Kolman building, she brightened, waved me inside, and closed the door. 'You're back more quickly than I expected. Did you not find the place? I hope.'

'It was there,' I said. 'Right where Alex said it would be. But somebody got there first and broke in.'

She sighed. 'Thieves everywhere. Well, anyhow, congratulations. Now you know how the rest of us feel when you and Alex have taken over a site.' She paused, smiled as if she wanted me to think she didn't want to hurt my feelings, just kidding, you know how it is. But she was enjoying herself. 'Were you able to make off with anything at all?'

I ignored the phraseology. 'The place was cleaned out,' I said.

Her eyes slid shut. I saw her lips tighten, but she said nothing. Windy was tall, dark, passionate about the things she believed in. No halfway measures. Me she tolerated because she wasn't going to throw a friendship overboard that went all the way back to when we were both playing with dolls. 'No idea who they were?'

'No. It happened recently, though. Within the last year. Maybe within the last few days.'

Her office was big. There were pictures from various missions on the paneled walls, as well as a scattering of awards. Winetta Yashevik, Employee of the Year; Harbison Award for Outstanding Service; Appreciation from the United Defenders for contributions to their Toys for Kids program. And there were pictures from excavations.

'Well,' she said, 'I'm sorry to hear it.'

'Windy, we were trying to figure out how it happened.' I took a deep breath. 'Don't take this the wrong way, but as far as we

14

can figure, you're the only one who knew in advance where we were going.'

'Chase,' she said, in a level tone, 'you told me to keep it quiet, and I did. You also know I would never help one of these *vandals*.'

'We know that. But we were wondering if the information got passed on in any way? If anybody else in the organization knew?'

'No,' she said, 'I'm sure I didn't tell anybody.' She thought about it. 'Except Louie.' That was a reference to Louis Ponzio, the director.

'Okay. That probably means somebody's listening in on us.'

'Could be.' She looked uncomfortable. 'Chase, we both know the director doesn't run the tightest ship on the planet.'

Actually I didn't know.

'That may or may not have been the problem. I'm sorry. I shouldn't have said anything.'

'It's okay. It was probably the comm system.'

'Whatever. Listen, Chase—'

'Yes?'

'I wouldn't want you to feel you can't tell me things.'

'I know. It's not a problem.'

'Next time—'

'I know.'

Fenn Redfield, Alex's old police buddy, was at the country house when I got back. Alex had told him what happened. Not an official complaint, of course. There was none to be made. 'But there's a possibility somebody's doing some eavesdropping.'

'Wish I could help,' he said. 'You guys just have to be more careful what you say over an open circuit.' Fenn was short, stocky, a walking barrel with green eyes and a deep bass voice. He had never married, loved to party, and played cards regularly in a small group with Alex.

'Isn't it illegal to eavesdrop on people?' I asked.

'Not really,' he said. 'Such a law would be unenforceable.' He made a face to suggest he was thinking it over. 'But it *is* illegal to own enabling equipment. I can keep an ear open, but what you *should* do, Alex, is install a scrambler system.'

That sounded good, but it wasn't very practical when you're trying to solicit calls from new clients. So Fenn assured us he'd let us know if they learned anything, which meant, of course, that we were on our own.

We had lunch before going back to the office. Alex is big on lunch. He thinks a good lunch is what life is really about. So we stopped at the Paramount House and decided over sandwiches and potato salad that we would opt for a cryptosystem that would secure calls between Alex and me, and between the office and our more significant clients. And to Windy.

Despite failing to capitalize at Gideon V, Rainbow was prospering. Alex had all the money he could possibly want, much of it deriving as a by-product of the celebrity status he'd achieved from the *Tenandrome* and *Polaris* affairs. But he'd have been wealthy even without those fortuitous events. He was a good businessman, and everybody trusted him. If you had an artifact you wanted to put a value to, you knew you could take it to Alex and get an honest appraisal. In our business, reputation is everything. Add his basic integrity to the fact that he's at least as knowledgeable as any of his competitors, and throw in his genius for public relations, and you have the formula for a profitable operation.

Rainbow is headquartered on the ground floor of his home, an old country house that had once served as an inn to hunters and sight-seers before civilization – or development – washed over it. Tradition has it that Jorge Shale and his team came down hard nearby, the first landing on Rimway. Alex, who grew up there, claims he used to go looking for evidence of the event. After several thousand years, of course, there wasn't going to be any, even assuming the location was correct. But it got the young Alex interested in history, and especially that part of it that involved digging and produced artifacts. Leftovers. Pieces of another time.

I'm his pilot, social director, and sole employee. My title is executive assistant. I could have taken any title I chose, up to and including chief of operations. It was midwinter when we got back from the Celian base. We let our clients know we were home and fielded hopeful queries about new artifacts. No, I spent the afternoon explaining, we hadn't brought anything home. We'd had a washout.

It was one of those slate gray days warning of impending snow. The wind was out of the north, literally howling against the house. I was still hard at work when Alex wandered down from his quarters upstairs. He was wearing a thick gray sweater and black slacks.

He's about average height, average everything really. He is not by any stretch an imposing figure, until the lights come on in those dark brown eyes. I've said elsewhere that he doesn't really care that much about antiquities for their own sake, that he prizes them exclusively as a source of income. He has seen that comment and strongly objects to it. And I'll admit here that I may have misjudged him. He was, for example, still angry over what he called the looting of Gideon V. And I understood there was more to it than simply the fact that someone had beaten us there.

'I found them,' he said.

'What's that, Alex?'

'The artifacts.'

'The *Celian* stuff?'

'Yes,' he said. 'What did you think?'

'They showed up on the market?'

He nodded. Yes. 'They're being offered for sale by Blue Moon Action.' He brought up the inventory and we looked at a gorgeous collection of plates and glasses, some pullovers, some work uniforms, all carrying the Celian characters for Gideon V, and the familiar mountaintop. There was also some electronic gear. *'This magnetic coupler,'* read the advertising, *'would look elegant in your living room.'* The coupler was labeled with a manufacturer and a date seven centuries gone.

Alex directed Jacob to get Blue Moon on the circuit. 'I wanted you to hear what they say,' he told me. I took station back near the bookcase, where I wouldn't be visible. An AI answered.

'I'd like to speak to whoever's in charge,' Alex said.

'That'll be Ms Goldcress. May I tell her who's calling?'

'Alexander Benedict.'

'One moment, please.'

A blond woman about my age appeared. White blouse, blue slacks, gold earrings and bracelet. She smiled pleasantly. *'Hello, Mr Benedict. What can I do for you?'*

'You have some Celian artifacts for sale.'

An armchair blinked on beside her and she lowered herself into it. *'That's correct. We haven't closed the bidding yet. Actually, we won't do so until next week.'* She hesitated. *'Which of the pieces were you interested in?'*

'Ms Goldcress, may I ask how you came by the artifacts?'

'I'm sorry. I'm not at liberty to say. However, the objects will come with a fully documented certificate of authentication.'

'Why can't you tell me?'

'The owner doesn't wish his name known.'

'You're simply acting as his agent?'

'That's correct.' They stared at each other across the open space of the office, she in her armchair, Alex standing, leaning back against my desk. *'By the way, the catalog shows only a fraction of what's available. If you're interested, the entire inventory of Celian antiques will be on display at the Antiquarian Caucus this weekend. In Parmelee.'*

'Excellent,' he said. 'Would you be willing to put me in touch with him?'

'With whom?'

'With the owner.'

'I'm sorry, Mr Benedict. I really can't do that. It would be unethical.'

He casually produced a transmit card and laid it on the desk. 'I'd be extremely grateful.'

'I'm sure you would. And I'd help if I could.'

18

Alex smiled. 'It's a pleasure to know there are still professionals in the business.'

'*Thank you,*' she said.

'Might I ask you to pass a message to him?'

'*Of course.*'

'Ask him to call me.'

'*I'll take care of it.*'

She signed off, and he made an irritated sound. 'It's a fool's errand,' he said. 'You can bet we won't hear from him.'

I was looking up the Antiquarian Caucus. 'Bolton's guest of honor this year,' I said. Ollie Bolton headed Bolton Brothers, a historical recovery firm for more than half a century. 'The Caucus has several exhibitions scheduled.'

It was a two-hour train ride. 'Book it,' he said. 'You never know who might turn up at one of these things.'

The event was being held at Medallion Gardens, among breeze-ways and glass enclosures and a hundred varieties of flowering plants. We arrived during the late afternoon, shortly after the antiquities exhibit had opened. It featured the Rilby Collection, which was in the process of being transferred to the University Museum; and several pieces of three-thousand-year-old electronics from the *Taratino,* the first manned vessel known to have left the galaxy. And, of course, the Celian artifacts.

That was painful, knowing they could – and should – have been ours. In addition to the material we'd seen in the catalog, there were musical instruments, chess and suji sets, a lamp, and three framed pictures (still remarkably sharp despite their age), all with backdrops from the base. One was of a woman, one of an elderly man, and the third of a pair of young children, a boy and a girl. The boy's name was Jayle. Nothing more was known about anybody.

Ms Goldcress was there and was every bit as uncommunicative in person as she had been on the circuit. How was she doing? Quite nicely, thank you. Had she ever been out to a site herself?

19

No, too busy, unfortunately. When Alex wondered aloud whether the owner of the display items was present, she replied she was sure she didn't know.

She smiled politely at me in a manner that suggested she would appreciate it if I'd find something for Alex to do other than waste her time.

'Did you pass my message to the owner?' he asked.

We were standing by the Celian display, and she never took her eyes from it. 'Yes,' she said. 'I passed it on.'

'What did he say?'

'I left it with his AI.'

As we walked away, he said quietly, 'I'd like to brain her.'

The attendees were antiquities dealers, with a sprinkling of academics and a few journalists. At seven we gathered in the Island Room for a banquet. There were approximately four hundred people present.

The other guests at our table were impressed to discover they were sitting with *the* Alex Benedict. They were all anxious to hear details of his forays, and Alex, who loved every minute of it, was only too pleased to comply. Alex was a decent guy and he usually kept a level head on his shoulders, but he *did* enjoy having people tell him how well he'd done, and what remarkable contributions he'd made. He blushed with all good grace and tried to give me some credit, but they weren't having it. And I could see he believed he was being appropriately modest. Humility, he once told me, is the trademark of greatness.

When we'd finished the meal, the emcee rose to present a few toasts. The late Maylo Rilby, whose priceless collection had been donated by his brother, was represented by a vivacious young niece. She stood and we drank solemnly to her. We raised our glasses also to a commissioner from the University Museum. And to the outgoing president of the Antiquarian Caucus, who was retiring after seven years of service.

There was some formal business to be taken care of, and

eventually, they got around to the guest speaker, Oliver Bolton, the CEO of Bolton Brothers and a man of extraordinary celebrity. The odd thing about Bolton Brothers was that there were no brothers. Not even a sister. Bolton had founded the company twenty years earlier, so it wasn't as if it had descended to him from an older generation. He'd been quoted as saying he'd always regretted that he had no siblings. The corporate name, he explained, was a concession to that sense of loss. I'll admit here I had no idea what he was talking about.

He was a tall man, graying, with a majestic presence, the kind of guy people reflexively make room for. And simultaneously like. He would have made an effective politician. 'Thank you, Ben, thank you,' he said, after the emcee had piled on a solid five minutes of praise. Ollie Bolton, it seemed, was responsible for the reclamation of substantial pieces of the 'Lost Centuries,' for the work that had allowed historians to rethink their conclusions about the Time of Troubles, and for a wide array of other accomplishments.

He outlined a couple of his more celebrated experiences, apportioning credit among his associates and introducing them as he did. Then he told stories about himself. How unsettling it had been at Arakon when the workers went home and took their ladders with them and he'd remained stranded overnight in the tombs. And his night in jail at Bakudai, charged with grave robbing. 'Technically, they were correct. But leave it up to the authorities, and the crystal basin over there, now headed for the museum, would still be buried in the desert.'

More applause.

He was by turns angry, impassioned, poetic. 'We have fifteen thousand years of history behind us, much of it in a medium that preserves everything. The footprints of the first man to walk on Earth's moon are still there,' he said. 'I know we all share the same passion for the past, and for the relics that survive the ages, that wait for us in the dark places where no one goes anymore. It's an honor to be here with you this evening.'

21

'How come,' I whispered to Alex, 'you're not more like him?'

'Maybe,' he said, 'you'd prefer to work over at Bolton. I could arrange it.'

'What's he pay?'

'What difference does it make? He's a much more admirable figure than your current boss.'

I was surprised. He was pretending to be kidding, but I could see I'd struck a nerve. 'No,' I said. 'I'm happy where I am.'

Alex had looked away, and he needed several seconds to turn toward me again. 'I'm sorry,' he said.

Bolton played to his audience. 'It's always a privilege to speak to Andiquar's antiquities dealers. And I understand we have a few guests from around the globe, and even two from off-world.' He took a minute to recognize visitors from the Spinners, and from Earth. 'The home world.' (Applause.) 'Where it all began.' (More applause.)

I'd expected him to speak exclusively about himself, but he was too smart for that. Instead, he described the work 'we all do,' and the benefits that accrue to all.

'Fifteen thousand years,' he said, 'is rather a long time. Punctuate it with war and rebellion, with dark ages and social collapse, and things have a tendency to get lost. Things that we should never forget. Like the Filipino women who, during a forgotten war, defied enemy soldiers to give food and drink to their own men and their allies during the Death March. Ah, I see some of you know about the Death March. But I wonder how much we'd know were it not for the work of Maryam Kleffner, back there in the rear.' He waved in that direction. 'Hello, Maryam.'

He picked out several more for personal kudos. 'Historians do the brute work,' he said. 'Their contribution cannot be overstated. And there are people like Lazarus Colt up front. Lazarus is head of the archeology department here at the university. Without Lazarus and his team, we wouldn't know yet whether the Mindans on Khaja Luan were real or mythical. A golden civilization for a thousand years, and yet somehow it drifted into a backwater and was almost forgotten.

'Almost.' He had the audience in his grip. He paused, and smiled, and shook his head. 'But here is an example of where those of us who pursue and market antiques make our contribution. I spoke with Lazarus earlier this evening. He'd be the first one to tell you that they would never have found the Mindans, would never even have gone looking for them, had Howard Chandis not discovered a wine vessel buried in a hill. Howard, of course, is one of us.' He looked around to his left. 'Stand up, Howard. Let everybody see you.'

Howard stood and applause rolled through the room.

Bolton spoke about twenty minutes. He finished with a flourish, observing that one of the more pleasant aspects of his profession was the company he got to keep. 'Thank you very much.' And he bowed, preparatory to stepping down.

One of the diners, a thin little man with black hair and pugnacious features, got up. There were a few whispers, and a woman one table from us said, 'Uh-oh.' The applause died. Bolton and the little man were left staring at one another.

Someone near him was trying to get him to sit back down. He resisted and straightened himself. Bolton smiled and remained congenial. 'Did you have a question, Professor Kolchevsky?' he asked.

Casmir Kolchevsky. The near-legendary archeologist who'd been pursued by the security bot. 'I do,' he said.

Alex reached for his wineglass. 'This should be interesting.'

'Why? What's going on?'

'He doesn't approve of people in our line of work. At least not those of us who go out and dig up their own merchandise.'

'You take credit for a great deal,' Kolchevsky said. He was not the natural speaker Bolton was, but what his voice lacked in timbre, it more than made up in passion. He swung around to encompass the audience.

He had a lined, windblown face, a long jaw, and eyes that, at the moment, blazed with anger. 'I suppose nothing should surprise me anymore, but here I am, listening to you people honoring this

23

thief, this *vandal*. He stands up there talking as if he's an honest man. As if he makes a contribution. You applaud him because he tells you what you like to believe about yourselves.' He turned back to the speaker. 'I'll tell you what you contribute.'

I could see movement at the doors. Security people were spreading out into the room and weaving among the tables, closing on Kolchevsky.

'You people have wrecked countless sites across the Confederacy, and beyond its borders. And if you haven't done it personally, you've done it by proxy. You've done it by supporting—' Someone grabbed him and began pulling him away from the table. 'Let go of me,' he demanded.

A tall woman with the security detail had moved in behind him along with two or three others. She was saying something to him.

'No,' he said, 'we certainly can't have this, can we? It doesn't do to confront the truth, does it?' He continued to struggle. Reinforcements arrived. Someone at his table began struggling with one of the guards. Somebody else fell down. Kolchevsky by then had both arms pinned against his sides. 'I'm leaving on my own,' he roared. 'But this is a den of thieves. Nothing more.'

They began dragging him toward the exit while he continued to resist. I'll tell you, I couldn't help admiring the guy.

For several minutes after they got him outside, we heard raised voices. Bolton never moved from his position at the speaker's table. When the disturbance seemed at last to have subsided, he straightened his jacket and smiled at the audience. 'All part of the show, folks. Wait'll you see what's up next.'

You might say the evening's mood had been dampened. We wandered among the guests, and when the official proceedings ended, attended several of the parties. Alex was certain Goldcress's client was on the premises. That he'd have to be there somewhere. 'No way he could resist this.'

'But how do you expect to find him?' I asked.

'He knows us, Chase. I've been hoping he'd give himself away, maybe show a little too much interest in us. Maybe allow himself to watch too closely while we talked with his agent.'

'And did you see anybody?'

'I saw a lot of people keeping an eye on us,' he said. 'But primarily on *you*.' That was a reference to my cherry red evening best, which was maybe a bit more revealing than I was accustomed to allow.

But if anyone was there, he stayed clear of us. At the end of the evening, we went back to our hotel empty-handed.

The day we returned home, I slept late. When I walked into the office at midmorning, Jacob posted a list of the day's callers. Among them was a name I didn't recognize. '*Local woman*,' he said. '*Wants an appraisal*.'

Where antiquities are concerned, serious collectors prefer to do things face-to-face, especially if they think they have a potentially valuable artifact. In fact, where that kind of merchandise is concerned, Alex refuses to do a remote appraisal. But the vast majority of the stuff they show us is of minimal value, and you don't need to see it up close to realize it.

We get a lot of people directly off the street. They tend to be folks who've picked up something at an estate sale, or it's maybe an inheritance, and they've begun wondering if it's worth more money than they'd been told. When they do, under the assumption there's nothing to lose, they call us. I take a look, then offer my assessment. Diplomatically, of course. The truth is that I'm no expert in matters *antiqua*, but I know junk when I see it. If I'm not sure, I pass it to Alex.

Ninety-nine percent of the calls off the street are pure refuse. That's a conservative estimate. So when, a couple hours later, I returned the call and her image blinked on in the office, my first thought was to take a quick look at what she had and send her on her way.

She was a tiny, blond woman, nervous, not particularly well

25

dressed, unable to look me in the eye. She wore gold slacks that would have fit better on someone with narrower hips. A creased white blouse was open at the throat and would have revealed a lot of cleavage if she'd had any. She had a blinding red neckerchief and a smile that was at once aggressive and shy. She was seated on a worn Springfield sofa, the kind that you get free if you buy a couple of armchairs.

Greetings were short without being abrupt. *'My name's Amy Kolmer,'* she said. *'I have something here I'd like you to look at. I was wondering if it might be worth some money.'* She reached out of the picture and came back with a cup, which she held up to the light.

It was a decorative piece, the sort of thing you might buy in a souvenir shop. It was gray. A green-and-white eagle was etched into its side. There was something antiquated about the style in which the eagle was drawn. It was in flight, wings spread, beak open in an attack posture. A bit overdramatic. It might have been popular in the last century. A small banner was unfurled beneath the eagle, and something was written on it. It was too small to make out clearly, but I could see it wasn't the Standard alphabet.

She turned the cup so I could see the back side. It featured a ringed globe, with inscriptions above and below. Same type of symbols.

'What do you think?' she asked.

'What's the language, Amy? Do you know?'

'I've no idea.'

'Do you know what it is?'

She looked puzzled. *'It's a cup.'*

'I mean, what *kind* of cup? Where did it come from?'

'My boyfriend gave it to me.'

'Your boyfriend.'

'My ex-*boyfriend.'* Her eyes narrowed, and I could see things had come to a bad end. She was trying to turn whatever remained of the relationship into cash. *'He saw me admiring it one time so he told me I could have it.'*

'Good of him,' I said.

'*I liked the eagle.*' She stared at it for a long moment. '*He gave it to me the night before we broke up. I guess it was supposed to be a consolation prize.*'

'Maybe.'

'*The cup's worth more than he is.*' She smiled. One of those smiles that tell you she wouldn't feel especially upset if the boyfriend fell off a bridge.

'Where did *he* get it?'

'*He always had it.*'

I could see I wasn't going to get far with her. I was tempted to tell her what I believed, that the cup was worthless. But Rainbow has a code of ethics that requires me to know what I'm talking about. I fell back on our AI. 'Jacob,' I said. 'What's the language?'

'*Searching,*' he said.

There was really nothing outré about the cup, nothing to set it apart, aside from the strange symbols. But I'd seen a lot of odd lettering during my years with Rainbow, and, believe me, it didn't necessarily mean anything.

Jacob made a sound as if clearing his throat. It signaled he was surprised. Had Amy Kolmer not been on the circuit, I knew he would have made an appearance of his own. '*It's English,*' he said. '*Mid-American.*'

'Really?'

'*Of course.*'

'Fourth Millennium,' I guessed.

'*Third. Nobody spoke English in the Fourth.*'

Amy came to life. She'd not expected any good news from me. But she'd overheard enough to raise her hopes. She looked at the cup, looked at me, looked back at the cup. '*This thing is nine thousand years old?*'

'Probably not. The inscription uses an old language. That doesn't mean—'

'*Hard to believe,*' she said. '*It's in good shape for all those years.*'

'Amy,' I said, 'why don't you bring the cup over here? Let us take a close look at it?'

The truth is that Jacob can give us all the physical details remotely. But Alex insists that a computer-generated repro is not the same as holding the actual object in his hands. He likes to imply there's a spiritual dimension to what he does, although if you ask him point-blank he'd say it was all nonsense, but that there are qualities in a physical object that computers cannot measure. Don't ask him to specify.

So I made the appointment with Amy Kolmer for that afternoon. She showed up early. Alex came down and ushered her into the office personally. His curiosity had been piqued.

I didn't particularly care for the woman. On the circuit, I'd sensed that she expected me to try to cheat her. In person, she went a different direction, playing the helpless but very sexual female. I suppose it was Alex's presence that set her off. She fluttered and primped and cast her eyes to the floor. *Poor me, life is hard but maybe I've gotten lucky and I surely would be grateful for whatever assistance you can lend.* If she thought Rainbow's asking price to broker a transaction would go down as a result of her efforts, she didn't know Alex.

She'd wrapped the cup in a piece of soft linen and carried it in a plastic bag. When we were all seated inside the office, she opened the bag, unwrapped the cup, and set it before him.

He studied it closely, bit his lip, made faces, and placed it on Jacob's bulk reader. 'What can you tell us, Jacob?' he asked.

The lamp in the top of the reader blinked on. Turned amber. Turned red. Dimmed and intensified. Went pretty much through the spectrum. The process took about two minutes.

'The object is made of acrylonitrile-butadiene-styrene resins. Coloring is principally—'

'—Jacob,' said Alex, 'how old is it?'

'I would say the object was constructed during the Third Millennium. Best estimate is approximately 2600 C.E. Error range two hundred years either way.'

28

'What does the inscription say?'

'*The banner says* New World Coming. *And the lines on the back of the cup seem to be a designator.* IFR171. *And another term I'm not sure about.*'

'So the cup is, what, from an office somewhere?'

'*The letters probably stand for* Interstellar Fleet Registry.'

'It's from a ship?' I asked.

'*Oh, yes. I don't think there's any doubt about that.*'

Amy tugged at my arm. 'What's it worth?'

Alex counseled patience. 'Jacob, the other term is probably the ship's name.'

'*I think that is correct, sir. It translates as* Searcher. *Or* Explorer. *Something along those lines.*'

The lamps went off. Alex lifted the object gently and placed it on the desk. He looked at it through a magnifier. 'It's in reasonably good condition,' he said.

Amy could hardly be restrained. 'Thank God. I needed *something* to go right.' Alex smiled. She was already thinking what she would be able to buy. 'How can it be that old?' she asked. 'My drapes are new, and they're already falling apart.'

'It's a plastic,' he told her. 'Plastics can last a long time.' He produced a soft cloth and began gently to wipe the thing.

She asked again how much we would pay.

Alex made the face he always used when he didn't want to answer a question directly. 'We're not normally buyers,' he said. 'We'll do some research, Amy. Then test the market. But I'd guess, if you're patient, it will bring a decent price.'

'A couple hundred?'

Alex smiled paternally. 'I wouldn't be surprised,' he said.

She clapped her hands. 'Wonderful.' She looked at me, and turned back toward Alex. 'What do I do next?'

'You needn't do anything. Let's take this one step at a time. First we want to find out precisely what we have.'

'All right.'

'Have you proof of ownership?'

Uh-oh. Her face changed. Her lips parted and the smile vanished. 'It was *given* to me.'

'By your former boyfriend.'

'Yes. But I own it. It's mine.'

Alex nodded. 'Okay. We'll have to provide a document to go with it. To certify that you have the right to make the sale.'

'That's okay.' She looked uncertain.

'Very good. Why don't you leave it with us, and we'll see what more we can find out, and get back to you.'

'What do you think?' I asked when she was gone.

He looked pleased. 'Nine thousand years? Somebody will be delighted to pay substantially for the privilege of putting this on the mantel.'

'You think it's really from a ship?'

He was looking at the cup through the magnifier again. 'Probably not. It comes out of the era when they were just getting interstellars up and running. It's more likely to have been part of a giveaway program or to have been sold in a souvenir shop. Not that it matters: I doubt it would be possible to establish whether it was actually on shipboard or not.'

What we really wanted, of course, was that yes, it had traveled with the *Searcher*, and that preferably it had belonged to the captain. Ideally, we would also find out that the *Searcher* was in the record somewhere, that it had accomplished something spectacular, or better yet, gotten wrecked, and, to top everything, its captain would be known to history.

'See to it, Chase. Put Jacob on the job, and find out whatever you can.'

3

There is an almost mystical attraction for us in the notion of the lost world, of an Atlantis out there somewhere, a place where the routine problems of ordinary life have been banished, where everyone lives in a castle, where there's a party every night, where every woman is stunning and every man noble and brave.

—Lescue Harkin,
Memory, Myth, and Mind, 1376

The Third Millennium was a long time ago, and the record is notoriously incomplete. We know who the political leaders were, we know when and how the wars started (if not always *why*), we know the principal artists, literary movements, religious conflicts. We know which nation threatened to do what to whom. But we've little idea what people's lives were like, how they spent their time, what they really thought about the world in which they lived. We know of assassinations, but we don't always know the rationale. Or even whether, when they happened, ordinary citizens mourned or breathed a sigh of relief.

Nine thousand years is a long time. And nobody except a few historians really thinks much about it.

So Jacob went looking for the *Searcher*. When he found nothing, he started recovering detailed accounts of the more famous interstellars, on the possibility we'd find mention of a similar name. *'Maybe we don't quite have the translation right,'* he said. *'English was a slippery language.'*

So we went through accounts of the *Avenger*, which had played a prominent role in the first interstellar war between Earth and three of its colonies in the early thirty-third century. And the *Lassiter*, the first deep-space corsair. And the thirtieth century *Karaki*, the largest ship of its time, which had hauled a record load of capital goods out to Regulus IV to get that colony started. And the *Chao Huang*, which had taken a team of doctors to Maracaibo when, against all expectation, human settlers had been stricken by a native plague. (This was at a time when the experts still believed disease germs could only attack creatures evolved in the same biosystem.)

There was endless information about the *Tokyo*, the first interstellar to vanish into the transdimensions. Never heard from again. There were pictures of its captain and first mate, and of various passengers, of the dining area and the engine room. Everything you wanted to know. Except where it went.

And the most famous of all the starships, the *Centaurus*, which made the first transdimensional flight to Earth's neighboring star, requiring seven weeks to complete the journey one way. You have to smile at that: Seven weeks to go four light-years.

But there was no mention of a *Searcher*. Or an *Explorer*. There was a *Voyager*. Three of them, in fact. A popular name, obviously. And even a *Hunter*.

Few physical objects have survived from the Third Millennium. Most of them tend to be either ceramic, like Amy Kolmer's cup, or plastic. There's an axiom in our business that the cheapest stuff lasts longest.

I didn't know anybody who was an expert on the era, so I checked the Registry and picked one at random, an assistant professor at Barcross University. His name was Shepard Marquard.

He looked young, but he'd written extensively on the period and been recognized by his peers.

I called and had no problem getting through. Marquard was a good-looking guy, tall and redheaded, more personable than his pictures had led me to expect. *'Most of the naval and shipping records from that era are lost,'* he told me. *'But I'll see what I can do. I'll look through what I have and get back to you.'*

The following day, I took virtual tours of half a dozen museums and spent a lot of time wandering through third-millennium artifacts. I saw a plastic case that might once have been a container for makeup, an electronic device whose use could only be guessed at, a woman's pair of high-heeled shoes, a couple of pens, a lamp, a sofa, a sheet of paper in laminated plastic described as a 'classified section from a newspaper.' I didn't know what a newspaper was, and neither did anybody else I was able to talk to. (Marquard told me later that it was information printed on paper and distributed physically across a wide area.) There was a man's hat with a visor to keep the sun off. And a coin with an eagle on one side. Metal money. *United States of America.*

In God We Trust. It was dated 2006, and the data display said it was the second-oldest coin in existence.

I wandered through the exhibits, and when I'd seen everything I cared about, I settled into a reading room and opened one of the data files.

The Third Millennium was a turbulent era. Earth was crowded well beyond capacity. Its inhabitants seemed to be constantly at war with each other, over politics, real estate, or religion. Political systems were generally corrupt and prone to collapse.

There were serious environmental problems left over from the Industrial Age, and the deterioration of the global climate seemed to coincide with political leaders who grew increasingly ruthless. The worst of these was Marko III, known to his American subjects as The Magnificent.

Midway through the twenty-fifth century, while Marko was jailing and killing as his mood dictated, Diane Harriman did her groundbreaking work in the dimensional structure of the space-time continuum, and twenty years later Shi-Ko Han and Edward Cleaver gave us the interstellar drive.

Another four years, and we'd discovered the first habitable world. It's not surprising to read that a lot of volunteers signed up to head for the frontier.

I was getting ready to go home for the day when Jacob passed a call to me. '*Chase,*' said a familiar voice. '*I think I have what you want.*'

It was Marquard. 'You've identified the *Searcher,*' I said.

'*Yeah.*' There was an odd intonation. '*May I ask why you wanted to know?*'

I told him about the cup. He listened without comment, and when I'd finished, the silence stretched out. 'Your turn,' I said finally. 'What have you got?'

'*A surprise. Could you arrange to come by the school?*'

'Can't you just tell me what you have?'

'*I'll tell you what. Why don't you join me for dinner?*'

Subtle as an avalanche. 'Dr Marquard, I really haven't time to go all the way out to Barcross.' Not that I wouldn't have enjoyed it, but it's a long run.

'*Call me* Shep. *And I guarantee you'll find it worth your while.*'

Barcross is a large diamond-shaped island, probably best known as a summer resort for singles. Years ago I went through a phase during which it was an occasional part of my social calendar. It was part surf, part moonlight, part dream. The kind of place that felt as if the love of your life was in the wings somewhere. I'm a bit more realistic now, but I still felt a touch of regret as I came in low over the ocean and looked down at the empty beaches and the villas beyond. The sun had just dipped below the horizon, and lights were beginning to come on.

The island is engineered. It's arranged with consecutively rising terraces as you move inshore, so that everyone, theoretically, has a view of the sea. It was off-season. A few hardy souls moved along ramps and walkways. Most of the shops and restaurants were closed.

Base population was forty thousand, with an additional forty distributed among surrounding islands. The university served seven thousand students, who came from all over the archipelago and from the mainland. It had a good reputation, especially for the sciences. If you planned to be a physician, it was exactly the right place to start.

The campus spread across two broad terraces, immediately below the municipal buildings, which occupied the highest point on the island. I turned the skimmer over to the guide, which brought me down onto a landing pad adjoining a dome. The dome housed a student center, several shops, and a restaurant. The restuarant was Benjamin's. I remembered it from a long time ago, when it had been down near the beach.

Marquard surprised me by appearing from a side door. He strode quickly out onto the pad, opened the hatch, and provided a hand to help me down. In an age when chivalry ranks up there as just one more antiquity, it was a good way to start things off.

Barcross has probably the loveliest campus on the planet. It's all obelisks and tortoiseshell buildings and pyramids, with a spectacular command of the sea. But it was cold that day, and a sharp blast of wind stayed at our backs and all but blew us into the student center.

'It's good to meet you, Chase,' he said, steering us into Benjamin's. 'I appreciate your coming.' He was wearing gray slacks and a blue seashell shirt beneath a white jacket. He looked good, a tall, dashing type with a sense of humor and maybe a little bit shy, out for a night on the town.

We sat down and picked up our menus. Benjamin's hadn't changed much over the years. The dining area was bigger than in the old days, when the restaurant was located on a pier. And the selections had changed, of course. But it was still cozy, still subdued, and it still featured a seafaring ambience. There were sails and wheels and compasses scattered about, and one wall opened onto a virtual lighthouse and storm. In addition, they still had images of celebrity entertainers, including the classic one of Cary Webber standing outside the restaurant on the pier, with the ocean at her back. She looked lost. Cary had been a romantic favorite, but she died young, of course, and thereby became immortal.

We ordered wine and some breadsticks. When the server had gone, Marquard leaned across the table and whispered that I was striking. 'But of course,' he said, 'you already know that.'

I wondered if I was in for a long evening. I said thanks, propped my elbows on the table, folded my hands, and rested my chin on them. 'Shep,' I said, 'what do you have on the *Searcher*?'

'Wrong translation, Chase.' He looked around as if to ensure that we were alone – we were, save for a group of three or four students seated over by the window – and lowered his voice. 'It's *Seeker*.' He said it as if it had special significance.

'*Seeker*,' I said.

'That's correct.'

'Okay.'

'Chase, I don't think you understand. This might be *the Seeker*.'

'I'm sorry, Shep. I have no idea what we're talking about. What's the *Seeker*?'

'It's one of the ships that carried the Margolians off to their colony.'

'The Margolians.'

He smiled at my ignorance. 'They left Earth during the Third Millennium. *Fled*, I guess, is a better term. They told nobody where they were going. Went out on their own with five thousand people. And we never heard from them again. They're the lost colony.'

Atlantis. Intava. Margolia. Light dawned. 'They're a myth, aren't they?'

'Not really. It *happened*.'

'They didn't care much for the home world.'

36

'Chase, they lived in a society that was nominally a republic—'

'—But—?'

'—It controlled the churches, and used the schools to indoctrinate rather than teach. Patriotism was defined as unwavering support for the leader and the flag. Anything short of that was disloyal. The decisions of those in authority were not to be questioned.'

'What happened if you did? You got jailed?'

'Hellfire.'

'What?'

'You had a divinely imposed responsibility to submit to the will of the president. Render to Caesar.'

'That's not what "Render to Caesar" means.'

'It got twisted a bit. Failure to support the political establishment, and for that matter the social establishment, in thought as well as in act, constituted a serious offense against the Almighty.'

'Weren't there any skeptics out there?'

'Sure. But you don't hear much about them.'

It was hard to believe people could ever have lived like that. 'So it's a famous ship?'

'Oh, yes.'

'Are you telling me the *Seeker* never came back, either?'

'That's correct.' He leaned toward me, and the candlelight flashed off a row of white teeth. 'Chase. If this cup you told me about is really from the *Seeker*, you couldn't have done better.' The wine and breadsticks arrived. 'You say a woman walked in off the street and just presented you with it? Without any explanation?'

'Yes. That's pretty much what happened.' I was thinking how pleased Alex would be.

'I don't suppose you have it with you?'

I smiled. 'If I'd tried to take it off the premises, Alex would have had cardiac arrest.'

'And you're sure it's nine thousand years old?'

'That's the reading we got.'

'Incredible.' He handed me my glass and lifted his own. 'To the Margolians,' he said.

Indeed. 'So what really happened to them?'

He shrugged. 'Nobody knows.'

The wine was good. Candles. Firelight. And good wine. And good news. It was a hard combination to beat. 'They vanished completely?'

'Yes.' The waiter was back. I tend to eat light meals, even when someone else is buying. I settled for a fruit salad.

The waiter asked whether I was certain, and assured me that the Cordelia breakers were excellent.

'The *Seeker*,' Marquard continued, 'left Earth December 27, 2688, carrying approximately nine hundred people. Two years later they were back, and took off another nine hundred.'

'There was a third trip as well, wasn't there?' I was beginning to remember the story.

'Yes. The other ship was the *Bremerhaven*. They made three flights each. Carried more than five thousand people out to the colony world.'

'And nobody knew where it was? How's it even possible? You can't leave the station without filing a movement report.'

'Chase, we're talking about the beginning of the interstellar age. They didn't have many rules then.'

'Who owned the ship?'

'The Margolians. According to the record, it was refitted after each flight.'

'That doesn't sound as if it was in the best of shape.'

'I don't know what it took to maintain an interstellar in that era.'

'Was a search conducted for them?'

'Hard to say. The records aren't clear.' He finished off his wine and gazed at the rim of the glass, which sparkled in the candlelight. 'Chase, the authorities probably didn't try very hard. These were people who didn't want to be found.'

'Why not?'

An easy smile spread over his features. He *did* look good. He sat a few moments, admiring my charms, or my physical attributes, or the breadsticks. He signaled his approval as the waiter showed up with a dish full of nuts and grapes. 'They were perceived as troublemakers. They wanted to stay out of sight, and the government was happy to oblige them.'

'How were they troublemakers?' I asked.

'You ever been to Earth, Chase?'

'No, as a matter of fact. I've been wanting to make the trip for years. Just never got around to it.'

'You should do it. That's where it all began. For an historian, the trip to Earth is *de rigueur*.

'You go there, and you see the great monuments. Pyramids, statues, dams. The Kinoi Tower. The Mirabulis. Stop by Athens, where Plato and his colleagues launched the civilized world. Visit London, Paris, Berlin. Washington, and Tokyo. St Petersburg. Famous places, once. Centers of power in their day. You know what they're like now?'

'Well, I know they're not capitals anymore.'

'Except Paris. Paris is forever, they say. Chase, Earth has always had a problem: It's loaded with more people than its resources can support. It's always been that way. Ever since the Industrial Age. The results of too many people are that someone's always hungry, there's always a plague running loose somewhere. Ethnic jealousies always get worse when times are hard. Nations become unstable, so governments get nervous and impose strictures. Individual freedoms break down. One thing the place has never been short of is dictators. People there have old habits, old hatreds, old perspectives that they keep passing down from generation to generation, and never get rid of.

'The planet's population today is about eight billion. When the Margolians left, it was more than twice that. Can you imagine what life must have been like?'

'So,' I said, 'the Margolians were, what, downtrodden? Trying to find a place where they could feed their kids?'

39

'No. They were at the other end of the scale. They were intellectuals, by and large. And they had their share of the wealth. But they didn't like the noxious environment. *Noxious* meaning both physically and psychologically. They had a dictator. A theocrat by the name of Carvalla, who was relatively harmless as dictators went. But a dictator nevertheless. He controlled the media, controlled the schools, controlled the churches. You attended church or you paid the consequences. The schools were indoctrination centers.'

'Hard to believe people would consent to live like that.'

'They'd been trained to take authority seriously. In Carvalla's time, if you didn't do what you were told, you disappeared.'

'I'm beginning to see why they wanted to clear out.'

'They were led by Harry Williams.'

Another name I was obviously supposed to know. 'Sorry,' I said.

'He was a communications magnate, and he was connected for years to various social and political movements, trying to get food for hungry kids, to make medical care available. He didn't get into trouble until he started trying to do something about education.'

'What happened?'

'The authorities didn't like his basic notion, which was that kids should be taught to question everything.'

'Oh.'

'They called him unpatriotic.'

'I'm not surprised.'

'An atheist.'

'Was he?'

'He was an agnostic. Just as bad.'

'In that kind of society, I suppose so. You said it was a theocracy?'

'Yes. The head of state was also effectively the head of the Church.'

'What happened to Williams?'

'Fifteen years in jail. Or seventeen. Depends on which sources you trust. He'd have been executed, except that he had powerful friends.'

'So he did get out?'

'Yes, he got out. But it was while he was in jail that he decided something had to be done. Revolution wasn't possible. So the next best thing was to escape. "Joseph Margolis had it right," he's reported to have said at a meeting of his associates. "We'll never be able to change things."'

'I take it Joseph Margolis is the guy they're named for?'

'Right.'

'Who was he?'

'A British prime minister. A hero, and apparently something of a philosopher.'

'What was he right about?'

'That communication technologies lead easily to enslavement. That it is very difficult to maintain individual freedoms. He was fond of citing Benjamin Franklin's comment to the American people: "We have given you a republic. Now see if you can keep it."'

He saw I didn't recognize Franklin's name either. He grinned and offered to explain, but I got the drift. 'There *were* no colonies at the time, were there?'

'Two small ones. But both were under control of the home world. There were no independents.'

'And the government acquiesced?'

'They encouraged him to go and offered assistance.' He stared through the window at the ocean. 'Good riddance to trouble-makers. But that meant they'd know the location of the colony. Williams wanted out from under their thumb. So he and whoever was with him had to go it alone.'

'Not possible,' I said.

'Some of the Margolians thought the same way. But he persuaded them to make the attempt. They believed they could create an Eden. A home for humanity that would embody freedom and security. An ideal place to live.'

'That's been tried any number of times,' I said.

He nodded. 'Sometimes it's happened. Anyhow, they were desperate. They sent people out to look for the right world. When they found it, they kept its location secret, bought the two ships, and headed out. Five thousand of them.'

'That's an incredible story,' I said.

'Harry went with the last group, more than four years after the first Margolians left. He's reported to have told the media that, where they were going, even God wouldn't be able to find them.'

The server refilled our glasses. 'And nobody ever *did*,' I said.

'No. Not as far as I can tell.'

Alex was not very demonstrative. If the building were burning, he'd suggest it might be prudent to make for the door. So the news that the cup was associated with both a famous ship and a celebrated mystery did not send him reeling with joy around the office. But I saw a glint of satisfaction in those brown eyes. 'Jacob,' he said.

Jacob responded with a few bars of Perrigrin's *Eighth*. The kind of majestic chords with which heroic figures in the sims customarily make their entrances. Alex told him to knock it off.

'*How may I be of assistance?*' Jacob asked, in the deepest baritone he could muster.

Alex rolled his eyes. 'Jacob,' he said, 'we'd like to know whether any artifacts from the two ships associated with the Margolians, the *Seeker* and the *Bremerhaven*, are currently available, or have been on the market at any time.'

'*They'd be quite old,*' said Jacob. '*I'll need a few moments.*'

We made small talk for about a minute, then he was back. '*I see nothing of that nature. Nothing associated with either vessel. There are six verified items connected with the Margolians themselves. And numerous suspect objects.*'

'Name them, please. The ones that are verified.'

'*A communications link of some sort. A pen with Jase Tao-Ki's name engraved on it. Tao-Ki was a prominent member of the group, and a substantial contributor. There is also a wall plaque on which is inscribed a commendation to the Margolians from a social welfare group. A lapel pin bearing their symbol and name. The symbol is a torch. A portrait of Harry Williams himself. And a copy of* Glory Run, *signed by its author, Kay Wallis. It's an account of how they put the mission together. The signature is faded but can be seen in ultraviolet light. All six were left behind. There is nothing from them after their departure.'*

'Who was Kay Wallis?' asked Alex.

'One of the founders of the organization. One of its prime defenders when people began to laugh at them. The record's unclear, but it looks as if she died just before the final round of flights. She never left Earth.' He paused, perhaps expecting a comment. But none came. 'Wallis laid out their objections to various governmental policies in* Glory Run. *Basically they were concerned that each generation was subjected to a series of ideologies which, once imposed, were hard to get rid of, hampered independent thought, and led to various hostilities. She spells everything out. Get the religious groups under control. Reign in the corporate types. Recognize that dissent is healthy. Provide a level playing field so no one is disadvantaged.'*

'If American society – that was America, right? – Yes, if American society was so oppressive, how'd she get it published?'

'It was published in China,' said Jacob, 'one of the last strongholds of democracy on the planet.'*

'The Margolians,' I said, 'weren't really disadvantaged.'

Alex's eyes narrowed. 'They had resources. But if you don't have freedom of action, *disadvantaged* is the right word.' He scribbled something on a pad. 'Let's talk about the artifacts.' He requested a list of the amounts paid the last time the six Margolian objects had changed hands. Jacob reported two had been secret transactions. The other four printed out. Alex sighed. 'Not bad,' he said.

Indeed. Tao-Ki's pen went for several years' worth of my income. And I was well paid. The others were higher.

Alex rubbed his hands together. 'Okay. She'll have to produce ownership documentation before any of this goes public.' He was, of course, speaking of Amy.

'You'll take care of that?' I said. There would also be some negotiation involved, and that line of work was his specialty.

'Get through to her when you can. Find out if she'd be willing to meet us at the Hillside for a drink.'

I called Amy. She decided good things had happened and pressed me for information. I explained that we were still gathering data, but that Alex wished to ask a few more questions. She wasn't having it, of course. But that was okay. When we got to the Hillside, Alex would caution her not to pass the good news to anyone until we were sure nobody would dispute her ownership claim. We had to do that to protect ourselves since we would be facilitating the sale.

'I'll be there,' she said.

Alex had placed the cup in our vault. I brought its image up and wondered about its history.

Probably, someone had collected it as a souvenir during the *Seeker*'s early years, before it became associated with the Margolian migration. Or, it might have made one or two of the early flights to the colony world and come off the ship when it returned for the third mission. It was unlikely, but it could have happened that way. Were that the case, and we could show that it was, the cup would then become enormously valuable. But it was hard to see how we could take it that far.

When I mentioned it to Alex, he told me not to get excited. 'FTL travel was a big deal in the twenty-seventh century,' he said. 'What probably happened is that somebody got the trademark rights and produced cups and uniforms and all sorts of *Seeker* souvenirs for sale to the general public.'

The English characters looked especially exotic. Marquard had pronounced the ship's name for me, in both Standard and in English. He'd admitted at the same time that there was some uncertainty about pronunciation. No original audio recordings remained from the period, so even though we could read the language, nobody knew for certain what it had actually sounded like.

See-ker. Accent on the first syllable.

Outward Bound.

Where had they gone?

'So far away even God won't be able to find us.'

Several accounts existed of various aspects of the story, the background of Harry Williams, the roots of the Margolian movement, contemporary attacks accusing the Margolians of being elitist, their probable destination, and, eventually, theories about their disappearance. They had done precisely what they said they would do, suggested some. They had gone so far out, that even now, thousands of years later, the world they'd selected remained undetected.

The common wisdom was that something had gone wrong and the colony had perished. Some thought that Margolia, over the ages, might have sidestepped the various bumps and reversals suffered by the mainline civilization, and moved so far ahead of it that they would not be interested in communicating with us. Me, I thought the common wisdom had it right.

Margolia had been the subject of several sims. Jacob showed me one. It was titled *Invader*, and had been produced less than a year earlier. In it, the hero discovers that Margolians *have* returned quietly to the Confederacy. They are highly advanced, they walk unrecognized among us, and they actually control the machinery of government. They consider ordinary humans to be inferior and are planning a takeover. When the protagonist tries to warn the authorities, his girlfriend disappears, people begin dying, and there are lots of chases down dark alleys and through the corridors of an abandoned space station. The plot dissolves into a major shoot-out at the end, the young lady is rescued, and the good people of the Confederacy are alerted.

No one ever explained what conceivable reason the Margolians could have had in trying to take us over. But I'll give the producers this: I was hanging on to my chair during the chase scenes.

4

Drink deep the cup of life;
Take its dark wine into your soul,
For it passes round the table only once.

—Marcia Tolbert
Centauri Days, 3111 C.E.

The Hillside was an exquisite, posh club along the Riverwalk. The kind where they don't put any prices in the menu because you're not supposed to care. They had a human hostess, which is standard in most of the better restaurants, and human waiters, which of course is not. They also had a piano player.

The tables were well supplied with jasmine candles. Walls and tables were dark-stained wood. Prints in the style of the last century provided a sense of nostalgia. I noticed a couple of senators with their spouses (I assumed) across the room. One, a well-known champion of corporate benefits, recognized Alex and came over to say hello.

Amy walked in a few minutes later, looking around as if she were lost. Then she spotted us and strode briskly over. 'Good evening, Mr Benedict,' she said, still taking in her surroundings. 'This is really nice.'

Alex rose, pulled her chair out for her, and said he was glad she was pleased. She said hello to me and sat down.

47

She wore a pressed lavender suit and seemed to have had something of a makeover. Her hair was pulled back and in better order. Her eyes were more alert, and she stood a bit straighter than she had at the office. She wasn't at ease, but that of course was the reason we were there. The Hillside was the place Alex used when he wanted to put a client on the defensive. Which is to say, when he wanted something he wasn't sure he could get.

She went immediately to business: 'Chase said you have good news for me.'

That was her imagination at work. Alex looked at me, read my face, and smiled. 'The cup is associated with a famous, and very early, interstellar,' he said. 'We think it's reasonably valuable.'

'How much?' she asked.

'We'll have to let the market decide, Amy. I'd rather not guess.' He produced a chip. 'When you get time, complete this document. It will establish your ownership of the property.'

'Why do I have to do that?' she asked. 'It's mine. It was given to me.'

'And possession is ninety percent. But disputes have a way of appearing in these cases. It's a formality, but it might save problems later.'

She was annoyed, but she took it and dropped it in a side pocket. 'I'll get it back to you tomorrow.'

'Good,' said Alex. 'As soon as you've done that, we'll put the cup on the market and see what happens.'

'All right.'

He leaned forward and lowered his voice. 'Now,' he said, 'while we don't know its precise value, we should establish a minimum bid.'

'How much?'

He gave her a number. I've been through these things before, but it took my breath away. It was more than I'd been able to earn so far in a lifetime. Amy's eyes squeezed hard shut and I saw a tear run down her cheek. I may have been getting a little damp myself.

48

'Wonderful,' she said, with a breaking voice.

Alex beamed. He was the picture of philanthropic content. It was so nice to be of assistance. Our cut, of course, would be the standard ten percent of the eventual sale price. I knew him well enough to be aware that his minimum bid was conservative.

I thought for a minute she was going to come apart. Fluttering handkerchief, brave smile, giggle, and an apology. Sorry, it's such a shock.

'Now,' said Alex, 'I want you to do something for me.'

'Of course.'

The waiter arrived, and we took time to order, although Amy was no longer paying much attention to the menu. When he was gone, Alex leaned across the table. 'I want you to tell me where it came from.'

She looked startled. Fox and hounds. 'Why, I told you, Mr Benedict. My ex-boyfriend gave it to me.'

'When would that have been?'

'I don't know. Several weeks ago.'

Alex's voice dropped even lower. 'Would you be kind enough to tell me his name?'

'Why? I told you, it belongs to me.'

'Because there might be more of these objects around. If there are, the owner may not be aware of their value.'

She shook her head. No. 'I'd rather not do that.'

Breakup city. Alex reached across the table and took her hand. 'It could mean a great deal to you,' he said. 'We'd arrange things so you got a finder's fee.'

'No.'

He looked at me, shrugged, and changed the subject. We talked about how nice it was to have an enormous amount of money fall out of the sky, and how the cup was a valuable artifact. The meals came, and we continued in that vein until Alex caught my eye again. I understood what he wanted, and a few minutes later he excused himself.

Time for girl talk. 'Bad ending?' I asked in a sympathetic voice.

She nodded. 'I hate him.'

'Another woman?'

'Yeah. He had no right.'

'I'm sorry,' I said.

'It's okay. I let him get away with it a couple times. But promises don't mean nothing to him.'

'You're probably better off. He sounds like a jerk.'

'I'm over it.'

'Good.' I tried to look casual. 'If he has more of these around somewhere, it could mean a lot more money for you.'

'I don't care.'

'We could handle it so he wouldn't know where the information came from. It would not involve you. He'd never know.'

She shook her head. Absolutely not.

'How about this? If he has any more artifacts like the cup, we'll keep you out of it, and we'll make him an offer without telling him what they're really worth. Then you and I can split whatever we make.'

That would have been a trifle unethical, and Alex would never have gone for it. Me, I wouldn't have had a problem. I was beginning to feel some sympathy for Amy, so I had no trouble taking her side.

She started having second thoughts. 'You're sure he'd never find out? About me?'

'Absolutely. We've handled these things before.' If we could get a name, it would be easy enough to look into the situation without alerting him. If it turned out there were actually more souvenirs from the *Seeker* lying around, then we could go back and negotiate some more with Amy.

'He would know it was me the minute you mentioned the cup.'

'We'd be careful.'

'It doesn't matter. He'd know.'

'We wouldn't mention the cup.'

'Don't bring it up at all.'

'Okay. We won't. We won't say a word about it.'

She thought about it some more. 'His name's Hap.' Her face tightened and I thought she was going to cry again. It was turning into a weepy evening. 'Actually, it's Cleve Plotzky. But everybody calls him Hap.'

'Okay.'

'If you tell him, he'll come after me.'

'He's assaulted you,' I said.

She wouldn't look at me.

'Does he live in Andiquar?'

'Aker Point.'

Aker Point was a small community west of the capital. Most of the people who lived there were either unable to hold a job or satisfied subsisting on the minimum ration.

I saw Alex loitering across the room, pretending to examine the artwork. He figured out that the negotiation had ended, lingered another minute or two, said something to a waiter, and rejoined us. Moments later a fresh round of cocktails arrived.

Cleve (Hap) Plotzky *did* work for a living. He was a burglar. But not a very successful one. We got that much from the public record. He was good at rigging devices that shut down security systems, but he always seemed to make a beginner's mistake. Sometimes he got caught trying to move the merchandise. Or because he sneezed and left his DNA on the property. Or because he bragged to the wrong people about his skills. He also had a record of assorted assaults, mostly against women.

So we went back to see Fenn Redfield. The police inspector had been a burglar himself at one time, sufficiently prone to the profession that the courts eventually ordered a mind wipe. He knew none of this, of course. His memories of his past life, up to about fifteen years earlier, were all fictitious.

He let Alex look through the court documents regarding Hap but could not show him the police reports. 'Against the rules,' he said. 'Wish I could help.'

The court documents didn't go into sufficient detail about what had been stolen. 'How about,' Alex said, 'if I tell you what I'm looking for, and you tell me if it was among the stuff this guy took?'

So Alex described the cup with its English inscription, and Fenn looked at the record and said no. 'It's not listed.'

'Is anything like that on the list? Any kind of drinking vessel?'

Fenn explained that Hap Plotzky only took jewelry. And ID cards if he found any. And maybe electronic devices that were lying around loose. But pots and dishes and collectors' items? 'No. Not ever.'

Our next step was to talk with Plotzky himself.

We put together a mass-distribution ad. Jacob gave us an attractive female avatar, dark-skinned, dark-eyed, lithe, long-legged, with spectacular bumpers, and we had her sit in a virtual office surrounded by virtual antique dishware. We used my voice, which Alex told me was sexy, then smiled to let me know he was kidding. And we wrote a script.

'Hello, Cleve,' the avatar would say, *'do you have some old pottery or other similar items that have been around a long time and are just gathering dust? Turn them into instant cash with us . . .'*

We used 'Cleve' instead of 'Hap' because we wanted to be sure he concluded this was a mass mailing and not a message directed specifically at him. We figured this guy wasn't very bright.

'Will it get past the AI?' I wondered.

'Sure,' said Alex. 'Plotzky will have a basic, no-frills model.'

So we sent it off.

We got no response, and after a couple of days we went to Plan B. If Hap had given the cup to Amy, he had no idea of its value. That made it likely any similar object he owned wouldn't be locked away. It would be on a shelf somewhere. All we really had to do was gain entry.

Jacob connected me with Hap's AI. I introduced myself as a researcher with the Caldwell Scientific Sampling Survey and asked to speak with Mr Plotzky. The AI gave me an avatar to look at, a large, hostile, ill-kempt female. The sort of woman you might find enjoying a good fight. That image told me everything I needed to know about Hap. In fact, you can tell quite a lot about people from the images their houses show you. Anyone who calls Alex, for example, first sees a well-dressed, polished, impeccably polite individual. It might be a male or female figure. That's left to Jacob's discretion. But there's no question it holds a master's degree from New London.

'*Why?*' she asked, making no effort to mask her owner's hostility. '*What do you want?*'

'I'd like very much to ask Mr Plotzky some survey questions. I'll only take a few minutes of his time.'

'*Sorry*,' she said. '*He's busy.*'

'I could call back later.'

'*You could, but it wouldn't matter.*'

Alex was sitting back out of range of the image pickup so he couldn't be seen. But he was nodding vigorously, egging me on. Don't lose your patience. 'There's money in it for him,' I said.

'*Oh? How much?*'

'Enough. Please tell him I'm here.'

She ran the idea through her software. Then the picture froze. She had her arms folded and was staring directly at me. That sort of thing tends to hold your attention. A minute later she blinked off and I was looking at Hap himself. '*Yeah?*' he said. '*What's the problem?*' He looked as if he'd been asleep. We knew he was thirty-two, but he had the battered, caved-in features of someone much older.

'I'm conducting a survey for the entertainment industry. We want to make a determination about what people are watching. It would only take a few minutes.'

'*Lulu tells me you said something about money.*'

'Yes,' I said. 'There's a modest stipend.'

'*How much?*'

I told him.

'*Okay,*' he said. '*What do you want to know?*'

'Well, I'd need to come by the house, Mr Plotzky. We need to complete a document on your equipment as well.'

'*I can tell you what I have, lady. Save you the trip.*'

'Sorry. We can't do it that way. I'd like to, but I have to certify that I've made the visit.'

He nodded and took a long look. It was as if he hadn't noticed me before. Then he said okay, and tried a come-hither grin. It was crooked and repulsive but I smiled back.

Actually the place wasn't the hovel I expected. Plotzky lived nineteen or twenty floors up in one of the vertical cities that made Aker Point infamous. There wasn't a lot of space, but it was reasonably clean, and he had a pretty good view of the Melony. I mean it was well south of lush, but if you'd decided just to drift through life, you could have done worse.

He opened the door and attempted a smile. There was a woman with him, hard-eyed, short, solid as a bowling ball. It struck me he should have tried to keep Amy on board. This one made the avatar look good. She watched me suspiciously, the way women do when they think you're out to steal their guy.

Hap was wearing a workout suit with a top that said DOWN-TOWN AND LIKE IT, under a picture of a shot glass and some bubbles. He was short and barrel-chested with thick black hair, lots of it, growing everywhere. He indicated the chair I could use. I complied and took out my notebook.

Hap Plotzky was more congenial than he'd been on the circuit. Maybe it was because I'd become a money source, but I decided he was trying to figure out how to make a play for me while the steamroller was sitting there. I was willing to bet he'd tried unsuccessfully to get her out the door prior to my arrival, and that was what explained the woman's animus.

'So what did you want to know, Ms Kolpath?'

I asked him about his favorite programs, how much he participated, what he would prefer to do other than what was available, and so on. I recorded his answers and admired the furniture, which allowed me to get a good look around the living room. The decorations were, you could say, sparse. What he had, essentially, was a sofa, a couple of chairs, and walls. The walls were lemon-colored. There was a cheap laminex shelf adjacent the front door, but the only thing on it was a pile of data chips.

'Yeah,' he said, 'I like cop shows. Nothin' much else worth a damn.' He thought he'd cut off the angle on his female guest – or roommate – and he tried leering.

I felt sorry for the guy. Don't ask me why.

When we'd gotten through my list of questions, I took out a monitor that's designed to interact with the AI in my skimmer. It's in a small black case and it had red and white status lamps. It doesn't do anything else, and it certainly wasn't capable of what I was about to claim for it, but he had no way of knowing that. 'If you don't mind, Hap, I'm going to record the capabilities of your system now.' We were on first-name terms by then.

'Sure,' he said.

I pointed it in the general direction of the projectors and squeezed. The monitor lit up and the lights chased each other around the case. 'Good,' I said. 'Uh-huh.' As if I'd picked up a significant piece of information. The kitchen opened off the living room. I could see a table, two chairs, and a mounted plate that said YOU'RE IN MY KITCHEN NOW. SIT DOWN AND SHUT UP. And another that said I'M THE BOSS HERE. There was no sign of an antique.

The bedroom – there was only one – opened through a door to my right. I got up and walked coolly into it.

'What the hell,' demanded the woman, 'do you think you're doing?'

'Just checking the projection system, ma'am.' Hap had thrown her name in my direction but I hadn't caught it. 'Have to be thorough, you know.' I saw nothing of interest. Unmade bed. More bare walls. A clothes chute stuck open. A full-length mirror with a chipped frame.

I aimed at the projectors and set the lights running again. 'What does that do?' Hap asked.

I smiled. 'Damned if I know. I just point and press. Somebody else does the download and analysis.'

He grinned at me, looked at the monitor, frowned, and for a moment I thought he was getting suspicious. 'I'm surprised Dora hasn't said something about being probed.' Dora would be the AI.

'They tell me it's noninvasive,' I said. 'Dora probably hasn't noticed.'

'Is that possible?' He looked as if I were introducing gremlins.

'Anything's possible these days.' I shut the instrument down. 'Well, thank you very much, Hap.' I strolled back into the living room and picked up my jacket. The woman never took her eyes from me. 'Nice to have met you, ma'am,' I said.

Hap got the door. He could have told Dora to open it, but he got it himself. It was a gesture that didn't get by his companion. I smiled, wished him good afternoon, and slipped into the hallway. The door closed, and I immediately heard raised voices inside.

'Hap has a sister,' Alex said after I'd told him I didn't think Hap had any more pieces from the *Seeker*.

'Do we care?' I asked. 'About the sister?'

'She might be able to tell us where he got the cup.'

'That's a long shot.'

'Maybe. At the moment it's all we have.'

'Okay.'

'She lives on Morinda.'

'The black hole?'

'The station.'

Interstellar flights had become a lot less inconvenient with the arrival of the quantum drive. It was near-instantaneous travel within a range of a few thousand light-years. After a jump, you had to spend a few hours recharging, then you could go again.

Theoretically, you could have jumped all the way to Andromeda in maybe a year or so, except that the equipment would require maintenance and would wear out long before you got there. And you couldn't carry enough life support, or enough fuel. Nevertheless, the trip is feasible if we're willing to make some adjustments. But nobody's come up with a good reason yet to go. Other than a few politicians looking to find an issue to run on that won't alienate people. The Milky Way is still ninety percent unknown territory, so it's hard to see the point of an Andromeda mission. Other than to be able to say we did it. But in case anyone in authority is reading this and has plans along those lines, don't look at me.

'I take it you want me to go talk to her,' I said.

'Yes. Woman to woman is best.'

'We promised Amy we wouldn't let the family know we're interested in the cup.'

'We promised her that Hap wouldn't find out. Chase, the woman is on *Morinda*. Moreover, she and her brother haven't spoken for years.'

'Where's the mother?'

'Dead.'

'And the father?'

'Dropped out of sight early. I can't find anything on him.'

5

There's something about having a black hole in the neighborhood that leads to sleepless nights.

—Karl Svenson,
Strumpets Have All the Fun, 1417

Morinda is one of three black holes known to exist inside Confederacy space. The name also serves the large armored orbiting space station that was home to a thousand researchers and their support staffs, who were measuring, poking, taking the temperature of, and throwing assorted objects into, the beast. Most of them, according to the info tabs, were trying to learn how to bend space. There were even a few psychologists conducting experiments related to the way people perceive time.

I had never been there, nor had I ever seen a black hole before. If that's the correct terminology, since you don't really *see* a black hole. This one wasn't particularly big, as these things go. It was maybe a couple hundred times the mass of Rimway's sun. A ring of illuminated debris, the accretion disk, enclosed it, firing off X-ray jets and God-knows-what other kinds of radiation, and sometimes even rocks.

That's why the station is armored and equipped with Y-beam projectors. Most of the action is predictable, but the experts claim you never really know. They don't worry much about the rocks, which they can dissolve. But radiation is a different kind of problem.

I jumped into the system at a range of about 70 million kilometers from the hole. That was closer than I should have been, but still a safe distance. Quantum travel is convenient because it's instantaneous. But the downside is that there's a larger degree of uncertainty to it than there was with the old Armstrong engines. It's a modest difference, but it's there, and it's enough to get you killed if you don't give yourself plenty of room so you don't materialize inside a planet, or for that matter in the same space as anything too big for the prods to push out of the way.

I needed three days to coast into the station. While en route I arranged billeting, called my old friend Jack Harmon who was there on assignment and let him know I was coming and he could expect to buy me a drink, and checked out what I could find on Hap's sister.

Her name was Kayla Bentner. She was a nutritech, whose chief responsibility was to see that food supplies at the station were healthful. Her husband Rem was a lawyer. I know you're wondering why a space station needs a lawyer, but this is a big operation. People are always renegotiating contracts and quarreling over assigned time on the instruments. They also get married, make out wills, file for separation. And occasionally they sue one another.

At a place like that, the lawyer is the neutral party, the guy everybody trusts. Not like back home.

I thought about letting Kayla know I was coming, but then decided it would be best not to make a big deal of it. So I cruised into my assigned berth on the evening of the third day, checked into my hotel room, met Harmon in a small bistro, and spent the evening recalling old times and generally enjoying myself. I'd hoped he might know either Kayla or her husband. That would have made the job easier, but no such luck.

In the late morning I planted myself outside the offices of the

Support Services, where Kayla worked, and when she came out to go to lunch, I fell in behind.

She was with two other women. I followed them into a restaurant called Joystra's, which was a no-frills place. The tables were too close together and management expected you to eat up and move on. Furniture, curtains, and tableware all looked as if they had been made on the run. But it was located on the station's outer perimeter, and there was a wall-length window with a view of the accretion disk. It wasn't much to look at, a large shining ring that under other circumstances would have been just another shining ring, of which the Orion Arm has plenty, but it was ominous because you couldn't get out of your mind what was at the center of the thing.

Kayla didn't look much like her brother. She was tall, trim, serious. Civilized. You looked into her light blue eyes, and you could see somebody was home. Half the people in the restaurant seemed to know her, and exchanged greetings with her as she passed.

She and her friends were shown to a table, and I was next in line, wondering how to manage getting an introduction when I caught a break. Sharing tables during peak hours was a common practice at the station. 'Would madam mind?'

'Not at all,' I said. 'Perhaps the three ladies who just came in—'

'I'll attend to it.' The autohost was tall, lean, black mustache, constantly smiling, but it was the kind of smile that looked glued on. I've never understood why the people who arrange these things can't get the details right. He strode over to the table where Kayla and the others were seated and made his request. The women looked my way, one of them nodded, and Kayla raised a hand in my direction.

I went over. Introductions all around. I gave my name as Chase Dellmar. 'I know you from somewhere,' I told Kayla, putting on my best puzzled frown.

She studied me. Shook her head. 'I don't think we've ever met.'

I pressed an index finger against my lips and creased my brow, thinking deeply about where we might have connected. There was some back and forth about places we'd both worked. No link there. Different schools. Must be my imagination. We ordered, lunch came, we talked aimlessly. The women were all assigned to the same facility. There was a problem of some sort with the boss, who was forever taking credit for other people's ideas, who wouldn't listen to anyone, and who didn't spend enough time with the software. That was station-speak for someone who didn't socialize, a capital crime in a small society. The usual cautions about supervisors fraternizing with the help didn't apply to the same degree in places like Morinda.

I waited until we were finished and dividing the check. Then it struck me. I brightened, looked directly at Kayla, and said, 'You're Hap's sister.'

She went white. 'You know Hap?'

'I was Chase Bonner when you knew me. I used to come by the apartment.'

She frowned.

'Years ago, of course. I can understand you might have forgotten.'

'Oh, no,' she said. 'I remember you. Of course. It's just that it's been so long.'

'I can't believe I'd run into you here.'

'Yes. That's a wild coincidence, isn't it?'

'How's Hap? I haven't seen him in a lot of years.'

'Oh. He's okay. I guess. Actually, I haven't seen him myself in a long time.' We were out of the restaurant by then, trailing behind her companions. 'Listen,' she said, 'it's been a pleasure to see you again, uh . . .' She had to struggle for the name. '—Shelley.'

'Chase.' I smiled gently. 'It's okay. We didn't spend that much time together. I wouldn't expect you to remember me.'

'No. I remember you. It's just that I have to get back to work, and I guess my mind is on other things.'

'Sure,' I said. 'I understand. How about letting me buy you a drink while I'm here? Maybe this evening?'

'Oh, I don't know, Chase. My husband—'

'Bring him along—'

'—doesn't drink.'

'Dinner then. My treat.'

'I can't let you do that.' Still backing away from me.

'It's okay. It's something I'd really like to do, Kayla.'

'You have a number?' I gave it to her. 'Let me check with him, and I'll get back to you.'

'Okay. I hope you can make it.'

'I'm sure we can manage it, Chase. And thank you.'

We met at the same place where Jack and I had eaten the evening before. I brought him along to balance the sides.

Remilon Bentner was a pleasant enough dinner companion, easygoing, plainspoken, a good conversationalist. He and Jack, it turned out, both played a game that had become popular at the station. It was called Governance, and required participants to make political and social-engineering decisions. We have, for example, implants that will stimulate intelligence. No known side effects. Do we make them available to the general public? 'I did, and I got some unpleasant surprises,' said Rem. 'High IQs aren't all they're cracked up to be.'

'In what way?' I asked.

Jack was drinking coffee. 'Beyond a certain level, roughly one-eighty, people, young ones especially, tend to become disruptive. Rebellious.'

'But that,' I said, 'is because they become restless, right? Their peers are slower, so the brighter ones lose patience.'

'Actually,' said Rem, 'they're simply harder to program. You ever wonder why human intelligence is set where it is?'

'I assume,' I said, 'it's because the dumber apes walked into the tigers.'

'But why not *higher*?' asked Jack. 'When Kasavitch did his Phoenician study at the beginning of the last century, he concluded there was no evidence humans are any smarter now than they were at the dawn of history. Why not?'

'Easy,' said Kayla. 'Fifteen thousand years is too short a time for evolutionary effects to take hold. Kasavitch – did I get his name right? – needs to come back in a hundred thousand years and try again. I think he'll see a difference.'

'I don't think so,' said Bentner. 'There seems to be a ceiling.'

'Why?' I asked.

'The experts think that once you get past one-eighty, you become too much of a social problem. Uncontrollable. Herd-of-cats syndrome. Authority tends to be a bit mindless no matter how you structure the political system. The high-IQ types have a hard time tolerating it.' He grinned. 'That puts them at a serious disadvantage. These people get to about seven years old and after that they have to learn everything the hard way. Where a truly superior intelligence should help them, it becomes a handicap. In the old days, the tribe would get sick of it and wouldn't protect them. So the tigers got them.'

'The same thing,' said Jack, 'seems to be true among the Mutes. They have more or less the same range we do. And the same ceiling.' The Mutes were the only known alien race. They were a telepathic species.

'I'd expect,' I said, 'that the rules would be different for telepaths.'

Bentner shook his head. 'Apparently not. Jack, what did you do? Did you use the implants?'

Jack shook his head. 'No. I didn't think a whole society full of people who thought they knew everything would be a good idea.'

'Smart man. My society became unstable within two generations. I've a friend whose state collapsed altogether.'

'Did you know,' said Jack, 'that the suicide rate among people with genius-level IQs is almost three times what it is among the general population?'

'We're dumb for a reason,' I said.

'That's right.' Bentner grinned. 'And thank God for it.' He lifted a glass. 'To mediocrity,' he said. 'May it flourish.'

A few minutes later, I mentioned as a by-the-way that my hobby was collecting antique cups. That caught nobody's interest. But I turned to Kayla. 'Now that I think of it, you guys had one.'

'One what?'

'An antique cup. Remember? It had that strange writing on it.'

'Not us,' she said. 'I don't remember anything like that.'

'Sure,' I said. 'I remember it clearly. It was gray, with a green-and-white eagle. Wings spread.'

She considered it. Pursed her lips. Shook her head. Then surprised me. 'Yes. I remember. It was on the mantel.'

'You know,' I said, 'I always admired that cup.'

'I hadn't thought about it in years. But that's right. We *did* have one like that.'

'Those were good days, Kayla. I don't know why that cup sticks in my memory. I tend to associate it with happy times, I guess.'

'That sounds as if you're having problems.'

'No. Not at all. But that was a more innocent age. You know how it is.'

'Of course.'

She and I were drinking tea, and we each took a sip. 'I wonder where it is now,' I said. 'The cup. Do you still have it?'

'I don't know where it is,' she said. 'I don't have it. I haven't seen it since I was a girl.'

'Maybe Hap has it.'

'Could be.'

'You know,' I said, 'when I get home I think I'll look him up. It would be nice to see him again.'

Her features hardened. 'You wouldn't like him now.'

'Oh?'

'He's too much like his father.' She shook her head in disapproval. 'Well, let it go.'

We talked about her work on the station, and when I saw an opening, I went back to the cup: 'You know, I was always intrigued by it. By the cup. Where did it come from originally, Kayla? Do you know?'

'I've no idea,' she said.

'Hap never struck me as someone interested in antiques.'

'Oh,' she said, 'I doubt it's an antique. But you're right about Hap.' A darkness drifted into her eyes. 'He wasn't interested in anything this side of alcohol, drugs, and money. And women.'

She regretted having said that, and I tried to look sympathetic and moved the conversation along. 'Somebody probably gave it to him.'

'No. We had it up on the shelf as far back as I can remember. When Hap and I were both kids.' She thought about it. 'I suspect he *might* still have it.'

'You know,' I said, 'I seem to recall there were a couple other pieces like it.'

'No, Chase,' she said. 'I don't think so.' Dinner finally arrived. 'I'm pretty sure it's the only one we had. Now that I think of it, I believe Mom told me once that my father gave it to her.'

Alex's celebrity has spilled over, to a degree, on me. I seem to have not quite enough to draw autograph seekers, but I do get the occasional crank. Next morning, I was standing in a souvenir stall picking up a snack to take back to my room when a small, sharply dressed, middle-aged man with disheveled black hair asked whether I wasn't Chase Kolpath. The tone was already vaguely hostile. And it took me a moment to realize this was the same guy who'd disrupted Ollie Bolton's remarks at the Caucus. Kolchevsky.

I could have denied who I was. I've done that in the past, but I didn't think it would work with this character. So I owned up.

'I thought so,' he said.

I started edging away from him.

'No offense intended, Ms Kolpath. But you seem like a capable young lady.'

'Thank you,' I said, grabbing a cherry cheesecake more or less at random and pointing my key at the reader to pay for it.

'Please don't run off. I'd like a moment of your time.' He coughed lightly. 'My name is Casmir Kolchevsky. I'm an archeologist.'

'I know who you are,' I said. Kolchevsky, despite his hysterical behavior on that earlier occasion, was *not* small potatoes. He had done major excavations on Dellaconda, in Baka Ti. It was a civilization that had prospered for almost six hundred years before going into a sharp decline. Today it was nothing more than a handful of villages. The reasons behind its collapse remained very much a subject for debate. Some thought their technological development had outrun their good sense, others that they'd been victimized by a cultural revolution that had split them into a series of warring subgroups, and still others that their dinnerware had contained too much lead, leading to widespread infertility. Kolchevsky had done much of the fieldwork at Baka Ti, had in the process recovered a substantial number of antiquities that were now housed in museums. And he'd established a reputation for both brilliance and bellicosity.

'Good. No need then to stand on ceremony.' He looked up at me as he might have looked at a cat with a broken leg. 'I've read about you,' he said. 'You're obviously talented.'

'Thank you, Professor.'

'May I ask what in heaven you're doing working for Benedict?'

'I beg your pardon?'

'Oh, come now. You know what I'm talking about. You and your partner are a pair of temple thieves. I'm sorry to be so blunt, but I'm really quite appalled.'

'I'm sorry you disapprove of what we do, Professor.' I tried to get by him, but he blocked my exit.

'The day will come, young lady, when you'll look back over these years and regret your actions.'

'Professor, I'd appreciate it if you would let me by.'

'Of course.' But he didn't move. 'Benedict,' he went on, warming to his subject, 'is a grave robber. A looter. Objects that should be the property of everyone wind up as showpieces in the homes of the wealthy.' His voice softened. 'You know that as well as I do.'

'I'm sorry you feel that way,' I said. 'You don't sound as if you're open to other opinions, so why don't we just agree to disagree and let it go at that? Now, I'll ask you again, please stand out of my way.'

'I *am* sorry,' he said. 'I really didn't mean to give offense. But I wonder whether you're aware what your association with him does to your own reputation?'

'I'm inclined to wonder, Professor, who appointed you guardian of the world's treasures?'

'Ah, yes. By all means, when no defense will suffice, go on the attack.' He stood aside. 'That's not a very satisfactory response, is it?'

'It wasn't a very satisfactory question.'

I'd decided to spend a couple of days with Jack. But before going down to meet him for lunch, I sent a message to Alex, advising him that the mission had been futile. I was coming home with nothing. I didn't mention Kolchevsky.

6

Talent is important, perseverance good. But in the end there's nothing quite like blind luck.

—Morita Kamalee,
Walking with Plato, 1388

When I got home, Alex had news for me. He'd been to see Fenn and had information about Hap's father. 'His name was Rilby Plotzky. Known to his associates as *Rile.* Like his son, he was a burglar.'

'With a name like that, I can understand it.' Skills ran in the family, I guessed. 'You say he *was* a burglar. Did he reform? Or die?'

'Mind-wiped.'

'Oh.'

'I asked whether we could talk to him.'

'Alex, you know they'd never let us do that. And it wouldn't do any good anyhow.'

It was snowing again. We were sitting in the office watching big wet flakes come down, and it didn't look as if it was ever going to stop. Snow was hip deep out to the landing pad. 'Mind wipes aren't always complete,' Alex said. 'Sometimes it's possible to reverse the effects.'

'They wouldn't let you do that either.'

'I know. I've already inquired.'

'What did they say?'

'It didn't get past the official filters.'

I was surprised that Alex would even consider going that far. If the elder Plotzky had established a new life under a new name, he had a complete set of false memories and the lifetime habits that came with them. He would be a solid citizen. Break through that wall and it was anybody's guess what might happen.

He resented my disapproval. 'We're talking about objects of enormous value, Chase,' he said. 'I can't say I'd have all that much sympathy for him. If he was worth a damn, they wouldn't have had to do the procedure in the first place. And, anyhow, they could put him under again.'

'Are we assuming he *stole* the cup?'

'You think he was likely to have been a lover of the finer things in life?'

The first Plotzky's burglary career had ended almost twenty years before, in 1412, when he was convicted for the third time, on seventeen counts. That was when they imposed the wipe. His first arrest had been in 1389. The evidence indicated he'd been active in his chosen profession during most of the intervening twenty-three-year span.

'So,' I said, 'how does any of this help us?'

'We try to pin down which burglary might have produced the cup.'

'How do we do that? Are there police reports?'

'Yes. Of all the unsolved burglaries in Plotzky's area of operation. But they can't be made available. Privacy laws.'

'So we have to go through the media.'

'I'd say so.'

'There's no point. He must have taken it because it caught his eye. He obviously didn't realize the value of the thing or it wouldn't have sat on that shelf all those years. If somebody had reported the theft of a nine-thousand-year-old cup, Plotzky would have known what he had.'

'That's a good argument,' said Alex.

'Okay. Look, I hate to point this out, but we now have reason to suspect we're aiding and abetting. We're helping unload stolen property.'

'We don't know that, Chase. It's guesswork.'

'Right. This family of burglars, on the side, has a taste for antiques.'

He was getting uncomfortable. Frustrated. Outside, the wind was picking up, and the storm was growing worse. 'Let's do *this*,' he said. 'We'll set some parameters for Jacob and let him run a search through news reports covering the period. If we can't find a break-in where the cup might have been taken, what have we lost?'

Actually, that wasn't as unlikely a possibility as it sounded. Burglary's a rare phenomenon. Most people have high-tech security. And criminal behavior itself is relatively unusual. We're living in a golden age, although I doubt most people realize it.

It got me thinking about the Margolians, and the kind of world that would drive five thousand people to clear out, to jump on the *Seeker* and the *Bremerhaven* and make for an uncertain frontier. What had it really been like to live in the twenty-seventh century? Widespread criminal behavior. Intolerance. Political oppression. Environmental problems. Religious crazies. You name it.

'Jacob,' said Alex, 'check through the news stories relating to burglaries in the Andiquar region from 1389 to 1412. You're looking for any reference to the *Seeker* or to a nine-thousand-year-old drinking cup.'

'*Commencing search,*' he said.

Alex was sitting in the big, soft, hand-tooled sofa facing the desk. He was wearing a frumpy gray sweater and looked distracted. He picked up a book, closed it, wandered over to the window, and stared out at the snowstorm. 'I can call you,' I told him, 'when he finishes.' I'd have liked to see him go upstairs to his office.

'It's okay,' he said.

Ten minutes later Jacob was back. '*Negative,*' he said. '*No matches.*'

'All right.' Alex closed his eyes. 'Try any thefts involving antiquities.'

Jacob's lights went on and the electronic hum in the walls picked up.

I'd been going over the latest items coming onto the market, looking for objects that might be of interest to our clients. Someone had found an eighty-year-old handmade clock. None of our customers would care, but I liked the way it looked. It wouldn't cost much, and it would give my living room a bit of cachet. I was trying to make up my mind about it when Jacob reported negative again.

'All right.' Alex sank back into the sofa and crossed his arms. 'What we need to do is find thefts from homes whose occupants would have been likely to own antiques.'

'How do we do that?'

'Hang on a second.' He flipped open a notebook. 'Jacob, would you see if you can get Inspector Redfield on the circuit for me?'

Fenn and a slice of his desk appeared in the middle of the office. '*What can I do for you, Alex?*' He sounded as if he were having a long morning.

'The case we were talking about yesterday—?'

His brow furrowed. '*Yes?*' He looked as if he'd already heard enough about that one.

'I wonder if you could tell me whether the burglaries were limited to a single area?'

'*Wait one.*' He made weary sounds. '*What was the name again?*'

'Plotzky.'

'*Oh, yes. Plotzky.*' He gave instructions to an AI, reminded Alex that that week's card game would be at his place, and took a bite out of a sandwich. Then he looked up at a monitor. '*Bulk of the cases were in Anslet and Sternbergen. There were a few elsewhere. Pretty well spread around, actually.*'

'But all in the region immediately west of Andiquar?'

'Oh, yes. Plotzky didn't travel much.'

'Okay, Fenn. Thanks.'

In his final trial, Plotzky had been charged with seventeen counts of theft by breaking and entering. We had the names of the property owners from the court records. The prosecutors had tagged him with more than a hundred over his career. 'What we do is use the media to track down every burglary we can find in the target area while Plotzky was active.'

'That's going to be a lot of burglaries.'

'Maybe not. The records don't indicate that he had much competition.' He got up and went over to the window and looked out at the snow. 'Jacob?'

'Yes, Alex?'

'How many burglaries were there during the period?'

More lights. *'I count two hundred forty-seven reported instances.'*

'I thought you said he didn't have much competition.'

'Chase, we're looking at twenty years.' He shook his head at the weather. 'Doesn't look as if it'll ever quit snowing.' It was the kind of day that left me wanting to curl up in front of a fire and just go to sleep.

'Jacob,' he said, 'we need the victims' names.'

A list rolled out of the printer.

'Now what?' I asked.

'We check each of them. Try to find people likely to have owned antiques.'

Easy to say. 'This is forty years ago. Some of these people won't even be alive.'

'Do your best.'

What happened to the 'we'? 'Okay,' I said. 'Who's likely to own antiques?'

'Think what our clients have in common.'

'Money,' I suggested.

'I would have preferred *exquisite taste*. But yes, they will have

73

to have money. Get the addresses. Look for people who live in the more exclusive areas.'

'Alex,' I said, 'we're talking about burglars. They're going to *favor* the more-exclusive areas.'

'Not necessarily. Security systems are less effective elsewhere.'

Alex pitched in, and we spent the next few days making calls. Most of the people who'd been burglarized had since moved or died. Tracking down the survivors, or relatives, was another big job.

We *did* connect with some. Did your family ever own an antique cup with English symbols?

Actually, several thought they might have had one once. But nobody could describe it accurately. And nobody sounded serious.

'Alex,' I complained, 'there have to be better things we could be doing.'

After a few days had passed without result, he was tired of it, too. By the fourth evening, we were near the end of the list. 'It's a wild-goose chase,' I told him. 'I'd be willing to bet the majority of burglaries didn't even make the news.'

He was chewing a piece of bread, looking as if his mind were somewhere outside in the night. The lights in the room had been dimmed, and Jacob was playing something from *Sherpa*. It was a quiet rhythm, adrift in the somber mood of the evening.

'Plotzky didn't know what he had. Maybe the original owner didn't either.'

'It's possible,' I said.

'Maybe the victim wasn't somebody who collected antiques. Maybe it was a guy who collected cups.'

'Cups. Somebody who collects cups.'

'Jacob,' said Alex, 'let's see the cup again. Close up.' It appeared in the center of the office, the image about my size. 'Turn it, please.'

It began to rotate. We looked at the eagle, at the banners, at

74

the registry number. At the ringed planet. 'No way,' I said, 'you could miss that it's connected with interstellars.'

'My thought exactly. Jacob, let's go back to the time period of the burglaries. Same geographical area. How many families can you find with a connection to the interstellar fleet?'

Families on record as having been burglarized?'

'No,' he said. 'Anybody with a connection to interstellars.'

We found nine families in the target area with fleet connections. Five had moved during the intervening years. Of the remaining four, two were military, and one was connected with a corporation that maintained orbitals. The fourth was the sole survivor of her family, a female who still owned the house but who was now married to a journalist and living in the eastern Archipelago. Her name was Delia Cable.

She'd been Delia Wescott at the time Plotzky was active. Her parents, and the owners of the property at the time of the burglary, were Adam and Margaret, who had lost their lives in an avalanche in 1398. Margaret had been a class-two pilot for Survey, and Adam had been a researcher who'd made a career of the long-range missions.

The connection with Survey caught Alex's attention, and Delia Cable went directly to the top of the list. Jacob made the call, and she materialized in the office.

It's difficult to determine qualities like height over the circuit. People have a tendency to adjust settings, so the projection may be considerably different from the reality. But you can't do much with eyes other than change their color. Delia Cable's eyes filled the room with their intensity. I suspected she was tall. She had chiseled cheekbones, and the kind of features that you associate with models. Her black hair swept down over her shoulders.

Alex introduced himself and explained that he represented Rainbow Enterprises. He had a few questions about an antique. Her expression was polite although it let us know she had better things to do than talk to strangers, and she sincerely hoped Alex wasn't trying to sell her something.

Her clothes, a soft gray Brandenberg blouse and matching skirt, with a white neckerchief – I couldn't see the shoes – indicated she was not wanting for resources. Her diction was perfect, the accent Kalubrian, that happy mix of detachment and cultural superiority that derives from the western universities.

'Did your family,' he asked, 'ever own an antique cup?'

She frowned and shook her head. No. *'I've no idea what we're talking about.'*

'Let me ask a different question, Ms Cable. When you were a girl, you lived in Andiquar, is that correct?'

'In Sternbergen, yes. It's a suburb. That was before my parents died.'

'Was your house ever robbed?'

Her expression changed. *'Yes,'* she said. *'There was something about a burglar. Why do you ask?'*

'Did the items get returned?'

She considered the question. *'I really don't know. It was a long time ago. I was pretty young when it happened.'*

'Do you recall an antique cup? An ordinary-sized drinking cup with odd symbols on it? And an eagle?'

She closed her eyes, and a smile touched those austere lips.

Bingo.

'I haven't thought about that cup for more than thirty years. Don't tell me you have it?'

'It has come to our attention, yes.'

'Really? Where was it? How did you connect it with me?'

'That's a long story, Ms Cable.'

'It would be nice to have it back,' she said. *'Are you planning to return it?'*

'I'm not sure what the legal ramifications are. We'll check into it.'

She indicated he shouldn't go to any trouble. *'It's not a major issue,'* she said. *'If it can be returned, fine. If not, don't worry about it.'*

76

'If I may ask,' he said, 'were there other objects in the house like it? Other antiques?'

She thought it over. '*Not that I recall. Why? Is it valuable?*'

Alex would have liked to avoid getting the corporation into the middle of a legal dogfight. 'It might be,' he said.

'*Then I would most certainly like to have it back.*'

'I understand.'

'*How much is it worth?*'

'I don't know.' Market values on objects like that tended to fluctuate.

'*So how do I get it returned?*'

'Easiest way, I suppose, would be to get in touch with your local police. We'll make a report on this end.'

'*Thank you.*'

I didn't feel comfortable with the way this was playing out. 'You're sure there was nothing else around the house like the cup?'

'*Of course I'm not sure. I was seven or eight years old.*' She didn't say *idiot*, but it was in her tone. '*But I don't recall anything else.*'

'Okay.' Alex pushed back in his chair, trying to ease the tension. I didn't especially like the woman and would have preferred to let Amy keep her prize. In fact I was already regretting that we'd stuck our noses into the business at all. 'Your parents, I understand, died in an avalanche in 1398.'

'*That's correct.*'

'Do you have any idea where they might have gotten the cup?'

'No,' she said. '*It was always there. As far back as I can remember.*'

'Where did they keep it? If you don't mind my asking.'

'*Their bedroom.*'

'And you're sure you don't know where it came from originally?'

She bit her lower lip. '*I had the impression,*' she said, '*that they brought it back from one of their trips.*'

'What kind of trip?'

'*One of their flights. They worked for Survey at one time. Used to go together on exploratory missions.*'

'How sure are you? That it came back on one of the flights?'

She shrugged her shoulders. '*I wouldn't want to bet on it, Mr Benedict. Keep in mind that was all pretty much before my time. I was about two years old when they left Survey.*'

'That would have been—?'

'*Around 1392, I guess. Why? What has any of this to do with anything?*'

'Aside from the *Survey* missions, were there other flights?'

'*Yes.*' She smiled. '*We traveled quite a lot.*'

'Where did you go? If you don't mind my asking?'

A love seat appeared, and she sat down in it. '*I don't know. Not anywhere special, I guess. Middle of nowhere. I don't think we ever made landfall.*'

'Really.'

'*Yes. It always seemed odd. We'd go to a station. It was pretty exciting stuff for a kid.*'

'A station.'

'*Yes.*'

'Do you know which one?'

She was getting annoyed again. '*I have no idea.*'

'You're sure it was a station.'

'*Yes. It was off-world. What else could it have been?*'

'How big was the station? How busy was it?'

'*Too long ago,*' she said. '*Anyhow, I don't think I ever left the ship.*'

'Why not?'

'*I don't know. I suspect my memory's playing tricks on me. I wanted to leave the ship. But they—*' She stopped, trying to recall. '*It's odd. I never understood, to be honest. They told me it wasn't a good place for little girls.*'

'You're right. That *is* odd.'

'That's the way I remember it. I've always thought it didn't really happen that way. Makes no sense.'

'Did you get a look at the station?'

'Oh, yes. I remember it. It was a big long cylinder.' She smiled. 'It looked scary.'

'What else can you remember about it? Was there any unusual structure anywhere?'

'Not that I remember.'

'Did you dock in a bay?'

'I don't know.'

'How about the lights? Could you see lights anywhere?' Some stations advertised hotels and other services on marquees that were visible on approach.

'It had lights, Mr Benedict. Spots playing across the station.'

'Okay.'

While they were talking, Alex was looking through the family information that Jacob had made available. 'You were with them at the time of the avalanche, isn't that right?'

'Yes. I was lucky. We were at a ski resort, in the Karakas, when there was an earthquake and the mountain came down. Couple hundred dead.'

'Must have been a terrible experience for a little girl.'

She stared off to one side. 'There were only a handful of people at the hotel who survived.' She took a deep breath. 'The burglary you're talking about happened about a year before we left on that trip.'

I looked at the data screen. After the accident, she'd gone to live with an aunt on St Simeon's Island. 'Ms Cable,' Alex said, 'what happened to your household possessions? The stuff your folks owned?'

'I have no idea,' she said. 'I never saw any of it again.'

'Okay.'

'Maybe that's not precisely true. My aunt Melisa, she took me in, salvaged some odds and ends. Not much, I don't think.'

Alex leaned forward. 'Can I persuade you to do me a favor?'

'*What do you need?*'

'When you have a chance, take a look at your older possessions and see whether you have anything else remotely like the cup. Anything with English characters. Or anything at all that doesn't seem to belong.'

'*All right.*'

'Thank you.'

'*Mr Benedict, there's something else.*'

'Yes?'

'*I remember my mother telling him, telling my dad, once when they were getting ready to go outside, over to the station, when they thought I was not close by, that she was scared.*'

I ran a search on the Wescotts. Adam had earned a degree in mathematics at Turnbull, a small western college, then gotten his doctorate in astrophysics at Yulee. He declined going into academia and opted instead for a field career with Survey. A fair number of postdocs take that route. It means they're less interested in making a reputation for themselves, or in doing serious work in their fields, than they are in simply getting up close to stars and visiting worlds that nobody has ever seen before. You don't usually think of scientific types as being romantics, but these guys seem to qualify. I spent two years piloting Survey ships, and I met a few of them. They are unbridled enthusiasts. Normally a mission is assigned a section of maybe eight to ten stars. You go into each system, do a profile of the central sun, get more information about it than anybody's ever going to care to read, then run a survey of the planets if there are any. And you look especially close at worlds in the biozone.

I looked at Adam's graduation picture from Turnbull. He was twenty-two, good-looking, with brown hair, blue eyes, and a confident smile. This was a kid who might or might not have been bright, but he himself had no doubt he was going to be top of the class.

I dug out whatever else I could. Adam Wescott doing grunt work at Carmel Central Processing Lab. Wescott entering the *Lumley*, the first time he'd gone on board an interstellar. I found him as a thirteen-year-old accepting an award as an Explorer, smiling as if recognizing it would be only one of many. He looked good in the uniform, everything tucked neatly in place, beaming while an adult, also in uniform, handed him his plaque. He turned and I got a look at the audience, composed of about fifteen other boys, all brushed and sharp in their uniforms, and maybe three times as many adults. The proud parents of the little group of Explorers at, according to the banner strung across one wall, the Overlook Philosophical Society, which apparently sponsored the corps.

I even got to hear him speak. '*Thank you, Harv,*' he said, and immediately corrected himself: '*Mr Striker.*' Smile for the audience. We all know he's really good old Harv. He took a piece of paper out of his pocket, unfolded it, and made a face at it. '*The corps wants me to say thanks to all the parents, and to Mr Striker, and the Society,*' he said. '*We're grateful for your help. Without you, we wouldn't be here.*'

The kid was on his way.

And there was a middle-aged Adam as an observer at the table of Jay Bitterman when Bitterman received the Carfax Prize. And Adam again during a birthday celebration for a politician with whom he'd developed a passing relationship.

And Adam's wedding. He'd shown good taste and married his pilot, Margaret Kolonik. Margaret looked gorgeous the way brides inevitably do because they are happy and emotional and celebrating a premier moment. In fact, though, she'd have looked good in an engine room. She had the same highlighted black hair I'd seen in her daughter, framing perfect features and a smile that lit up the room.

The routine at Survey is to interchange pilots and researchers after each mission. The average mission now lasts about eight or nine months, and I doubt things were much different forty years ago. It was done because the missions usually carried only the pilot and one or two researchers. People locked away like that for extended periods of time tend to get on each other's nerves.

But the background information indicated the happy couple had been together ten consecutive flights. On the last two, their baby daughter Delia had been along. I assumed there was no problem arranging that if you wanted to do it.

I sat in my office and watched Margaret Kolonik stride purposefully up the aisle to take charge of her guy. No wilting flower, this one. The data prompt informed me that her father was dead, and she was given away by an uncle, an overweight man who kept looking around as if he wanted to escape. Not somebody she'd have been very close to, I thought.

It was a religious ceremony. A priest requested the blessings of the Almighty on the happy couple, and led them in their vows. The best man produced the ring, Adam slipped it on her finger, she waltzed into his arms, and they kissed.

I envied them that moment. I've had a good life and can't complain. But I don't think I've ever approached the sheer joy I saw in Margaret's eyes as she let go of him, and they started back down the aisle.

The best man was described as a lifelong friend of Adam's, Tolly Weinborn. I recognized him immediately and switched back to the Explorer ceremony. And there he was, about thirteen, standing at attention with his comrades, with all due intensity and innocence.

I found Tolly after a quick search. He was living in Barkessa, on the northern coast, where he was an administrator at a public service office, the kind of place people go to when they're in trouble. He was not available at the moment, the AI told me. Could they have him return the call?

I found other tasks to occupy my time while I waited, among them looking for books that dealt with the Margolians and their flight from Earth. I came across *The Golden Lamp*, by Allie Omar. Omar looks at the causes of humanity's long history of starting and stopping, taking three steps backward, turning left, going forward, and doing lots of pratfalls. Her basic question: What might have happened if, since the twenty-seventh century, the human race had been able to avoid the infighting, the economic dislocations, the collapses? Had we sidestepped the three distinct sets of dark ages that set in during the Fourth, Seventh, and Ninth Millennia? Assume a straightforward dead-ahead unimpeded progress. Where would we be?

She doesn't answer her own question, but is satisfied with speculating on what the result might have been had the Margolians succeeded. The bottom line: They would be technologically three or four thousand years ahead of us. *They'd regard us, not as barbarians, but as distinct inferiors.*

In the early years of interstellar travel, people worried about meeting aliens who would prove to be vastly superior. *In technology. Perhaps ethically. Possibly both.* And the fear was that, faced by a hypercivilization, however benevolent its intentions might be, humans would simply lose heart. Similar effects had been observed time and again during the early years as man spread around his home world.

But, where the Margolians were concerned, the fears were, of course, unfounded. After leaving Earth, they were never seen again. And, across thousands of years, the only aliens we've encountered are the telepathic Ashiyyur, the Mutes, sometime friends, sometime rivals, occasional enemies. We discovered to our surprise that we were their technological equals. And since they still engaged in war among themselves, and occasionally against us, we were further gratified to conclude they were no better than we were.

There was no one else. Visits to star systems over the millennia produced numerous living worlds, but none with anything you could call recognizable intelligence. Of course there were some species out there with potential. If you were prepared to wait around a few hundred thousand years, you might have someone to talk with. But the galaxy, as Art Bernson famously said, has a lot of empty rooms.

* * *

Tolly never called back, so I tried him at home that evening. When I mentioned Wescott's name to his AI, he immediately agreed to talk to me. He still looked relatively young, despite the accumulation of years. The features, cherubic in the twelve-year-old, congenial in the best man, had assumed a kind of world-weariness.

He'd gained weight, and his face was lined, his once-red-blond hair gone mostly gray. He wore a beard, and he had something of a haunted look. Too many years of public service, maybe. Too many sad stories.

I identified myself and explained that I was doing some historical research. 'Did you keep in touch with Adam after he got married?' I asked.

He couldn't suppress a grin. *'It was impossible to stay in touch with him. He was away too much.'*

'Did you see him at all?'

He bit his lip and pushed back in his chair. *'A couple of times. During the early years.'*

'What about after he left Survey? When his career was over?'

No hesitation this time: *'His career never ended,'* he said. *'He might have left Survey, but he and Margaret kept making flights. Did it on their own.'*

'You mean they paid the bills?'

'Yes.'

'Why did they do that?'

Shrug. *'Don't know. I always assumed they'd gotten hooked and just had to keep going. I asked him that question once.'*

'What did he say?'

'"The world is too small."'

'But why wouldn't they have stayed with Survey if that's what they wanted to do?'

'He said Survey always gave him a prepared itinerary. He liked being able to go wherever he wanted.'

'That make sense to you?'

'Sure. They had plenty of money. They'd saved all those years, and Margaret had access to a trust of some sort.'

'Did you ever think about going along with them?'

'Who? Me?' The grin spread across his face. 'I like to keep my feet on the ground. Good old terra firma. Anyhow, I had a career to take care of. Such as it was.'

'Did they ever invite you?'

He rubbed his jaws. 'I just can't remember, Chase. It's too long ago. I'm sure they'd have made room for me if I'd asked.'

'Do you know where they were going? On the private flights? Did they go to different places? Or was it the same destination all the time?'

He reached for a glass half-filled with a colorless liquid and ice cubes. He took a sip and put it back down. 'I always assumed they went to different places.'

'But you didn't ask?'

'What would be the point of going back to the same place all the time?'

'I don't know,' I said.

'You must have had something in mind when you asked the question.'

I let him see I was talking off the top of my head.

'Why does it matter?' he asked.

'We're trying to put together a history of the missions during those years.' The answer seemed to satisfy him. 'And he never said anything to you at all about those flights?'

'I didn't see him that much, Chase. And no, I can't really remember anything he might have said. Except probably, when he got back, that he was glad to be home.'

'Tolly, is there anybody else he might have spoken to? Anyone who might know what those later missions were about?'

He needed a minute or two to answer that one. He mentioned a couple of names. Someone who might have known, maybe, but he died a few years back. And there was a friend of Margaret's, they might have talked to her, but she's dead, too.

'Let's try a different approach, Tolly. Did Adam, or Margaret, either of them, ever tell you they'd found something out there? Something unusual?'

'Like what?'

'Like an old starship. *Really* old.'

'*No, I don't know about anything like that.*' He shook his head. '*Well, maybe he did say something once or twice.*'

'What did he say?'

'*He was kidding around. Said they'd found something that would blow the socks off everybody.*'

'But he didn't say what?'

'*Wouldn't tell me. Just smiled and said how they were going back out eventually and I was going to get the surprise of my life. But he kidded a lot. You know what I mean?*'

I reported the conversations to Alex. 'Good,' he said. 'We're making progress.' He rubbed his hands and told me I'd done brilliantly.

I couldn't see it. 'In what way?' I asked. 'The only thing I can see that we've done is compromise the interests of our client.'

'We'll find a way to make it up to her.'

'How are we going to do that?'

'Buy her a nice birthday present. Point out to her the possibility of a major find out there, and that if we can come up with it, she'll get a generous share.'

'I don't think she's the type to let the cash go and settle for an outside chance.'

'I know.' He sucked in some air. 'We bungled that part of things, I guess.'

'*We?*'

'Okay. I did. Look, Chase, we've been doing what we had to.'

'We could have just moved the merchandise, taken our commission, and made the lady happy. Now, if we're lucky, maybe we'll have to settle for some reward money. And I don't like the way this is working out for Amy.'

'I know.' He looked unhappy. 'Ms Cable appears to be generous. If nothing else develops from this, I'm sure she'll compensate us for our trouble.'

'I'm sure.'

'Chase, we had an ethical responsibility here. We don't market stolen goods.'

'I'd like not to be here when you explain it to Amy.'

7

Where did they go? Into the glade, or along the river? Back to the sea, or beyond the moon?

—Australian children's fable,
twenty-third century C.E.

We debated taking Amy back to the Hillside, but we were both concerned she might make a scene. It was better to talk things out at the office, *then* see whether she'd be receptive to a meal.

I'll say one thing for the woman: She was no dummy. She knew as soon as she walked in the door it was bad news. 'What?' she demanded of Alex, bypassing the customary greetings, and ignoring me altogether.

Alex directed her to the sofa and sat down behind the desk. Would she like something to drink? Thanks, no.

'It's beginning to appear,' he said, 'the cup was stolen.'

Her nostrils quivered. 'That's crazy. Hap gave it to me. It was a peace offering after I caught him screwing around. A goddam *cup*.'

That wasn't quite the same story she'd told us initially.

'It seems odd,' said Alex. 'Ordinarily you'd expect flowers or candy.'

'Yeah. Well, Hap wasn't your ordinary kind of guy. It was the cup I usually drank out of when I was over there, and he wasn't going to go out of his way.'

'You *drank* out of it?' Alex was horrified.

'Yeah. Is that a problem?'

'No.' Alex cast a quick glance my way. 'No, not at all.' We lapsed into an uncomfortable silence.

'I didn't steal it,' she said. 'I asked you not to contact him. Is that what he's saying? It's a lie.' She finally looked over at me. 'It's just like him. Now that he knows it's worth something, he wants it back.'

'Hap doesn't know anything,' Alex said smoothly. 'Hap isn't the problem.'

'Who is?' she demanded.

'There's a fair chance that Hap didn't have legitimate ownership.'

'You mean Hap stole it from someone? Is that what you're saying?'

'Not Hap. Probably his father.'

Color flowed into her cheeks. 'Maybe you should just give it back to me and we'll forget the whole thing.'

'We can do that, if you like. But the person we think was the original owner knows that we know where it is. I expect she'll be taking action.'

'Thanks. You've been a big help, Mr Benedict. Now please give me my cup.'

Alex's tone never changed: 'In order to be able to get it back, though, the other party will have to be able to establish ownership. I don't know whether she can do that.'

Amy stared at Alex. 'Please get me the cup.'

He sighed. 'Have it your way, if you must. But it's a mistake.' He excused himself and left the office. Amy sat stiff as a board.

'We can probably arrange a finder's fee,' I said.

She nodded violently.

'We really had no choice,' I continued. That was hedging a bit, but there was some truth to it.

90

She was on the verge of tears. 'Just leave me alone.'

Alex came back with the cup, showed it to her and packed it in a container. 'You won't want to let anything happen to it, Amy.'

'I'll take care of it. Have no fear.'

'Good.' She got up, and he opened the door for her. 'I suspect you'll be hearing from the police.'

'Yeah,' she said. 'Why am I not surprised?'

'I don't feel very good about that,' I told him, when she'd gone.

'The law is what it is, Chase. These things happen.'

'It wouldn't have happened if we'd not poked our noses into it.'

He took a deep breath. 'Our code of ethics requires us to look into the source of anything that seems doubtful. If we start moving stolen merchandise around, we become liable. Suppose we'd sold it to somebody, *then* Ms Cable showed up.'

'She'd never have known.'

'It would have been on the open market, Chase. She might have found out.' He poured two cups of coffee and handed me one. 'No. We do things by the book.' He used a tone indicating that part of the conversation was over. 'I was looking at your interview with Delia Cable.'

'—And?'

'I've done some research on them. The parents. You know what they were doing for income after they left Survey?'

'I've no idea.'

'Nothing. Margaret had an inheritance that left her independent.'

'Must have been considerable if they could afford skiing vacations and flights to God-knows-where.'

'Apparently, it was. She came into it early in the marriage. They were able to do whatever they wanted. And in the end they left Delia pretty well provided for.'

'Okay. Is this leading somewhere?'

'Maybe. How much does it cost to lease an interstellar?'

'A lot.'

'They did it on a regular basis. But there's no record they ever stopped anywhere with it. They made a number of flights, according to Delia, but she can't remember getting off the ship. All she has is the recollection of a station. Doesn't that strike you as odd?'

'People working for Survey don't usually disembark.'

'But they weren't working for Survey. This was after they'd left the organization. Did you know that at the time they quit they only had six years remaining before Wescott would have been eligible for retirement from the program? Why do you think he left early?'

'Well, for one thing, they had a baby daughter. Maybe the Survey lifestyle wasn't working.'

He thought about it. 'You might be right,' he conceded. 'But then they start making flights on their own.'

'I know.'

'So where were they going?'

'I have no clue.'

'Might have been a good idea to press Delia a bit more.'

'She was a kid at the time, Alex. You couldn't remember things very well. That they were sight-seeing tours.'

'Chase, this is more than thirty years ago. It predates the quantum drive. It's back in the days when it took weeks to go anywhere. Would you travel a couple of weeks in a closed cabin with a six-year-old if you didn't have to?'

'Actually, having a six-year-old aboard might be fun.'

He plunged ahead as if I hadn't spoken. 'They weren't away from Survey six months before they were out making more flights. On their own money.'

'Okay. I'll admit it makes no sense to me. So where does that leave us?'

He looked at a point somewhere back of my left shoulder. 'They were doing something other than sight-seeing. I think they found something. On one of the Survey missions. Whatever it

92

was, they wanted to be able to claim it for themselves. So they kept quiet about it. Left early. And then went back.'

'You're not suggesting they discovered Margolia?'

'No. But I think they were looking for it. That's why they made *several* flights.'

'My God, Alex. *That* would be the find of the century.'

'Of all time, love. Answer a question for me.'

'If I can.'

'When you're out with Survey researchers, who determines where the mission goes?'

'As I understood it, the researcher was responsible. If there was more than one, their head guy did it. In either case, they submitted a plan to the operational people. It targeted a given area, laid out objectives, and stipulated any special reasons for the flight, other than general survey. If Ops approved, the mission went forward.'

'Could they change their minds en route? Change the plan?'

'Sure. Sometimes they did. If they saw a more interesting star, they thought nothing of making a side trip.'

'They kept a log, of course.'

'Of course. The researcher turned a copy over to Ops at the end of the mission.'

'Was the log validated in any way?'

'How do you mean?'

'How would Survey know the researcher had actually gone where he said he had?'

Strange question, that. 'Well,' I said, 'the ship comes back with data from the systems that were visited.'

'But the AI also maintained a record, right?'

'Sure.'

'Did they check the log against the AI?'

'Not that I know of. What reason would they have to do that? I mean, why would they be concerned that someone would lie?'

'I'm just saying *if*. If somebody found something they didn't want to make public, didn't want to report to Survey, Survey would never know. Right?'

'Probably not.'

'Chase, I think they found the *Seeker*.'

'The space station? But she said it had lights.'

'A child's memory.'

'I think she'd remember if it had no lights. I think that would be a striking feature.'

'She might have been looking at reflections from their navigation lights.'

'All right. But if they did – and I don't for a minute believe it – they would also have found Margolia.'

'Not necessarily.'

I was on the sofa, and I felt the air go out of it as I leaned back. 'It's only a cup,' I said. 'They could have got it anywhere. It might have been lying around for thousands of years.'

'In somebody's attic?'

'More or less.'

He tried to smother a laugh, then gave up.

'If they found the *Seeker*, why didn't they find Margolia?'

'I don't know. That's a question we'd want to answer.'

'Why didn't they report finding the ship?'

'If they had, Survey would have owned it. And everybody in the Confederacy would have been out there poking around. I'm guessing the Wescotts didn't want that. And if they discovered it later, on their own, they could claim it for themselves.' He looked excited. 'So we proceed on that assumption. First thing is to find the *Seeker*. Which is going to be in one of the systems they visited.'

'Their last Survey mission,' I said. 'How many planetary systems were involved in that last flight? Do we know?'

'Nine.'

'Well, that should make it simple enough. Margolia will be a terrestrial world located in the biozone. Nine systems will take a while to look at, but it can be done.'

'I don't think it would be that easy.'

'Why not?'

'Because if we're right, the Wescotts knew where the *Seeker* was. Yet they apparently had to make a number of flights. No landfall, though, according to Delia. So they didn't find the lost colony. Why not?'

'Beats me.'

'It suggests the colony isn't in the same system as the *Seeker*.'

'Maybe they found the place and just didn't let Delia out of the ship.'

'Don't you think they'd have said something if they'd come across Margolia? Discovery of the age? There'd be no reason to sit on that. No, I think, for whatever reason, the *Seeker* and Margolia aren't located in the same place.'

'That means we'd be hunting through nine planetary systems for a *ship*?'

'Yes.'

'Well, we can do that, too. But it would take some time.'

'Chase, we can't even be sure they made the discovery on the last mission. They might have found it earlier and thought it a good idea to do nothing for a while. After all, how would it look if they left Survey prematurely, then a couple years later, or whatever, they make a major discovery in one of the systems they'd recently visited officially?'

That would pile up the numbers. 'How many systems did the previous mission visit?'

'Eleven.' He went over to the window. It was a cold, gloomy day. And a storm was approaching. 'We have to pin things down a bit. I think what we need to do is talk with the Wescotts.' He folded his hands together and braced his chin on them. 'Jacob?'

'Yes, Alex?'

'Be good enough to get us Adam and Margaret Wescott.' Since they were long dead, he was of course referring to their avatars, which might or might not exist.

Even if no avatar were available, it was possible for a reasonably competent AI to cobble together what the records implied about a given individual and create a personality, within a given margin of error.

For almost three thousand years, people have been constructing their own avatars as 'gifts' to posterity. The net is full of them, mostly creations of men and women who'd lived their lives and moved on to the hereafter leaving no other trace of their existence than their natural offspring and whatever they'd installed in cyberspace. This latter type of avatar was of course notoriously unreliable, because it tended to be a wish-fulfillment ideal. It was usually the embodiment of wit, or virtue, or courage, constructed of qualities its original never approached. I doubt anybody has ever put an avatar into the system without improving it substantially over the original model. They even *look* better.

Neither Margaret nor Adam had submitted an avatar, but Jacob told us he had enough information on both to provide credible mock-ups.

Margaret blinked on first, near the door. Her black hair was cut short in a style long since abandoned. Clearly a woman of the nineties. She stood looking around like the person in charge, which was a good thing when you were a pilot and might run into problems a thousand light-years from home. She wore a dark blue jumpsuit with a shoulder patch marked *Falcon*.

Adam appeared moments later in the center of the room. He was formally dressed, red jacket, gray shirt, black slacks. He was in his midforties, with a long face and a set of features that looked as if they didn't smile much.

Alex did the introductions. Chairs appeared for both avatars, and they sat down. There were some comments about the weather, and how nice the office and the house looked. That sort of thing happens all the time. Obviously it's of no significance to the avatars, but Alex seems to need the process to get into the right frame of mind. He's used avatars on several occasions to confirm or negate data regarding the existence and/or location of various antiquities. But there's a method to it, and if you ask him, he'll tell you that you have to go the whole route, accept the illusion you're talking to real people and not just to mock-ups.

The country house was positioned atop a low hill, where it got a lot of wind. We were getting strong cold gusts out of the northeast, rattling windows and shaking trees. There was a taste of more snow in the air. *'Storm coming,'* said Margaret.

The trees were close to the house, and on some days the wind was so bad that Alex worried that one of them would come down on the roof. He said something to that effect to Margaret and moved on to the missions. How long had Adam been employed by Survey?

'Fifteen years,' Adam said. *'I was part of those projects for fifteen years. I held the record for most years in the field.'*

'How much of that time,' Alex asked, 'did you actually spend in the ship?'

He looked at his wife. *'Almost all of it. We did a mission a year, on average. A mission generally lasted eight to ten months. Sometimes more, sometimes less. Between flights, I usually accepted academic and lab assignments. Sometimes I just took the time off.'*

'Obviously, Margaret, you weren't always his pilot. You're too young.'

She smiled, pleased with the compliment. *'Adam had been making the flights for four years before he showed up on the* Falcon.'

'That was your ship all along?'

'Yes. I had the Falcon *from day one with Survey. I was in my second year with them when I met Adam.'*

'On our first mission together,' Adam said, *'we decided to get married.'* He exchanged glances with her.

'Love at first sight,' Alex said.

Adam nodded. *'Love always happens at first sight.'*

'I was fortunate,' said Margaret. *'He's a good man.'*

Alex looked my way. 'Chase, when you were with Survey, did you ever think about marrying any of your passengers?'

'Not a chance,' I said.

He grinned and turned back to Adam. 'You say nobody has spent more time than you in Survey's ships. Fifteen years out there, usually with only one other person on board. Nobody else is even close. The runner-up is at eight.'

'Baffle.'

'I'm sorry?'

'Emory Baffle. He was the runner-up.'

'Did you know him?'

'I met him.' Adam smiled. 'He was a hard worker. And I know what you're thinking. You and Chase over there.'

'What are we thinking?'

'That we're antisocial. But it's not so.'

'Never thought it was,' I put in.

'Look. The truth is, I liked company. We both did. Especially Margaret. But I had a passion for the work.'

Margaret nodded. 'He was the best they had.'

Most pilots don't stay long with Survey. You go in, get some experience, and go elsewhere. Money's better in other places, and you get more company. Long flights with, at best, a handful of people on board can be wearing. When I was working for them, I couldn't wait to transfer out.

'Were you both skiing enthusiasts?' Alex asked.

'I was,' said Margaret. 'God help me, I talked him into going to Orinoco—'

'The ski resort?'

'Yes. We'd been there before. A few times. For how little skiing he did, he was quite good at it.'

'What actually happened at Orinoco?'

'It was an earthquake. It was ironic. They were putting out avalanche advisories, telling us to stay off the slopes. Conditions were bad. But the quake hit instead.'

'No advance warning?'

'No. They'd never had a problem there, and nobody was paying attention, I guess.'

'How long had you been retired from Survey at that time? When the accident happened?'

'*Six years.*'

'Why did you leave?'

They looked at each other. And here was the crunch. If the Wescotts had been hiding something, they'd not have made it available on the net, and the avatars wouldn't know.

'*We just decided we'd had enough. We were ready to stop. To go home.*'

'So you pulled the plug.'

'*Yes. We settled down in Sternbergen. It's outside Andiquar.*'

Alex sat quietly for a moment, drumming his fingertips on the arm of the sofa. 'But within a short time after leaving Survey, you were making more flights.'

'*Yes.*'

'Why?'

Adam, who'd been quietly watching Margaret field the answers, took that one: '*We missed the old days. We both loved going out alone like that. You know, until you've cruised past some of those worlds, you don't really know what it means. We started feeling earthbound.*'

'It looks,' said Alex, 'as if you started feeling earthbound right after you moved into Sternbergen.'

Margaret grinned. '*Yes. It didn't take long.*'

'*We discovered,*' said Adam, '*we couldn't just go out and sit on the porch. We both loved what we'd been doing for a living. We missed it.*'

'Then why not come out of retirement? Let Survey pay the bills?'

'*Yeah,*' said Adam, '*we could have done that. But I think we liked just being able to do things at our own pace, without clearing projects with anyone. Without needing permission. We had the resources to do what we wanted, so that's what we did.*'

'*I think, too,*' said Margaret, '*we wanted Delia to see what was out there.*'

'She was very young.'

'*That's right.*'

'Too young to understand.'

'No,' said Adam. '*She was old enough to see how beautiful it is. How tranquil.*'

'She could have gone along on the Survey missions.'

'*Actually, she did,*' said Margaret. '*She made two with us. But we felt it was important to be able to manage our own schedule.*'

Alex looked from one to the other. 'Is it possible you were searching for something?'

'*Like what?*' asked Margaret.

'Like Margolia.'

They both laughed. '*Margolia's a myth,*' she said. '*There's no such place.*'

'No,' said Alex. 'It's not a myth. It happened.'

Both of them protested that we couldn't be serious.

'When you were running the Survey missions,' Alex continued, 'did you ever discover anything unusual?'

'*Sure.*' Adam lit up. '*We found two suns closing on each other in the Galician Cloud. They'll impact in less than a thousand years. Something else, too, during, I think, the next mission—*'

'Hold it,' Alex said. 'I'm talking about artifacts.'

'*Artifacts?*'

'Yes. Did you ever come across any artifacts? Anything from another age?'

'*Once.*' Adam's features clouded. '*We found an abandoned lander one time. At Arkensfeldt. It was from a Dellacondan ship. Couple centuries old.*'

'I don't think that's what we're looking for.'

Adam shrugged. '*With a pilot and a passenger on board.*'

'You had, in your home, a drinking cup that we were able to date from about the twenty-eighth century, terrestrial calendar.'

They replied simultaneously, Adam saying he knew nothing about an antique cup and Margaret saying it wasn't so.

'We think it was in the bedroom. At your home in Sternbergen.'

'Not *that I can recall*,' said Adam.

Margaret shook her head vehemently. '*I'm sure I'd know if we'd had anything like that.*'

'Let it go,' said Alex. 'It apparently wasn't included in your programing.'

Which to my mind proved that the Wescotts knew they had something to hide. They'd put it up there in tribute to themselves, but apparently no mention of it was made outside the house.

Shortly before closing time, Jacob informed me a visitor was approaching. '*Descending now,*' he said.

There was no one on the appointments calendar.

'Who is it, Jacob?' I asked.

'*It's Mr Bolton. Calling for Alex.*'

I went to the window and looked out. The storm that had been threatening all day had finally arrived. Light snow had begun falling, but I knew it was going to get worse. 'Patch it here, Jacob,' I said. 'He's busy at the moment.'

A black-and-yellow corporate vehicle drifted down out of the gray sky. The *BBA* logo was displayed in heavy yellow letters on its hull. I hit the intercom. 'Boss,' I said. 'Ollie Bolton's here. Making for the pad.'

He acknowledged. '*I see him. Be right down.*'

An image formed in the office. Bolton, seated in the back of the aircraft. '*Hello, Chase,*' he said, cheerily. '*It's a pleasure to see you again.*'

'Hello, Ollie.'

'*I apologize for dropping by without warning. I happened to be in the neighborhood.*'

I mentioned earlier that Bolton possessed the kind of gravitas that you associate with the occasional serious political leader. He never forgot a name, and he had a reputation for being both methodical and persistent. He was, an associate once told me, the kind of guy you wanted to have on your side when things weren't going well. Still, there was something about him that put me off.

Maybe it was a sense that he thought he could see things that people around him were missing.

'What can we do for you, Ollie?' I said.

I was hoping to have a few moments with Alex.

'I'm right here.' Alex strode into the room. 'What are you up to, Ollie?'

Not much. I was sorry I didn't get a chance to talk with you at the Caucus.

I was still standing by the window. The skimmer touched down and a door opened.

'To be honest,' said Alex, 'I thought you had your hands full fending off the true believer.'

Kolchevsky? Yes, and unfortunately we shouldn't take him lightly. He's been in touch with me since.

'Really? About what?'

He's pushing legislation to put us out of business.

'I've heard that before.'

I think he's serious this time.

'He won't get anywhere,' said Alex. 'We both satisfy the public's taste to own a piece of history.'

I hope you're right. The Bolton image blinked off, Bolton himself climbed out of the aircraft, pulled on a white-brimmed cap, and started leisurely up the walkway, pausing to frown at the threatening skies. He tugged his collar up, glanced in my direction, waved, and proceeded to the front door, which opened for him.

Alex met him, brought him back to the office, and poured him a drink. 'Social call?' he asked.

'More or less. I wanted you to know about Kolchevsky. We need to present a united front.'

'I don't think there's too much to worry about. But sure, I'm with you.'

'To be honest, Alex, there's something else. I was on my way back to my place when an idea hit me.'

'Okay.'

'It involves you.'

They sat down on opposite sides of the coffee table. 'In what way?'

Bolton glanced in my direction. 'It might be best if we talked privately.'

Alex waved the idea out of the room. 'Ms Kolpath is privy to all aspects of the operation.'

'Very good.' Bolton brightened. 'Yes, I should have realized.' He complimented the wine and made a comment about the weather. Then: 'We've been in competition for a long time, Alex. And I can't see how either of us benefits from that situation. I propose an alliance.'

Alex frowned. 'I don't think—'

'Hear me out. Please.' He turned his attention to me. 'Mr Benedict has a flair for locating original sites.' He took a deep breath and cleared his throat. 'But Bolton Brothers has the resources to exploit that capability to the fullest. If we were to combine Rainbow Enterprises with BBA, we'd have far more financial muscle to work with. And you'd have a Confederacy-wide network of researchers behind you. None of them is in your league, of course, but they could do the grunt work. It would be to everyone's advantage.'

Alex sat quietly a moment. Then: 'Ollie, I appreciate the offer. But the truth is, I prefer to work on my own.'

Bolton nodded. 'I'm not surprised you feel that way. But why don't you take some time? Think it over? I mean—'

'No. Thanks, Ollie. I like having my own organization. And anyhow, you don't need me. You seem to be prospering nicely.'

'It's not so much what I need,' he said. 'It's just that I'd enjoy working with you. Side by side with the best in the business.' He sat back. 'I need not mention there'd be an appropriate position for Chase.'

Alex was getting to his feet, trying to end the conversation. 'Thank you, but no. Really.'

'All right. Should you change your mind, Alex, don't hesitate to get in touch. The offer's open.'

* * *

At Alex's direction, I checked to see which corporate entities were leasing superluminals during the 1390s. The only company then in the business on Rimway was StarDrive. But it had since crashed. I tracked down a former executive of StarDrive, Shao Mae Tonkin, currently with a food distribution firm.

It took the better part of a day to get through to him. He was reluctant to talk to me, too busy, until I told him I was working on a biography of Baker Stills, who had been StarDrive's CEO. Tonkin was a massive individual. He may have been the biggest human being I've ever seen. He was maybe three times normal size. But it didn't look like fat so much as concrete. He had solemn features and small eyes that peered out from under thick lids. His forebears had inhabited a low-gravity world, or maybe an orbital. Or maybe he just ate too much. In any case, he'd probably live longer if he retreated off-world.

It wasn't just physical size and weight that impressed me. There was a heaviness of spirit, a kind of concrete demeanor. I asked him about StarDrive.

'*Went down twenty years ago,*' he said. His tone was so serious an eavesdropper would have thought the fate of the world hinged on the conversation. '*I'm sorry, Ms Kolpath, but everything other than the financial records were destroyed. Long ago. I can tell you all you need to know about Baker.*' He'd been competent, creative, a hard driver. Et cetera. '*But I can't provide much in the way of details on the day-to-day operations. It's been too long.*'

'So there's no record of any kind where your customers took the ships?'

He seemed to be running about five seconds behind the conversation. He thought my question over while he massaged his neck with his fingertips. '*No. None whatever.*'

'How many ships were in the company fleet?'

'*When we closed operations, in '08,*' he said, '*we had nine.*'

'Do you know where they are now?'

'*You're thinking that AIs might have made a permanent record of everything.*'

'Yes.'

'Of course. Unfortunately, our fleet was old at the end. That's one of the reasons we shut down. We would have had to upgrade or buy new vehicles. Either way—' He moved his head from side to side, as if to loosen joints in his neck. 'So we terminated. Most of the ships were recycled.'

Broken down and recast. 'What about the AIs?'

'They'd have been downloaded and filed. I believe the requirement is nine years from the destruction of the ship.' He pondered it for a long moment. 'Yes. That's correct. Nine years.'

'And then?'

He shrugged. 'Expunged.' A frown formed slowly, like a gathering cold front. 'May I ask why you're interested? None of this seems germaine to the biography.'

I mumbled something about statistical research, thanked him, and disconnected.

'I think the trail's gone cold,' I told Alex.

He refused to be discouraged. Despite the negative results, he was in an ebullient mood. Later I discovered he'd been contacted by a prospective client who'd come into possession of the Riordan Diamond, which, in case you're one of the few people in the Confederacy who doesn't know, was once worn by Annabel Keyshawn and supposedly was cursed. It eventually became one of only three items we've ever carried in our inventory officially designated in that category. It served to drive up the value. 'We haven't exhausted the possibilities yet,' he said.

I could see it coming. 'What do we do next?' The *we*, of course, at Rainbow Enterprises was strictly a pejorative term.

'Survey doesn't destroy its records,' he said. 'It might be interesting to see whether the Wescotts reported any unusual findings, especially during their later missions.'

I was getting tired of the runaround. 'Alex, if they found anything connected to the cup, like maybe Margolia, don't you think Survey would have acted on it by now?'

He gave me that you-have-a-lot-to-learn look. 'You're assuming they read the reports.'

'You don't think they do?'

'Chase, we've been assuming that if the Wescotts found something, they omitted putting it into their report.'

'I think that's a safe assumption. Don't you?'

'Yes. In fact, I do. But still we can't be certain. And there's always a possibility there'll be *something* on one of the reports that gives the show away. In any case, we lose nothing by looking.'

8

Might the Harry Williams group have succeeded in building a society that had actually banished the various imbecilities that have always plagued us? The reflex is to say no, that it could not be done so long as human nature itself remained unchanged. But this view denies that we can learn from history, that we can sidestep the inquisitions, dictatorships, and blood-letting of past ages. That the programing of false values into our young can be stopped. That people can learn to live reasonably. If they were able to establish themselves on their chosen world, and to pass on their ideals to succeeding gener-ations, if they could avoid forgetting who they were, then success might have been achieved. Maybe we have not heard from them since their departure six centuries ago because they did not want to be contaminated. I'd like to believe it's so.

—Kosha Malkeva,
The Road to Babylon, 3376 c.e.

The administrative offices of the Department of Planetary Survey and Astronomical Research were located in a complex of glass-and-plasteel buildings on the north side of Andiquar, along the banks of the Narakobi. Its operational center was halfway across the continent, but it was here that policy was set, politicians were entertained, missions approved, and resources allocated. This was where personnel decisions were made and where researchers came to present and ultimately defend their projects. The public information branch was located here, and this was where the records were kept.

The grounds were mostly parkland, although in midwinter the place looked a bit desolate. There was a move on to put a dome over the entire complex, but the proposal, as of this writing, is still stalled in committee somewhere.

The visitors' space was filled, so I dropped down onto a parking area half a kilometer away and walked in. We'd had a break in the weather, and it was almost warm, with a hazy sun and a few clouds spread across a yellow sky. There were a few people out with their kids, and I passed a chess game being played by two shivering middle-aged guys on one of the benches. Ahead, I could see the three-story parabolically shaped Trainor Building that housed the personnel offices. To my left, in a cluster of trees, was the Central Annex, which looked more like a temple than a structure intended for scientific research. The Annex housed Survey's museum and exhibits.

I veered right, strolling past stone memorials to old glories, circled the Eternal Fountain (which is supposed to symbolize the notion that exploration will never cease, or that the universe goes on forever, or something like that), passed a couple of bureaucratic types arguing and looking annoyed, and approached the Kolman building, which housed Survey's director and his immediate staff.

I climbed the eleven steps at the front entrance. Alex tells me they signify the eleven interstellars that formed the original Survey fleet. Eight Doric columns supported the roof. At the far end of the portico, a child was charging down the steps with a red kite in tow while his mother watched.

The front doors opened onto a stiff, uncomfortable lobby, filled with plants and armchairs and tables. It had a vaulted ceiling and a long array of windows, both real and virtual. They were framed by lush silver curtains. The walls were lined with paintings of Survey vessels cruising past exploding suns or serene ring systems, and of people getting out of landers and standing heroically gazing across alien landscapes. PUTNAM ARRIVES ON HELIOTROP IV, an attached plate said. Or, THE *JAMES P. HOSKINS* DOCKS AT STARDANCE. It was the kind of place specifically designed to make the occasional visitor feel insignificant.

And there stood Windy, in conversation with someone I didn't know. She saw me, waved, and signaled me to wait. A moment later she came over. 'Social call?' she asked.

'Not this time. I just wanted to get authorization to look at some records.'

'Can I help?'

'Sure,' I said.

'Good.' She smiled. 'By the way, did you ever figure out who the thief was?'

'At Gideon V? No. We have no idea.'

'I checked on this end. There were several people who had access to my report.'

'Okay.'

'I'm sorry. There's a good chance that's where things went wrong.'

'Well, we'll know better next time.'

'It infuriates me,' she said.

'Let it go.'

'Well, I can't quite do that. Not if we have someone giving out information that allows people to descend on archeological sites.' Her mouth was a thin line. God help whoever it was if she caught him. 'What did you want to see?'

Adam Wescott had completed a total of fourteen missions for Survey over a fifteen-year period, beginning in 1377 and ending in 1392.

I started with the most recent and worked backward through

each of the missions he'd shared with Margaret. That might have been overkill, but I didn't want to miss anything.

Most of the Survey flights are general purpose. You pick a group of stars, go in, take pictures, get sensor readings, measure everything in sight, and move on. Adam had a special interest in the mechanics of G-class stars as they approach their helium-burning phase. Three of his missions, including the last one, had been focused on that subject. That wasn't to say they didn't also look at other aspects of the central luminary and also survey the planetary system. But helium was the watchword. Consequently, all the stars on the itinerary were old.

I visited every system with them. I looked at the images, paged through the details of each sun, its gravity constant, mass, temperature ranges, whatever. And of course I got to see the planetary families. During their joint career, they'd found four living worlds, one their first time out together, one on the third mission, and *two* on their seventh. I heard their voices, his low in the register, the voice of a professional researcher, always calm and methodical, hers soft and subdued, much in contrast, I thought, to her take-command appearance.

I heard them on the one occasion when they thought they'd discovered evidence of intelligence, in a forest that looked remarkably like a city. They'd retained the professional tone, but I could feel the electricity. Until, a few minutes later, they realized they were looking at something quite natural. Then the disappointment was evident.

There probably *is* somebody else out there. Other than the Mutes. But there are just so many places to look. Some experts think that, by the time we find a third player, we'll have evolved away from being human.

Nowhere was there any mention of a derelict, or of Margolia.

I made a copy of the record. Next I needed somebody with some insight into Survey procedures.

Shara Michaels was an astrophysicist, employed on Survey's analytical staff. Her responsibility was to advise upper management about submitted projects: which were worth pursuing, which could be put on the waiting list, and which could be safely dismissed.

I'd gone to school with her, partied with her, and even introduced her to a future husband. A future ex, as things turned out, but we'd remained friends through it all although in recent years we hadn't seen much of each other.

She'd been the queen of the walk in those early days, the woman you didn't want your date to see. Blond hair cut in an elfin style, sea-blue eyes, and a talent for mischief. Everybody loved her.

She still looked good when she came to the door of her office. But the old cavalier attitude had disappeared. She was all business. Polite, glad to see me, commented how we needed to get together once in a while. But there was a level of reserve her younger self had never known.

'You should have called,' she said, showing me to a chair and taking one herself. 'You almost missed me. I was on my way out the door.'

'I hadn't expected to come by today, Shara,' I said. 'Do you have a few minutes?'

'For you? Sure. What's going on?'

'Alex has had me on the run. I was over at the archives.'

'Still doing slave labor?'

'Pretty much.' We did several minutes' worth of small talk. Then I got down to cases. 'I need your help.'

She got drinks for us. Wine from the islands. 'Name it.'

'I've been looking at some old mission reports. From forty years ago.'

'Why?' she asked. 'What are you looking for?'

'Survey used to have a husband-and-wife team, Adam and Margaret Wescott. There's a possibility they found something unusual on one of the missions.'

'People often find unusual things on the missions.' She meant planets with odd orbits or gas giants with unusual mixes of, say, carbon and methane.

I looked at her over the rim of my glass. 'No,' I said. 'Not like that.'

'Like what, then?'

'Like an artifact. A derelict ship. Connected with Margolia.'

'With *what*?'

'Margolia.'

She still had a great smile. 'You're kidding.'

'Shara, a woman showed up at our place a week or so ago with a drinking cup that might be from the *Seeker*.' When the frown reappeared, I explained.

When I'd finished, she looked amused. Maybe disappointed that I could jump to an obviously silly conclusion. 'Chase,' she said, 'anybody can manufacture a cup.'

'It's nine thousand years old, love.' Her eyes widened. 'We've been able to trace it back to Wescott. It was taken from his home in the 1390s. By a burglar.'

'But you don't know where Wescott got it?'

'No.'

'He probably bought it somewhere. Do you have reason to suspect it actually came off the ship? Or from' – she couldn't suppress a smile – 'Margolia.'

'It's a possibility.'

'A remote one.'

Her office was on the third level. The walls were decorated with pictures of stars in collision. That was her specialty. She'd done her thesis on interstellar traffic accidents and remained disappointed that she'd come along too late to see the crash between Delta Karpis and a dwarf star sixty years earlier.

One image was particularly striking. It was a computer graphic done from behind and above a yellow star that was about to do a head-on with a white mass of some sort. A dwarf, probably. 'How often do these things happen?' I asked.

'Collisions? There's always one going on somewhere. There's one happening at this moment. Somewhere in the observable universe.'

112

'Well, the observable universe is pretty big.'

'I was just trying to answer your question.'

'It's still a lot of wreckage,' I admitted. 'I've only heard of one in my life.'

'The *Polaris* incident.'

'Yes.'

She smiled again, letting me know how uninformed I was. 'They happen all the time, Chase. We don't see much of it around here because we're pretty spread out. Thank God. Stars never get close to one another. But go out into some of the clusters—' She stopped and thought about it. 'If you draw a sphere around the sun, with a radius of one parsec, you know how many other stars will fall within that space?'

'Zero,' I said. 'Nothing's close.' In fact the nearest star was Formega Ti, six light-years out.

'Right. But you go out to one of the clusters, like maybe the Colizoid, and you'd find a half million stars crowded into that same sphere.'

'You're kidding.'

'I never kid, Chase. They bump into one another all the time.' I tried to imagine it. Wondered what the night sky would look like in such a place. Probably never got dark.

'I have a question for you,' I said.

She tucked a wisp of hair back in place. 'I thought you might.'

'If I want to do a mission, I come to you with a plan. You look at it, and if it's okay, you approve it, assign me a ship and pilot, and I'm on my way. That's the way it works, right?'

'It's a little more complicated than that, but that's the essence of it, yes.'

'Okay. The plan I submit tells you which star systems I want to look at. It includes a flight plan, and, if there are special reasons for the mission, it mentions those also. Is *that* correct?'

'Yes.'

'I used to do the preliminary missions. And I know there were follow-up flights, with specialists.'

She nodded.

'How often? If I came back from a mission on which I'd visited, say, a dozen systems, what are the chances somebody would actually go back and look at one them?'

'Usually, you could expect maybe half of them would get follow-ups.'

'Really? That many?'

'Oh, yes. Sure.'

'So if I found something and wanted to keep it quiet—'

'You'd want to leave that system off the mission report. Substitute something else.'

'But if I did that, you guys would notice, right?'

Shara looked uncomfortable. 'I doubt it. I don't know how we were doing things thirty, forty years ago. But there's no reason to backcheck the report against the proposal. Nobody has a reason to lie about any of that, and to my knowledge there's never been a problem.'

'Do the proposals still exist?'

'From 1390? I doubt it.'

'Would you check for me?'

'Hold on.'

She put the question to the AI. And we both heard the response: *'Proposals are retained three years before being discarded.'*

'That's longer than I would have thought we keep them,' she said. 'You think the Wescotts found the *Seeker* and falsified the report?'

'It's possible.'

'Why would they do that? They'd get full credit.'

'But if they found the *Seeker*, could Margolia be far away? What would Survey have done if they'd announced their discovery?'

She thought about it. 'Oh.'

'That's right. You'd have assigned a small fleet to go looking for Margolia. So the big discovery would probably get made by someone else.'

'I suppose so. Yes.'

114

'That's why it doesn't go into the report, Shara. They wanted to be the ones who found Margolia. Biggest discovery ever. But to do that they had to keep quiet about the *Seeker*.' I became aware of voices in the corridor. 'But the ship's AI,' I said, 'would record where the mission actually went.'

'Yes.'

'So you'd have to doctor that as well, if you were going to falsify the record.'

'Yes.'

'My experience is that it wouldn't be that hard to make the change.'

'I wouldn't think so. I'm sure Margaret Wescott would have known how to do it. Penalties are severe if you get caught, though.'

'But they wouldn't be likely to get caught.'

'Probably not.'

'Can we get access to the AIs from their missions?'

'No,' she said. 'They get wiped periodically. Every few years. I'm not sure of the exact timing, but it's nowhere near thirty.'

'What did you come up with?' Alex asked, when I'd called in next morning.

'Not much,' I said. I explained, and he said that was what he'd expected. 'Alex,' I added, 'maybe we're letting our enthusiasm run away with us.'

'Maybe. I don't know. I have a question.'

'Go ahead.'

'We know which systems they looked at. Or at least, what the claims are.'

'That's correct.'

'Do we know what the order of the star systems was on each flight? Where they went first, where next, and so on?'

I looked at the records and shook my head. 'Negative.'

'It would be nice to know.'

'Why? What does it matter?'

'It always helps to have a complete picture of what happened.'

115

He scratched his temple. '*By the way, Fenn tells me they did find more burglary records. The Wescotts were among them. And the report included the cup.*'

'So Amy will have to give it up.'

'*I'm afraid so. But it tells us the Wescotts understood it was more than just a drinking cup.*'

'But that still doesn't lead to anything.'

'*Maybe not.*' He looked hesitant.

'What's wrong?' I asked.

'*Amy called to tell me she'd talked with Hap.*'

'She told him about what's been happening?'

'*Yep. I think she was taking a little revenge. Telling him how much the cup was worth so he'd eat his heart out.*'

'And—?'

'*Apparently he got annoyed. Started making threats. Against her and against us.*'

'Against us? She told him we were involved?'

'*By name. I doubt there's anything to worry about, but I wanted you to know. Keep your security systems on.*'

Next day was my day off, but I wasn't quite ready to let go of Margolia. I had an early breakfast and settled in to watch *Sanctuary*, which was a thirty-year-old thriller about the lost colony.

It was one of the Sky Jordan adventures, which were hugely popular in their time. Sky was played throughout that long series by Jason Holcombe, who always struck me as the sexiest leading man in the business. In this one, his ship gets too close to an alien device that sucks the power out of everything, and he's rescued by Solena, a beautiful Margolian.

She's played by a popular actress of the period. But I pulled her out, put myself in her place, and settled back to watch the action.

Solena patches up the battered hero, pulls him out of his dead ship, and, using a force shield that negates the power drain, heads for home.

Margolia is a world of gleaming cities and impossible architecture.

Its citizens enjoy a life of absolute leisure. (How they'd stand it isn't explained.) The place looks great. The mountains are higher, the forests greener, the oceans wilder than anything you might see on Rimway. There are twin suns, which seem to move through the sky together, three or four moons, and a set of rings.

If the Wescotts had found anything like that, I would surely have liked to visit.

But this Margolia is under threat by Bayloks, a horde of malevolent aliens. It was the Bayloks who had planted the power drain. They come complete with lizard snouts and bursts of tentacles and malignant red eyes that glow when the lights go down. Whatever evolutionary advantage accrued from this, I couldn't imagine. But they were ugly and stomach-churning in the manner of most special effects monsters.

Despite their advanced technology, the Margolians, because they have been cut off from the rest of the human race for so long, have forgotten how to defend themselves. They have no warships and no knowledge how to build any. They have nobody trained in the military arts. (At some point, they apparently decided that the armed forces had no place in an enlightened society.) And, to cap things off, they're averse to killing.

There is also Tangus Korr, who is Solena's boyfriend. Tangus becomes jealous of Sky and begins plotting against him.

Solena sees through his tricks and casts her lot with the hero, who is meantime providing engineering advice. The aliens are coming fast, and there is a race to put together a defense force. You get a tour of Sky's new ship, which they name *War Eagle*. It's small but of course it packs a wallop.

Solena meantime falls in love with Sky and takes him into her bedroom. It is the night before the face-off with the enemy, and Sky may not come back, *probably* will not come back. He wants her to stay out of harm's way, but she won't have it. In the end, tears running down her cheeks, she releases the clasps on her blouse, opens it wide and gives him a choice. '*You want me,*' she says, '*then promise you will take me with you tomorrow.*'

Well, what's a guy going to do?

I might as well confess right here that my favorite part of these sims is watching myself get taken by the right leading man. I know women generally deny that, at least when there are men in the room, but there isn't much that gives me a better ride than watching Jason Holcombe perform his magic with me.

Things run off the track a bit when Tangus turns out, incomprehensibly, to be in the pay of the Bayloks. He very nearly destroys the nascent fleet in dock, but after a desperate shoot-out and slugfest with Sky, the ships get safely launched.

What the audience knows, but the Margolians do not, is that the Bayloks can teleport over short distances. At the height of the battle they explode onto the bridge of the *War Eagle*.

So I'm sitting there, enjoying the action, when one materialized, screeching, fangs bared, directly in front of me. I shrieked and fell out of my chair.

'*That's unnerving,*' said Carmen, the AI.

I sat in the middle of the floor, watching the battle rage around the living room. 'We need a little more restraint,' I said, 'by the people who make these things.'

I slept most of the afternoon, went out for dinner with a friend that evening, and got back just before midnight. I showered and got ready for bed, but paused to look out at the river and the sleepy countryside. I was thinking how fortunate I was, and all the things I was taking for granted. A good job, a good life, and a good place to live it. It wasn't Margolia, but it had taverns and live theater. And if you bottled yourself up watching sims night after night, whose fault was it?

I killed the lights, draped my robe across a chair, and climbed into bed. The room was dark except for a few squares of moonlight on the floor, and the illuminated face of a clock on top of my bureau. I pulled the blankets up around my shoulders, snuggling down into their luxurious warmth.

Back to the office in the morning.

I was trying not to enumerate the next day's tasks because that would wake me up, when Carmen told me we had a visitor.

At this hour? I immediately thought of Hap.

'*A woman,*' she said. I heard voices at the door, Carmen, and someone else. '*Chase, she says her name is Amy Kolmer.*'

That couldn't be good news. I reached for a robe. 'Let her in,' I said.

9

Perception is everything.

—Source unknown,
approximately twentieth century C.E.

Amy looked distraught. Her blouse was half-hanging out of her belt, her hair was disheveled, her colors clashed. She looked as if she'd gotten dressed on the run. She sighed when I opened the door, thank God I was home, looked back down the corridor, then pushed past me into the apartment. Her eyes were wild.

'He was behind me,' she said. 'Just a few minutes ago. He was right behind me.' She was carrying something wrapped in red cloth.

'Hap?'

'Who else?' She went to the window, stood to one side, and looked out. Then she fussed with the drapes. 'I'm sorry,' she said. 'I know it's late.'

'It's okay. Are you all right?'

'I didn't know where else to go.'

'Okay. Sit. You're safe now. How'd you find me?'

'You're the only Chase Kolpath listed.'

'All right. Good. You did the right thing.'

'He showed up at my place. Pounding on the door. Yelling

121

about the cup.' She wiped away tears and tried to straighten herself.

'What did you do?'

'I told him it was *mine*.' She started to tremble. 'I went out the back. When he gets like that he's out of his mind.' She unwrapped the red cloth, which was a blouse, and produced the cup. 'If it's okay, I wanted to leave it with you.'

'Sure. If you want.'

'It'll be safer here. If he gets his hands on it, I'll never see it again.'

'You said you saw him behind you?'

'A few minutes ago. As I was coming up the walk. I don't know how he found me here.'

It might have had something to do with your mentioning my name to him, you nitwit.

'Okay,' I said. 'Just relax. Everything'll be okay. We'll get you some protection.'

'He says it's not really mine. That he didn't mean for me to keep it.'

'Why didn't you call the police, Amy?'

'He'd kill me if I did something like that. You don't know what he's like when he gets mad.'

'Okay.'

'He goes crazy.'

I was thinking how much trouble people get into because they can't keep their mouths shut. 'Listen,' I said, 'you better stay here tonight. Tomorrow we're going down to report this and get some help.'

She shook her head violently. 'Won't do any good. He'll be out again in a couple of days.'

'Amy, you can't live like this. Eventually, he's going to hurt somebody. If not you, somebody else.'

'No. It's not like that. We just need to give him time to cool down.'

Carmen's voice broke in: '*Chase, we have another visitor.*'

Amy began to tremble. 'Don't let him in,' she said.

'Relax. I won't.'

'He's on something.'

The door has a manual bolt. Extra security because I've never completely trusted electronics. I threw it just as the lights went out.

'He did that,' she said. 'He has a *thing*—'

'Okay.'

'It kills power—'

I immediately thought of the Bayloks and their power drain. 'I know. Take it easy. We're okay. Carmen, are you there?'

No response.

'It shuts everything down—'

A fist pounded on the door. It sounded heavy. *Big.*

'Open up, Amy.' It was Hap's growl. No question about that. 'I know you're in there.'

'Go away,' she said.

More pounding. The door, barely visible in the glow of the moon and a streetlamp, literally bent. She was off the sofa, cowering near the window. But we were on the third floor. We weren't going to get out that way. And there was no back door. 'Don't open it,' she pleaded. Her voice squeaked.

It sounded as if Hap was using a sledgehammer. I took a quick look out the window and saw that the other lights in the building were out, too. 'Get into the bedroom,' I told her. 'There's a link on the side table. Use it. Get the police.'

She stood looking at me. Paralyzed.

'Amy,' I said.

'Okay.' Her voice was barely audible.

'Go away,' I told the front door. 'I've called the police.'

Hap returned a string of profanity. 'Open up, bitch,' he added. 'Or I'll do you, too.'

Amy disappeared into the bedroom and the door closed behind her. It had no lock. Hap went back to pounding, and the latch started to come loose. I tossed the cup on the sofa and threw a

123

cushion over it. Not much of a hiding place. Then, stumbling around in the dark, I drew the curtain across the kitchen entrance and closed the bathroom door.

'I have a scrambler,' I said. 'You come in here, and you're going down.' In fact I did have one, but it was up on the roof, in the skimmer. Good place for it.

He responded with a final hammerblow and the door flew open. It ripped around on its hinges and banged against the wall and he stumbled into the room, big and clumsy and ugly. He was an unnerving sight. I hadn't taken much notice when I'd visited him under more peaceful circumstances. He was a head taller than I was and maybe two and a half times the weight. He wore a thick black sweater with enormous side pockets. The side pockets bulged, and I wondered whether any of them contained a weapon. Not that he'd need it.

He turned on a flashlight and stuck it in my face. 'Where is she?' he demanded.

'Where's who?'

I heard voices in the corridor. And doors opening. I thought about calling for help but Hap read my mind and shook his head. 'Don't do it,' he whispered.

My neighbor across the hall, Choi Gunderson, showed up in the doorway. Was I okay?

Choi was thin, fragile, old. 'Yes, Choi,' I said. 'We're fine.'

He stared at the broken door. And at Hap. 'What happened?'

'Had a little accident,' Hap growled. 'It's all right, Pop.'

'I wonder what happened to the power,' Choi said, and I thought for a moment he was going to try to intervene. I hoped he wouldn't.

'Don't know,' said Hap. 'Best you go back to your room and wait until the repair people get here.' The lamplight fell across his open door.

Choi asked again whether I was all right. Then: 'I'll call Wainwright.' The property owner. He withdrew, and I heard his door close.

'Good,' Hap told me. 'You're not as dumb as you look.' He swept the room with the lamp. 'Where is she?'

'Hap.' I tried to keep my voice calm. 'What do you want?'

He started to say that I knew what he wanted, but stopped in mid-sentence to stare at me. 'You're from the survey.'

I took a step toward him. 'Yes.'

'You're the bitch who came to the house.' The veins in his neck bulged.

'That's right.' No use denying it.

I was going to say something more, not sure what, I was making it up as I went along. But he broke in before I got started. 'You're helping her cheat me.'

'Nobody's cheating you, Hap.'

He grabbed my shoulder and threw me against a wall. 'I'll deal with you in a minute,' he snarled. Railing about what he was going to do to 'these goddam bitches,' he looked in the kitchen, used his elbow to knock some glasses to the floor, checked the bathroom, and headed for the bedroom.

He scratched his armpit and yanked the door open. Had to do it manually since he'd killed the power. He pointed the lamp inside. 'Come on out, Amy,' he said.

She squealed, and he went in after her. I looked for a weapon while his light bounced around the inside of my bedroom. Amy alternately pleaded with him and shrieked.

He dragged her out by her hair. She was holding my link in one hand.

'The police are on their way, Hap,' I said, in the steadiest voice I could muster. 'Best thing for you is to clear out.'

But Amy would never win a prize for brains. She shook her head. No. 'I didn't call them,' she said. And, to Hap: 'I didn't want to cause you any trouble.'

'You've already caused me a lot of trouble, slut.' He took the link from her, dropped it on the floor, and stomped it. Then he hauled her to his side, twisted her arm behind her, dragged her backward to the front door, and kicked it shut. It banged open again, and a second kick didn't improve things, so he shoved Amy in my direction, pushed the door closed and dragged a chair in front it. When he was satisfied nobody would come in and break up the party, and that no one was going to get out, he returned his attention to us. 'Now, *ladies*,' he said, 'let's talk about the cup.'

He set the flashlight on a side table and tossed Amy onto the sofa, without ever taking his eyes off me. He was quicker than he looked. 'It's nice to see you again, Kolpath,' he said. 'You're the antique dealer. You never had any connection with a survey group, right? What did you want at my place?' His hands were balled into big meaty fists. If it came to a fight, it was going to be over in a hurry.

I could hear other people in the hallway.

'I thought there might be more where the cup came from.' No use lying.

'Stealing the cup wasn't enough for you, huh?' He seized Amy's arm and twisted it. She cried out. 'Where is it, love?'

'Turn her loose,' I said, starting toward him, but all he did was tighten his grip. Tears ran down her face.

I needed a weapon.

There was a hefty bronze bust of Philidor the Great on a shelf behind us. I didn't look at it, didn't want to draw his attention to it. But I knew it was there. If he could be distracted . . .

He leaned over Amy. 'Where's the cup?'

She looked around the room, uncertain what had happened to it. 'I must have left it in the bedroom,' she said.

He pulled her to her feet and shoved her toward the open door. 'Get it.'

She wobbled off. I was listening to the voices in the hallway. Other than Choi, my neighbors were a young, timid woman, and a guy who was about ninety. No prospect of help there. I hoped someone had called for police.

Amy returned to report she couldn't find the cup. Couldn't remember what she'd done with it. Before he could hit her, I pulled the cushion away and showed it to him. Hap broke into a large toothy grin, picked it up, admired it, shook his head like who would have thought this piece of junk would be worth money, and shoved it hard into a pocket. It banged on something, and I winced. The thing had traveled nine thousand years to get mashed by this barbarian.

'What's it worth?' he asked. He was more or less talking to the wall, his words directed to a blank spot between me and Amy. Anybody who wanted to could reply.

'Probably twenty thousand or so,' I said.

'All right.' He glanced down at the pocket. 'Good.'

We stood there while he thought what to do next. He signaled Amy to sit back down on the sofa, and she complied. Hap pointed his flashlight directly at me. I had my hand over my eyes, trying to shield them from the glare. 'If you leave now,' I told him, 'I'd be willing to forget about this.' You bet. Right after I'd found a way to take him out.

'Yeah,' he said, with a smile that was absolutely cold. 'I know you will, because if you make any trouble for me, ever, I'll break your sweet neck.' He let me see nothing would give him more pleasure. 'All right,' he said. 'Here's what's going to happen.' Another smile. Then before I even realized it was coming, I caught a stinging slap across the jaw. It knocked me off my feet.

'Get up,' he said.

I was following flashing lights, and the floor felt unsteady.

'You want another one?' He lifted his foot and aimed it at my ribs. *'Get up.'* I looked at him. Philidor showed up in my peripheral vision, hopelessly out of reach. I staggered to my feet, holding on to the arm of the sofa to keep my head from spinning. 'Now here's what we're going to do, Kolpath.'

No two ways about it. This guy was loaded with charisma. I had to admire Amy's taste in men.

'I want you to make a call. Call whoever you have to. And transfer twenty-two thousand into my account.' He produced a card. 'Here's the number. I'm going to sell you back your cup. Nice honest transaction.'

I decided not to argue with him.

'It was mine, you know. It's been in our family my whole life. Shouldn't be anybody else getting that money.'

Absolutely not.

He dug into the same pocket the cup was in and produced a link, which he held out to me. 'Make the call,' he said.

'I don't have the account numbers memorized. I need the AI.'

He raised his fist and I backed away, but he thought better of it. Put me out of business and he can't get his money. So he went into the other pocket, the left one, and withdrew a dark blue waferlike object. He fiddled with it for a minute, and the lights came back. Carmen's status lamps blinked.

'It won't work,' I said. 'The police will trace the money.'

'No.' He smiled at my naïveté. 'It's a network. The money moves around. Nobody'll ever know.'

He hadn't meant to say that, because it meant Amy and I had a short future. He went back into the sweater and came out with a scrambler and pointed it in my direction. 'Do it,' he said.

'Carmen?'

'Yes, Chase.' She was using a different tone than normal, deeper, almost masculine, signaling she would help any way she could.

I took his card and held it up for the reader. 'We're going to transfer twenty-two thousand,' I said.

'Wait a minute,' Hap said. 'How much you got in your account?'

'I don't know without looking.'

He hit me again. This time I was ready and managed to sidestep some of the impact. Still, it knocked me off my feet again.

'Let her alone,' said Amy. 'She didn't do nothing to you.'

'How much?' he demanded.

I didn't know. But I gave him a ballpark. 'Enough to cover. About twenty-four.'

'Make it thirty.' He jammed the scrambler against my belly, grabbed my hair, and hauled me back onto my feet. 'Truth is,

Kolpath, you've put me to a lot of trouble.' He twisted my hair. 'Empty the account.' He desperately needed a shower. And some mouthwash. 'Put it all in there.' He jabbed a finger at his card. If there'd been any doubt about his plans for Amy and me, that settled it.

He was standing in front of the sofa, where he could watch both of us. But I didn't think he was really worried.

'*Which account do we make the transfer from?*' Carmen asked, in a flat disinterested tone. I only had one. She was suggesting a course of action. '*Perhaps the Baylok account?*'

Baylok? And Sky Jordan?

Jordan fighting off the teleporting monsters.

Nobody will ever again tell me household AIs are not sentient. 'Yes,' I said, trying to sound subdued. 'Let's do it that way.'

'How much you got in the Baylok account?' demanded Hap.

'Forty-two. Plus change.'

'Maybe you should show me.' He was standing, facing the center of the room, watching the two of us, and moving his weapon casually back and forth to keep us both in the line of fire. He was looking simultaneously malevolent and pleased with himself when the Baylok leaped into the room, snarling and spitting.

Hap jumped.

The thing roared and charged. Amy shrieked. Its jaws gaped and a tentacle sliced toward Hap's head. Hap fired once and fell backward over a footrest.

I should have gone after the weapon. But I was fixated on Philidor and I swept it off the shelf as he went down. The phantom roared past and I brought the statuette down on Hap's skull with everything I had. It produced a loud *bonk* and he screamed and threw both hands up to protect himself. Carmen shut off the VR and I nailed him a second time. Blood spurted. Amy was off the sofa in an instant, begging me to hold fire. The people in the hallway pounded on the door. Was I okay?

I was trying to get another clear shot at Hap. Amy went to

her knees on the floor beside him and blocked my angle. 'Hap,' she sobbed. 'Hap, are you okay, love?'

Maybe I don't understand these things, but I could have bopped her, too.

10

I was there when the *Seeker* left orbit, December 27, '88. I'd made my decision and stayed behind. So I watched my sister and some of my lifelong friends start out for a distant place that had no name and whose location had not been disclosed. I knew, as I watched the monster ship slip its moorings and begin to move into the night, that there would never come a time that I would not question my decision to stay behind. And I knew, of course, that I would never see any of them again.

—*The Autobiography of Clement Esteban*, 2702 C.E.

When I walked into my office next morning, Alex asked what had happened to my lip. By then I'd pretty much had it with the *Seeker*, the cup, and the Margolians.

'Hap paid me a visit.'

'*What?*' Alex turned purple. 'Are you okay? Where is he now? Here, sit down.'

How wobbly did I look? 'I'm fine,' I said. 'A few bruises, nothing more.'

'Where's he now? That son of a bitch.'

I believe that was the only time I ever heard Alex use the term.

'I talked to Fenn this morning. He says they'll probably put him away for a while. This one is over the top. He's assaulted Amy twice now, plus a couple of other girlfriends. Maybe they'll finally decide he's not responding to treatment.'

I described what had happened. He broke into a huge grin when the Baylok showed up. 'Good,' he said. 'That was a brilliant idea.'

'Yes. It was Carmen's.'

'Who's Carmen?'

'My AI.'

He squinted at my bruises, told me he hoped they got Hap off the streets. Then he sat down beside me. 'How about Amy?'

Usually, when I check in, he says good morning, tells me what our priorities are for the day, and goes upstairs to look over the markets. But this time he seemed at a loss for words. He told me he was glad it was nothing serious, that I hadn't been injured, that it must have been a scary experience. He bounced out of the chair and came back minutes later with coffee and toast.

He made a few more comments about how glad he was I'd come through it okay, and was I sure I wasn't hurt, had I been to see a doctor. And before I'd quite locked in on him again he got one past me. 'Before we give up on the Margolians,' he said, 'we have another lead I'd like you to follow. If you feel up to it.' He waited while I ran it through a second time and realized I was receiving an assignment among all the well wishes. 'Last one,' he promised. 'If nothing comes of this, we'll write the whole thing off.'

'What do you need?' I asked.

'Mattie Clendennon. She trained at navigation school with Margaret and stayed close to her.'

'Okay,' I said. 'What's her number? I'll talk to her first thing.'

'It's not that easy.'

Another off-world run, I thought.

'No.' He looked guilty. It takes a lot to make Alex Benedict look guilty. 'She's apparently a bit strange.'

'Stranger than Hap?'

'No. Nothing like that. But it looks as if she likes to live alone. Doesn't much talk to anybody.'

'She's off-line.'

'Yes. You'll have to go see her.' He put a picture up. 'She's in her eighties. Lives in Wetland.'

It was hard to believe Mattie Clendennon was that young. Her hair had gone white; she appeared to be malnourished; and she simply looked worn-out. The picture was two years old, so I wondered if she was even still alive.

Alex assured me she was. So I took the misnamed nightflyer next morning and arrived in Paragon by midafternoon. From there I caught the train to Wilbur Junction, rented a skimmer, and went the last hundred kilometers to Wetland. Despite its name, it was located in the middle of the Great Northern Desert; Wetland was a small town that had been a major tourist draw during the last century when desert sports were all the rage. But its time had come and gone, the tourists had left, the entrepreneurs had bailed out, and fewer than two thousand inhabitants were left.

From a distance it looked big. The old hotels were clustered on the north side around the water park. The gravity works, where dancers and skaters had free-floated, resembled a large covered bowl in the downtown area, and the Egyptian replicas, pyramids, Sphinx, and stables, lay windblown on the western edge of the city. Here, in the good days, you could bring your friends, mount a drome (the closest thing Rimway had to a camel) and set off to explore the glories of the ancient world. The Temple of Ophir toward the sunrise, the Garden Palace of Japhet the Terrible a few kilometers farther on (where, if you stayed alert and rode with skill, you might be able to get out with your valuables and your life). This was a place where you came to escape from VR, where the adventure was *real*. More or less.

It was all before my day, of course. I'd have enjoyed spending some time there during those years. People today sit in their living rooms too much. Everything's vicarious, as somebody said. No wonder most of the population's overweight.

The streets were quiet. A few people wandering around. No sign of kids.

I had an address. Number one Nimrud Lane. But Carmen had been unable to match it with a location. So I had no idea where I was going. There were only a few landing pads, and those all seemed to be private. You wanted to come down, you came down on the desert.

I descended near a stone building designed to look like an enhanced pagoda, climbed out, and dropped down onto the sand. The sun was in the middle of the sky, bright and unblinking, but it was cold rather than hot. Not at all what you'd expect.

I tried my address out on a couple of passersby, but they shrugged and said they had no idea. 'Try City Center,' one said, pointing to the pagoda.

I walked into it five minutes later and stood in the lobby, which felt like a place bypassed by history. A bank of elevators lined the far wall. Worn chairs and divans were scattered about. There was only one other person there, an elderly man on a sofa peering at a notebook.

I approached a service counter and a male avatar appeared, looking fresh and helpful. Dark hair brushed back, amiable features, eyes a bit larger than you'd see in a normal human. 'Yes, ma'am,' he said. 'My name's Toma. May I help you?'

I gave him the address, and he looked puzzled. 'It doesn't seem to be in the atlas. May I ask you to wait a moment while I consult my supervisor?'

He was gone less than a minute. 'I should have realized,' he said. 'It's out at the Nimrud exhibit. Or at what used to be the Nimrud exhibit. It's in private hands now.'

It was nine kilometers northwest of the city. One of the old stops from the days when caravans filled with tourists ran out of Wetland.

* * *

Mattie Clendennon lived in a palace. High stone walls, spires at each of the four corners. Arched entrance, up a flight of broad stairs, everything guarded by sculptures of people in antique dress. Enormous windows. Angled skylights. Flags and parapets. There was a large interior courtyard filled with more statuary, shrubs, and trees. A fountain threw spray across the walkway. The only sign of decay was a dust-filled pool in a portico on the eastern side of the building.

I debated landing in the courtyard, thought better of it, and set down in front of the main entrance. I used my link to say hello, but got no response.

I got out, pulled my jacket tight against a cold wind, and stood admiring the building for several moments. The town officially claimed that the various ancient outposts surrounding Wetland were authentic, in the sense that this was how Nineveh and Hierakonopolis and Mycenae had actually looked, and *felt*, in their glory days. Nimrud, according to my notebook, had been part of the Assyrian Empire.

The truth was that the only thing I knew about Assyrians was the line from Byron.

I went up the front steps (cut at the actual dimensions from the original, according to the claims), walked beneath the arch, and stopped before a pair of ornately carved wooden doors. They were big, maybe twice my height. Iron rings were inset at about eye level. I pulled on one.

'Who's there, please?' Female voice. Not an AI, I decided.

'Chase Kolpath. I was looking for Mattie Clendennon.'

'What about? I don't know you, Kolpath.'

'You're Ms Clendennon?'

'Who else would I be?'

A grump. 'I was wondering if you'd be willing to talk to me for a few minutes about Margaret Wescott.'

Long pause. 'Margaret's gone a long time. What could there possibly be to talk about?'

The wooden doors remained shut. Hunting cats were carved

into them. And guys with war helmets and shields. And lots of pointed beards. Everybody had one. 'Might I come inside?'

'*I'm not alone,*' she warned.

'That's fine. I mean you no harm, Ms Clendennon.'

'*You're too young to have known her.*'

'That's so. I did not know her. But I'm doing some research about her.'

'*Are you a journalist?*'

'I'm an antiquarian.'

'*Really? That seems an odd way to make a living.*'

'It's been a challenge.'

Another long pause. One of the doors clicked and swung out. 'Thank you,' I said.

'*Come straight ahead until you reach the rear of the passageway. Then turn left and go through the curtains.*'

I crossed a stone floor into a shadowy chamber. The walls were covered with cuneiform, and stone cylinders mounted around the room depicted kings accepting tribute, archers stationed atop towers that looked exactly like the ones surrounding the palace, warriors going head-to-head with axes, shining beings handing tablets down from the sky. Weapons racks, filled with axes, spears, and arrows, ran along two sides of the chamber. Shields were stored near the entrance.

Following her directions, I passed through another door into a broad passageway, took an elevator up to the fourth level, and turned left into a waiting room. I heard footsteps clicking on the stone, and Mattie Clendennon joined me. Her pictures didn't do her justice. I'd expected a feeble, half-deranged old woman. But Mattie was ramrod straight. She radiated energy and strolled across that stone floor like a cat. She was tall, imperious, with gray-green eyes and thin, intense features. A smile played about her lips.

'Welcome, Chase Kolpath,' she said. 'I don't get many visitors.'

She wore sand-colored clothes and a trooper hat, the sort of thing you might have wanted if you were going out to do some excavations. Somehow this eighty-year-old woman did not look at all absurd in the outfit.

'It's a pleasure to meet you, Ms Clendennon,' I said.

She shifted her gaze to the engravings that surrounded us. 'This is where they found the *Gilgamesh Epic*,' she said.

'Really?' I tried to sound impressed, thinking that the woman was out of her head.

She read my reaction. 'Well, of course, not literally. This is a replica of the palace at Khorsabad. Which is where George Smith found the tablets.'

She led the way down a long corridor. The stone gave way to satin curtains, thick carpets, and lush furniture. We turned into a room furnished with modern chairs and a sofa. Curtains were drawn across two windows, softening the sunlight. 'Sit down, Kolpath,' she said. 'And tell me what brings you to Sargon's home.'

'This is a magnificent place,' I said. 'How do you come to be living here?'

One silver brow arched. 'A mixed compliment? Is there a problem?'

'No,' I said. 'It just seems a bit unusual.'

'Where better?' She studied me, making up her mind whether I was friend or whatever, and came down on my side of things. 'Would you like a drink?'

She mixed us a couple of black bennies while I drew one of the curtains aside and looked out the window. Wetland, which should have been on the horizon, was missing. In its place I saw a city with minarets and towers. 'Baghdad,' she said, 'in its glory days.'

It was a projection. 'It's lovely,' I said.

'You should see it at night, when it lights up.' She handed me my drink. 'I decided I didn't like life on Rimway very much. So I've gone back to a better time.'

I looked around the room, with its climate control and its synthetic walls and its VR capability.

She laughed. 'That doesn't mean I'm an idiot. I get the best of both worlds here. Baghdad is romantic, but needs to be kept at a distance.'

I sampled the black benny and complimented her on it.

'It's my favorite.' She started to sit but changed her mind. 'Here, Kolpath, let me show you something.' We walked back out into the passageway, made a couple of turns, passed through several rooms, and came into an enormous chamber. Just enough sunlight filtered into it to cut through the gloom. It was filled with clay pots and more stone cylinders. All were engraved. 'Each group tells a story,' she said. 'Over there, the deeds of Sennacherib. To your right, the glories of Esarhaddon. There—' She produced a lamp, turned it on, and directed the beam onto a podium. 'The Crystal Throne itself.'

It glittered brilliantly in the lamplight.

'What's the Crystal Throne?'

'Sargon, my dear. My, they did neglect your education, didn't they?'

'Sometimes I think so.'

She laughed, a pleasant sound like tinkling ice cubes. 'You're a security officer of sorts, aren't you?' I asked.

'Of sorts. Actually, the AI handles the security.' She smiled. 'Just in case you had any ideas.'

'I wouldn't think of it,' I said. 'I've no use for a crystal throne.'

We returned to the sitting room, where she produced another round of drinks. 'Now,' she said, 'what is this about Margaret that brings you to the palace?'

'She was a close friend of yours, wasn't she?'

'Margaret Wescott.' She looked around the room, as if trying to locate something. 'Yes. I never knew anyone else like her.'

'In what way?'

'She was a marvelous woman. She cared about things. You got her for a friend, you knew she'd always be there if you needed her.'

'How about Adam? How well did you know him?'

She thought it over. 'Adam was okay. He was like most men. A bit slow. Self-absorbed. I don't think he ever appreciated what he had. In her, I mean.'

'He took her for granted?'

Smile. 'Oh, yes. Adam was too busy looking at the stars, worrying about things that were far away, to see what was under his nose.'

'But he didn't mistreat her?'

'Oh, no. Adam wouldn't have harmed a fly. And he loved her. It was just that it was a kind of limited love. He loved her because she was physically attractive, and she enjoyed the same kinds of things of things he did, and because she shared his passion for the outer boundaries. And because she was the mother of his daughter.' She looked around the room again. 'It's depressing in here. Why don't we open the curtains, dear?'

I helped, and sunlight streamed in.

'Much better,' she said. 'Thank you. Have you met their daughter? Delia?'

'Yes.'

'Sweet young thing. She has a lot of her mother in her.'

She paused, obviously lost in the past. I took advantage of the opening: 'Did Margaret ever suggest to you that she and Adam might have discovered something unusual during one of their flights?'

'Oh, yes,' she said. 'Of course. Did you know about that?'

'I know they found something.'

'She always told me to keep it quiet.'

'What did they find?' I asked.

She drew back into the present and looked at me closely, trying to decide whether she could trust me. 'Don't you know?'

'No. I know there was a discovery. I'm not sure what it was. Did they find Margolia?'

Her eyes locked on me. 'They found the *Seeker*,' she said.

'The *Seeker*.'

'Yes.' She nodded. 'Do you know what I'm talking about?'

'Yes.'

'They went back several times, trying to extract information from it. But everything was too old.'

'I'd think so.'

'They hoped it would tell them where Margolia was.'

'And it didn't.'

'No. But they didn't have enough time. They were still working on the problem when they went out on that damned skiing vacation.'

'Where is the *Seeker*?'

'I don't know. She told me once, but I really have no recollection. Just coordinates. Numbers, and who remembers them?'

'Are you sure?'

'Oh, yes.'

'Did she write it down?'

'If she did, it's a long time gone.' She managed another smile. 'I'm sorry. I know this isn't what you hoped to hear.'

'No, it's okay. But they actually found the *Seeker*.'

'Yes.'

'Why didn't you tell somebody?'

'I didn't think they'd want me to. I wouldn't have told you if you hadn't mentioned Margolia. You already had part of the story. So I figured no harm done.' She looked cautiously at me. 'I hope I'm right.'

'I've no interest,' I said, 'in damaging anyone's reputation. I understand they boarded it.'

'That's correct.'

'Can you tell me what they saw?'

'A dead ship.' She lowered her voice, as if we were in a sacred place. 'It was carrying a full complement.'

'Of crew?'

'Of passengers. I'll never forget the look on Margaret's face when she told me.'

My God, I thought, the ship's capacity was, what, nine hundred people?

'Lost together,' she said. 'Whatever happened, they were lost together.'

When I got back to the office, a call from Delia Wescott was waiting for me. *'I have something you might want to see. Can you come to the island?'*

Delia lived on Sirika, which was several hundred kilometers southeast of Andiquar. I got directions from her and grabbed a southbound train for Wakkaida, which is a seacoast community. From there I took a cab, settled into the backseat and relaxed while it rose above the shoreline and headed out to sea.

It was early evening by then. The skies were clear, and the first stars had shown up in the east. The cab passed over a pair of large islands and joined some local traffic. Sirika appeared on the horizon. It was an unremarkable place, mostly just a refuge for people with a lot of money and an inclination to get away. Its population was only a few thousand.

Its houses were all outrageously big, and they came with columns and colonnades and pools. They all had boathouses, which looked better than most people's homes.

We angled down toward a villa situated on a hilltop. It was modest, as things went in that neighborhood, located amid a vast expanse of lawns. There was a decent guesthouse off to one side. We drifted toward the landing pad, and Delia got on the circuit. *'Welcome to Sirika, Chase.'* A door opened below, and two kids, a boy and a girl, charged out onto the walkway. Delia followed behind.

The cab touched down, the kids cheered, and I disembarked. She introduced the children. They wanted to look inside the cab, so I held it a minute before paying up. Then they ran off, accompanied by a peremptory warning from their mother not to go far, dinner's about ready. Delia looked proudly after them until they disappeared into a cluster of trees. 'It's a long way from Andiquar,' she said, 'but I'm glad you could make it.'

'I had a good book,' I said.

We went inside. It was a showy home, with high ceilings, lots of original art, marble floors. 'My husband's away on business,' she said. 'He asked me to tell you he was sorry not to be here.'

She directed me into a sitting room. It was small, cozy, obviously the place where the family hung out. Two armchairs, a sofa, and a dark-stained coffee table, on which stood a metal box. Music was being piped in. I recognized Bullet Bob and the Ricochets.

'I know you're anxious to hear why I asked you to come,' she said. 'After Alex asked me about the cup, I called my aunt Melisa. She took care of me after my folks died. She didn't know anything about a discovery, but she and my father weren't all that close anyhow. Aunt Melisa wasn't interested much in outer space.

'I'd talked to her as I told you I would, and she said at first there wasn't anything we'd care about. From my parents. But she went looking and she called me the other day to tell me about something she'd found.' Delia indicated the box.

I followed her gaze and she nodded. Open it.

Folded inside was a white shirt wrapped in plastic. It was marked with the same eagle emblem I'd seen on the cup. 'Beautiful,' I said.

'Melisa tells me she remembers now that there was other stuff. Clothes, boots, electronic gear. Data disks.'

'My God. What happened to it?'

'It got tossed. She said she kept it a few years, but it looked old, and the electronics didn't seem to do anything, weren't compatible with anything, and she couldn't see any reason to store it. She kept the shirt as a memento.'

'Did she get rid of the disks, too?'

'She says everything went.' She sighed. Me, too. 'Which brings us to the other reason I wanted to talk to you.' She looked worried.

'Okay.'

'If you're right, if they really did discover the *Seeker*, they must not have reported it. It's going to turn out my parents hid information from Survey.'

'Yes,' I said. 'Actually, that's the way it looks.'

'How serious is that?'

'I don't know.' I told her why we thought they'd have kept it quiet. That they might have felt it was necessary to protect the artifact. I put the best light on it I could. But Delia was no dummy.

'No matter,' she said. 'If that's what happened, it won't look good.'

'Probably not.'

'Chase, I don't want to be part of anything that's going to harm their reputations.' She paused. Looked around the room. 'You understand what I'm saying?'

'Yes.'

'So I'm not sure where I go from here.'

'I'll do what I can to protect them,' I said.

'But you won't be able to do much, will you?'

'Probably not,' I admitted.

On the way home, I watched *Insertion*, the classic horror show in which superphysical emotionless humans from Margolia have infiltrated the Confederacy. They've come to regard the rest of us as impediments to progress, which they define in terms of enhanced intelligence and a 'higher' set of moral values. These, of course, don't seem to include prohibitions against murdering people who discover the secret or simply get in the way.

If you've seen it, you haven't forgotten the desperate chase through the skyways and towers of New York City, during which the narrative's hero, fleeing a dozen bloodthirsty Margolians, tries to get to the authorities to warn them. En route he has to use lubricating oil, electrical circuits, an automatic washer, and several other devices, to escape. The Margolians could do all the super-intelligent double talk they wanted, and bend metal, and the rest of it, but when it came to the crunch, it was obvious that good old native Confederate ingenuity would win out every time. I especially liked the lubricant gig, which he used to send one of his pursuers sliding off a partly constructed terrace.

I don't care for horror shows. In this one, twenty or so people are killed off in an astonishingly wide range of ways, most involving lots of blood, gouging, and impaling. (I couldn't figure out why the Margolians carried those long pokers when they could far more easily dispatch folks with scramblers.) That's a lot more murder victims than I can normally tolerate in an evening. But I wanted to get a sense of what other people had been making of the Margolian story.

Well, there you are. *Insertion* was fun, in a childish way. But it seemed unlikely anything like that could actually happen.

11

We are leaving this world forever, and we intend to go so
far that not even God will be able to find us.
—Ascribed to Harry Williams
(Remarks as Margolians prepared to depart Earth)

I'd taken pictures of the white shirt to show Alex. 'You think it's
legitimate?' he asked.

'No way to be sure just looking at it. But she'd have no reason
to lie.'

'I guess.' Alex couldn't restrain a smile that illuminated the
entire room. 'Chase, I can hardly believe it. But we really do have
a ship out there.'

'Pity we don't have the Wescotts' data disks.'

'The aunt really threw them out?'

'That's what Delia says.'

'Did you check with her? With the aunt?'

'No. I didn't see any reason to.'

'Do it. Maybe she kept *something*. Maybe she knows where
they were taken. Maybe we can still find them.'

'You're sounding desperate, Alex.'

But I made the calls. Delia gave me the aunt's code. The aunt wondered if I'd lost my mind. 'Put them in the trash thirty years ago,' she said.

The earliest serious efforts to settle other worlds had been made two hundred years before the *Seeker* and *Bremerhaven* flights. The pioneers, according to the history books, had been driven, not by desperation, but by a sense of adventure, of wanting to escape the monotonous and sometimes deadly routines of civilization. They'd hoped to make their fortunes on a remote frontier. They'd gone out to Sirius, and Groombridge, Epsilon Eridani, and 61 Cygni.

Those first interstellars had been slow, requiring months to make the relatively short flights to nearby stars. But thousands of people had gone, taken their families, and settled worlds deemed to be hospitable.

But none of those early efforts had prospered.

The colonies, theoretically self-supporting, encountered difficulties, weather cycles, viruses, crop failures, for which they were unable to make adjustments. Technological assistance from the home world, at first steady, became sporadic, and eventually went away.

The survivors came home.

The first successful settlement, in the sense that it actually prospered, waited another thousand years. Eight centuries after the Margolian effort.

The *Seeker* had been designed originally, during a burst of unbridled optimism, to move whole populations to colony worlds. On the Margolian mission it was captained by Taja Korinda, who had been the pilot of the *LaPierre* when it discovered a living world in the Antares system. Her second chair was Abraham Faulkner. Faulkner had been a politician at one time, had seen where things were going, and switched careers so that, if the legend was true, he could get out when he needed to.

I found holograms of Korinda and Faulkner. When I showed them to Alex, he commented that Korinda looked like me. She was an attractive woman, and it was Alex's ham-handed way of passing a compliment. He's good with the clients, but for whatever reason when he gets around to me he seems to have problems.

Faulkner looked the part of a guy with a mind of his own. Big, brawny, wide shoulders, obviously accustomed to command. About forty. The kind of guy you took seriously.

'But Harry's the one we want to talk to,' said Alex. 'He's the heart and soul of the Margolians.' There weren't any avatars back that far. But Jacob could assemble one from what was known about Williams. The problem was that it might not be very accurate. But then that was always the problem with avatars.

'There is not a wealth of data,' Jacob complained. *'And the validity of what is known about Williams is suspect.'*

'Do the best you can,' Alex said.

'It will take a few minutes. I have to make some judgment calls.'

'Good. Let me know when it's ready.' Alex seemed distracted that morning. While he waited, he wandered around the house straightening chairs and adjusting curtains. He stopped in front of one of the bookcases and stared at the volumes.

'You all right, Alex?' I asked him.

'Of course.' He strolled over to a window and gazed out at a ruddy, cloud-swept sky.

'You're thinking about the disks.'

'Yes. Idiot woman throws them out.'

'Not her fault,' I said. 'She had no way of knowing.'

He nodded. 'Lucky she didn't toss the shirt.'

'Do you think,' I said, 'there's any possibility the colony might have survived? Might still be out there somewhere?'

'The Margolians? After nine thousand years?' He looked wistful. 'It would be nice to find something like that. But no. There's no chance.'

Stupid question. Had they lived, how would you explain the fact nobody had heard from them in all that time? 'If they *were* out there, it might be they wouldn't want to be found.'

147

'If trees could fly,' he said.

'If I were writing a novel,' I said, 'they'd have arranged the earthquake that killed the Wescotts and ended their search.'

'And why would they want to keep their existence secret?'

'We're barbarians in their eyes.'

'Speak for yourself, Chase.' He made a sound deep in his throat and lowered himself onto the sofa. 'They not only died out, but they must have gone quickly.'

'Why do you say that?'

'Because later generations wouldn't have shared the grudge Harry Williams and his friends had. It just wouldn't have happened. They'd have gotten back in touch. At some point. It would have been to everyone's benefit.' His eyes slid shut. 'They'd have had to. For one thing, after a few centuries, they'd have been as curious about us as we are about them. But the colony site is out there somewhere. And I'll tell you, Chase, if we can bring back some artifacts from *that*, we are going to make some serious cash.'

There was a long silence. I became gradually aware of someone standing behind me, near the office door. It was a tall, dark-skinned man of middle age, dressed in clothing from another century. Cream-colored vest, loose black shirt open to the navel, the sort of white slacks you might wear at sea. Everything a bit more garish than you could get away with today. He smiled, looked at me, then at Alex, and said hello in the deepest baritone I'd ever heard.

'Harry Williams,' said Alex, sitting up.

'At your pleasure, sir. And, Chase, I would not be too quick to dismiss the possibility they survived.' He crossed the room, and took a seat in the armchair closest to Alex. *'Do you think you can find the colony world?'*

I froze the picture. 'Alex, I understood no likeness of him had survived.'

'You just have to persevere.' He grinned. 'Never give up. That's my motto.'

'Where'd you find it?'

'In fact, there are a few of them. This one came from a set of memoirs by a contemporary.'

The guy looked good. Noble aspect and all that. I could understand why people were willing to follow him. Even to distant places that didn't have restaurants. Alex flipped through his notebook and reactivated Harry. 'The goal was "to create free minds in a free society." Right, Harry?'

'Your words?' I asked.

'Yes.'

'Noble sentiment.'

He nodded. *'Unfortunately, the truth is it's pure hyperbole. Nobody lives in a free society.'*

'We do.'

'I doubt it. We all believe what our parents believed. You get filled up during the first few years when the mind is open to everything, and you assume adults know what's going on. So you're vulnerable. And if later on you decide to reject the local mythology, whatever it might be, you pay a price. Parents frown, old friends are shocked, you get ostracized. There's no such thing as a completely free society.' A sofa appeared and he unwound into it.

'You're not talking about us,' I said.

He smiled. *'Freedom's an illusion.'*

We looked at one another across the expanse of the office. At that moment we might have been separated by light-years. Alex grinned at me. Are you really going to argue philosophy with *this* guy?

I plowed ahead. 'Harry, aren't we exaggerating a trifle?'

'We're tribal, Chase. We talk about freedom, but you better not say things the tribe doesn't care to hear. Or act outside approved norms.'

'For example?'

'I don't know where I am.' He looked around the room, at the antiques on display for clients. At the several framed commendations. *'You collect artifacts.'*

'Yes.'

'*That is your profession.*'

'That's correct,' I said.

'*On-site? You recover some of them personally?*'

That much was evident from the framed scroll presented us by Coryn University. 'Yes. Sometimes.'

He looked over at Alex. '*Have you and your associate been accused of being grave robbers?*'

'That's very good,' Alex said.

'*So much for your free society.*'

'That's different.'

'*How is it different? You're making an honest living, are you not? But there's this tribal instinct about burial places being sacrosanct. Unless you work for a museum.*'

Alex broke in. 'Maybe we can hash this out another time. Harry, we'd like to find the colony world. Do you know where it is?'

'*I have no idea. None whatever. The sources Jacob tapped to create this program did not have that information.*'

'Pity.'

The guy had charisma. Or maybe that's the wrong word. Presence. I sat there knowing I was in the company of a heavyweight. The way he smiled, the way he crossed one leg over the other, the way he engaged with us. He was accustomed to giving direction, taking charge, confronting what he had to. And I know that's all part of the installation program, and the real Harry Williams might have been quite different. But nevertheless, his dialogue and persona were both extracted from what was known about him. '*How long has it been?*' he asked.

'Nine thousand years.'

His eyes widened at that. He took a deep breath. Swallowed. And I saw fear in his expression. '*Are you telling me you don't know where they are?*'

'No.'

'*How's that possible?*'

'Nothing's been heard from them. *Ever.*'

'Since when?'

'Since they left Earth.'

He'd almost stopped breathing. *'My God.'* He threw his head back. *'I don't understand how that could be. May I ask where we are?'*

'We're not on Earth,' said Alex.

'Amazing.' He smiled. *'This isn't a joke, is it?'*

Alex shook his head. No.

Harry got up, went to the window, and looked out. *'It looks like home.'*

'Most of the garden is designer plants. Everything else, trees, grass, you name it, is native to Rimway.'

'And that is the name of this place? Of this world?'

'Yes. We are well out toward the edge of the Orion Arm. At one time, no human world was farther from Earth.'

'Wonderful,' he said. But there were tears in his eyes. *'And you never came across the colony?'*

'No.'

'In nine thousand years?'

'No.'

'Incredible.'

I felt sorry for him.

'Was there any contact at all after they left Earth?'

'None that we know of.'

'Well,' he said, *'that* was *the plan. I thought we were being optimistic.'*

I listened to voices outside. Kids playing somewhere close by.

'You kept your secret too well, Harry. It's not available to us. And therefore not to you.'

'Something went wrong.'

'Yes. I think so.'

'It's hard to understand what could have happened. We planned to be on our own until we put together the kind of society we wanted. But to disappear forever? That's inconceivable. It couldn't have happened.'

151

'It was a risky venture,' I said. 'Surely you knew that.'

'*We considered every eventuality.*'

'You missed something.'

'*Yes. It would seem so.*'

Alex shook his head, puzzled. 'Harry, you did not have FTL communications, did you?'

'*No.*'

'So if a major problem *did* develop, you had no way to get help. Other than sending back either the *Bremerhaven* or the *Seeker*.'

'*That's correct.*'

'Which meant help was two years away.'

'*Yes.*'

'What are you driving at, Alex?' I asked.

'Mattie Clendennon says the Wescotts found the *Seeker* adrift. That at the time it broke down, or whatever, it was loaded with passengers.' He returned his attention to Harry. 'Were there any plans to move large chunks of the population elsewhere? After you colonized Margolia?'

'*We thought it might happen. In time. But no, we had no relocation plans. There weren't enough of us even to consider anything like that.*'

'So where were they going?' When Harry shook his head, Alex asked whether there were other ships in the group.

'*No. Only the two transports.*'

'The two interstellars were old when you bought them, right?'

'*Yes, Alex. That's correct. But they were certified for us. We spent the money to have them inspected and maintained.*'

'But according to the record, after each of the missions they made for you, they had to be refitted. If they'd both broken down, or maybe were allowed to fall into disrepair, your people might easily have been stranded.'

'*The odds against both of them breaking down were pretty long, Alex.*'

'I'm not so sure. They'd have required maintenance. Were you prepared to maintain them? Over an extended period of time?'

'Yes. We had a service organization.'

'What about after the first generation died off? Was there a program to ensure replacements?'

'*Not when we left, of course. It wasn't one of the things we were especially worried about. Look, we had a hospitable world to go to. It was safe. We took all the technology with us that we could possibly need. We wanted no contact with Earth, and we set things up deliberately so that none would be necessary.*' He seemed to take a deep breath. '*I can't get hold of the time,*' he said. '*Nine thousand years is just too long. Is there still an organized political system on Earth?*'

'Yes, Harry,' said Alex.

'*What kind of system is it? What kind of system do you live under?*'

'We have a republic. As does Earth. We're spread out now across more than a hundred worlds. And you'll be happy to know we live well, we have free institutions, by any reasonable definition. And life is good.'

'*That amazes me.*'

'You didn't think we would do well?'

'*We weren't doing well in my time.*' He looked out across the lawn. It was getting late in the day, and the sky was gray and cold. '*It feels so much like home.*'

Something flapped past too quickly to allow a good look. He stared after it. '*I just can't believe I'm actually on another world.*'

'We don't think of it that way.'

'*I guess not. Is that a cemetery over there?*'

'Yes. It's just off the property line.'

'*It looks old.*'

'It was there when I was a boy, growing up here.' Alex smiled. 'I was always scared of it.'

'*How long have we been here? On Rimway?*'

'A long time. More than six thousand years.'

He shook his head. '*You've been here longer than we'd had civilization on Earth.*'

153

'About the same length of time.' Alex's gaze was locked on him. 'So you didn't like life in the American Republic?'

'We were looking for a better place.'

'Where'd you get the starships?' I asked.

'The Seeker *was bought from Interworld. A salvage dealer. The* Bremerhaven *was built by the Chinese. It was a famous ship in its time. It was part of the fleet that hauled people and equipment to Utopia.'*

'Utopia?' I asked.

Harry sighed. *'It was an early effort to colonize. It didn't go well. Either.'* He wandered over to the bookcase and began examining the titles. *'I never heard of any of these people,'* he said.

Alex waved the comment aside. 'Was it your idea to head out to the stars?'

Harry looked tired. *'I doubt it was the idea of any single individual.'* He seemed to be trying to remember. *'It was probably an idea that grew out of the group. I don't recall any one person coming forward with it. There was a lot of talk about getting away. Could we get a ship? Could we find a place of our own? In the beginning, it was just talk.'* He looked overcome with emotion. 'A place of our own. *It became our mantra.'*

'How did you find five thousand people willing to go?'

'Fifty-three hundred is closer to the correct figure. We started with eighty. But the genetics wouldn't work, so we opened the plan to friends. Others who were tired of the kind of society they lived in.'

'And they joined?' I said.

He laughed. *'Not many people, even the bravest, are willing to leave home permanently. But there was a steady stream until finally we had to cut it off.'*

'There'd been other settlement attempts. You mentioned Utopia.'

'Yes. By the time we were ready, there was already a history of failure. They'd been at it for a long time when we launched.'

'How'd the government react? Did they make an effort to stop you?'

'*They were glad to see us go. We were branded as unpatriotic by unofficial spokesmen, and eventually by the general population. But we were actually given whatever assistance we needed.*'

'Who decided which world you'd settle?'

'*No one person. We sent out a few of our people, a group of scientists, and some other specialists. They found the place—*'

'And were sworn to secrecy.'

'*Yes.*'

'I wouldn't have thought it possible to keep such a secret.'

'*Alex,*' he said, '*we all understood that if anyone compromised the location of the colony world, we would be followed by all the evils and stupidities we were trying to leave behind. Do you know where Margolia is?*'

'You know I don't.'

'*It appears we were successful.*'

'So what do we do now?' 'I don't know,' Alex said. 'You have any ideas?'

'We could hunt through every system in the Wescott record. But we have no guarantee the *Seeker* wasn't somewhere else.'

'Chase, you said they were allotted a specific area of sky for each mission. How big is the area?'

'*Big.*'

'Can you be more specific?'

'Out where the Wescotts were, it probably holds thirty thousand class Gs.'

'Well, at least that narrows it down.' He glanced at Jacob's control panel. 'What about the AI?'

'How do you mean?'

'Maybe we've been taking the wrong tack. Instead of trying to find their leased vehicle, maybe we should have been looking for the Survey ship they used.'

'The *Falcon.*'

'Was that its name?'

'Yes.'

'Would the AI have recorded everything?'

'Yes. But the Wescotts could have deleted whatever they didn't want known.'

'That's a pretty serious offense, isn't it? If they get caught?'

'Yes.'

'You said nobody ever checks the AIs. So why bother changing it?'

'That's a point,' I said. 'But before you get excited, Survey reconditions the things every few years. They come in, clear the system, maybe upgrade it, and reinstall it.'

'Every few years?'

'Yes. The AI the Wescotts had would have been cleared a long time ago.'

He sat quietly and made a few offhand comments about the weather and the cemetery, and on a few business-related matters. I thought the subject had been dropped until he said, abruptly, 'Let's give it a try anyhow.'

'Give *what* a try?'

'The AI. Maybe we'll get lucky.'

'Alex, there's no point.'

'There's nothing to lose. Let's get on the circuit and ask. Maybe they download everything into a master file. Who knows?'

He went off for lunch with a client. I called Survey and got one of their avatars. Elderly man, this time. A bearded eminence. *'Yes, young lady,'* he said, *'how may I be of service?'*

I told him what I wanted, that I was looking for details on the Wescott flights during the 1380s and early '90s. That I hoped that data from the *Falcon* AI might be available.'

'We have the official logs on file, you know,' he said, as if that solved everything.

'Yes, of course. But we think there might have been an error. We'd like to recover the AI, if that's possible.'

'Really?'

'Yes.'

'Can I ask you to hold a moment, please?'

He was gone. Survey is like most other bureaucracies. When

156

they ask you to hold, they pump images of waterfalls and sandy beaches and mountaintops at you, throw in some soft music, and keep you waiting an hour. This was different. I got the waterfall, but they were back within a minute. A human being this time.

'Hi, Chase,' he said. 'I'm Aaron Winslow. You wouldn't remember me but we met at the Polaris event last year.'

'The one that blew up.'

'Yes. What a terrible thing that was. But I was glad to see most of us came through it okay. How can I help you?'

'Aaron, I work for Rainbow.'

'Yes, I know. Alexander Benedict's company.'

'Right. I was doing some research on the deaths of the Wescotts, back in '98. I was hoping that the AI from their ship, the Falcon, might have survived.'

'After thirty years? I don't think so, Chase. They're absolutely religious about reprogramming them at six-mission intervals.' He was biting his lower lip. 'You say they used the Falcon?'

'Yes.'

'Doesn't ring a bell.' He looked off to one side, probably at a data screen. 'Hold on a second.'

'Okay.'

'The Falcon's before my time. In fact, it was sold off after its last mission with the Wescotts.'

'Was there a problem?'

'No. It had forty years' service. That was as long as they kept them then.'

'They keep them longer now?'

'Fifty-five. We buy better stuff now.'

'What happens to a ship when its time is up?'

'We sell it if we can. Junk it if we have to.'

'Do they clear off the AI when that happens?'

He looked puzzled. 'You know, I really have no idea. It's not something I ever thought to ask.' He made a face and drummed his fingertips on a flat surface. A desktop, probably. 'Hold on a second, Chase.'

The scenic images came back. Sand dunes this time. And music designed to make you feel affectionate toward Survey. Then he reappeared. *'They tell me we do now. But at the turn of the century, we don't know whether they bothered. There was a court case eighteen years ago. That's what got us serious about it, so now everything gets cleared.'*

'Can you tell me specifically what happened to the *Falcon?'*

'Let me check,' he said. *'I'll get back to you.'*

You should understand I had no hope whatever that anything would come of the inquiry. But Alex expected me to be thorough.

When Aaron called back, he had a piece of paper in front of him. *'Chase,'* he said, *'it was purchased in 1392 by the Hennessy Foundation.'*

'Hennessy,' I said.

'Dedicated to peace with the Mutes.'

12

Takmandu is the loveliest of human worlds. Its forests are deep, its seas veiled in mist, its triple moons breathtaking. It is remote from the mundane skywalks and crowded parks of the Inner Confederacy, and its proximity to the demon-haunted Ashiyyur suggests it will remain that way.

—Hyman Kossel,
Travels, 1402

The ski slopes are great, too.

—Leslie Park,
quoted in *The Ultimate Tourist*, 1403

The Hennessy Foundation was headquartered on Takmandu, in the Coroli Cluster. Takmandu had been, for centuries, the political center of the outlying worlds. I'd been there once, with my class, when I was a teenager. It was the first time I'd been off Rimway, and it was one of those life-changing events. I wasn't all that caught up visiting the historical sites, which was the purpose of the field trip, but I loved the ship. The *Starduster*. And the flight itself. I came back with the determination to be a pilot.

In an era during which you could communicate more quickly over interstellar distances by traveling physically than by any other means, I knew I'd be hitting the road again. Alex pleaded the pressure of business. Appointments with clients. Have to keep them happy. You know how it is, Chase. 'Anyhow,' he said, 'I don't know anything about shipboard AIs. Find the *Falcon*. And let's see what the AI has to say for itself.'

'If anything,' I said.

He gave me his most optimistic gaze. 'Nothing ventured,' he said.

So I packed a couple of good novels, picked up a blank chip that would be compatible with the *Falcon* AI data dump, and boarded the *Belle-Marie*. On the first day of the new year I set out for Takmandu and the Josef Hennessy Foundation, which was dedicated to creating a better understanding between us and the Ashiyyur.

I'd never seen a Mute in the flesh. Alex had talked with one once. If that's the right word. They're telepaths, and there's something about their physiognomy that creeps people out. Not to mention the fact that they can see into your mind. Alex describes the experience in his memoirs. His comment to me was that what humans and Mutes need isn't understanding, but distance. *We're just not designed to get along.* 'The Foundation's been at it for half a century,' he'd said. 'They should understand the realities by now.'

'I guess they keep trying,' I told him.

'Yep. Makes me wonder if they're not really con men collecting money from idiots.'

I read what I could about the Hennessy Foundation on the way out. They supervised some exchange programs, and conducted seminars in how to communicate, the nature of Mute psychology, and how to control your own natural revulsion in their presence. Mutes didn't really look that bad. They were humanoid, but there was something insectile about them. Their pictures didn't look all that unsettling; but Alex warned me that the common wisdom was correct. Get close to them and your hair stands on end.

The AI produced a Mute avatar for me to talk with. It *did* look pretty revolting, like one of those things that show up in horror sims. Red eyes, fangs, claws, and a smile that suggests you're next on the menu. Still, I didn't feel the kind of revulsion that I'd been warned about.

'That's because,' Alex said, 'it wasn't really there, and you knew that.'

Whatever Alex might think, the Foundation seemed to be having a degree of success. The sporadic sniping and occasional warfare between Mute and human had stopped. Visitors from each side were spending time with receptive groups, and there was even an Ashiyyur-human friendship society. The Foundation's stated goal: *Two intelligent species with a single objective.*

The objective, Alex commented, was to keep well away from each other.

The historian Wilford Brockman has argued that we were fortunate to find the Mutes, because they had the effect of uniting the human race. Since they arrived on the scene centuries ago, there had been only one major war between human powers. The last few centuries have been the most sustained period of internal peace in millennia.

Interestingly, the same effect had been noted on the Mute side. They, too, had a long history of internecine struggle, which had slowed perceptibly. Nothing like a common enemy to bring people, or Mutes, together.

I came out of jump status three days away from Takmandu. I let their ops people know I was in the neighborhood and started one of the mysteries I'd brought along.

But I've never been able to read six or seven hours at a crack, so I found myself watching more sims inspired by the Margolian legend. In *Tiger-Men of the Lost World,* a mission finds the lost colony, but it is covered with trackless forests and the colonists have devolved into ravenous beasts. (How that could happen in a few thousand years isn't explained.) *Vampire Below* posits a freighter that encounters a Margolian ship with a lone pilot, who turns out to be – Well, you guessed it.

The majority of books written on the subject weren't serious. Most of the authors were true believers of one kind or another, generally pushing occult visions of what had happened and sometimes claiming that the lost colony exercises a mystic influence over certain individuals. *(Send money and learn how to apply Margolian power in your own life.)*

The most popular theory by far was the demon star notion that had arisen shortly after the colonists had departed. Harry Williams's celebrated comment that they would travel so far that even God couldn't find them gained notoriety as depicting an antireligious spirit. The notion took hold that the Margolian mission was therefore doomed from the start. Someone launched the idea that a red star would arrive over their chosen world, the eye of God, and that it would herald the destruction of the colony.

Stories began to circulate that many of the people who had donated money and time to the Margolians had died prematurely. As the years passed, and no message ever came back, talk of a curse became widespread. The eye of God no longer sounded so far-fetched.

I thought about what a truly free society might accomplish in nine thousand years. Harry Williams's refugees had started with the intention of avoiding the old mistakes and applying the lessons of history. Their society would throw off all strictures except those imposed by compassion and common sense. Education would emphasize the sciences and philosophy and stress the value of independent thought. Everything would be open to question. Professional politicians would not be allowed.

It sounded good. But we're all conditioned to assume that utopian notions are, well, *utopian*. Not practical. Utopias always collapse.

I sat on the bridge of the *Belle-Marie,* watching Takmandu gradually grow into a disk. To port, I could see the vast star-clouds of the Veiled Lady, including one small gauzy group near the tip of what was perceived as her right ear. It was the Versinjian Cluster, in which, according to completely unsupported legend, the Margolians had planted their colony. But there were tens of thousands of stars in the group. I wondered whether, at that moment, I was seeing light from the Margolian sun.

The Josef Hennessy Foundation maintains an operational office in orbit. I called ahead and made an appointment, citing research. They told me they'd be delighted to see me.

Takmandu is an outpost. Nothing in the Confederate polity is closer to Mute country. The Ashiyyurean world Kappalani is less than three light-years away. Consequently I'd expected to see some signs of their proximity. Maybe a docked ship. Or even a couple of Mutes loose in the concourse.

But it didn't happen. I found out later that there were occasional Mute visitors, but that the experience seemed to unsettle everybody on both sides so much that there was a mutual agreement in effect. If they came, they were escorted off the ship, their path was cleared, and nobody got to see them except the escorts, who are specially trained.

The Takmandu station is probably the biggest functioning orbiter I've seen. There's a magnificent view of the Veiled Lady that draws thousands of visitors, and nearby Gamma is a naval base, so there's a lot of traffic, and a lot of accommodation for tourists. The concourses are crowded with clubs, VR sites, souvenir shops, and even a live theater.

I checked into one of the hotels, showered, dressed, and went out to take care of business.

There's a plethora of industrial, operational, and scientific offices scattered around on several decks. They line wide, garishly painted, gently curving passageways.

The Foundation was located between a travel agency and a first-aid station. I could see one woman inside, seated at a desk, apparently absorbed by a data screen. A banner dominated the wall behind her. It read OUR FRIENDS THE ASHIYYUR. I paused in front of the door and told it who I was. It said that it was glad to see me, and opened.

The woman inside looked up and smiled. 'Ms Kolpath,' she said, 'welcome to the Hennessy Foundation.' She tilted her head. 'Or is it *Dr* Kolpath?'

'*Ms* is fine. *Chase* works, too.'

'Well, hello, Chase.' She extended a hand. 'I'm Teesha Oranya.' She had red hair and animated blue eyes, combined with the suppressed energy of a social worker. 'How can we help you?'

'I'm interested in the Foundation,' I said. 'I wonder if I may ask some questions.'

'Of course. Ask away.'

'You're trying to foster better relations with the Mutes. How exactly do you go about that?'

'The *Ashiyyur*.' She looked briefly pained, as if another bigot had surfaced in front of her. 'Basically, we try to keep communications open. We talk with them. We train others to talk with them. And we learn to overlook the differences.'

'What sort of people? Diplomats? Tourists?'

She motioned me to a seat. 'Traders. Fleet people. Researchers. Sometimes people who just want to meet them. To say hello.'

There was a framed picture on her desk: Teesha standing with a Mute under a tree. She followed my gaze, and smiled. 'That's Kanta Toman,' she said. '"Kanta the Magnificent," he calls himself.'

'Is he serious?'

She laughed and shook her head at my provincialism. 'He's my counterpart. He works for an organization much like this one. They have bureaucracies, too, Chase. He's stuck in his, and he feels invisible.'

'That sounds like a human reaction.'

'Ashiyyureans and humans have far more in common than what separates them. Don't let the fangs fool you. Or the telepathy. They take care of their kids, they want to be good at whatever it is they choose to do, they want affection. They expect to be

164

treated decently. And they abide by a code of principles as ethical as anything we have.'

Kanta the Magnificent was half again as tall as she was. He had gray skin and red-rimmed eyes set far apart. A predator's eyes. His mouth was open in what was probably supposed to be a smile, but it was hard to look past the dagger bicuspids. He wore a ridiculous-looking broad-brimmed hat, baggy red trousers, and a white pullover. The pullover said BELLINGHAM UNIVERSITY.

'The director's school,' she explained.

'Where was it taken?'

'During a visit here two years ago.' She sighed. 'It's a good thing he had a sense of humor.'

'Why's that?'

'You ever been in the same room with an Ashiyyurean?'

'No,' I said.

'When he was here, I invited a few people in off the concourse to say hello. Ordinary travelers. I was new then.' She smiled and shook her head. 'A couple of them had to be helped out.'

'Really?'

'It was probably from trying not to think about anything. Trying to keep their minds blank. If there's a major difference between the species, it has to be that you and I are more easily shocked. And are less honest. In a society where everybody's thoughts are open, you don't have many hypocrisies.'

'Naked on the street corner.'

'That's about it.'

'You seem to be doing okay.'

'Good training,' she said. 'Now, let's get back to you. What else did you want to know?'

'I'm interested in a superluminal that the Foundation purchased from Survey in 1392.'

Her eyebrows rose. 'In 1392?'

'Yes. If the AI is intact, it might have some information that would be of value to me.'

'Well, that's interesting.' She sat back in her chair and asked me to explain.

'It's a complicated story,' I said. 'It has to do with a research project.'

She nodded. 'I should tell you that it's against Foundation policy to allow unauthorized persons aboard our ships.'

'Can I persuade you to grant me authorization?'

'Would you like to tell me specifically what you're looking for?'

Well, it wasn't as if it was a military secret. So I told her there was reason to suspect the *Falcon* might have seen a derelict ship. That the record at Survey was incomplete.

'Okay.' She shrugged. 'We don't have a *Falcon* in our fleet, but that's no surprise because we would probably have rechristened it. Let me see what I can do.'

'Thank you.'

'You understand, we'll have to have one of our technical people go on board with you.'

'Of course. That's no problem.'

'All right. Let's see where the *Falcon* is.'

She gave directions to the data screen. Information swam into view. She tapped the screen, said something to herself, and brought up another page. She obviously wasn't seeing what she expected. 'Not here,' she said.

'You mean it's out somewhere?'

'No. It's not on the inventory.'

'How many ships do you have?'

'Seven.'

'And none of them is, or was, the *Falcon*?'

'That seems to be the case.'

A door opened. A man and woman stood just inside an adjoining office, in the process of saying good-bye to each other. The man wore a white beard, carefully clipped. The lines in his face suggested he'd eaten something that disagreed with him. Permanently. The woman came out, the man retreated back inside, and the door closed.

She was diminutive, probably twenty years older than Teesha, and carefully packed into a blue business suit. She walked past me without noticing I was there. Teesha caught her eye and nodded toward me. She took a quick look in my direction, and let me see she had more important things to do.

'Emma,' Teesha said, 'have we ever had a ship called the *Falcon*?'

Emma's eyeslids half shut. She was too busy for trivia. 'No,' she said. 'Not as long as I've been here.' She sailed out through the door and was gone.

'How long has she been around?' I asked.

'About fifteen years. A long time. She's our director of inter-species relations.'

'She manages the diplomacy?'

'You could put it that way.'

I strolled down onto the maintenance deck and said hello to the duty boss. He was a short, olive-skinned guy in his sixties with too much weight and a distinct wheeze. His name was Mark Woolley. Mark needed medical help, and I hoped he was getting it.

'*Falcon?*' he said, screwing up his face and shaking his head. 'Not here. Not ever, that I know of.'

'This would have been a long time ago, Mark.'

He was wearing coveralls with STARTECH INDUSTRIES stenciled over one pocket and MARK over the other. He looked tired. 'I been here all my life,' he said. 'We never had a ship with that name.'

'Okay. Hennessy acquired it in 1392 from Survey. They might have changed the name.'

He led me back to his office, which was crowded with parts, disks, tools, and instruments. It overlooked one of the docks. Two ships with Foundation markings were out there at the moment, tied to umbilicals. The engine room of one, a *Monitor* class, had been opened, and a team of robots were working on it.

He sat down, wheeled over to his right, brought up a data screen, and asked for any maintenance record or fleet information they had regarding a ship either currently or formerly named *Falcon*. 'Take it back fifty years,' he added.

The AI replied in the same voice: '*No record of a* Falcon *during the indicated period. Or of a ship previously carrying that name.*'

'Okay,' I said. 'Something's wrong somewhere.'

Mark shrugged. 'Don't know.'

I could have started back that evening and told Alex it was a dead end. But I'd just spent several days in the *Belle-Marie,* and I needed a break.

I changed clothes again, opting for something a bit more intriguing than the business suit I'd been wearing. Something black and clingy. Then I headed for the Outrider Club, which, judging from the information I had available, was the most posh eating place on the station.

Time doesn't change on space stations. At a restaurant like the Outrider, it's always evening, because flights are always arriving and departing, and everybody's in a different time zone. The fact that people operate on varying clocks – some on an eighteen-hour day, others on thirty hours, and with all sorts of variations between and beyond – adds to the confusion. So restaurants specialize. Some always serve breakfast. At others, it's always 8:00 P.M. Or whatever passes for 8:00 P.M. in your part of the Confederacy.

I picked a table near a flowering tree of a type I'd never seen before, ordered a drink, and tried to look accessible. I was hoping not to spend the evening alone.

The Outrider had everything, soft music, dim lights, candles, musky scents, a spectacular view of the Veiled Lady. It was a glowing cloud, consisting of millions of stars. You needed an imagination to make a female form out of it. But it didn't matter. Below, on the planetary surface, it was just getting dark and the cities were beginning to light up.

I switched my attention to the guys coming in, looking for someone interesting, when I spotted the pained-looking man with the white beard from the Foundation office. He was in a dinner jacket, accompanied by an older woman, standing at the host's station.

I tried to remember if his name had been on the door, or if Teesha had mentioned it. But I couldn't come up with anything. He and his companion were shown to a table across the room. My waiter returned, and I ordered a light meal.

I tried calling Teesha's office number, but she was gone for the day, and the AI would give me nothing. Let me say up front I had no real hope that this guy could provide any information on the *Falcon*, but you just never knew.

So I collected my drink and wandered over to their table. They looked up, and he frowned as if trying to recall where he might have seen me before. 'Pardon me,' I said. 'My name's Chase Kolpath. I couldn't help noticing you in the Foundation office today.'

A smile appeared. 'Oh, yes,' he said, rising. He introduced himself and his companion. He was Jacques Corvier. 'I hope you got whatever you needed.'

So I told him. I explained how far I'd come, that I was involved in a research project, that the *Falcon* had been sold to the Foundation, and that I wanted very much to talk to its AI.

He pretended to be interested. I got the impression that was for the benefit of his companion. 'I think I know what might have happened,' he said, when I'd finished.

I had the distinct feeling that, had the other woman not been present, he'd have invited me back to the office to take a look at the files. As it was, he spoke into his link and offered me a chair. He listened for a moment to the response. Said *yes*. Then he looked at me. 'Chase,' he said, 'the *Falcon* was never part of the Foundation fleet. We got it from Survey for the express purpose of turning it over to the Ashiyyur.'

'To the Ashiyyur?'

'It was before my time, understand. But yes. They wanted a ship for an exhibition they were putting together, or a museum. I don't know which. But the ship was turned over to them

169

immediately. We took possession only long enough to make the transfer.'

'Turned over to whom, exactly? Do you know?'

He repeated the question into the link, listened, and shook his head. 'We don't know.'

There was a Mute passage office in the main concourse for those traveling on to Ashiyyurean worlds. The station information packet indicated that flights left every four days for Xiala, which was the entry world to that other domain. I should mention here that Xiala is a made-up human word. We know what the term looks like in its written form, but because the Mutes do not speak, there is no such thing as a correct pronunciation, or indeed any pronunciation. However all that may be, I thought we could have done better than *Xiala*.

I went to the passage office, where I was greeted by a human avatar. She was reticent, polite, conservatively dressed in a silver-trimmed red uniform. She smiled and said hello as I walked in. Could she help me?

The office was plain. A counter, a couple of chairs, an inner door. Two posters saying ASHIYYUREAN TRAVEL and PASSAGE DOCUMENTATION HERE. An electronic board provided the schedule for incoming and outgoing flights over the next two weeks.

I was tempted to ask to speak to the Mute-in-charge. But I restrained myself. 'I have a question. Is there someone here I might talk to? Someone who's been around a while?'

'Are you sure I can't answer your question?'

I tried her. Starship contribution by the Foundation decades ago, possibly to an Ashiyyurean museum. The *Falcon*. Did she know where it might be? She had no idea. Had never heard anything about it. 'Just a moment, please,' she said. 'I'll check with my supervisor.'

She blinked off. Moments later I heard sounds behind the door. And a chair scraping the floor.

Footsteps.

I braced myself for first contact. Noted how many people were strolling past just outside. Reminded myself it couldn't possibly be as bad as I'd heard.

The door opened. And I was looking at a young woman. The model, I thought, for the avatar. Except that the original looked a trifle more agreeable. 'Good afternoon,' she said crisply. (Despite everything, it was still middle of the day in the station business world.) 'My name's Indeila Caldwell. You wanted to know about a starship?'

'Yes. Please.'

'It was sold to an Ashiyyurean organization by the Foundation?'

'That's correct.'

'And the Foundation doesn't know who?'

'They don't know what happened to it after it was turned over to' – slight pause – 'the Ashiyyureans.'

She stood in the doorway, trying to decide how to get rid of me. 'I really don't know where you'd get that kind of information. Thirty-plus years—' She focused intently on the poster that said PASSAGE DOCUMENTATION HERE, as if the answer might be contained in the lettering. 'We just do the electronic work to get people in and out. Of Xiala.'

'I understand,' I said. 'Is there by any chance an Ashiyyurean office here? Maybe an embassy? Someone I could speak to who might be able to access the information? Or who might even remember?' It struck me before I'd finished the sentence that I might be making an impolitic remark since Mutes don't speak. Couldn't speak, except with the assistance of voice boxes.

'I'm the entire staff,' she said.

'I see.'

'At the moment, of course. There are four of us. We work a rotating schedule. But we have no Ashiyyurean.'

'Is there an embassy anywhere?'

She nodded. 'Groundside.'

13

It is good to learn to look without wonder or disgust on
the weaknesses which are to be found in the strongest minds.
—T. B. Macauley 'Warren Hastings,'
Edinburgh Review, October 1841

I was tempted to send a message to Alex, suggesting if he was
determined to proceed with the investigation, he'd be the obvious
person to do it since he had experience dealing with the Ashiyyur.
The problem was that I knew how he'd respond: You're already
there, Chase. Pull up your socks and go talk to them. See what
you can find out.

So I bit the bullet. I sent a message telling him what I knew,
and that if I could learn who had the *Falcon* I would proceed to
Xiala. I also told him I was underpaid.

Then I linked through to the Mute embassy and was surprised
when a young man answered the call. I figured they'd want a
human face up front, but I'd expected an avatar. The guy on the
circuit *felt* real, and when I flat out asked him if it were so he
said yes. *'I think,'* he added with a laugh, *'that we want to impress
everyone that there's really nothing to fear.'* He grinned. *'Now,
Ms Kolpath, what can I do for you?'*

He had the unlikely name Ralf, and when I told him I needed some information, he invited me to go ahead. He was graceful, amiable, well-spoken. Auburn hair, brown eyes, good smile. Maybe thirty. A good choice for the up-front guy.

When I finished explaining he shook his head. *'No,'* he said. *'I wouldn't know anything about that. Wait, though. Let me check.'* He looked through a series of data tables, nodded at a couple of them, and tapped the screen. *'How about that?'* he said. *'Here it is. The* Falcon, *right?'*

'That's correct.'

He read off the date and time of transfer. And the recipient. Which was another foundation.

'Good,' I said. 'Is there a way I can get access to the ship?' I went into my research-project routine.

'I really have no idea,' he said. *'I can tell you where it is. Or at least where it was shipped. After that you'll have to deal with them.'*

'Okay,' I said. 'Where is it?'

'It was delivered to the Provno Museum of Alien Life-forms. On Borkarat.'

'Borkarat?'

'Yes. Do you have a travel document?'

He was talking about authorization from the Confederacy to enter Mute space. 'No,' I said.

'Get one. There's an office on the station. Then check in with our travel people. We have an office, too. You'll have to file an application with us as well. It may take a few days.'

I hung around the orbiter for two weeks thinking all kinds of angry thoughts about Alex, before the documentation was completed and my transport vessel arrived. I wasn't permitted to take the *Belle-Marie* into Mute space. That was a Confederate prohibition, dating back to a few years ago when we first came into possession of quantum-drive technology. The Confederacy wanted to keep the system out of the hands of the Mutes. But of course that proved impossible. You can't have hundreds of ships using a given drive system, much better than anything anyone had had previously, and not expect the neighbors to come up with it pretty quickly. The Mutes have always claimed that their version was independently developed, but nobody believes it.

Curious thing: There'd been an assumption when we'd first encountered them that a species that used telepathy in lieu of speech would be unable to lie, would never have known the nature of deceit. But of course they turned out to be no more truthful than we are. Not when they discovered humans couldn't penetrate them.

I'd kept Alex informed. I pointed out it would be expensive to take the connecting flight to Xiala. I would be on board the *Diponga,* or, as the station people called it, the *Dipsy-Doodle*. I also let him know I wasn't happy with the fact this was becoming a crusade. I suggested if he wanted to call a halt, I wouldn't resist. And I'd wait for his answer before going any farther.

His response was pretty much what I expected. He sat at my desk, looking serene, with the snow-covered forest visible through the windows, and told me how well I was doing, and how fortunate he was to have an employee with such persistence. '*Most people would have simply given up, Chase,*' he said.

Most people were brighter than I was.

I thought about signing up for the Hennessy Foundation's seminar on How to Control Psychological Responses When Communicating with Ashiyyureans. But it was hard to see that it would be helpful if they didn't have an actual Mute come into the conference room. Anyhow, it seemed cowardly.

So when everything was in order, I boarded the *Dipsy-Doodle,* along with eight other human passengers. They settled us in the ship's common room, and an older man in a gray uniform inscribed with arcane symbols over the left-hand pocket – MUTE TRANSPORT, I guessed – welcomed us on board, and told us his name was Frank and he'd be traveling with us and anything he could do to make things more comfortable we should just ask. We would be leaving in about an hour. He explained that the flight to Xiala would take approximately four standard days. And were there any questions?

My fellow passengers looked like business types. None was especially young, and none seemed very concerned. I was surprised, though, that all were human. Were there no Mutes returning home?

Afterward, Frank showed us to our compartments, and asked if, after settling in, we would all return to the common room. At 1900 hours. And thank you very much.

I stowed my gear. Four days to Xiala. Then it would be another four days to Borkarat, which was halfway across Mute space. (An odd aspect of quantum travel was that any destination requiring only a single jump tended to be three or four days away. Depending on how far you were from your destination when you emerged from the jump.) I began to wonder if I wanted to look at something else in the way of career employment.

When we rejoined Frank, he talked about procedures for a few minutes, how the meal schedule would run, use of washroom facilities, and so on. Then he explained that the captain wanted to introduce himself.

On cue, the door to the bridge opened and the first Mute I had ever seen in person walked into the room. It had gray-mottled skin, recessed eyes under heavy ridges, arms too long for the body, and the overall appearance of something that needed more sunlight. It wore a uniform similar to Frank's.

I had expected, judging from everything I'd heard, to feel a rush of horror. Accompanied by the knowledge that my thoughts lay exposed. But none of that happened. I would not have wanted to meet the captain on Bridge Street at night. But not because it, he, had a fearsome appearance. (He did appear to be a male, but he didn't look as if he were ready to try me with his hors d'oeuvres.) Rather, there was something about him that was revolting, like a spider, or insects in general. Yet the captain certainly bore no resemblance to a bug. I think it was connected with the fact that his skin glistened.

'Good evening, ladies and gentlemen,' he said, speaking through a voice box. 'I'm Captain Japuhr. Frank and I are pleased to have you on board the *Diponga*. Or, as Frank and the people at the station insist on calling it, the *Dipsy-Doodle*.' The pronunciation wasn't quite right. It sounded more like *Dawdle*. 'We hope you enjoy your flight, and we want you to know if there's anything we can do, please don't hesitate to tell us.' He nodded at Frank, and Frank smiled.

Every hair I owned stood at attention. And I thought, *He knows exactly what I'm feeling. He picks up the revulsion.* And, as if to confirm my worst fears, the captain looked my way and nodded. It wasn't a human nod, it was rather a lowering of the whole head and neck, probably because he didn't have the structural flexibilty to do it the way you or I would. But I understood the gesture. He was saying hello. He understood my reaction, but he was not going to take offense.

That was a good thing. But what would happen when I was away from the captain and dealing with ordinary run-of-the-mill street-level Mutes?

What had I gotten myself into?

While I was worrying myself sick, Captain Japuhr came closer. Our eyes connected, his red and serene and a bit too large, and mine – Well, I felt caught in somebody's sights. At that moment, while I swam against the tide, thinking *no, you have no idea, you can't read me,* his lips parted in an attempt to smile. 'It's all right, Ms Kolpath,' he said to me. 'Everyone goes through this in the beginning.'

It was the only time I saw his fangs.

During the flight, the captain, for the most part, confined himself to the bridge and to his quarters, which were located immediately aft the bridge, and separated from the area accessible to the passengers. My fellow travelers explained that the Ashiyyur – nobody used the term *Mute* on shipboard – were conscious of our visceral reaction to them, and in fact they had their own visceral reaction to deal with. They were repulsed by us, too. So they sensibly tried to defuse the situation as much as they were able.

Frank explained that there were no Ashiyyurean passengers for much the same reason. Flights were always reserved for one species or the other. I asked whether that also applied to him. Had he made flights with alien passengers?

'No,' he said. 'It's against the rules.'

We were about twelve hours out when we made our jump. One of the passengers got briefly ill. But the reaction passed, and she had her color back a few minutes after transition was complete. Frank informed us that we were going to arrive at Xiala sixteen hours ahead of schedule. That would mean a nineteen-hour layover at the station before I could catch my connecting flight. 'I was looking at the passenger list,' Frank said. 'You'll be traveling on the *Komar,* and you'll be the only human passenger.'

'Okay,' I said. I'd suspected that might happen.

'Have you traveled before in the Assemblage?' That was the closest approximation in Standard of the Mutes' term for their section of the Orion Arm. I should add here that they have a looser political organization than the human worlds do. There is a central council, but it is strictly a deliberative body. It has no executive authority. Worlds, and groups of worlds, operate independently. On the other hand, we've learned the hard way how quickly and effectively they can unite in a common cause.

'No,' I said. 'This is my first time.'

He let me see that he disapproved. 'You should have someone with you.'

I shrugged. 'Nobody was available, Frank. Why? Will I be in physical danger?'

'Oh, no,' he said. 'Nothing like that. But you'll be a long time without seeing anybody else.'

'It won't be the first time I've been alone.'

'I didn't mean you'd be alone. You'll have company.' He jiggled his hands, indicating there was no help for it now. 'And I don't want to give you the wrong impression. I think you'll find your fellow travelers willing to help if you need it.' More hesitation. 'May I ask where you're headed? Are you going anywhere from Borkarat?'

'No,' I said.

'When will you be coming back?'

'As soon as my business is completed.'

'Good,' he said. 'I'm sure you'll be fine.'

The first night I stayed up until midmorning. Everybody did. We partied and had a good time. And when we'd all had a bit too much to drink, the captain came out, and the atmosphere did not change.

When finally I retired to my cabin, I was in a rare good humor. I hadn't thought much about Captain Japuhr during the previous few hours, but when I killed the lights and pulled the sheet up, I began to wonder about the range of Mute abilities. (Think *Ashiyyur*, I told myself.) My quarters were removed from the bridge and his connecting cabin by at least thirty meters. Moreover, he was almost certainly asleep. But if he was not, I wondered, was he capable of picking up my thoughts at that moment? Was I exposed?

In the morning I asked Frank. Depends on the individual, he said. 'Some can read you several rooms away. Although they all find humans tougher than their own kind.'

And was the capability passive? Or was there an active component? Did they simply read minds? Or could they inject thought as well?

There were about five of us in the common room, eating breakfast, and Frank passed the question around to Joe Klaymoor. Joe was in his seventies, gray, small, and I would have thought introverted, but I could never make myself believe an introvert would head for Mute country. Make it maybe reticent. And a good guy. He kept his sense of humor through the whole experience. Laughed it off. 'I have nothing to hide,' he said. 'To my everlasting regret.

'It was a big philosophical issue for them at one time,' he continued. 'Same as the question we once had, whether our eyes emitted beams of some sort which allowed us to see. Or whether the outside world put out the beams. Like our eyes, the Ashiyyur are receivers only. They collect what gets sent their way. And not just thoughts. They get images, emotions, whatever's floating around at your conscious level.' He looked momentarily uncomfortable. '"Floating around" is probably an inadequate expression.'

'What would be adequate?' asked one of the other passengers, Mary DiPalma, who was a stage magician from London.

'Something along the lines of an undisciplined torrent. They'll tell you that the human psyche is chaotic.'

Great. If that's really so, no wonder they think we're all idiots. 'The conscious level,' I said. 'But not subconscious?'

'They say not,' said Joe. He laid his head on the back of the chair. 'They didn't settle the transmission/reception issue, by the way, until they encountered us.'

'Really. How'd that happen?'

'They understood a lot of what we were thinking, although a fair amount of it was garbled because of the language problem. When they tried to send something, I gather we just stared back.'

Somebody else, I don't recall who, asked about animals. Can they read animals, too?

Joe nodded. 'The higher creatures, to a degree.'

'And pain?' asked Mary DiPalma.

'Oh, yes. Absolutely.'

'That must be a problem for them.'

Frank took a long breath. 'What's the survival advantage in that?' he asked. 'I'd expect that a creature that feels pain around it would not last long.'

Joe thought it over. 'Evolution happens along two tracks,' he said. 'One track is individually based, and the other assists survival of the species. Or at least, that's the way it was explained to me. It's not my field.'

'Then they're not predators,' I suggested.

One of the women laughed. 'Not predators? You get a look at those bicuspids? And the eyes? They're hunters, no doubt about that.'

'That's true,' said Joe. 'From what I understand, they don't make the connection with their natural prey. It also seems to be the case that they developed the telepathic capability relatively late. They're a much older species than we are, by the way.'

'I wonder,' said one of the guys, 'if we'll develop psi abilities eventually.'

One of the women drew herself up straighter. 'I certainly hope not,' she said.

Mary laughed. 'I can already do it.'

'Show me,' said Larry, the youngest guy on the ship.

Mary turned to me. 'Can't you read his mind, Chase?'

'Oh, yes,' I said.

Nobody seemed in a hurry to make port. Frank broke out drinks every evening, and we partied. Mary warned me that she still remembered her first flight into alien space and how unnerving it had been. 'But just relax and enjoy it,' she said. 'You'll never experience anything like it the rest of your life.'

They were good times on the *Dipsy-Doodle*.

I should say up front that during my visit to Mute country, no Ashiyyurean mistreated me in any way, or was anything but courteous. Still, we were aware of the *thing* on the bridge, that it was different, not only physically, but in some spiritual way. And that sense of the *other*, however nonthreatening it might be, drove us together. Herd instinct in action.

I made several friends on that flight, people with whom I'm still in contact. Like Joe Klaymoor, a sociologist from Toxicon, studying the effects on a society of widespread telepathy. And Mary DiPalma, from ancient London. Mary showed me enough to make me believe in magic. And Tolman Edward, who represented a trading company. Tolman, like me, had never been in the Assemblage before. He was headed into the interior to try to straighten out a trade problem.

I've thought since that the entire effort, trying to chase down the *Falcon*, was worth it just for the few days I spent with them. It had all started with a drinking cup from an interstellar. I have another one on my desk as I write these words. The characters, once again, are unfamiliar. The eagle is replaced by a seven-pointed star with a halo. It belonged, not to the *Seeker*, but to the *Dipsy-Doodle*.

But it had to end. When Captain Japuhr came back to inform us that we would be docking in fourteen hours, we all felt as if something was being lost. I've been on a lot of flights, a lifetime's worth, but I've never known anything quite like it. He asked if we were comfortable, and if there was anything he could do. Then he withdrew.

Frank took me aside. 'Have you figured out how you're going to get around?' he asked.

'How do you mean?'

'There'll be a language problem.'

'Why?' I'd assumed I was dealing with mind readers, so communication should be easy.

'You think in Standard. They'll read images, but not the language. Even if you can get them to understand *you*, you still won't be able to understand *them*.'

'What do you suggest?'

He opened a cabinet and took out a notebook. 'This will help,' he said. He turned it on and spoke to it. 'Help me, I'm lost, I have no idea where I am.' A group of Mute words appeared on the screen. 'Just show them this. They'll read it, and they can input an answer for you.' He smiled. 'Don't expect them to be wearing voice boxes.'

'How do I read the reply?'

It had a Mute keyboard. 'They can poke in whatever they want to say. It will translate and put it on the display.' He frowned at it. 'It's not practical for long conversations, but it will help you order food and find your hotel.'

'May I borrow it?'

'You can *rent* it.'

'Absolutely,' I said. It wasn't cheap, but I put it on Rainbow's account. 'What about food? Will I have trouble?'

'Some of the major hotels can provide a menu for you. Don't try to eat the stuff the Ashiyyur do. Okay?'

I'd seen pictures of what they eat. There was no danger of that.

'One other thing, Chase. There'll always be somebody who can speak Standard at our service counter. We're also as close as your link. They'll be able to direct you where you want to go.'

We disembarked that night at the Xiala orbiter, picked up our bags, and did a last round of good-byes. Good luck and all that. Captain Japuhr came out to wish us farewell. Everybody shook hands and hugged. We clung together for a few steps as we moved out into a concourse filled with Mutes. They towered over us and they had six digits on each hand and they liked solemn clothing (except one female with a yellow hat that looked like a sombrero). They eyed us as if we were, as the old saying goes, from Bashubal. Frank lingered with us and told us we'd be fine and wished us luck. He seemed especially concerned about me. And then, finally, I was alone.

I've watched lovers walk out of my life twice, guys I was seriously attached to, and about whom I still have regrets. But I never watched anybody walk off with quite the same level of misgiving as on that occasion.

A female with two children passed me, and she moved to put herself between them and me as if I might be dangerous. I wondered if she – and they – picked up the sudden resentment I felt. What was the point of having telepathic abilities if empathy didn't come with them?

The concourse was almost empty, for which I was grateful. I wandered over to one of the portals and looked down. The sun

183

was just rising over the curve of the planet. Directly below, it was still night over a major landmass. I could see a single big moon. It was setting in the west, and its soft glow illuminated a series of mountain peaks.

The service counter surprised me. The avatar was a duplicate of me. *'How may I help you, Chase?'* she asked.

She confirmed my booking to Borkarat. The ship would leave next afternoon. She recommended a hotel, made my reservation, and wished me a pleasant evening.

Actually, she looked pretty good.

Overall anatomical structure of the Mutes is similar to our own, at least as far as things like waste disposal are concerned. I suppose there are only so many ways an intelligent creature can function. There'll necessarily be gravity, so energy-source intake has to happen near the top of the anatomy, the processing functions midway, and elimination near the bottom of the working area. What I'm saying is that the rooms assigned to humans at the Gobul Hotel were Mute rooms. Everything was bigger, and I'll confess I found the toilet something of a challenge.

I took my first meal in the restaurant, in an effort to accustom myself to my hosts. And I sat there like an idiot convinced everyone was watching me, the *real* me, not simply the external shell that we're accustomed to putting on display. What was most difficult, I hated being there, thoroughly disliked being in their company, struggled to hold down my emotions, and knew that all of it was visible to any who cared to look. Joe Klaymoor tells me Mutes are able, to a degree, to shield their minds from each other. They are, he says, probably evolving into an entity that will eventually possess a single consciousness. But not yet. And he adds the scary possibility that we may go the same way.

One or two came over to introduce themselves, and I said hello through the notebook, but it was a clumsy business. They told me they had never seen a real human before, and I knew they were trying to be complimentary. But I felt like a show animal.

They left after a couple of minutes. My food came and I hurried through it, tried smiling at the surrounding Mutes who persisted in staring at me when they thought I wasn't looking. I was glad to get back to my room.

I thought about calling it off. Let Alex track down the *Falcon* himself.

Which he would do.

He wouldn't say anything to me, wouldn't criticize me, but I knew how he was. Send a boy – or a woman – to do a man's job.

I boarded the *Komar* in the morning. Direct flight to Borkarat, one of the major worlds of the Assemblage. It was eighty-six light-years from Xiala.

I had twenty-one fellow passengers, all Mutes. Most were in the common room when I made my entrance. Which is the right word. A young male saw me. Nobody else turned in my direction, but they all came to alert. Don't ask me how I knew. But I was suddenly aware they were all watching me through that single pair of eyes.

A kid buried his head in his mother's robe.

I could see right away this was going to be a thoroughly enjoyable flight. I smiled lamely at the young male. Mutes don't smile well. Maybe they don't need to. Some, who've lived among us, have picked it up, but they don't do it naturally, which is the reason it always scares the pants off you when they try.

Another aspect of spending time with Mutes is that they don't talk. You're in a room with more than twenty people, and they're all sitting quietly, looking at one another. And nobody is saying *anything*.

They tried to be sociable. They made gestures in my direction. Made eye contact with me. Several raised their hands in greeting.

After a few minutes, I did what I'd promised myself I wouldn't: I ducked into my compartment and closed the door, wishing with all my heart I could shut the door on my conscious mind. Outside, a short time later, hatches closed. I heard the engines come to life. And there was a knock at the door.

I opened up and looked at a Mute in the same gray uniform Frank had worn. He handed me a white card. It said, *Welcome aboard. Please belt in. We are ready to launch.* And then a second card: *Do you require assistance?*

I leaned forward and pointed at my forehead, like a dolt. I wanted him to know I was thinking. And I formed the word *No* in my mind. *No, thank you. I'm fine.*

Then I remembered he probably didn't understand Standard. He bowed.

I know there's a harness attached to my chair. I'll use that. I visualized myself secured by the harness.

He bowed again and walked away.

I am a little blue cookie box.

I hid in my cabin. Went out just long enough to use the washroom facilities, or grab my meals, which were okay. (I understood there were special preparations on board for me.) Four days wasn't terribly long. I could live with that.

We were about an hour into the flight when the knock came again. This time, though, it wasn't the attendant. It was a male, of indeterminate age, tall even for a Mute. Too tall for the passageway, forcing him to hunch down. He looked at me with stone-cold eyes and I wondered whether he was reading my discomfort. He wore dull blue leggings and a loose shirt, an outfit not uncommon among the Mutes I'd seen, although they usually preferred robes.

I stood staring up at him. Then I heard a click, and an electronic voice said, 'Hello. Are you all right?'

I tried to push everything out of my mind, save a return greeting. 'Hello,' I said. 'Yes, I'm fine, thank you.'

'Good. I know this sort of thing can be unsettling.'

'No. I'm fine. No problem at all.' And I thought about the logic of trying to lie to a mind reader.

'Can I be of assistance?'

'I think you just have been.'

'Excellent.' The voice was coming from an amulet. 'May I point out that, whatever you may think, you are among friends.'

Naked among friends. And I tried to pull that one back.

He hesitated. I began to understand he didn't want to let me see he could actually probe me.

I was trying to decide whether to invite him in. 'I appreciate your concern,' I said.

'Do not take any of this experience seriously. We will be together four days, more or less. At the end of which we will go our separate ways. So nothing you do here can harm you.'

'You're right, of course.'

'Would you like to join us? We would be very happy to make your acquaintance.'

'Yes. Of course.' He backed away, making room for me. I followed him, closing the door behind me. 'My name is Chase.'

'You would probably find mine unpronounceable. Call me—' I literally felt his presence in my head. 'Call me Frank.'

Had I been thinking about the flight attendant on the *Dipsy-Doodle*? 'Okay, Frank.' I extended my hand.

I passed my notebook around and the other passengers used it to ask questions. Where was I from? Had I been in the Assemblage before? Where was I headed? Why was I so afraid? (This last came from a child who had participated reluctantly and seemed almost as fearful as I was.)

Frank was quite good. 'There is nothing that can pass through your mind that we have not seen before,' he said. 'Except, perhaps,' he added, 'your squeamishness in our presence.'

Don't hold back, big fella. Just let me have it.

Several of them poked one another and bobbed their heads in what must have been laughter.

I asked Frank whether it wasn't distracting to be constantly experiencing a flow of thought and emotions from others.

'I can't imagine life without it,' he explained. 'I'd be cut off.' His red eyes focused on me. 'Don't you feel isolated? Alone?'

Over the course of the trip, I learned that a blending of minds lends an extra dimension to what lovers feel for each other. Or friends. That telepathy facilitates a deeper communication. That no, there is not any evolution that any of the Ashiyyur are aware of toward a group mind. In fact they laughed when I relayed Joe's theory. 'We are individuals, Chase,' said one of the females, 'because we can see so plainly the differences between ourselves and others.'

'We can't hide from what we think,' Frank told me on the second day. 'Or what we feel. And we know that. My understanding is that humans are not always honest even with themselves. I can't understand how that could be, but it's a fascinating concept. On another subject, we're aware of your struggle against your coarser notions. But we all have them. So we think nothing of it. It is part of what we are, what *you* are, so we accept it.

'And by the way, there is no need to be embarrassed by your reflexive reaction to our appearance. We find you unappealing also.' He stopped and looked around. I had by then picked up some of the nonverbal cues they used, and several signaled their displeasure at his statement. 'I should amend that,' he said, 'to *physically* unappealing. But we are coming to know your interior, your psyche. And there we find that you are one of us.'

14

Man has always considered himself the peak of creation, the part of the universe that thinks, the purpose for it all. It's no doubt a gratifying view. But the universe may have a different opinion.

—Marik Kloestner,
Diaries, 1388

Although Borkarat was not the Mute home world, it was influential. This was where policy toward humans was formulated and, when possible, sold to the various independent political units of the Assemblage. This was the place where representatives met. And from which, during the recurring periods of hostility with the Confederacy, action had been directed.

No shots had been fired between Mute and human warships for a few years, but the long conflict still simmered. Nobody really knew what it was about, any longer. Neither side was interested in real estate belonging to the other. Neither side actively threatened anyone. And yet there it was, a living antipathy, drifting down the centuries. Politicians on both sides got support by promising the voters to be tough with the aliens. (I wondered how the Mutes could have politicians when their minds were more or less open to all.)

The term *Assemblage* was a misnomer. The loose group of Mute states, worlds, duchies, outposts, orbital cities, and whatever else, were more a social grouping than a formal political entity. But they could react in concert with stunning efficiency. Some observers argued they could already see the stirrings of a group mind.

I was relieved to get off the *Komar*. I stopped at the service desk, where another human avatar in my image presented herself and gave me directions to get to the museum at Provno.

The shuttle I wanted was marked with a lightning bolt designator. It was crowded, and I had to push in. There was nothing more revelatory of the alien nature of Mute society than boarding that vehicle and watching the Mutes interract with each other, make way, stow their packages, move their children into seats, quiz each other over who gets the window, and do it all in absolute silence. Well, maybe not *absolute*. There were of course the sounds of rustling clothing, closing panels, and air escaping from cushions. Harnesses clicked down into place. But there was never a voice.

I had by then been more than a week in the exclusive company of Mutes, and I was learning to ignore the sense of being exposed to the public gaze. Just don't worry about it, I told myself. But I couldn't resist occasionally glancing over at a fellow passenger and picturing myself waving hello.

There was usually a physical response, a meeting of eyes, a lifting of the brow, something. Occasionally they even waved back.

I tried to think warm and fuzzy. And in fact, my reaction to these creatures, the primal fear and revulsion I'd felt in their presence, was dwindling every day. But as I sat on that shuttle, trying to read and comprehending nothing on the page, I was a long way from being comfortable.

We dropped into the atmosphere, descended through a twilit sky, ran into some turbulence and a storm, and finally sailed out of the clouds beneath a canopy of stars. Below, cities blazed with light.

A female flight attendant stopped by my seat. 'We'll be landing in seven minutes,' she said. I couldn't tell where the voice was coming from.

I spent the night at a hotel just off a river walk. Ashiyyurean architectural styles, at least on Borkarat, are subtly different from anything we've employed. Human structures, whatever their cultural tendencies, are static. They are symmetrical, and however eclectic the design, one always detects balance and proportion. Mute buildings, on the other hand, are a study in motion, in flow, in energy. The symmetry is missing. Seen from a distance, my hotel looked incomplete, as though part of it projected into another dimension.

I ate in the restaurant, surrounded by Mutes. And I'm proud to say I held my own. Stayed at my table, worked my way casually through my meal, and never flinched when a nearby infant took one horrified look at me and tried to burrow into its mother's mammaries.

I wondered how early in life the telepathic capability began. Could a child in the womb communicate?

Two humans, male and female, showed up. They saw me and came over. You'd have thought we were the oldest of friends. At my invitation, they sat down and we exchanged trivia for the next hour. They were from St Petersburg, one of the ancient terrestrial capitals.

I think I've mentioned that the Ashiyyur do not use spirits of any kind. I read somewhere that there are no comparable drugs for them, and they do not understand the human compulsion to drown our senses. So the glasses we raised to each other that night were tame, but we made promises that we'd get together back home. Amazing how close Andiquar and St Petersburg became.

I slept well, except for waking in the middle of the night after an especially realistic sexual dream. And there I was again, wondering if the Mutes could pick up nocturnal stuff as well.

Had I frightened the children on three floors? No wonder they didn't like having people around.

I thought about the couple I'd met at dinner. They were young, recently married. But I bet myself that tonight they were sleeping apart and probably drumming up more emotional vibrations for any Mute antennas paying attention than a good old-fashioned romp would have. Mute-world is not a place for a honeymoon.

The Museum of Alien Life-forms was located on an expanse of parkland on Provno, in a long island chain in one of the southern seas. The parkland area is largely devoted to public buildings and historical preserves. Landscaped sections are blocked off, often commemorating historical figures, sometimes simply devoted to providing quiet places for reflection. There are streams and myriad small creatures that come begging for handouts from visitors.

The architecture was hyperbolic, rooftops that surged like ocean waves, angled spires, soaring stalks. Crowds wandered through the area on long curved walkways that sometimes ascended to the upper levels. Everywhere there were leafy porticoes to which you could retreat simply to enjoy the play of nature. Everything seemed light and fragile, as ethereal as the sunlight.

Private vehicular traffic was banned in the parks. Visitors could enter by aircab, although the bulk of traffic was handled by an overwater maglev train. I'd never seen one before, and I have no idea how they handled the engineering.

The museum stood between two similar but not-quite-identical obelisks. It was made of white marble and incorporated arcs and columns and rising walkways so that it was reminiscent of one of those children's puzzles that you can take apart and reassemble but always looks different. A moving ramp took me up to the front entrance, where I came to a wall engraved with Mute characters. I turned my translator loose on it, and it told me that the museum had been founded on an indeterminate date. (The translator wasn't good at converting dates and times.) And that life-forms from all over the galaxy were welcome.

I went inside, while Mute children looked alternately at me and the sign and gaped, while others just gaped and still others drew back in alarm. But I smiled politely and pushed ahead.

You might expect that a museum devoted to off-world biological systems would give you lots of holograms of the various life-forms in action. But it wasn't that way at all. Maybe there was a sense that visitors could get the holograms at home. So what they had were display cases and exhibits filled with stuffed skins and heads.

They'd probably been picked for shock value. Giant creatures with maws big enough to swallow a lander. Snakes that could have used me for a toothpick. Predators of all sizes and shapes, some fearsome beyond belief. And the prey, cute little furred creatures that could run fast. And damn well better.

There were plants capable of gobbling down a fair-sized technician, and multilimbed creatures that lived in the trees of Barinor, wherever that was, and stole children. I wondered why anybody would choose to live under such conditions. At least, with kids.

I'm happy to report there were no stuffed people. Maybe that was a concession to the fact that they occasionally had human visitors. They did have a couple of birds and lizards from Rimway, and a tiger from Earth. But the only human was an avatar, a bearded guy who looked like a Neandertal. He even carried a spear. When I approached him, he grunted.

Best foot forward, I always say. I wondered how many Mute kids were getting their first impression of the human race from this guy.

He was guarding the Hall of the Humans, an entire wing dedicated to us. *The only other known technological species.* It was big, circular, with a vaulted ceiling three stories high. Display cases and tables supporting exhibits stood everywhere. There were primitive and modern weapons on display, representations of various deities, musical instruments, clothing from various cultures, a chess game in progress, and dishware. An alcove was fitted out to look like a business office. Many of the displays, where appropriate, were marked with a date and world of origin. There were headsets that allowed you to plug into the history of the various objects. And an array of books, all translations into basic Mute. I scanned them and found *The Republic*, Burnwell's *Last Days of the American State*, *Four Novels by Hardy Boshear*, and a ton of other work. On the whole, they didn't have a very representative collection. Most of the writers were modern, and there were desperately few classics.

In the center of the room, on a dais, was my target. The *Falcon*. Mutes were queued up on a ramp, waiting their turns to enter the airlock. They were coming out the other side, through an exit that had been cut through the hull.

DEPARTMENT OF PLANETARY SURVEY was inscribed up near the bridge, along with its designator TIV114. And, of course, FALCON. Its navigation lights were on. That was good news because it meant the thing had power. I'd brought a small generator on the possibility I'd have to supply my own.

There were maybe forty Mutes in the hall, but none of them was moving. They were all looking straight ahead, pretending to examine the various displays at hand, but the fact they were frozen in place gave them away. One female, standing near a statue of one of the ancient gods, was watching me, and everyone there was sitting behind her eyes.

She raised a hand. *Hello.*

I smiled and switched my attention back to the *Falcon*, telling myself what lovely lines it had and how I'd enjoy piloting it. I tried to keep my mind off the actual reason for my visit. Gradually my fellow visitors began moving again. As far as I could tell, not one ever turned for a surreptitious look.

I strolled among the displays, fingering the data chip I'd brought for the download.

There were guide stations where you could learn about humans. I used my translator and discovered that we were high on the evolutionary scale, but remained a step below the Ashiyyur. We thought of ourselves as sentient, the guide explained, and in a limited sense we were, even though our primary mode of communication was *yapping*. Okay, *yapping* is my translation. They said 'by making sounds or noise.' Take your pick.

We were described as having some admirable traits. We were loyal, reasonably intelligent, compassionate, and could be friendly. On the other hand we were known to be dishonest, vile, violent, licentious, treacherous, hypocritical, and on the whole we ran a society that had lots of police and needed them.

Individuals tend to be docile, said the guide, *and may usually be approached without fear. But when humans form groups their behavior changes and becomes more problematic. They are more likely to subscribe to a generally held view than to seek their own.* Elsewhere: *There seems to be a direct correlation between the size of a group and its inclination to consent or resort to violence or other questionable behavior, and/or the predilection of individuals to acquiesce when leaders suggest violent or simplistic solutions to perceived problems.*

This is the collective reaction phenomenon.

Several of the books were described as providing an especially incisive view of human mental limitations. I was beginning to get annoyed.

I kept an eye on the *Falcon* as I circled the hall, trying to damp my thoughts, wondering again about telepathic range. More Mutes came in, and while I was wandering among the exhibits looking as casual as possible, they joined the line.

Realizing the line was not going to go away, I took my place at the rear. There were about a dozen in front of me, including two younger ones, not quite adult, but not children either. Both female. I saw them react, saw one touch the other's elbow and pull her robe more tightly around her.

I'd had it by then. I tried to send a message. To all who were listening. *People who need to feel superior by accident of birth usually turn out to be dummies.* I didn't know how to visualize it, so I don't imagine much of it got through, but I felt better afterward.

* * *

The hatchway onto the bridge was open so I could see the instruments and the pilot's position. But a blue restraining cord was drawn across the entrance and a sign read DO NOT ENTER. There were two chairs, one for the pilot, one for a visitor or technician. I thought, this is where they had been, Margaret Wescott at the controls and Adam in the auxiliary seat. I looked through the viewport at the gray museum walls and wondered what had been visible to *them*.

In front of the pilot's seat, and to its right, was the reader. I reached into my pocket and touched the chip.

The AI's name had been James.

I leaned over the cord, acutely conscious of the others around me. I would have liked a few minutes alone. 'James,' I said in a whisper, 'are you there?'

There was no vocal reply, but a green lamp came on. I wasn't familiar with the *Falcon* instrument panel. Still, some aspects remain identical from ship to ship, and from one era to another. The green lamp always means the AI is up and running. First hurdle cleared. (I assumed they'd disconnected the voice so James wouldn't startle anyone.)

The cord was too high for me to get *over*, so I lifted it and went *under*, and proceeded directly to the reader, ignoring the stir behind me. I inserted the chip. 'James,' I said, 'download the navigation logs. Any that are connected with Dr Adam Wescott.'

Another lamp came on. White. I heard the data transmission begin. I turned and smiled at the Mutes standing behind me. Hi. How you doing? Enjoying your visit? I tried to think how this was routine maintenance. Instead, it occurred to me that the Mutes might suspect I was trying to steal the ship, that I was planning to take off with it, blast out of the hall, and head for Rimway. Trailing Mutes all the way. I could see the *Falcon* rising over Borkarat's towers, then accelerating for deep space. No matter how hard I tried, I couldn't get the image out of my mind.

No such scenario of course was even remotely possible. The museum had removed a bulkhead to admit the ship, and then replaced it. The engines were at least disengaged and probably missing. And there wouldn't have been any fuel anyhow.

The chip whirred and hummed while the data collected over more than a decade flowed through the system. I looked over the other instruments, the way a technician might, just doing a little maintenance, got to adjust the thrust control here.

More Mutes were crowding up to the guide rope to see what was going on. I imagined I could feel them inside my head, checking to see whether I was deranged. It occurred to me they might conclude this was the way inferior species behaved and think no more of it. And I wondered whether that had been my own thought, or whether it had arrived somehow from outside.

A couple of them moved away but others took their places. I watched the lights, waiting for the white lamp to change color, indicating the operation was complete.

I straightened the chairs. Looked out the portals. Checked the settings on the viewscreens. Straightened my blouse.

I wished I'd thought to bring a dust cloth.

I looked out the portals again. Two Mutes in blue uniforms were converging on the *Falcon*.

The lamp stayed white.

The crowd began to shuffle, to clear out of the way. I heard heavy footsteps. And of course no sound of a voice anywhere.

Then the authorities arrived. Both in uniform. Both looking severe. But then, with an Ashiyyurean, how could you tell? I tried to cut that idea off at the pass. Tried to transmit *Almost done. Just be patient a moment more.*

They stepped over the cord. One took my arm and pulled me away from the reader. I looked back. The lamp was still white.

They wanted me to go with them and I was in no position to decline. They half carried me back out through the airlock, and through a gawking crowd that now made no effort to hide the fact that they were watching. We exited the hall, went down a ramp, across a lobby, and into a passageway.

I was helpless. I was projecting all the protests I could manage.

But nothing worked. You couldn't talk to these guys. Couldn't use nonverbals. Couldn't even use the old charm.

They hauled me through double doors and into a corridor lined with offices. I realized I wasn't simply being ejected. We were headed into the rear of the museum.

The doors were made of dark glass, and Mute symbols were posted electronically beside them. One opened, and I was ushered inside. It was an empty office. I saw an inner door, a couple of tables and three or four chairs. All standard Mute size. My guards released me and set me down.

They stayed with me, both standing, one near the door by which we'd entered, the other by the inner door. I wondered whether my chip had finished loading yet.

We waited about five minutes. I heard noises on the other side of the inner door. Then it opened. A female emerged, wearing clothing that resembled a workout suit. The color was off-white. The suit had a hood, but it lay back on her shoulders.

She looked at me, then at my escorts. They seemed to be exchanging information. Finally, the escorts got up and left the room. Apparently I was not considered a threat.

The female reached into a pocket, produced a translator on a cord, and draped it around her neck. 'Hello, Chase,' she said. 'I'm Selotta Movia Kabis. You may call me Selotta.'

Even under the circumstances, it was hard not to laugh. I gave my name and said hello.

She stared at me. 'We are pleased you decided to visit us today.'

'It's my pleasure,' I said. 'This is a lovely museum.'

'Yes.' She circled me and took a chair opposite. 'May I ask what you were doing in the *Falcon*?'

No point lying. The translator wouldn't help her read my thoughts, but I wondered whether she really needed it. 'I was trying to download the navigation logs.'

'And why were you doing that? The *Falcon* has been in the Human Hall as long as I've been here. It must be twenty-five years.'

'It's been a long time,' I agreed.

She concentrated on me. Made no effort to hide the fact she was in my head. 'What's the *Seeker*?' she asked.

I told her. I described its connection with Margolia, then explained what Margolia was.

'Nine thousand years?' she said.

'Yes.'

'And you hope to find this place? Margolia?'

'We know that's a trifle optimistic. But we do hope to find the ship.'

Gray lids came down over her eyes. And rose again. The corneas were black and diamond-shaped. She considered me for a long moment. 'Who knows?' she said, finally. 'Find one, and it might lead you to the other.'

'As you can see,' I said, 'I need your help to get the information from the *Falcon*.'

She sat quite still while she considered it. Then she seemed to come to a conclusion. The door to the passageway opened. I turned and saw one of the guards. Selotta motioned him forward. He had my chip in his right hand. I wondered if it might be possible to grab the chip and run.

'No,' said Selotta. 'That would not be a good idea.'

He handed it to her, turned, and left. She inspected it, switched on a lamp, and took a longer look. When she'd finished she turned those diamond eyes directly on me. I got the distinct feeling she thought she was talking to me. Suddenly she seemed surprised. She shook her head in a remarkably human gesture and tapped the translator. 'It's hard to remember sometimes I have to speak.'

'I guess,' I said.

'I was asking whether you don't have some qualms about the possibility of a living civilization out there. Your own people, after nine thousand years. You have no way of knowing what you might find.'

'I know.'

'No offense intended, but humans tend to be unpredictable.'

199

'Sometimes,' I said. 'We don't expect to find a living world. But if we could find the original settlement, we could retrieve some artifacts. They'd be quite valuable.'

'I'm sure.'

I waited, hoping she'd give me the chip and wish me god-speed.

'Perhaps we can make an arrangement.'

'What did you have in mind?'

'You may have your chip.'

'If—?'

'I will expect, if you find what you're looking for, a generous bequest.'

'You want some of the artifacts?'

'I think that would be a reasonable arrangement. Yes, I will leave the details to your generosity. I believe I may safely do that.' She got up.

'Thank you, Selotta. Yes. If we succeed I will see the museum is taken care of.'

'Through me personally.'

'Of course.'

She made no move to hand over the disk. 'Chase,' she said, 'I'm surprised you didn't come to us first.'

I stood there trying to look as if attempted theft had been a rational course of action. 'I'm sorry,' I said. 'I should have. To be honest, I didn't know whether you would allow it.'

'Or try to grab everything for ourselves.'

'I didn't say that.'

'You thought it.' She put the chip on the tabletop. 'I'll look forward to hearing from you, Chase.'

15

Those decisions that are truly significant are only confronted once. Whether it's the choice of a life partner, or of an invasion route, the opportunity never returns. You must get it right the first time.

—Mara Delona,
Travels with the Bishop, 1404

Back in my hotel room, I used my notebook to run the chip. First I scanned for any reference to Margolia, to a derelict, or to any kind of artifact whatever.

'*Negative search,*' it said.

'Okay. Just print the damned thing out and let's see what we have.'

'*Very good, Chase. The data covers ten missions, beginning in 1381 and ending in 1392.*'

The hotel made several versions of assorted nonalcoholic drinks available for its guests. While I waited for the printout, I tried one with a lime taste that was actually quite good.

The *Falcon* had visited nine suns on its last flight with the Wescotts. None had been binaries. We had the usual details on each – mass, temperature, and age, along with a wealth of associated data. We also had the details of the planetary systems, where they existed. (One of the targets, Branweis 4441, had none.) We had everything that had been on the original report and, as far as I could see, nothing more.

And everything was consistent.

I took it back one mission, conducted in 1390–91. They'd inspected ten systems on that one, and again all the data checked out.

I went over the rest of the flights, all the way back to Adam's first mission on the *Falcon*. I saw no anomalies.

A week later I was at Takmandu, where a message was waiting from Alex. *Spare no effort,* he'd written. *Come back with the prize and consider yourself a junior partner.*

Sure, Alex. What we have is a copy of what we already had.

I was glad to check out of the hotel and get the shuttle up to the orbiter. And I can't adequately describe my feelings, ten days later, at seeing the *Belle-Marie* again.

I got on board, said nice things to the guys in ops to get a quick clearance, told Belle I'd missed her, sat down on the bridge, and started going through my checklist. Fifteen minutes later I was on my way home.

It was a four-day flight. Mostly, I sat stewing over the amount of time and effort invested to come up with nothing. I read, watched some sims, and when I got within radio range of Rimway I called Alex.

'*How'd you make out?*' he asked.

'I got the AI download. But there's nothing new in it.' We were audio only, with a twelve-minute total time delay while the transmission traveled out and back. I made myself comfortable.

'*Okay. Hang on to it. Maybe we can find something.*'

Did he really think I might toss it overboard? 'I'm not optimistic,' I said.

He was waiting at Skydeck when I docked, all smiles and reassurances. Not my fault nothing was there, he said. Not to worry. We'll take another look. Who knows what we might see? 'Don't know where I'd be without you, Chase,' he added. He thought I felt terrible. What I mostly felt was frustration. Three weeks of mostly inedible food and playing mental dodge ball with Mutes, and we had nothing to show for it.

'Where's the download?' he asked finally.

It was in one of my bags.

'Okay.' He was trying to sound reassuring. 'Why don't you get it out so we can look at it on the way down?'

'It's no different from the official record.'

He waited for me to comply. I did, and when he had the printout in his hands, we headed for the shuttle deck. We'd gone maybe five steps when his eyes lit up and he rolled the documents into a cylinder and waved them over his head.

'What?' I said.

'The individual operations are dated. We've got the sequence in which they visited each system. Good show, Chase. You're a genius.'

'Why's that important?'

'Think about it. You did your Survey time before the quantum drive became available. When distance really mattered.'

'Okay.'

'You've got, say, a dozen stars to visit on a given mission. How did you determine the sequence?'

That was simple enough. 'We arranged things so the overall distance to be traveled was kept to a minimum.'

'Yes.' He squeezed my arm. 'So now we can find out whether the record reflects where they actually went. If they didn't take the shortest routes among the target stars, that'll tell us they changed something. And maybe we'll be able to figure out where the *Seeker* is.'

When I pressed him how this would happen, he talked to me about fuel economy. 'Your friend Shara is on vacation. Off on an island somewhere. When she gets back, we'll present the matter to her and see whether she can pin things down.'

'Okay,' I said.

'By the way, you had a call from Delia. Get back to her when you can, okay?'

The following evening I met her at the Longtree, a downtown bistro located just off Confederate Park. Dark corners, stained paneling, candles, soft music. It was her suggestion, but it was one of my favorite places.

She was already seated when I got there. Dark hair framing attractive features that held a hint of anxiety. She was modestly dressed in a powder blue skirt, white blouse, and sleeveless lace jacket. Only her comm link suggested wealth: It was encased in a gold bracelet on her wrist. 'So good to see you, Chase,' she said. 'I'm glad you could come.'

We talked about the weather for a few minutes. Then I let her know I was surprised she was in Andiquar.

'I came specifically to see you,' she said.

Our autowaiter showed up, introduced himself, took drink orders, and hurried off.

'I should tell you,' I said, 'that we've located the AI record for the *Falcon*. It backs up the official reports.'

'Good.' She smiled defensively. 'It's just a matter of time, though, isn't it?'

'I don't know.'

'I hate this.'

'I'm sure.'

Our drinks came. She studied hers, then raised it. 'To the *Seeker*,' she said. 'Wherever it is.'

'To the *Seeker*,' I agreed.

'They'd want you to find it,' she said. 'I know they wouldn't have wanted it to stay lost.'

'I think you're right.'

Delia adjusted her jacket collar, tugging it together, pulling it around her as if to fend off something. 'Chase, I know my parents have been part of your investigation. Bits and pieces of it are getting back to me.'

'We haven't really been investigating your folks,' I said. 'It's the missions we've been looking at.'

'Phrase it however you like. It's the same thing. Word's getting around, and people are calling me to ask what kind of cover-up they were involved in.'

'I'm sorry to hear that,' I said. 'We've tried to be circumspect. I know no one's accused anybody of anything.'

'The investigation is enough. It constitutes an accusation. I'm sorry to say this, but I'd be grateful if you would stop.'

I looked out through the window. People hurried by, bundled against a cold night. 'I can't do that,' I said.

'I'm willing to make it worth your while.'

'You just said your mom and dad would want the *Seeker* found.'

'That's what *they* would want. But *I* don't want the family name destroyed.'

'I'm sorry,' I said. 'I really am.'

She no longer looked friendly. 'They're not alive to defend themselves.'

'Delia, there are no charges. Nobody's claiming they did anything wrong.'

'Doctoring the record, if that's what happened, would be a criminal offense, wouldn't it?'

'Yes. I suspect so.'

Tears were rolling down her cheeks. 'Please take a minute and think about what you're doing to us.' The waiter was back to take the dinner orders. The way things were developing, I wasn't sure we were going to get to dinner. She looked at me, looked at the menu, started to say something, and shook it away. 'The special,' she said. 'Rare.'

Red meat.

I ordered a boca casserole, which, for my off-world readers, tastes much like tuna. I also asked for a second round of drinks and settled in for the duration.

'Incidentally,' she said, 'I had another visitor who was interested in my parents.'

'Oh? Who was that?'

'His name was Corbin. *Josh* Corbin, I think.' She bit her lip. 'Yes, that's right. Josh. Young guy. Midtwenties.'

'Why was he interested?'

'He said he was doing a history of Survey operations.'

'Did he ask about the *Seeker*?'

'As a matter of fact, yes.'

That was a jolt. Somebody else knew. 'What did you tell him?'

'I didn't see any point keeping things quiet. I told him pretty much everything I told you.'

While I was having a big time with Delia, Alex received a call from the producer of *The Peter McCovey Show*. They had heard about the search for Margolia and were going to 'highlight it' next day. Several guests were being invited. Would he care to appear?

Alex was not happy that word of the effort was getting out, but it seemed impossible under the circumstances to keep a secret. He tried to beg off, but they told him he was the center of interest and would be essential to what they wanted to do. If he persisted in refusing to participate, the producer said, they would have no choice but to inform their audience he had been invited but had declined. And they would be forced to put an empty chair on the set to represent him.

Alex had been on these kinds of shows before and always got attacked. 'They don't let you talk,' he'd complained to me afterward. 'The hosts load the questions, control the flow of conversation, and never let you finish an answer if they don't like the way you're going.' The fact that they consistently went after him as someone more interested in making money than in revealing the truth didn't help. They'd made it sound as if there was something wicked in turning a profit.

But Alex thought the empty chair wouldn't look good. So he agreed.

I went with him to the station the following evening. They

could have done the show by remote, of course. But they prefer that you come physically so they can arrange your makeup and do what they like to call the personal touch, which always seemed to involve laying on a lot of charm and trying to put him off guard before they go to broadcast. This was the same guy who, when the Christopher Sim information came out, had openly accused him of being unpatriotic.

Peter McCovey is short and stocky with a black beard and a smile that never goes away and never changes. He wore his trademark blue jacket with a white neckerchief and a white sash. A little pretentious, he admitted to me, but his audience expected it.

There were two other panelists, Dr Emily Clark, who doubted that the Margolian colonists had ever managed to get a foothold on the world of their choice, wherever it might have been. And one Jerry Rhino, who insisted that Margolia had not only survived its early years but had affected our daily lives through subliminal influences and magnetic manipulation. 'It's the source of our spiritual strength,' he said. Rhino had written several books on the subject and was wildly popular with the occult crowd.

The show took place on a set designed to resemble a book-lined den. McCovey introduced his guests and opened things up by asking Alex what had really happened to the Margolians.

Alex, of course, didn't know. 'Nobody knows,' he added.

Rhino claimed he knew, and the show developed rapidly into an argument. McCovey liked having guests quarrel with one another. He was, and remains, among the highest-rated media hosts.

Clark smiled relentlessly throughout the performance, success-fully implying that anyone who took any of this seriously was an idiot. When Alex tried to argue that for all we knew they could still be alive and prospering out there somewhere, she rolled her eyes and wondered aloud where common sense had gone. She could not tolerate Rhino at all and simply dismissed him with icy sarcasm.

But Jerry plunged on, unaffected. The Margolians had gotten caught up in the spiritual flow of the cosmos. Cut off from the more mundane activities of the home world, they had reached a kind of nirvana. And so on. Occasionally he glanced at Alex for confirmation. I got the impression Alex was trying to hide.

McCovey's standing claim was that he took no sides. He was not reluctant to call people names. At one point he asked Alex to explain how he wasn't a vandal, and he told Rhino he was deranged. I've noticed since that he makes it a point to invite people on who are easy to assault because they're reluctant to yell back. I've never mentioned that to Alex.

In any case, Alex left the studio in a bleak mood. He swore he'd never again allow himself to be caught like that. We stopped at the Silver Cane, and he tossed down three or four drinks, which was well past his usual limit.

The real attack came the following day, when Casmir Kolchevsky showed up on *Jennifer in the Morning*. 'There should be legislation to put people like Benedict out of business,' he insisted. 'They're thieves. They take treasures that belong to all of us and sell them to the highest bidder. It's contemptible.'

He went on like that for the better part of fifteen minutes. At the segment's conclusion, Jennifer invited Alex to appear and defend himself. Alex admitted he'd already received a call. 'They told me I'd want to watch.'

'What are you going to do?'

'I don't know,' he said. 'I'm not sure going on doesn't just make things worse.' He sighed. 'I'm tired of it. These guys are never satisfied. People like Kolchevsky, who could never find anything on his own, get on and claim we're stealing things that belong to the audience. But none of it belongs to anybody. It belongs to whoever is willing to show some ambition and do the legwork. If it weren't for us, a lot of this stuff would still be lying around out there.'

'Okay,' I said, 'but you have to go on and *say* that, Alex. You can't just let him make those charges and not respond. It looks like a concession.'

He nodded. 'Book me. And by the way, your pal Shara is due back tomorrow. I've already made an appointment for you.'

'Okay.'

'Show her the AI log. I'll be surprised if she can't tell us where the *Seeker* is.'

I got a call that evening from Windy. *'I didn't want to talk to you from the office, because I was concerned about being over-heard,'* she said.

'What's wrong?' I asked.

'I think I know who was putting out information. One of my people saw a member of the director's staff downtown last night. She was in a bar with one of Ollie Bolton's specialists.'

'Bolton?'

'There's no proof anywhere. But—' She shrugged.

'Do you have confidential information that Bolton would be interested in?' I asked.

'Sure,' she said. 'We always have stuff on projects and specula-tions that I'm sure, for that matter, you and Alex would like to see.'

'It doesn't prove anything,' I said.

Her voice hardened. 'No, it doesn't. But we're going to call her in tomorrow morning and talk to her.'

I hesitated. 'No. Why not leave her in place? Just be careful what she sees.'

Windy didn't take well to disloyalty. 'I hate to do that, Chase. If this woman is collaborating with him, giving information away, she should be *terminated*.'

I decided I wouldn't want to get on her wrong side. 'You don't know for sure. So you can't really act anyhow. Let it go for now.'

16

Time is a river of events, and its current is strong. No sooner does a thing appear in its flow than it is swept away, and another takes its place, until that too is carried from sight.
—Marcus Aurelius,
Meditations

I was at Shara's office next morning to explain what we wanted. The mission reports showed the stars visited by the Wescotts on their various flights. Thanks to the *Falcon* AI record, we now knew, for each mission, the order in which those visits had occurred. 'Alex thinks you might be able to determine whether that sequence coincides with the original proposal.'

'But the proposals have been discarded,' said Shara. 'We already went over this.'

'I know,' I said. 'But hang on. Before the quantum drive was developed, a Survey ship always computed the shortest total route for a given mission.'

I saw the perplexed look give way to a smile. 'Oh,' she said.

'And we know that Wescott was interested in G-type stars near the end of their hydrogen-burning cycle.'

'Okay.'

'We're pretty sure they found something in one of the systems and deleted that star from the report. They went somewhere else and substituted *that* for the one that had been in the original proposal. If we can establish which star was deleted—'

'—You'll know where the *Seeker* is.'

'Can we do it?'

'Without having the proposal in our hands—'

'Yes.'

'Sure.' Her eyes focused elsewhere. A flock of colbees floated past, riding the wind. Her AI broke in to inform her of an incoming call.

'Not now,' she said to it. Then: 'Chase, let me see what you have.'

I passed the disk over. She put it in the reader and darkened the room. 'Can we assume it probably happened during the final mission?'

'That's a good place to start.'

She directed the AI to bring up a projection of the search area for the 1391–92 flight.

The office vanished, and we were adrift among the stars. *'I've blanked everything outside the subject area,'* the AI said. *'There are thirteen hundred eleven stars in the field.'* Most were yellow G-types. One, near the bookcase at the far wall, brightened. *'That's Taio 4776, where they made their first visit.'* A line grew out of it and connected to a second star, a half meter away. *'Icehouse 27651.'* It angled off to a third, near the desk lamp. *'Koestler 2294.'* And up to a star near the overhead. From there it skimmed along the sofa, touching two more, and turned sharply to cross the room. In the end we were looking at a glowing zigzag. *'Distance across the field is thirty-two point four light-years. Total distance covered by the mission is eighty-nine point seven light-years. Ten stars visited.'*

'Mark.' Shara was addressing the AI. 'Keep this same field. I want you to show us which stars are near the end of their hydrogen-burning cycle. Say, stars in which helium burning would begin during the next half million years. Blank everything else.'

'*I will require a moment, Shara.*'

'Take your time.'

'Shara,' I said, 'wouldn't someone have had to visit these systems earlier for Adam to know which suns were at the end of the cycle?'

'Not at all. Spectrographic analysis would provide everything he'd need to plan the flight.'

'*Ready,*' said Mark.

'Okay.' The stars were beginning to wink out. 'Let's see what we have.'

We were left with about thirty target stars, including the ten visited by the Wescotts. The track of the *Falcon* was bright and clear.

'Store the pattern,' she said.

It winked off.

'Okay, Mark. Now I want you to plan a flight to the same ten stars, using minimal total travel time. Start from the same star the *Falcon* mission used. Taio Whatever. When you have it, put it up.'

Taio 4776 grew bright, and the line came out of it again, moved to Icehouse, then to the star near the lamp. When it had finished all ten, the zigzag pattern floated in front of us. 'Looks like the same one,' I said.

'Let's find out. Mark, shrink the pattern and let's see the first one again. Overlay them.'

He moved the patterns until they were side by side. Then he merged them.

Identical.

'Try the previous mission,' I said.

We found it in the 1386–87 flight.

The patterns were *almost* identical. Again, the mission had visited ten planetary systems. But this time, it had not used the most-fuel-efficient route. The deviation came at the sixth star.

Tinicum 2502.

It wasn't a major change, but it was enough to tell us something was wrong.

We sat looking at it. Had they remained consistent to the pattern, they would not have gone to Tinicum.

'Okay,' I said. 'Which star *should* they have visited? Which one fits with the rest of the pattern?'

Shara put the question to the AI. 'Assume,' she said, 'that after Tinicum 2502 they returned to the original track.'

'*Here,*' said Mark, brightening a nearby star.

Tinicum 2116.

'Brilliant, Shara,' I said.

She smiled. 'I have my moments.'

I took her to lunch. It seemed the least I could do. We went to the Hillside, got a table by a window, ordered drinks, and sat back to talk about lost interstellars.

'Tinicum's planetary system will probably have a diameter of about eight billion klicks,' she said. 'But the sun's gravitational influence will reach out several times that far. If the *Seeker*'s orbiting one of the planets, you should have no trouble finding it.'

'But if it's in solar orbit—'

'—You're going to want to pack a few meals.'

Yeah. That was the next order of business. It would take the *Belle-Marie*, which had only basic navigation equipment to conduct the search, a long time. Maybe years. 'Can Survey help?'

'I can let you have a piece of hardware, a telescope, that should move things along nicely.'

'Shara,' I said, 'you're a warm, wonderful human being.'

'Right. What do I get in return?'

'I'll pay for lunch.'

'You're already paying for lunch.'

'Oh.' I thought about it. 'You want to come along? Be there when we find it?'

She made a face as if I'd just offered a plate of chopped squid. 'I don't think so. I know it's historically big stuff, but I'm just not an enthusiast. Not enough to spend that much time on ship-board. You'll probably be out there a month or two.'

The food came. Sandwiches and drinks. There was a guy at a window table trying to catch Shara's eye. She seemed not to have noticed. 'When you find it,' she said, 'you publicly share credit with Survey—'

'Done.'

'—And agree to give us access to the discovery. Which is to say you and your boss don't strip the ship before we get there.'

'We'll want to take *some* stuff. Just a bit.'

'Keep it modest. Can you do that?'

'Of course.'

She looked at me. 'I mean it, Chase.'

'I know. It won't be a problem,' I said.

'Okay.' She tried her drink, but her mind was elsewhere. 'The truth about Survey,' she said after a hesitation, 'what we don't admit publicly, is that our prime interest is finding another civ-ilization. That's not official, of course. Officially, we want to inventory what's out there. Each system goes into the catalog. Physical details about suns and worlds. Characteristics and arrangements of the planets in each system. Any odd features, and so on.

'But the people in the ships know that most of the information they bring back goes into File and Forget. I mean, who really cares about the surface temperature of one more gas giant?'

'So you're telling me—?'

'—Inspection of gas giants is generally done at long range and tends to be hit-and-run. Ditto, worlds too close in, or too far out. The ships are required to survey everything in the system, but we generally will not go in close. You know that. You used to work for us. That means, if the *Seeker* is orbiting a planet, the planet would most likely be in the biozone. So you want to start there.'

'We don't even know for sure it's in the system.'

'That's what makes it a challenge.' She took the first bite out of her sandwich. 'Good stuff,' she said. 'I love this place.'

'Tell me about the telescope.'

'Okay, we'll need to coordinate getting it for you.' She spotted the flirt and looked bored. 'When are you leaving?'

When I got back to the office, I reported the conversation to Alex, who pumped a fist in the air. 'I believe we're in business,' he said.

I also told him about Windy's call.

'Ollie Bolton.' He made a face. 'Why am I not surprised?'

'I don't think there's much we can do. Short of physical assault.'

'I don't, either.'

'You don't seem all that annoyed.'

'It's part of the business,' he said. 'We got outsmarted.'

'It's *not* part of the business. It's bribery.'

'Let's not worry about it for the moment, Chase. We have bigger things to think about.'

The *Belle-Marie* didn't have a mount for the telescope, so there was a delay of several days while a cradle was prepared and installed on the hull.

While that was going forward, Alex tried to check on Josh Corbin, the man who'd visited Delia and questioned her about the *Seeker*. But we got no useful information beyond what we already knew: He was an occasional consultant for Bolton.

Meanwhile a package arrived for me at the office. It carried a greeting card: *Chase, I've never forgotten you. Letting you get away was the dumbest thing I've ever done. I'll call this evening. Jerry.*

There had been a Jerry Unterkefler in my life a few years back, but he hadn't struck me as the passionate type.

Last year, during the *Polaris* business, when several attempts were made on our lives, we bumped up to class-A security coverage. I was about to open the package when it paid off. Jacob told me to put it down, gently, warn Alex, and for both of us to get out of the house.

* * *

216

We stood on the lawn an hour later while police carried the box off. 'Clearance nanos,' Fenn told us. 'They'd have turned the house into a park with three stone benches in about four minutes' time.' He looked at me. '*You'd* have been one of the benches.'

That was unsettling.

'Who'd want you guys dead?' he asked.

We had no idea who would go so far as to try to *kill* us. We spent an hour with him, answering questions, trying to zero in on suspects. We told him about the *Seeker,* and about Josh Corbin. And about Ollie Bolton.

'You think Bolton's behind this?'

Alex said he didn't know. I'm no fan of Bolton's, but I couldn't believe he'd try to kill anyone. 'How would you get your hands on these things?' I asked. 'On the nanos?'

'We're looking into it. They're designed for industrial use. Not hard to get. Unfortunately.'

That night they located Jerry Unterkefler and hauled him downtown for an interview. Actually, it was good to see him again. But I knew he wasn't behind it.

Fenn called to warn us to be careful, take no chances, and not to hesitate to let him know if we felt threatened.

Truth was, we already felt threatened, and we were glad another flight on the *Belle-Marie* was coming up.

Two guys from Tech Support attached the telescope, which they called a Martin, after Chris Martin, who is believed to be the first to use this specific type. Back in ancient times. They connected it to the ship's AI, ran a couple of tests, and told us we were all set.

This time, of course, Alex was coming. We logged in for a morning departure, but couldn't get rooms at either of the Sky-deck hotels the night before, so we were forced to sleep on board. We had dinner at Karl's, a sedate Dellacondan restaurant. It's Alex's favorite at Skydeck. Whenever we're there, he tries to schedule time to eat at Karl's. Afterward, he returned to the ship, while I went looking for a party. I found one, and didn't get back to the *Belle-Marie* until we were within a couple hours of launch. Not that it mattered. Once we were away from the station, we'd need nine hours to build up a charge, so I'd have plenty of time to sleep. Alex was up when I got there, and he looked at me disapprovingly. But he didn't say anything.

I'd given Belle the target information before we'd gone to dinner. *Belle*'s maximum range on a single jump was just under a thousand light-years. Tinicum 2116, our destination, was sixteen hundred. So we'd have to stop and recharge. The entire voyage, from departure at Skydeck until our arrival in the vicinity of the target system, would take just under nineteen hours. As opposed to the six weeks the *Falcon* would have needed.

I showered and changed and was back in my seat when the fifteen-minute ready-signal came in from ops. The magnetic clamps took hold and moved us into the queue.

There was a passenger ship in front of us, capacity about thirty. People on vacation, maybe. I watched it launch. Then it was our turn.

Alex was in the right-hand seat. He'd been unusually quiet, and as we moved forward during those last seconds before departure, his eyes were on me. 'You sure you're awake?' he asked.

On the way out to our jump point, we ran an action sim and played some chess. I'm not really competitive with him. That's probably good, because he takes the game seriously. We also enjoyed the theatrical release of the musical *Second Time Around*.

By late afternoon, ship's time, the quantum drive was fully charged. So we made the first jump. It's actually a bit easier on the system not to go maximum range. In this case, with a target sixteen hundred light-years out, I just divided it in half.

We came out in the middle of nowhere, of course, in the deeps between the stars.

I started to recharge and told Alex we'd be ready to go at about 0200 hours. Not the best timing in the world.

I suppose if we'd thought we would be able to make the second jump and immediately home in on the *Seeker*, we'd have been up and ready to go. But it was going to be a long process and we knew it. So we decided to push the jump back, get a decent night's sleep, and bump forward to Tinicum in the morning.

Alex settled in after dinner to watch a panel of experts argue politics. (We'd brought a few chips with us to supplement the ship's library.) I entertained myself with the VR for a while, one of those interplanetary travel experiences where you sit in your chair and sail through the rings of a gas giant while a voice-over tells you how they formed and why they look the way they do. I descended into a nova, which was somehow less unsettling than dropping into the atmosphere of Neptune. The narrator thought it a gorgeous world. That told me he'd never been there. Actually, I hadn't either, but I've seen places like it, and when you look at them, up close, believe me, you're not thinking esthetics.

I read for an hour and fell asleep about midnight, after telling Belle not to wake me. 'When we've finished recharging,' I told her, 'I don't need to know about it.'

'*Okay, Chase,*' she said. She'd appeared beside me looking about twenty years old, demure, attractive, and sporting a pair of wings.

'Going somewhere?' I asked.

She smiled. '*I always thought people look more exotic with flyware.*'

I didn't know how to answer that. 'Don't call me,' I said, 'unless there's a problem.'

But it didn't do any good. When a recharge is complete, it produces a slight modification in the sound of the engines, and I'm constitutionally unable to sleep through it.

We made the second jump, as planned, as soon as we were both up and awake. Lights flashed, then went green. My insides churned a bit. They do that sometimes during the transition phase. We had a sun this time, and Belle identified it as Tinicum 2116.

This was the system the *Falcon* should have visited but, if you believed their report, had not.

'*We are three point one AU's out from the central luminary,*' said Belle. '*Half that distance from the biozone.*'

'Okay. Let's start the long-range scan. We need to see what the planetary system looks like.'

'*Adjusting course,*' Belle said. '*Inbound.*'

'And let's put the Martin to work. See if anything out there looks like a derelict.'

The technology for the Martin was simple enough. It used a three-meter telescope to survey squares of sky ten degrees on a side. It did one square every minute in ultraviolet through mid infrared, and recorded the results. Thus the entire sky was imaged in six hours, at which point the process started again.

That allowed us to build a catalog of all moving objects, planets, moons, asteroids, you name it. The object we were looking for would have a reflective hull. Which meant a high albedo. If it was really out there, we expected to be able to pinpoint it within a few days.

I invited Alex to punch the button to activate the system, but he declined. 'You've done all the brute work in this operation so far, Chase,' he said. 'You do it.'

So I did. Lamps flashed, and Belle showed up wearing khakis and a safari hat. '*Search is under way,*' she said.

I tied the Martin into the navigational display so we could watch. Alex stayed awhile, got bored, went back to the common room.

During the next few hours, our long-range scan spotted a gas giant ten AUs out from the sun, and another at fourteen. That was it for the day. Alex was visibly disappointed, but I reminded him there's a lot of space in a solar system and you can't expect to find everything right away.

I spent most of that first day on the bridge, watching the sun grow as we drew closer. Alex drifted between his quarters and the common room, mostly leafing through inventories of antiquities available on the market. After dinner, he joined me up front, as if that would prompt Belle to a greater sense of urgency.

'Belle,' he said, 'can't we see anything yet?'

'It's too soon, Alex.'

'How much time do we need to spot a *planet*?'

'Maybe another day or so.'

He looked at me. 'I don't suppose we've found anything with the Martin?'

'No,' I said. 'When we do, you'll be first to know.'

'I can't believe it takes the Survey ships this long to figure out what's in a planetary system.'

'We're not really equipped to do a planetary search,' I said. 'Our gear is designed to find small targets that reflect a lot of light. Derelicts or docking stations or whatever. Long-range scan is okay, but we would have been better off with something more specialized.'

'Why didn't you *get* something more specialized for this part of the work? I mean, we have the Martin to hunt for the *Seeker*. Why not get something that finds *worlds*?'

'I don't know,' I said, trying to keep the edge out of my voice. 'I was thinking about the derelict, and I guess I never gave much consideration to trying to map a solar system.'

'Well,' Alex said, 'no harm done, I guess. Whatever's out here, we'll find.' He looked dispirited, and it seemed to be more than simply having to wait around.

'You all right?' I asked.

'I'm fine.' He looked away from me.

'Something's bothering you.'

'No,' he said. 'Not really.'

He'd expected we were going to ride in and, within the first few minutes, spot a class-K, a world with liquid water and gravity levels that people would find comfortable. When it didn't happen, he began to suspect it wasn't going to be there.

We were not really looking for an ancient wreck. He wanted Margolia.

'You don't find these things right away, Alex,' I said. 'Have a little patience.'

He sighed. 'Chances are, if there were a class-K world in the biozone, we'd have seen it by now, right?'

I couldn't lie to him. 'Probably. But let's just relax.'

He shrugged. 'I'm always relaxed,' he said. 'They don't make them any more relaxed than I am.'

On the fourth day insystem, Belle reported another hit. *'It's a terrestrial,'* she said. *'We didn't see it earlier because it was on the other side of the sun.'*

'Where's it located?' asked Alex.

'In the biozone.'

Bingo. He jumped out of his chair and squeezed my arm. 'Let's hope.' He peered out the viewport. 'Is it visible?'

Belle pointed out a dim star.

'Let's go take a look.'

Belle acknowledged, and we changed course. We'd need another ten hours or so to recharge, after which we could jump in close.

'It has an atmosphere,' she said. *'Equatorial diameter thirteen thousand kilometers. Distance from the sun one hundred forty-two million.'*

'Beautiful,' said Alex. 'It's another Rimway.'

'No evidence of a satellite.'

'What about radio transmissions?' he asked. 'Are we picking up anything?'

'Negative radio,' said Belle. *'But it's quite far.'*

Nothing was going to dim his mood. 'It's asking too much to expect them to be alive after all this time.'

I agreed with that. 'Don't expect a miracle,' I said. I was getting a bad feeling.

'I am able to detect the presence of oceans.'

'Good!' Alex leaned forward like a racing hound.

'I have a question,' I said.

'Fire away.'

'If that's really Margolia, why didn't the Wescotts say something? They were here what, in 1386? Maybe '87? The proposals would have been destroyed by 1390 at the latest. But as late as 1395 they were still keeping quiet.'

'There would have been some suspicions,' he said.

'So what? They'd have to take the chance and come forward at some point.'

He shook his head. 'Maybe they were just giving it more time.'

'Alex,' I said, 'don't get your hopes up.'

It wasn't like him to get carried away like that. But the potential was so enormous, he simply couldn't contain himself. And I'm not talking about money. Beneath the hard-bitten profit-and-loss attitude, Alex was a romantic. And this was the ultimate romantic possibility.

We were still feeling the glow when, a few hours later, Belle said, quietly, *'Looks like bad news.'*

A pall fell over the bridge. 'What is it, Belle?' I asked.

'The world is not suitable for settlement. Probably not even for human life.'

Alex made a sound deep in his throat. 'I thought you said it was in the biozone, Belle?' he said.

'It's moving away from the sun.'

'What do you mean?' demanded Alex.

'It's in a highly elliptical orbit. I can't give you the exact numbers yet, but I estimate it goes out as far as four hundred million kilometers.'

'That would make for a cold winter,' I said.

'And it approaches to within forty million. There's a possible error of ten percent, but at those ranges it wouldn't matter.'

'I guess not,' said Alex.

'When it reaches perihelion, the planet's equatorial regions will get fourteen times more sunlight per square centimeter than Rimway does.'

'What happens to the oceans when it gets well out in its orbit?'

'*Not enough data yet.*'

The world was wrapped in white cumulus. The oceans covered more than half the globe. And the landmasses were green.

'*Axial inclination,*' said Belle, '*ten degrees.*'

She confirmed that there was no moon.

'It must boil over at forty million klicks,' said Alex.

'*As it approaches perihelion, Alex, it accelerates. It would be moving very swiftly during the period when it is receiving maximum radiation.*'

'Bat out of hell,' Alex said.

'*Oh, yes. Most decidedly. When it is farthest away, it moves much more slowly. This world spends most of its time in deep winter.*'

'But wouldn't the oceans dry up and disappear, Belle?' he asked. 'With this kind of orbit?'

'*I don't have relevant data,*' she said. '*I can tell you, however, that their presence provides some protection from the heat during the summer.*'

'Why is that?' I asked.

'*When the world passes close to the sun, there's substantial evaporation. Sea level may drop by thirty meters during the process. The vapor fills the skies with what you're looking at now: optically opaque thunderstorm clouds, which would block much of the incoming radiation.*'

The sensors were able to penetrate the thick atmosphere, and we got pictures. River valleys. Vast gorges. And snowcapped mountains.

'I suspect the oceans are losing water,' I said. 'A few million years of this, and they'll probably be gone.'

'*There appear to be large life-forms in the water,*' said Belle.

'Don't they freeze?' asked Alex. 'What kind of year does it have?'

'*It is approximately twenty-one and a half standard months in*

224

*length. For nine months, the temperatures are actually tolerable.
Even comfortable. During the coldest six months, the oceans will
freeze down somewhat. To what depth I have no way of deter-
mining. Possibly as much as a hundred meters. That would insulate
them against excessive heat loss.'*

'And provide a way for sea life to survive.'

'Yes.'

'Can you tell what kind of life it is?'

'No. I can discern movement, but I have no details yet.'

There was no sign of habitation. No indication anyone had
ever set foot on the world. The land was covered with vegetation.
Jungles, it looked like. We saw no large land animals. No animals
of any size, in fact.

We slipped into low orbit, and Alex stared down at the world.
From that altitude, it appeared warm and pleasant, an idyllic
place, ideal for settlement.

There were a few scattered patches of desert. Otherwise, everywhere we looked on land, we saw only jungle.

'I don't get it,' I said. 'This thing regularly moves within stone-
throwing distance of the sun. How does all this stuff survive?
Why isn't it a desert? Why isn't it just charred rock?'

*'The periodic proximity to the sun provides a hot, humid
climate. Perfect for jungles. And as I said, the clouds give it a
reasonably effective heat shield.'*

Alex had other things on his mind. 'Belle, do you see any
evidence of construction anywhere? Buildings? Roads? A harbor
facility, maybe? Anything like that?'

*'Negative. It will take a while to scan the entire planet, of
course.'*

'Of course.'

'At the moment, temperature in the midlatitudes,' she said,
'ranges from twenty-three to about fifty degrees Celsius.'

'A bit warm,' said Alex.

'The atmosphere is nitrogen-oxygen-argon. Breathable. Perhaps

a trifle oxygen rich. Air pressure at ground level is probably in the range of a thousand millibars.'

'Like home.'

'I see no reason why not.'

Alex looked at the jungle. 'What do you think, Chase?'

'I can't imagine anyone would want to settle here.'

Belle blinked on. In her elderly librarian/maternal figure persona. Lined face, white hair, reassuring smile. *'I'm getting volcanic activity in the southern hemisphere.'*

I needed somebody to talk to, so I called up Harry Williams. He appeared in the right-hand seat, smiled easily, and said hello. He was a big man, or at least the avatar was big. He looked around the bridge as if he owned it.

'This is a hell of a ship you have,' he said. *'I wish we'd had a few of these.'*

A white jacket with a high collar contrasted sharply with his dark skin. He was dressed casually, a man who was getting ready to go for a stroll in the park. There was an intensity about this guy that manifested itself in his eyes and the set of his jaw. Don't get in his way.

'Where are we?'

'Tinicum 2116.'

'Where?'

No way he could recognize the designation. The catalog system had been changed any number of times. I pointed him to the viewport. 'We thought maybe that was Margolia.'

'I don't know,' he said.

I showed him some of the close-ups. Jungle. And more jungle.

'No,' he said. *'That's not it. Margolia was a summer world. Green and wet with high skies and deep forests and broad oceans.'*

'I wish you knew where it was located.'

'So do I.'

'Would you recognize it if you saw it?'

'No. I've no data on it.' There was a pained reflection in his eyes. *'Why do you think it's in this system?'*

I tried to explain, but he got impatient. Told me to let it go. 'Doesn't matter. That's not it.' He fell silent for a time. Then: 'Margolia,' he said. 'Is that what you call it? Our world?'

'Yes. I guess we do.'

'We could have done worse. He was a great man. Have you read him?'

'No. Not really.'

'He was a twenty-fifth-century philosopher. And a British prime minister.'

'So what was there about him that appealed to you?'

'He measured everything against reason. No intricate abstractions. No sacred texts. Accept nothing on authority. As they said in an earlier age, "Show me the evidence."'

'That sounds sensible.'

'"Never lose sight of reality. The individual human life span is brief and, in the long view, inconsequential," he said. "We are children one day and signing out the next. Therefore, in the brief moment we are allotted, live reasonably, be compassionate, and when your hour comes, accept it without histrionics. Never forget that your handful of hours is a supreme gift. Use them wisely, do not fritter them away, and remember that your life is not an entitlement.

'"Most of all, live free. Free of social and political stricture. If there is such a thing as a soul, these surely are its components."'

'Would Margolis have gone with you?'

'I've spoken with his avatar. It was one of the first questions I asked.'

'What was his answer?'

'He said no. Most assuredly not.'

'Did he say why?'

A smile deepened the lines around the corners of his mouth. 'He called the plan grandiose.'

'Well,' I said, 'there you are.'

The moment stretched into one of those silences where you

could hear the murmur of electronics. Finally, I asked whether he had gone on the flight alone. 'Or did you have a family?'

'*My wife Samantha. And two boys. Harry Jr., and Thomas. Tommy.*'

'How long had you been married?' I asked.

'*Eight years at the time we left.*' His eyes became intense. '*I don't even know what they looked like.*'

'There were no pictures?'

'No. *Whoever did the reconstruction of my persona either didn't have a representation, or didn't think it was important.*'

'I'm sorry,' I said. Alex was forever reminding me that avatars have no more feelings than the chair I was sitting in. It's all an illusion. Just programing.

17

We know that time is elastic. That it passes more quickly on the roof than in the basement, or at rest than in a moving vehicle. We know there are objects that may have occupied a place in the cosmos for several hundred million years although they themselves are not 60 million years old. We are accustomed to watching time take its toll on the physical world. Buildings crumble. People vanish. The pyramids wear down. But in the great vacuum that surrounds us, time seems suspended. Footprints, left ten thousand years ago on a lunar surface, endure.

—Orianda Koval,
Time and Tide, 1407

We almost gave up and went home. If Margolia was not in the system, it seemed unlikely that the *Seeker* could be there. Somehow, we'd gotten it wrong.

But we'd gone to a lot of trouble. And we had noplace else to look. So we stayed, and turned the Martin telescope loose. Two days later, Belle reported a suspicious object. '*High-albedo source,*' she said. Highly reflective.

'Where?' I asked.

She showed me. *'Eight AUs from our present position.'*

'Can you give us any more information?' asked Alex.

'It's in solar orbit.'

'That's *it*? Can we get an image?'

A point of light appeared on-screen. A dull star.

'Enhance, please,' said Alex.

'It is enhanced.'

He didn't sound hopeful. But what the hell? 'Let's go take a look,' he said.

Belle adjusted course and began to charge the engines. During the next few hours, she was able to report some details: *'Preliminary analysis indicates long elliptical orbit. It's currently headed outward from the sun and will reach aphelion at seven point two AUs.'*

'Sounds like a comet,' said Alex.

'Albedo's not right.' We were belting down, getting ready to make the jump. *'It looks as if it would require approximately eighty years to complete an orbit.'*

Alex finished the coffee he'd been drinking and put the cup in the holder.

'It appears to be metal. Ninety-eight percent probability.'

The jump got us within two days' travel time, and after about four hours the scopes gave us our first real look at the object. It was, indeed, a derelict. Once we'd established that, Alex beamed. Knew it all along.

It was in a slow tumble, and its exhaust tubes were pointed in the direction of one of the gas giants, which was only a few million kilometers away.

Six hours in, we were able to make out details, the streamlined body, thrusters, sensor mounts. Amidships, it carried the soaring eagle that we'd seen on the cup.

Seeker!

'How about that?' said Alex. 'But what the hell is it doing out here?'

At nine hours, we were able to make out its name, in the now-familiar English characters, on the hull.

As we drew closer, we became more aware of the sheer enormity of the vessel. It was the size of a small *city*. Eight giant thruster tubes aft, any one of which could have swallowed the *Belle-Marie*. Six levels of viewports. A hull that would have taken twenty minutes to circle on foot. An army of pods and antennas.

And—

'Uh-oh.'

Alex turned my way. 'What is it, Chase?'

Two of the eight thruster tubes looked *bent*. They jutted at odd angles, off a few degrees from the others and from a line drawn down the center of the ship.

I'd seen pictures of the *Crossmeer* years before, after its jump engines exploded. Everybody had died, because the blast had ripped holes in the ship and the air supply blew out before the hatches could close. The exhaust tubes had looked like these.

'They had an accident,' I said.

Alex turned back to the monitors. 'Yes. That's what it looks like.' He exhaled, and asked an odd question. 'Do you think anybody might have survived?' He was speaking as though it had happened yesterday and there was still a chance to do a rescue. Being off-world can induce a sense of timelessness. Things don't change much when you get away from wind and rain.

'It's a big ship,' I said. 'I don't know. Depends on whether it got punctured in the wrong places.'

'Not a good way to go,' he said. 'Out here.'

I didn't think there *was* a good way to go, but I didn't say anything.

It was hard to understand how the *Seeker* had come to be where it was. There was no habitable world in the system. What was it doing there? 'It's been a long time,' said Alex. 'Maybe it just drifted in from somewhere else.'

'From where?'

'From wherever Margolia is.'

'The closest star is almost three light-years out. That's way too far for just floating over.'

'Chase, we're talking nine thousand years.'

'It's too far. Under power, without jumping, it would need twenty-five thousand years to travel that kind of distance. At least.'

He shook his head. 'Well, maybe they were in hyperspace. The engines blew, and the pilot pulled them out.' He looked the way he always does when confronted with a challenge. 'That *must* be the way it happened.'

'I suppose that's as good a guess as any. But it seems unlikely.'

There was nothing to be done until we got there, so Alex announced he was going back to his cabin. 'Let me know if you see anything more.'

'Okay.'

'I have to get back to work.'

'What work?'

'The Blackmoor Medallions,' he said. 'Looted during a civil disturbance three centuries ago on Morinda. Never seen since. They'd be worth millions.'

'You know where they are?' I said.

'I'm working on it.'

We pulled alongside, and even Belle was impressed by the size of the thing. The English symbols spelling out *Seeker* must have been twenty meters high. The ship was probably three times the volume of the *Madrid*, which was the biggest vessel currently in service.

The explosion had blown off large chunks of the after section. Several of the exhaust tube mounts had been mangled. A cluster of cables drifted out into the dark.

Belle took us within sixty meters of the damaged area, matched the roll and tumble of the derelict so that all motion relative to us stopped, and inched forward along the hull. I looked through blast holes into the interior.

'What causes engines to blow?' asked Alex.

'Any of a number of things could happen,' I said. 'This thing is pretty primitive, and they probably didn't have a lot of the safeguards we do. It might have been the fuel. Might have been an imbalance that can get created if you try to jump before the engines are ready.'

'It was the star drive?'

'Can't tell. Not from here. And I don't know enough about these things that I could be sure from the inside either. But that's where I'd put my money.'

The ship was pocked and torn. Belle trained a light on it, and occasionally it illuminated the interior through one of the holes, but we still couldn't make out much. We nosed past cargo hatches. Glided along rows of viewports. Past long narrow wings and a sail whose sole function would have been to serve as a mount for attitude thrusters.

The English letters, black and unadorned, slipped past. I saw a spate of other phrases and a splash of color. A flag symbol. I didn't recognize the flag. It seemed out of character for the Margolians, but I guessed it came with the ship.

Then we were passing the main airlocks. There were six of them. All sealed.

Finally, we approached the bow.

Alex pointed at an open hatch immediately to starboard. Maybe it was the way the Wescotts got in.

'Alongside,' I told Belle.

Attitude thrusters fired briefly, and we edged in close until I could almost have reached out and touched her.

I looked up at the sheer dark bulk of the thing, and found myself thinking about Delia Wescott, and I understood why she'd been frightened.

We suited up and went over. Alex likes to take charge in these situations, so he instructed me that we were to stay together at all times. He's entertaining when he gets like that. I'm not sure how much help he'd be if there were a real emergency, but it's always nice to have a protective male around.

The hatch had not been opened. It was cut. Apparently the Wescotts had been unable to get the manual release to work. But after so much time, I'd have been surprised if anything worked.

They'd also taken down the inner airlock door. We looked through it into a narrow chamber. A bench was fastened to the deck. Bulkheads were lined with cabinets. There was no gravity, of course. We were getting around in grip shoes.

Alex played his wrist lamp around the chamber, strolled over to a bank of cabinets, and tried to open one. But they were all warped. Frozen.

We moved out into a passageway. It had three doors on either side. Then it connected with a cross corridor with more doors. None of them would open.

Alex picked one arbitrarily and I used a laser to cut it down. When I pulled it clear of the frame, I saw movement inside. Alex jumped. I guess I did, too.

It was drifting debris, spread all over the room, and it took us several minutes to realize that it included a cadaver. Or what remained of one. We watched the pieces climb one bulkhead and start across the overhead as the ship rolled.

There wasn't enough left to know whether it had been a man or woman, or for that matter adult or child. We stood for a long minute, trying to ignore it, shining the lamps around the room. Other objects were afloat, bits of plastic, pieces of furniture, a comb, shreds of God knew what.

'Stay close,' said Alex. I wished we could have put the door back and resealed the room.

The cross corridor connected with more passageways with more doors. We opened a second cabin and found much the same sort of condition, but this time without the occupant. 'Looks like accommodations were for two to a room,' said Alex. 'Capacity was, what, about nine hundred?'

'Yes.'

'The quarters would not have been bad. I'd pictured them packed in a bit more closely.'

'Alex,' I said, 'why don't we move directly to the after section? See if we can figure out what happened.'

He stepped aside and made room. 'Lead the way.' He seemed unusually subdued. There's an inner cockiness about Alex. He's good, and he knows it. But he tries not to let that knowledge show. During that first hour on board the *Seeker*, though, it deserted him. He seemed almost overwhelmed.

We wandered aft. We found more pieces and bits of passengers adrift. Hard to know how many.

We also found washrooms, common rooms, VR areas, and a gym. English signs were everywhere. I showed them to Belle and she translated: exit, deck 5, press in case of emergency, ladies.

The interior airlocks had closed, presumably when the engines blew. But someone, very likely the Wescotts, had burned through. 'Other than that,' I said. 'there doesn't seem to be any damage in the forward sections that would date to the time of the accident. Anybody who was on board would have survived until the air ran out.'

The doors in the after section were generally spaced farther apart. We opened one and looked into what must have been an acceleration chamber. Twenty couches, four across, five deep.

All filled.

My God.

I recalled Mattie Clendennon. '*A dead ship.*' Her gray-green eyes had grown large as she said it. '*Carrying a full complement.*'

The remains, most of them, were still buckled down, although body parts had broken loose and were adrift in the room. A few of the victims had gotten loose.

We got a better idea who they'd been.

'Kids,' said Alex.

We found three more such places during the next few minutes. All were filled with children. After that we left the doors shut.

We were grateful, at last, to reach the engineering spaces. The bulkhead was peeled away by the force of the blast. The main engines were blackened, but otherwise relatively whole. The stardrive unit had erupted. The damage was so extensive, and the specifics of the ship itself so unfamiliar, there was no way to know for certain what had happened. 'I'd say they were trying either to enter or exit hyperspace.'

He nodded.

'Not that it matters,' I added.

'No,' Alex said. 'It matters. If we can figure out what happened here, maybe we can figure out where Margolia is.'

I didn't argue the point. I just didn't much care where Margolia was, not at that moment. And I know those kids died thousands of years ago, and it was foolish to feel anything at that point, but I kept thinking what the scene on the ship during those final moments must have been like.

'Don't,' said Alex. 'It was over quickly.'

We looked out through the ruptured hull at the stars and the nearby gas giant, and the distant sun, pale and cold at this range. It was barely more than a bright star in the firmament. When I leaned outside and looked toward the bow, I could see the *Belle-Marie*.

'Can you tell why it happened?' asked Alex.

I shook my head. 'Not really. The passengers were buckled in. That confirms that they were performing a maneuver. That's all I can say for sure.'

We descended to the lower decks and wandered the passageways. We came across a workout area. Devices that allowed passengers to jog, or to pump pedals, or to simulate weight lifting. The nature of the equipment suggested they hadn't had artificial gravity. I checked with Belle, and she told me it hadn't been developed for centuries after the *Seeker*.

Most of the equipment was still secured to the deck and bulkheads, but some was adrift. In addition there were towels and sweat clothes.

Acceleration chambers in the forward areas, away from the sections that had been damaged, were empty. The airlocks had saved them. Temporarily. Those sections were filled with floating human debris.

It was becoming apparent that the *Seeker* had indeed been carrying a full load of passengers. Nine hundred people. Had they all been kids?

'Where were they going?' I asked. 'I don't think any of the original flights out to the colony carried mostly children.'

'An evacuation,' said Alex.

'From what?'

'I've no idea.' He pushed away something that had floated in front of his helmet. 'It would have been slower up here.'

I knew what he meant, and I didn't even want to think about it.

He pressed a gloved hand against the bulkhead as if to read its secrets. 'Where were they coming from?'

Our air supply was dwindling, so we went back to the *Belle-Marie*. Neither of us said much. If I'd had my way, we would have called the whole thing off at that point and gone home. Let Survey or somebody else deal with it. It was odd. I've gone into more than a few archeological sites with Alex, but this was different from anything I'd experienced before. Or ever would again.

But he was determined to find out what had happened. So after an hour or so, and showers, we got fresh air tanks and went back.

First stop that trip was the bridge. We found it on deck four. It was smaller than I'd expected. And that surprised me. Big ship, you figure oversized bridge. There was nobody strapped in the seats, for which I was grateful. God knows what had gone through the captain's mind during all that.

I didn't recognize much about the equipment. There were some toggles and push buttons. But with the power off, the space wasn't much more than two chairs in an otherwise empty room with a blank control panel and blank bulkheads, and I couldn't have read the language without help anyhow.

'Any chance of getting the log?' Alex asked.

'No. Whatever was recorded isn't still there after all this time.'

'Pity.' He was looking around, hoping to find something reassuring in the midst of that disaster. There was a plaque mounted on the bulkhead to the left of the pilot's seat. It had a silhouette of the *Seeker*, and when we gave Belle a look, she said it was an award for carrying the first settlers to Abudai.

'Where?' Alex asked.

'*Abudai.*'

He looked at me. 'You ever hear of it?'

'Nope.'

'*The settlement shut down after forty years or so,*' said Belle. '*It consisted of a group that disapproved of technology. They were trying to hold on to the old days.*'

'What happened to it?'

'*It didn't work. As the children matured, they packed up and went back to Earth.*'

I'd brought a generator with me and managed to tie it in, but it was a fool's errand. The system wasn't going to take a charge. The ship was dead as a rock.

'I wouldn't be surprised,' said Alex, 'if Survey made a monument out of the thing. Or an historic preserve.'

I wasn't sure which was the pilot's seat. I imagined Taja and Abraham Faulkner sitting there during the long flights out from Earth. I wondered what they'd talked about. What they'd thought of Harry Williams. How they'd felt about their passengers. If either of them had been on board during this final flight.

I must have mentioned the pilots' names because Alex pointed out that we really didn't know when the *Seeker* had come to rest where it was. 'It might have been a long time after the settlers arrived,' he said. 'Taja and Faulkner could have been dead a hundred years before this happened.'

'I doubt it,' I said. 'It's not likely the *Seeker* would have lasted out here more than a century. Even with world-class maintenance.'

I opened some of the panels and looked inside, to see what condition the black boxes were in. These were the control systems for communication, navigation, power, life support, and so on. And probably for the AI. If they'd had one.

And I noticed something odd.

The boxes were marked. Plates carried symbols that probably indicated a manufacturer and a part number. And maybe a date. Some also had the group of characters that I now knew translated to *Seeker*. Several others had a different group of symbols, but done in the same style. It was always the same group. 'Belle,' I said, 'what's this mean?'

'*Please hold it higher so I can see. Ah, yes. That says* Bremerhaven.'

'*Bremerhaven?*' said Alex.

'*That is correct.*'

'The other ship on the mission.' He frowned. 'But this is the *Seeker*.'

'Yeah.'

'Then those are parts from the *Bremerhaven*? Is that what it means, Chase?'

'I'd say so, yes.'

'Are they critical parts?'

'I don't know anything about third-millennium ships. I mean this thing's an *antique*.'

'Best guess.'

'They're part of the basic package. On the bridge. Connected to whatever controls the captain has. Yeah. I'd say they were probably critical.'

There were storerooms, some filled with supplies that had never been used, others lined with cabinets. We broke into a few of the cabinets and found lots of baggage. It was all frozen rock solid.

There was no shortage of artifacts. Mugs and glasses, like the one Amy Kolmer had brought to the office, were stored in cabinets in the dining areas. Most of the glasses were cracked, but some had survived intact. We filled several containers with them. 'No problem about our deal with Shara,' he said. 'There's plenty here for everybody.'

Our customers were going to love this stuff. We took some lamps, dinnerware, pens, whatever. We especially liked anything that was marked with the *Seeker*'s name. The ship also had a substantial stock of toys. Stuffed animals and books designed for children and pull-toys and sets of blocks and play pistols. Not much of it was in what you'd call pristine condition. But considering the age of everything, it was pretty good.

I'd have preferred to complete an investigation before we started taking things out, but the ship was so big, and there was so much. We'd go from space to space, and Alex would say, look, there's a reader, or maybe a device that we didn't recognize, or maybe a towel – stiff as a board but still recognizably a towel – and we'd pick it up and soon we were hauling a lot of stuff around with us. We took what we had back to the *Belle-Marie*. When we got outside, Alex, his arms full, lost his grip on the load. Everything drifted away, but he managed to save the Abudai plaque.

I mention all this to impress on the reader that there was a fair degree of disorganization in the way we went about things. We were driven by competing motives, by our desire to know what had happened to the *Seeker*, and consequently to Margolia itself; and also by our hunt for salable artifacts. And maybe a little guilt associated with taking things from this particular site. Don't ask me why. We'd never had that problem before.

'I almost wish there weren't so much here,' said Alex. I knew what he meant. If only a limited number of artifacts from the *Seeker* existed, they would command extraordinary prices. But if a boatload came back, even if that boatload were restricted by Survey to museums and exhibits, their very existence would reduce the value of what we had to sell.

Well, no help for it.

We'd just gotten inside when Belle called over. '*I think I sighted another ship.*'

'Where, Belle?'

'*It's gone now. Might have been just a blip. It wasn't on the scope long enough to get a fix.*'

'Nearby?'

'*Thirty million klicks. There's an asteroid ring at that range.*'

'Okay. Let us know if it shows up again.'

18

Modern technology has made time travel possible. Not in the classic style, of course. Bouncing back and forth through the centuries appears to be forever beyond reach. We cannot go back to inform Caesar that it would be a good idea to stay out of the forum during March. But we *can* return to his world, and listen to his thoughts, and hear his heart beat.

—Jasmine Kalanna,
Voyages, 1365

You wander through something like the *Seeker* and you think about the federations and governments that have lived and died while that ship and its silent passengers moved along its solitary orbit. There had been dark ages and commercial revolutions and environmental disasters. Religions had been born, prospered, and vanished. There'd been wars, dictators, pogroms, rebellions, disasters. We'd seen golden ages, periods of extended prosperity, social and artistic triumphs. The great men and women had come and gone, as had the monsters, the visionaries, the rebels, and the artists. The sciences had advanced and retreated, Brooking had made his celebrated effort to reach M4 (and been lucky to come home alive). Trillions of human beings had been born and lived out their lives. More than half of recorded history had passed. 'You ever been to an older site?' I asked Alex.

'On the ground, yes,' he said. 'But not anything like this.' We were in one of the dining rooms. The bulkheads were gray and cold in the light from our lamps. On one, near the door, there was a barely discernible stain. Maybe caused long ago by leaking water. Maybe by spilled coffee. (Did they have coffee in those days?) It had the effect of reminding us that people had actually come into this room and talked, and munched on sandwiches. Drunk cold beer. I wondered whether Harry Williams had ever sat at one of the tables.

We took back another container of artifacts, our fourth. Among other things it contained a white pullover shirt and a jacket. The ship's emblem was emblazoned on the right-hand breast pocket of the shirt, and a silhouette of the *Seeker* had been embroidered on the back of the jacket. Both were in remarkably good condition. Stiff as boards, but when we got them to the *Belle-Marie*, they'd flex out.

We took inventory and stored everything in the common room. Despite our success, Alex remained in a dark mood. He'd made the discovery of his career, of *anybody's* career, but he showed no sign of self-satisfaction. 'It's not really our discovery, Chase,' he said. 'The Wescotts found it.'

That wasn't the issue, of course. But I played the game with him. 'Columbus wasn't the first guy to discover America, either,' I said. 'But he was smart enough to make the announcement, so he gets the credit. All of it.'

'Public relations,' Alex said.

What was the difference?

He was staring at the bulkhead. 'I think we need to talk to Harry again.'

'Why?' I asked. 'What do you expect to find out? He doesn't know any more about that' – I looked toward the *Seeker* – 'than we do.'

'I know. But I want to talk to him anyhow.'

Belle complied, and Harry Williams appeared, seated in a lush armchair. *'Hello,'* he said, cheerfully. *'Good to see you folks. Where are we now? Another oddball world?'* Before anybody answered, he noticed the *Seeker* through the bridge portals, and his eyes hardened. *'What happened?'* he demanded.

'The engines exploded,' Alex told him. 'That's all we know.'

Harry went over to the viewport and stared out. He looked scared.

'It appears they were carrying a full load,' Alex continued. 'We think most of the passengers were kids.'

'When did it happen?'

'We don't know that either,' Alex said. 'We don't know any more now than you do.'

'What about the colony?'

'We haven't even figured out where the colony was.'

His voice caught. *'You found the* Seeker, *but you don't know where the colony was? How's that possible?'*

'The ship is adrift in a system that has nothing approximating the kind of world you'd have needed. We don't have a clue why it's here or where it came from.'

'How hard can it be?' he demanded. *'Just look for a class-K.'*

'You're not listening, Harry. There is no class-K in this system.'

Harry shook his head. Can't be. *'Where are we now?'* he asked.

I told him. Tinicum 2116. Same as last time.

'Do *you* know where the colony was established?' Alex asked. I could hear growing impatience in his voice.

'No. I've told you, I'm only a composite.'

'I don't mean *you*, the avatar. I mean you, Harry Williams. When the first flight left Earth, taking the colonists out to wherever the hell it was, did Williams know the destination?'

'No.'

'You didn't?'

'No. Not in the sense you're asking. I couldn't have told anyone where it was. I'd been there. I knew what the world looked like. But I don't know anything about star travel.'

'You just knew it was out there, somewhere.'

'*Yes. There was no need for me to have specifics beyond that. They were irrelevant.*' In spite of everything he managed a smile. '*Tell me something was fifteen degrees west of Antares, and I would have no idea what you were talking about.*'

'All right. Let's try it this way. Who originally planned the details for the flights to Margolia?'

'*Clement Estaban.*'

The name meant nothing to me, but Alex nodded. 'The man who walked away,' he said.

'*Yes. At the last minute, he changed his mind. He wasn't the only one.*'

'How did that come about?'

'*Estaban was an engineer. Made some of the early exploratory flights. And he found a summer world.*'

'Was *he* the first to suggest the idea of a colony?'

'*No. I don't think so. To be honest, I don't remember who first suggested it. But—*' He was still having trouble with his voice. '*I hope they're okay.*' He spoke as if the original colonists might still be alive somewhere.

'Harry,' said Alex, 'what were the long-range plans for the *Seeker* and the *Bremerhaven*?'

'*You mean after they delivered the colonists?*'

'Yes.'

'*Simple enough. After the third voyage, the two ships were to remain with the colony. They were going to be put in orbit. Kept accessible in case we needed them.*'

'Okay. That means you intended to maintain them. But did you actually have the people to do it? And the equipment?'

'*Yes. We had both. We sent an orbital dock out with the colony. With all the parts and equipment we would need for the foreseeable future. And we had a few engineers. Not specialists in that kind of work, but willing to learn. But—*'

'—But what?'

'*I don't think we were that concerned about the ships. We didn't*

246

seriously expect to use them again. Our sense of the situation was that we were going to be a long time getting the colony up and running. Years. Maybe decades. We weren't much interested in maintaining an interstellar capacity. There was no need for it.'

'Okay.'

'We were going to keep the ships so we didn't lose the technology. So we'd be able to manufacture our own, when the time came.'

'Suppose the colony got into trouble? There was no long-range communication. You couldn't call for help.'

'What kind of trouble could we have gotten into?'

'Plague,' I suggested.

'We were going to be an off-world life-form. None of the local bugs could have touched us.'

'How could you possibly be sure?' demanded Alex. 'In the beginning of the interstellar age, the notion that disease could only affect life-forms from its own biosystem was only theory.'

'We talked to the top people. They said it wasn't possible.'

'They were wrong, Harry. There've been some incidents.'

He made a noise in his throat. His eyes were filled with pain. And I know. It was only an avatar. Not real. But you should have been there. 'Belle,' I said, 'can you cut the emotional levels? We need to be able to talk to him.'

'Sorry, Chase,' she said. *'If I make adjustments in the personality, I cannot vouch for the accuracy of the model.'*

'It's okay,' said Alex. 'Harry, you put, what, five thousand people out in the middle of nowhere. How could you be sure something wouldn't go wrong?'

'We were very careful. We knew the place we were going to. I assure you it was safe.'

'Suppose somebody changed his mind. Wanted to go home?'

'The colony would be home.'

'Come on, Harry. You know what I'm saying.'

His eyes closed for a moment. *'Actually, we knew that would happen and we made provision for it.'*

'What was the provision?'

'*Counseling. And, where necessary, a way to return.*'

'How did you manage that?'

'*We knew some people wouldn't be able to adjust. We also had a couple of crew members to take care of. Who were to go home. They weren't all members of the community, you know.*'

'I assumed—'

'*You assumed wrong.*' The voice was angry now. '*No. Abe was one of us. But that's because of his girlfriend. It wasn't a matter of principle with him. Two of the engineers were not staying. One on each ship. And Taja wasn't.*'

'The captain of the *Seeker.*'

'*Yes.*'

'So how were they going to *get* home?'

'*The* Boykins *was going to pick them up.*'

'The *Boykins.*'

'*Yes. They were to be taken back, as well as anyone else who wanted to return.*'

'So someone else *did* know where Margolia was?'

'*Of course. The pilot's name was Yurawicz. Marco Yurawicz.*'

'Did he actually make the flight? Did anyone go back? Other than the crew members?'

'*He made* three *flights. He returned almost four hundred people who'd changed their minds.*'

'Four hundred?'

'*Actually a bit more than that. We knew it would happen. We just didn't know how many. We didn't advertise our intention to provide an opportunity to return because we knew a lot of people would apply simply to see whether they'd like the experience. Give us a trial run. We wanted committed people only. But we knew we had to make provision.*'

'Wasn't that too many people to expect to keep a secret?'

'*They were like me, Alex. They had no idea where Margolia was. And I don't think anybody in the government cared where it was.*'

'And the crew members never told anybody?'

'As far as I know. That was the deal. They were well paid, and they were obviously as good as their word.'

'What about Taja?'

'She never did return to Earth. Must have liked the new world. Probably found someone and settled down.'

We went back next day for a final visit.

We broke into the captain's cabin, as well as those set aside for her executive officer and the other three crew members. The cabins were well preserved. Desks and chairs, at least the ones still secured to the deck, were reasonably intact. They'd had their own washrooms. I couldn't resist punching the pad over the shower, but of course there was no water. Outside, in the passageway, the bulkheads were stained where water lines had burst.

We found a few pictures on the bulkheads. In the compartment we guessed to be Taja's, there was one of a man, an adolescent girl, an older woman, and a child about five. In the adjoining cabin, we saw a picture of two attractive young women. Embossed on plastic. There were others. Family members, presumably. Kids. Even a dog. I'd brought a plastic sack in case we found anything else of interest. But Alex suggested we leave the pictures for Windy's people. 'Show up with those,' he said, 'and we'll be accused of crimes against humanity.'

The rooms had storage cabinets. We cut into a couple and found clothes. Work uniforms, for the most part. They were in poor condition. It was a pity because they carried the *Seeker* shoulder patch.

We also made a major discovery in the captain's cabin. Lying in a corner of a cabinet that was otherwise empty, we came across a small black case that might once have been leather. Inside, we found a plastic packet containing twelve lenses. I showed them to Alex.

They were stuck to the interior of the case, so we couldn't remove them. But the leather was open on both sides and, after we'd wiped them, we could see through the lenses. Alex examined them in the lamplight. Then he invited me to have a look.

Each of the lenses carried an image. But I couldn't make out what they were.

'Any ideas?' he asked.

'Not really.'

'You know what I think?' He took the case back and aimed his wrist lamp at it. Played it through the lenses. Blurry images appeared on the opposite bulkhead. He moved the makeshift projector forward and back. The pictures shifted but did not clear. 'Holograms,' he said.

I nodded. 'Could be. We can have Belle figure it out.'

He slipped the case into a cargo pocket. 'Damn, I wish people would keep better records. It would have been nice if one of them had left us some handwritten comments about what was going on.' He made an irritated noise. 'Can you imagine what something like *that* would be worth?'

Yeah. These people never think about the future.

'*We have company,*' said Belle. We hurried out to the bridge, but we couldn't see anything.

'*It appears to be a VTL.*'

'What's a VTL?' asked Alex.

'In the unofficial parlance,' I said, 'it's called a tracker. It's fully automated. They're usually used as probes.'

'Would it have been left by somebody?'

'Left or delivered.'

'Chase, I'm trying to ask whether it was capable of making the flight out here on its own.'

'Could it have followed us through a jump? No. No such technology exists. The experts say it can't be done.'

'Then either someone else *happened* to find this place, or—'

'—Someone knows about the *Seeker*. Belle, what's it doing?'

'*Approaching.*'

'ETA?'

'About eleven minutes. Coming at high velocity, by the way. It appears to be on a collision course.'

We looked at one another and I remembered the park-building nanos. 'Belle, start the engines. Alex, we have to assume it's hostile. We better get back to the ship before it gets here.'

He didn't need convincing. We moved quickly off the bridge and down through a half dozen passageways toward the airlock. While we scrambled as best we could through zero gravity, Belle gave me the bad news. 'It's hooked us.'

'What's she talking about?' asked Alex.

'It has a rider beam. It just latches on, and wherever *we* go, *it* will go. It gets a free ride and it can close on us at its leisure.'

'We'll have to jump clear.'

'Given eight hours, we could do that.'

We charged out through the airlock and onto the hull.

'It's probably a bomb,' he said.

'Maybe. But no need. All it would have to do is give us a good bump, and it'll be lights out.' We made the jump over to the *Belle-Marie*.

'ETA *just over eight minutes,*' said Belle.

'Let's see what we have,' I told her, scrambling onto the bridge and looking down.

The intruder was on the monitor. It was a small package, not much more than a set of linear engines and a drive unit with a few black boxes up front. But big enough to put us out of action.

'How fast is it coming?'

'*Eighteen hundred kilometers per hour.*'

'Yeah.' It was approaching the *Seeker* from directly forward.

'Chase,' said Alex, 'can't we use the HCS on it?'

The Hazard Control System was a particle-beam unit designed to take out rocks or ice that posed a danger. 'No,' I said. 'There's a safety feature to prevent its firing on ships and equipment.'

'Can't you override that?'

'If we had some time.'

'Then what do we do? You said we can't outrun it.'

251

'Watch and learn, boss. Watch and learn.' I took my seat, engaged the harness, and signaled for Alex to do the same. 'Belle,' I said, 'release the controls to me.'

Status lamps changed color. '*Done, Chase.*'

I moved the *Belle-Marie* forward, along the *Seeker*'s hull, in the direction of the approaching tracker.

'*Range two hundred ten klicks,*' said Belle.

A scarlet sunburst was emblazoned on the *Seeker*'s prow. I took station on a line between the intruder and the sunburst. 'These things are designed to chase asteroids,' I said. 'And comets. Space junk. They aren't made to contend with something that can move independently.'

'So we're going to—?'

'—Sit here and wait for it. When it rolls in, we'll step aside and it'll plow into the *Seeker*.'

'Isn't there a better way?'

'Be satisfied there *is* a way.'

He looked out at the ship. 'I hate to do any more damage.' His face grew hard. 'If I get hold of Bolton—'

'You think that's who it is?'

'Who else?'

'I guess. If he can get us out of the way, he could claim the *Seeker* and everything else for himself.'

'*Chase,*' said Belle. '*It's rotating. Looks like a three-sixty.*' I could see it on-screen. I watched it turn until its exhaust tubes were pointed in our direction. Then the engines fired.

'*Braking,*' Belle said.

'The thing's not as dumb as I'd hoped.'

'What do you mean, Chase?'

'It's recognized the danger. So it's slowing down.'

There was no place to hide.

Belle's status lamps flickered. '*What do you wish to do, Chase?*'

'I'm thinking about it.'

'*At current rate of deceleration, it will be moving at twenty kilometers per hour when it arrives.*'

'Give me the new ETA, Belle.'

'Ten minutes, forty-four seconds if current conditions hold.'

Well, at least we'd picked up some time. I fired the attitude thrusters and rotated the *Belle-Marie*. The tracker showed up in the viewport. Dead ahead. I pointed us at it, warned Alex we were moving out, and fired the main engines. We began to accelerate.

He wiped the back of his hand against his mouth. But he kept his peace.

I went to max sustainable thrust. We were both driven deep into our seats as the *Seeker* dropped behind.

'It has increased power to engines,' said Belle.

'It's gone to full braking,' I told Alex. 'It figures we're trying to get past it. It's trying to slow down enough so it can react.

'If we maintain present rate of acceleration,' Belle said, *'it will be moving at one point one kilometers per second when we reach it.'*

'I've a question,' said Alex.

'Go.'

'You're going to turn at the last minute, right? Slip by it on one side or the other?'

'Yes.'

'What happens if that thing turns the same way you do?'

'Odds are against. But that's the easy part. Alex, if it gets behind us, on our tail, it will make getting clear of it very difficult. I don't know that we can outrun it.'

'Okay.'

'So we have to take *it* out before it climbs up our rear end. I need you to do something.'

'Name it.'

'I'm going to shut down the engines in a moment. When I do, pick out one of the cases and load it with the heaviest artifacts we have.'

'Okay.'

It wasn't visible yet through the viewport. But the picture on the monitor was getting bigger.

'Belle,' I said, 'take the helm until I come back.'

'*I have it, Chase.*'

I released my harness and collected a tether and a pressure suit, which I took back to the common room, where Alex was shoving artifacts into a box.

'Here,' I said, 'I'll take over. You put this on.'

'Why?' he asked, puzzled. 'Am I going outside?'

'Talk later,' I said. I finished packing the case and secured it. Alex got into the suit, and I shortened the tether, cut it back to about a meter and a half, and connected it to his belt.

'*Six minutes,*' said Belle.

'Okay,' I told her. 'Kill the gravity.'

She shut it down and I picked up the case. 'Let's go.'

I opened the airlock and he went inside. I passed the case to him.

'What do you want me to do with this?'

'We're going to use it to save our necks.'

I closed the hatch, went back to my seat, and buckled in. There was a glow up ahead. '*That's it,*' said Belle. '*Engines are still firing.*'

'Okay.'

'*Five minutes.*'

'Alex, can you hear me?'

'*Loud and clear.*'

'Start depressurization.'

'*I already have.*'

'Good. Use the tether to secure yourself to one of the handgrips. We don't want you going out the door.'

'*Hang on a second.*'

I watched the glow getting brighter. 'Come on, Alex.'

'*How's this thing work?*'

'It's just a clip.'

'*I think it's defective.*'

'Just knot it if you have to.'

'*Four minutes.*'

254

'Okay, I got it.'

'Give it a good yank. Make sure it's secure.'

'It's fine.'

My instincts were all telling me to hit the brakes. 'All right. Air pressure will be zero in another minute.'

'Okay.'

'When it is, when the green light on the outer hatch comes on, open it.'

'All right. I know you're not about to tell me we're going to hit it with the artifacts.'

'How do you like breathing?'

'It's still on collision course, Chase,' said Belle.

'Didn't we have something else we could have thrown at it?'

'We could probably have used a sink if we'd had more time.'

'Two minutes.'

'Belle, power to the main engines. Let's be ready to move out.'

'Pressure's zero,' said Alex.

'It is still on collision course,' said Belle.

'One minute, twenty, Alex.' The tracker was still braking.

'Opening the outer hatch.'

The airlock was on the port side. 'When you push the case out, try to be gentle. Don't shove it.'

'Okay.'

'We want it, as much as possible, to continue ahead on our present vector.'

'Okay.'

'Just lay it out there. Let me know when it's done.'

'All right.'

'Ready?'

'Yes.'

'Do it.'

I heard him grumble. Then: 'Okay. It's gone.'

'Very good. Don't try to close the hatch. Just hang on. Turn in ten seconds.'

'Okay.'

'Nine, eight . . .'

The one serious risk was the one Alex had alluded to, that the tracker might guess what I was doing, or possibly even react quickly enough to change its course. But I doubted that was possible. More likely was that I'd cut it too close and would slam into the damned thing on my own.

'Four, three . . .'

Its engines were still firing, still trying to decelerate.

'. . . Two . . .'

I fired the port-side thrusters, turning hard to starboard. The tracker's starboard thrusters fired as it tried to match the move, but it was too late. We soared past, and the case of artifacts caught it right on the nose at a combined velocity close to two thousand kilometers per hour.

The sky lit up behind us. Alex complained that he couldn't believe he'd actually done that. Had to have been a better way. Now that there was time to think about it, I realized we might have filled the container with water. But I let it go.

We did a series of long- and short-range sweeps to assure ourselves nothing else was coming our way.

19

Orbits, vectors, and intersections. When you understand them rightly, all becomes clear.

—Korim Maas,
In the Lab, 1411

The next order of business was to clean the lenses. It was delicate work and I left it to Alex, who's the expert. When he was satisfied he'd done the best he could, we showed them to Belle. 'What do you think?' he asked her.

We watched lights playing through them. She commented that, considering their age, they were almost in decent condition.

'Can you reproduce the images?' asked Alex.

'I think so. Put one into the reader and let's see what we have.'

We retreated to the common room, and I loaded the first lens.

'That's good,' said Belle. Lights dimmed. We were looking at a field under a starlit sky. Dark trees crowded in on our left. In the foreground, two people stood by a gate in a wooden fence. A little girl, and a woman who seemed to be her mother. Beyond the gate were a lawn, a tree with a swing, and a house. Beyond the house lay a river.

Everything was somewhat blurred. *'Hang on,'* said Belle. *'I see the problem.*' The picture cleared, and the VR effect took hold. We were *standing* in the field. On the far side of the river, in the darkness, a ring of light glittered.

'A city, I think,' said Alex. 'Where are we, Belle? Can you tell? Is it Earth?'

'I don't know. It could be anywhere.'

The child was about nine. She wore a blue jumpsuit and a matching bow in her long auburn hair. She was looking directly at us, smiling, waving her hand. The mother's eyes were also fixed on us. She was dressed in khakis, her head canted, smiling self-consciously, patiently waiting for the picture-taking session to end.

I could feel rain coming. And the wind whispering in the trees. A yellow glow in a cloud-filled sky suggested the presence of a moon. The girl wanted to run toward us, to embrace us, but I suspected she'd been instructed to pose, and so she did.

'Okay?' Alex asked.

'Yeah,' I said. 'Next, Belle.'

Same two people. Standing on the front porch of the house. The house looked lived in. The front steps didn't fit quite right into the porch, and the post light leaned at an angle. The roof had some torn shingles, and one of several large windows needed its frame repaired. This wasn't the kind of place you used to impress friends. But there were lots of flowering bushes out front. And it looked comfortable.

The clouds had backed off a bit, and we could see the moon. It was full and bright, a fraction larger than Rimway's satellite. Light spilled through the windows. The woman was laughing now, more at ease, and seemed to be in the act of reaching down to catch the child in her arms. She was attractive. Her hair was like the child's, auburn tinged with red. She looked happy, a woman without a care in the world. She wore a white blouse and dark slacks. 'I wonder who they are,' Alex said.

I shrugged. 'Maybe she became the captain of the *Seeker*,' I said.

258

'She doesn't *look* like somebody who'd be piloting interstellars. She'll have her hands full with the little girl.'

'I was talking about the little girl,' I said.

It's not Earth,' said Belle.

The voice seemed to come out of a patch of trees. 'How do you know?' asked Alex.

'*It's not Earth's moon.*'

Three of the holograms were views of the river. It looked wide and tranquil. The woman appeared in one of them, standing beside a tree, gazing thoughtfully at the opposite bank.

Two were not recoverable. The other seven had been made in the vicinity of the house, including one with the mother and child standing in an open front door, providing our only real glimpse into the interior. I could make out an armchair and a table with a lamp on it. The girl appeared in each of the seven.

There were two chairs on the porch, and a table supporting a potted plant. Someone had draped a jacket on the back of one of the chairs. A toy wagon had been left out front on the lawn. And we saw the walkway that connected the house with the gate.

We went back to the river and looked more closely at the ring of light on the other side. 'Can we get closer?' I asked Belle.

She focused on the ring, then moved rapidly toward it. It expanded, broke into individual lights. The lights looked as if they might be traffic.

'Okay,' said Alex. 'Let's see the girl's jumpsuit again. Up close.' The child appeared front and center. Laughing. Pulling at the mother. The jumpsuit had a shoulder patch.

I recognized it. The suit and the patch. 'It's from the *Seeker*.'

'Made especially for kids,' he said. 'Probably a souvenir.' He looked up at the sky, but the stars were hidden. 'This is Margolia,' he said.

I'd gone to bed thinking how good it would be to get home again, and I was just drifting off to sleep when Alex knocked at the cabin door. I turned on a lamp, grabbed a robe, and told him to come in.

He was holding a cup of coffee. 'Sorry to bother you, Chase.'

'It's okay. What's wrong?'

'I just thought of something, and I wanted to run it by you.'

There was only one chair in the room, so I sat up on the bed and left it for him. 'Go ahead,' I said.

'We've been talking about a catastrophe of some kind. That's the only likely reason they'd have packed all those kids on the *Seeker*. It was a rescue effort.'

'Sure. Has to be. The colony ran into something. A virus. Famine. Maybe even aliens.'

'You're thinking small, Chase.'

'Small? Aliens show up and that's *small*?'

'We both know the planetary system here is screwed up, right? I mean, we've only been able to find three worlds, and one of them is in a lopsided orbit.'

'There's nothing unusual about that, Alex. There are lopsided systems everywhere.'

'But this is the one where we found the *Seeker*. That suggests at least the possibility of a connection.'

'Alex, what are we talking about?'

'Put the catastrophe on a planetary scale.'

'Oh.'

'Maybe something came through this system and either plowed into the colony world or ejected it.'

'Or knocked it into the sun. It's possible. But it seems pretty unlikely.' The chance of a collision was remote. But, if something had come this way—

His eyes looked distant. 'I think the odds are pretty good,' he said, 'that's *exactly* what happened. They arrived and set up on that pleasant world in the holograms. Built a city. Spread out a bit. Nice little places in the country with porches and swings. They were there long enough for the two ships to get old. The house we saw needed repair. Then they got an event.'

'Could be,' I said.

'Maybe a rogue world passing through. I don't know. I'm not a planetary scientist. We should have brought that friend of yours along.'

'Shara.'

'Yeah. Shara. She might have been able to give us a better idea.'

'It would explain everything. If they hadn't maintained the ships, or they'd simply gotten old—'

'—Neither was reliable. Neither could make it on its own. So they had to cannibalize one to give the other a chance. The plan would have been to send it to get help. Provided there was time. I mean, Earth was what, a year away? And another year back.'

'The fact that they loaded it up with kids suggests time was short,' I said.

'Or that they thought they'd solved the *Seeker's* problems.'

He took a deep breath. 'I'd like to know what actually happened.'

'If they got ejected from the system, we won't find them.'

'No, I don't suppose we would.' He tapped his fingertips on the navigation monitor. 'Why don't we run a test? See if we can confirm that this system was really home to the colony world.'

'What did you have in mind?'

'We look for the moon.'

'The moon?'

'Sure. Margolia had a moon. We have a picture of it.'

'Well, maybe we do. But even so, the moon would probably have gotten booted, too.'

'We don't know that. In any case, I don't see that it hurts to look.'

'Okay,' I said. 'If it's still in the system, it shouldn't be too hard to locate.' We knew what one side of it looked like. There was a lot of debris floating around, but not many spheres.

He went up to the bridge. I padded along behind him in bare feet, and we directed Belle to run through the images again.

The moon was actually visible in three of the holograms. She put them on display one by one. We had only the face of the satellite to work with, but it would be enough. We studied its details, craters here and here. Ridges over there and up toward the pole. Mountain range thus and so. 'Are we ready to do a sweep, Belle?' I asked.

'Say the word.'

We decided the moon would most likely be in a solar orbit and started our search accordingly.

We found four candidates the first day, but eliminated them quickly. Alex became engrossed in the effort. He talked with Belle incessantly, quizzing her about where we were looking, whether we were wasting time on one prospect or another, whether she was still following the search parameters that we'd set out for her.

She started getting irritable. By the beginning of the fourth day, when we were far from the sun and deep in the system with nothing resembling a moon anywhere on the scopes, she lost patience and told us she'd let us know when she had information of interest. *'In the meantime,'* she added, *'we need to be thorough. Even if this doesn't look like a promising area, we want to eliminate it so we don't have to come back here later when we start wondering if maybe we missed something.'*

He rolled his eyes. 'I'm annoying the computer,' he told me.

I'd done extended travel with Alex on numerous occasions, and if you're going on a long cruise, he's as good to have along as anybody. He can hold up his end of a conversation. He has a sense of humor. He's reasonably patient. And usually he knows when to be quiet. Nevertheless, when you put two people into a confined space over a long period of time, with no break, things do tend to get fractious. I've seen studies that indicate it's not so much being limited to seeing the same person day after day as it is the confinement within bulkheads. Put two people on a desert island, with sun, wind, and open sea, and you don't get the same effect at all.

262

So we made full use of the VR capabilities. We went to the theater, attended a concert, sat on the beach with hordes of other people, took our meals in virtual restaurants, went to sporting events and tried to scream along with the crowd. We played in a chess tournament in India, walked along the coast at Sea Gate, watched Parvis Kuney do his comedy act in the Royale, and wandered through the ancient Louvre.

The problem with all this is that it's *virtual*, and as the days pass, you become increasingly aware of that fact. There was nothing constructive to be done. Alex could spend time updating himself on the latest developments in the world of antiquities. I read mysteries. And after a while, it got old.

As any single female of the correct age will tell you, there's nothing quite like living with the possibility that on any given day you will meet The Guy. The one who sets your heart racing and whom you know from the beginning you will never forget. Well, okay. I've never seen one of those in the flesh, and there are moments when I doubt they really exist. But then an evening with the right sim, watching Choelo Tabor look into the soul of a Chase Kolpath avatar, watching the two of us fall desperately in love while the rain pours down on the cottage roof and the music swells and carries us away – Well, I can tell you that Choelo could have me anytime. But I knew that I wasn't going to see him, or anyone else for that matter, out here around Boopsilon Delta, or wherever the hell we were.

We were also beginning to use up our fuel. Short jumps are *short*, but we were doing a lot of them and they burn just as much fuel as the long-range insertions.

Eventually we transferred the search to the far side of the sun. By then, the plan was to take a quick look around, see if anything presented itself, then rethink our options.

Finally, on the ninth day, Belle announced she had spotted something.

'The moon?' I asked.

'*Not exactly,*' she said. Another oddly human trait: She loved being in charge of the moment and never hesitated to draw the situation out. *'How about that?'*

'What?' demanded Alex. 'What do you see?'

'Another high-albedo object.'

'Another tracker?' I held my breath.

'No. I don't think so.'

'Another *ship?*'

'Possibly.'

'The *Bremerhaven?*' I said.

'I cannot make that determination. Whatever it is, however, it's nearby.'

It *wasn't* the *Bremerhaven*. And it wasn't another visitor. It was a docking facility. It was about a kilometer long, with two enclosed bays for landers, a terminal, something that must have been a storage unit, and a collection of struts, crosspieces, and burst tanks. It was adrift, turning slowly, end over end, trailing spars and broken cables. The bays were open and empty.

We pulled alongside. Alex was already climbing into his suit. I asked whether we wanted to take a packing container with us.

'Let's just go look,' he said. 'See what we have.' He was still subdued.

I picked up a laser, and we made the crossing. There was a possibility the enclosed sections of the station were still holding air pressure, and that turned out to be the case. We went through one of the bays and had to cut our way through a bulkhead. There were no human remains this time. For which I was grateful.

We moved into a dark passageway, a bit more relaxed than we had been on the *Seeker*. But we didn't engage in our usual hunt for artifacts. To be honest, there wasn't much lying around.

Nor was there debris floating through the dark. We found an observatory, a maintenance station, and a galley. There were two boarding tubes. Both had been brought inside and retired to their cradles.

We went back out onto the dock, where, we assumed, the *Bremerhaven* and the *Seeker* had once tied up.

'How'd they do it?' asked Alex.

The ships would have dwarfed the station. We found tethers. They were thin, and it was hard to imagine either of the behemoths secured by them. 'The dock has magnetic skirts,' I said. 'They just locked it in and tied it down.'

'I'd have expected to find something broken,' he said.

'How do you mean?'

'Maybe I'm wrong. But I've assumed the *Bremerhaven* would not have been operational after they removed the parts we saw in the *Seeker*.'

'I don't really know for sure, but that's almost certainly right.'

'So what happened to it?'

I looked at the retracted tethers. Everything was in order. 'They released it,' I said.

'Why?'

'Maybe they didn't want the dock wrecked.'

'Chase, the dock got thrown a long way. You seriously think they didn't know that was going to happen?'

'I have no idea, Alex.'

He touched one of the tethers. It had lost its flexibility. 'Why bother releasing a ship that couldn't go anywhere?' he said.

'I don't know. Maybe they didn't want to have it come down on their heads during whatever it was that was happening. So they got rid of it.'

'Maybe.' He looked at me for a long minute, although I couldn't see his face inside the darkened helmet. 'It doesn't *feel* right.'

Belle called: '*We have a candidate for the moon.*'

As soon as we got within range, we saw that it was the satellite from the holograms. There was no mistaking the craters and the ridgeline and the mountain range.

Belle usually had a hard time understanding the vagaries of human behavior. She thought the discovery was reason to celebrate, so she showed up dressed in a black off-the-shoulder gown, looking like a model from *Sand and Sea*. She held both fists over her head while her bosom heaved, and she showered us with congratulations. But the mood on the ship remained gloomy.

Like the *Seeker*, and the dock, the former moon had gone into solar orbit.

'*Circumference at the equator is thirty-five hundred kilometers,*' Belle announced. Big for a moon, even by the standards of Rimway's oversized satellite. '*I do not detect any indication of catastrophic damage.*'

You've seen one moon, you've pretty much seen them all. This one was heavily cratered on one side, the side we'd seen in the hologram. The other was relatively smooth, the product of an ancient lava flow, I supposed. We went into orbit around it and began looking for anything that might tell us how it had gotten there.

Alex took pictures, and we mapped the object. We measured it and scanned it. We hoped to find signs that someone had walked on it. A base, a monument, a wrench dropped in the dust. Something. But if it was there, we didn't see it.

'*Orbital period approximately seven hundred thirty-five years. It is now inbound midway between aphelion and perihelion.*'

'We've got a dock and a moon,' I said. 'We might be able to use them to figure out where and when the event happened.'

He nodded. 'Do it.'

My chance to shine. 'Belle,' I said, 'track the orbits of the moon and the dock back nine thousand years. Do they at any time intersect?'

'*Working,*' said Belle.

'That's good, Chase,' said Alex. 'You may have a future as a mathematician.'

'That would be a step down,' I said.

Belle was back. '*No. They do not intersect. But there is a close approach.*'

'How close?'

'*They come within two point three million kilometers on March 3, 2745, in the terrestrial calendar.*'

'Fifty-five years after they'd first touched down,' said Alex.

'Let's see what it looks like, Belle. Show us the biozone, too.'

She dimmed the lights. Gave us the sun. Drew a wide circle around it to indicate the biozone. She added a bright yellow arc. '*This is the dock.*' And a second arc, passing well to one side of the dock. '*The moon.*' The approach took place on the inner edge of the biozone.

'Belle,' said Alex, 'show us where the terrestrial world was on that date.'

'*It's hard to be certain, because the planetary orbit might have been different prior to the event.*'

'It *would* have been different, Belle,' I told her.

'*Then what am I looking for?*' She sounded annoyed.

'Assume the terrestrial world originally had a standard orbit inside the biozone, near its inner edge. Where would it have been?'

'*One moment, please.*'

Nobody said anything.

A blinking marker appeared a hand's width away from the moon. Farther from the dock.

'Not exactly an intersection,' said Alex.

20

We will interrupt the ideological nonsense, whether it be political, religious, or social, that flows from generation to generation. We will begin anew, in a new place, with a new approach. We will learn from history, and we will discard the doctrines that have kept the human race anchored firmly to a cacophony of discord and confusion. We have always known the potential for greatness, because we have seen what can be done when individuals throw off the shackles of conformity. Now we will demonstrate what can happen when an entire society prizes, above all else, free minds.

—Harry Williams,
Remarks at the Freedom Day Celebration in Berlin,
March 3, 2684 C.E.

We were still orbiting the moon when Belle reported that she'd located the *Bremerhaven*. 'The final piece,' I said.

'We'll see.'

It was smaller, leaner, and longer than the *Seeker*. No blown engines this time. No sign of damage except dents where it had probably been struck by drifting rock and ice. It carried the same flag, and a more fluid style of lettering on the hull.

We saw no signs of human remains inside. There were some pieces that would have looked good on Rainbow's inventory, but Alex decided, without explaining why, that we would take nothing from the *Bremerhaven*. 'Leave it for Windy,' he said.

On the bridge, we opened the panels and looked at disconnected power lines. And at empty spaces once occupied by control boxes. Alex clomped around in his magnetic boots and poked his lamp into every open space. 'Chase,' he said at last, 'answer a question for me. After they transplanted the black boxes to the *Seeker*, would this thing have been capable of going anywhere? Under its own power?'

'I doubt it.'

'But you're not sure.'

'I'm not familiar enough with the ship. It's possible, for example, there's an auxiliary control center elsewhere on board.'

'All right,' he said. 'Is it possible for us to make a determination?'

I remembered a set of *Bremerhaven* power relays in the *Seeker*'s engine room. 'Let's go look at the drive units,' I said.

I've remarked elsewhere I don't know much about third-millennium technology. But you don't have to if you're just looking to see whether parts are missing and power cables are disconnected. I only needed a quick glance to know that the *Bremerhaven* wouldn't have gone anywhere on its own.

We removed nothing. Mostly we just made a visual record. Then we went back aboard the *Belle-Marie*, and poured ourselves some coffee.

Alex was adrift somewhere.

'What?' I asked, finally.

He took a long pull at his coffee. 'I think the jungle world is Margolia.'

'Even though the orbits didn't match up?'

'Yes. I don't know how, or why, but they're buried on that world somewhere.'

There was no indication there had ever been a settlement. But of course, give it a few thousand years, and the heavy vegetation we

270

were looking at would have buried Andiquar. We took the launch down and padded around a bit on the surface, looking for evidence. But there was nothing. Confirmation one way or the other would take specialized equipment.

'Chase?'

'Yes, Belle?' I was napping on the bridge while Alex looked over images from the surface.

'I've been examining the orbit of the Bremerhaven.*'*

'And—?'

'On March 3, 2745, it was thirty million kilometers away.'

'From this world?' asked Alex.

'Yes.'

We looked at each other. 'How do we explain that?'

'For now,' he said, 'let's just call it an anomaly.'

21

In the midst of celebration are we overtaken by calamity.
—Kory Tyler,
Musings, 1312

We slipped back into our home system at the end of a flight that people would probably be talking about a thousand years later. We'd found our Atlantis, but it had been a disappointment on a scale so vast that it weighed down every other consideration. Had we guaranteed ourselves a great bottom line? Absolutely. Were we going to be celebrities? I pictured myself being interviewed on every show from *Round Table* to *Jennifer in the Morning.* Money would pour in. And I was already thinking about a book. Still, we had hoped for an Atlantis that would be, despite all odds, up and running. Or at least, visible.

'What will you call it?' asked Alex, referring to the book.

'*Last Mission,*' I said.

He pressed his fingers against his temple and adopted the tone he might have used with a child. 'I hope you're not suggesting you're going to retire. And anyhow, titles shouldn't be about *you.*'

'It's *not* about me. I've no intention of retiring, Alex. It'll be about the *Seeker.* Trying to go for help, having a load of children

273

on board, and the engines go down. No rescue possible within light-years. Everybody on board dies, and Margolia loses its only hope. It's a tragic story.'

'Yes,' he said. 'It sounds like a downer. I think you need some daylight in there somewhere.' He was sitting in the common room, in front of a chess problem to which he paid no attention. When I asked how he planned to announce the discovery, he looked uncertain. 'I haven't decided,' he said. 'What do you think?'

'We could call a press conference, jointly with Windy.'

He picked up the black king, studied it, and put it back. 'I'm not anxious to do that. I don't want to stir up Kolchevsky and the other morons. Why don't we try to keep a low profile for now, and move our stuff as quietly as we can?'

'You know that's not going to work, Alex. Once it gets out that we found Margolia, every journalist in the world is going to be beating down our door. We need to know what we're going to say to them.'

We docked, made entry, and went in through the zero-gee deck because we had three containers filled with artifacts.

As we came out into the main concourse, a tall, young man was waiting for us. 'Charlie Everson,' he said. 'How was the trip, Mr Benedict?'

'Okay.' Alex looked in my direction. Did I recognize him? I'd never seen him before. He had black hair and a conservative bearing, but something about him reminded me of one of those guys who are always trying to impress you with their positions in the world.

'Windy sent me,' he said. 'She's anxious to know how things went.'

'Tell her,' said Alex, 'it was a productive operation. We'll get over to see her first thing tomorrow.'

'Good.' He seemed pleased. 'She'll be anxious to hear the details.' I expected him to press us, to ask whether we'd found what we were looking for, but he shoved his hands into his pockets and said she'd been talking about throwing a dinner in our honor. 'By the way,' he added, 'we've arranged your passage on the shuttle.' He had large brown eyes, and they focused on the containers. 'Compliments of Survey.'

'Well, that's good of you,' said Alex. 'Thanks.'

'It's our pleasure. Are those artifacts in the cases?'

'Yes,' Alex said.

'Wonderful.' He smiled again. Looked at me and looked away. This was a guy on the shy side, I decided. Someone who rarely had a good time. 'Congratulations, Mr Benedict.'

'Thank you.'

'I'll let Windy know. And I'll tell her to expect you tomorrow.' We all shook hands. 'It was good to meet you both.' He started away, paused, and turned back. 'Reservations are in your name, Mr Benedict. The shuttle leaves at six.'

Alex thanked him again, and he went on his way. Had other business to take care of, he said.

We stopped to arrange shipping for the containers. I was carrying a few of the more fragile artifacts in a box, which I intended to carry aboard the shuttle. At first they told us there was no room for more cargo, and they'd have to go down on a later vehicle. Alex showed them some money, and they found space.

We had almost an hour to spare when we left the kiosk. Alex was looking hesitant. 'What's wrong?' I asked.

'I'm hungry.'

There were plenty of snack shops. But Alex insisted we go to Karl's, with its candles, soft music, and sizzling Dellacondan chicken.

'We don't have time,' I said. It's true that an hour on Rimway is moderately longer than a terrestrial hour, but we'd still not come close to making the shuttle. At Karl's, you were expected to relax, enjoy the ambience, and let the food catch up to you, so to speak.

He frowned. 'There's another flight at nine.' He looked at me with those big eyes. Come on, Chase, we've been cooped up for weeks. Let's relax a bit. 'Why don't we just take it easy?' he said. 'Take advantage of the opportunity?' He was really asking whether I wanted a decent meal, or preferred the prepackaged stuff on the shuttle.

So he called the reservation desk to make the change, and we strolled up to B Deck, and poked our heads into a couple of the souvenir shops. I bought a shirt for a nephew, and Alex got some chocolate for the ride down. Then we wandered into Karl's.

Despite the mixed outcome of the mission, it was a night to celebrate. We got our table and sat down and I put the box and the souvenirs on the seat beside me and told Alex not to let me forget it. There was sultry music drifting from the piano at the far end of the dining room. We tossed off drinks and stared into each other's eyes like a couple of starstruck lovers. We told each other how good we were, and how the entire world was going to come to our doorstep to ask how we did it. We ordered seafood. White staple, supposedly from the Inland Sea. Whatever, I enjoyed every bite. It's funny, I can clearly remember the details of that meal, the way the salad looked, the dressing I used, the shape of the wineglasses, everything as if it happened yesterday. I can still see the chandelier, and the half-filled dining room. I can see Alex, swept away by the emotions of the evening, sitting at the apex of his career, simultaneously delighted and depressed. The plight of those people so long ago had gotten to him. Had I been behaving that way, he'd have told me to get my act together. Everybody dies eventually. It's ancient history.

Well, it *was* that.

I remember his joking about how there should be an antiquities dealers' hall of fame. About time they got the recognition that had long been withheld. And he took time to thank me for my contribution. I think by then he'd drunk a bit too much.

The piano player was real rather than virtual, a tall, serious-looking guy with a bristling mustache and gray eyes that didn't quite match the romantic music. I can still tell you what he played, and that he wore a red carnation and looked mournful. I remember thinking maybe it was a result of his wistful repertoire. 'Lost Without You.' 'Night with No Moon.' And 'Chandra.'

I'm not sure precisely when I became aware of a change in atmosphere. We'd gotten well past the meal and were simply sitting, drinking, and enjoying the evening. I was beginning to wonder if we'd make the nine o'clock flight. And gradually I noticed a change in the mood of the place. The spontaneity seemed to evaporate, and people were whispering and looking around and shaking their heads. Alex saw it, too. When our waiter came over to refill our glasses, Alex asked if something was going on.

'The shuttle,' he said. 'It blew up on the way down.'

I have to confess my first thought was not for the victims, but for us, how close Alex and I had come to being part of the disaster. Had it not been for his appetite, and his inclination to visit Karl's at every opportunity—

The victims. They'd been walking around the concourse a few hours ago brushing shoulders with us. And the guy with the shy demeanor. Charlie. Had he been aboard?

I don't recall that either of us ate or drank anything after that. The waiter had no details. I heard someone sobbing out in the concourse. I remember getting up from the table while Alex paid the bill. We wandered outside in a daze. 'These things happen,' I said.

He gave me a strange look and shook his head. I don't know how I got there, but I ended in his arms. 'It's okay,' he said.

I just hung on.

Alex shifted his weight.

'What?' I asked.

'The artifacts.' He called the shipping service. Yes, they were sorry, but the three containers *had* been on the six o'clock shuttle. '*But I see they're insured. No need to worry, Mr Benedict.*'

Insured for a nominal sum. Insuring them for their true value would have overwhelmed the shipping company and they'd have refused to accept the packages.

At that moment I remembered the box, the only remaining artifacts. Which I'd left at the table. I started back, only to see the host hurrying my way with the box and my purchases in his hands.

We tried to call Windy. Her AI informed us she was on another circuit, extremely busy, planning for a conference starting tomorrow.

I asked whether they knew about the shuttle.

'Yes,' he said. '*Dr Yashevik knows.*'

'I've a question,' said Alex. 'Is there a Charlie Everson on Windy's staff?'

'No,' said the AI. '*We do not have any such person on the rolls.*'

I broke the connection. He pulled me over to one side and looked anxiously at the crowd swirling around us.

'You think that was meant for us?' I asked.

'What do you think?'

'*No survivors,*' somebody was saying on a news spot. '*Names have not yet been released pending notification of next of kin.*' The reporter turned to another journalist. '*Bill, what do you have?*'

'*Lara, this is believed to be the first shuttle accident in more than a century. The last one occurred—*'

People were gathering to watch.

Alex called security. He gave them Charlie's description and told them he might be involved in what had happened to the shuttle. This was the guy I'd thought shy.

Two minutes later, a man and woman showed up and asked a lot of questions. After we'd given them what little we had, they looked skeptical. But they thanked us, assured us they'd make a full report, and asked us where we could be reached if additional questioning became necessary.

'Maybe they can get him before he gets away from the station,' I said.

'Let's hope.'

The media account continued: '—*Air and Space will be issuing a statement shortly*—'

A man standing beside us shushed his kids. A woman on the far side of the concourse collapsed.

'—*Twenty-two people, including the pilot*—'

I looked around, wondering if I might spot Charlie somewhere. Wondering if he might make a second attempt at us.

'—*Into the ocean. Rescue teams are just arriving on the scene*—'

Alex opened the box. Everything was accounted for. 'Try to hang on to it,' he said.

'—*They're telling us there was no hint of a problem, Lara. No distress call. Nothing like that. They just dropped off the scopes without warning*—'

The screen showed schematics of the L700, which was the shuttle model used at Skydeck. An analyst began explaining its safety features.

A pair of paramedics arrived to attend to the woman who'd collapsed. There were cries of *Look out* and *Give them room*. Then they carried her away.

'—*Tell us it's the safest shuttle in the fleet. It's been in service throughout the Confederacy for more than sixty years. And this is the first*—'

We disengaged from the crowd and found seats in one of the boarding areas. I think we were just beginning to grasp the reality of what had happened. Twenty-two dead. It would constitute one of the worst disasters of modern times. But I'm not sure that was what I was feeling. I pictured myself inside the cabin and suddenly blown into the sky.

'You okay?' Alex asked.

'Yeah.'

The security people came back and took us to a central location where we described Charlie again for an artist. 'Did you know,' Alex asked, 'there was a time they used surveillance cameras in places like this? Recorded everything.' In fact, he added, Rainbow had sold one of the devices to a collector years ago.

'Maybe we need to get them back,' I said.

By the time we were finished, we'd missed the nine o'clock shuttle, too. Assuming there'd been one.

22

Nothing quite shocks the system like murder. It reminds us that, even in this relatively enlightened time, there are still barbarians among us.

—Barringer Tate,
Civilized to a Fault, 1418

By morning they had the names of the passengers. I was not surprised to see there was no Charlie Everson among them.

'*He wasn't one of our people,*' Windy told me, speaking over the circuit. '*I didn't even know you guys were back until your call came in.*'

'We got in yesterday.'

'*Thank heaven you weren't on it. You really think this was an effort to kill you and Alex?*'

'It's the third attempt.'

'*My God, what's going on?*'

'Alex thinks somebody was hoping to put us out of the picture and claim the *Seeker.*'

She brightened considerably. '*You found it?*'

'Yes.'

'Tell me about it. What kind of condition is it in? Where is it? Did you find Margolia?'

I paused briefly for effect. 'We orbited the place.'

She caught her breath. *'Really? You wouldn't kid me.'*

'No, Windy,' I said. 'We were there.'

She clapped her hands, screamed 'Yes!' and came out of her chair with such force I thought she was going to charge physically into my office. *'Marvelous!'*

'It's a jungle now. Nothing left.'

'It's okay! But you found it? Wonderful! Are you sure? How do you know if there's nothing left?'

I needed several minutes to explain. Then another few minutes elapsed while we talked about the effect it would have on the archeological community. After she'd settled into a radiant glow, she switched back to the shuttle. *'What did Charlie look like?'*

I described him.

She shook her head. *'Rings no bells.'*

'I assume it's safe to say you don't know anything about a tracker either, right?'

'No. What tracker?'

'Somebody tried to play bumper cars with us.'

'This is crazy,' she said.

'Right. We think the danger's past now that we've filed the claim.'

'Be careful anyhow. When did you file?'

'First thing this morning.'

'You included us?'

'Wouldn't have it any other way.'

'Thank you.'

'You're welcome. We need two thing .'

'I'm listening.'

'We'd like to have an announcement made right away. With a big enough splash so we can be sure these lunatics know it's gone public. Just in case they're not following developments at the Bureau of Records. We want them to know Margolia is off the table.'

282

'Okay. I'll set one up for tomorrow morning. What else can I do for you?'

'I assume Survey will be sending a mission?'

'Of course.'

'Okay. You'll want to get moving on it. These people, whoever they are, have a head start. They could do a fair amount of looting before anyone gets there.'

As soon as I'd finished talking to Windy, I called Shara. 'I heard what happened,' she said. 'I'm glad you guys missed the flight.'

'There's more to it than that, Shara. Somebody tried to take us during the mission.' I explained about the tracker.

'How could that happen?' she asked. 'Who knew where you were going?'

I hesitated. 'Nobody except you.'

She covered her mouth with a hand. 'Hey,' she said. 'I didn't tell anybody.'

'That's what I wanted to ask. No one came around, asking questions?'

'No. Not a soul.'

'Would anybody have had access to the information you gave us?'

She took a deep breath. 'The staff.'

'What staff? Who, specifically?'

'Chase, anybody who works for Survey's administrative staff could have pulled it up.'

'Shara—'

'I used my office to run the program. That made it accessible.'

'To the whole world.'

'I'm sorry, Chase. You didn't say anything about a need for secrecy.'

'I thought it was obvious.'

'It wasn't. I'm sorry.'

'Okay. At least we know what happened.'

'If I'd realized, I could have put a security code on it.'

'It's okay,' I said.

'I didn't know—'

Fenn called us and that afternoon we got interviewed by two more investigators. We went over everything we'd told the first team, then went over it again. They asked who would want us dead and looked skeptical when we told them we didn't know. 'Not that I don't have enemies,' said Alex. 'Can't avoid it in my business. But I don't know of anyone who'd qualify as a homicidal maniac.'

'And you think they were after this *Margolia?*'

'Yes.'

'Sounds like the biggest claim jump of all time.'

They were male and female, very serious, thank you ma'am, are you absolutely certain? The male was short and dumpy, the female tall and trim. The male seemed to be in charge.

They called up images of every Charlie Everson on the planet. None of them was the guy. Then they showed us through a rogues' gallery. Nobody there, either.

'Was it a bomb?' I asked.

The woman nodded. 'Yes.' Her voice showed strain. Subdued rage, maybe. 'Hard to believe,' she added after a pause, 'anyone would put a *bomb* into a vehicle loaded with people. I don't know what we're coming to.'

'They've implemented all kinds of security measures,' said the male.

Alex asked whether the police had any idea who might have done it.

They replied they weren't in a position to comment.

They advised us to be careful and call if we saw anything suspicious. 'Don't assume you're safe,' the woman said, 'simply because you've filed a claim. It would probably be best if you didn't travel together. Until we sort this out.'

Nobody was much interested in archeological discoveries when the breakup of the shuttle was dominating the news. Windy tried anyway. She arranged the press conference for next day as she said she would, and Alex made the official announcement. He stood in front of a crowd of about fifteen writers and journalists – normally, for an event like this, there would have been close to a hundred – and told them Margolia had been found.

The immediate reaction was laughter and snorting. Surely he was speaking metaphorically.

No. 'It's actually there. We've been there.'

'Are they alive?' someone asked, to more laughter.

'No. It's a long time dead. It's jungle now.'

'Are you sure?' They started to calm down. 'You've got the right place, I mean?'

'Yes,' said Alex. 'There seems to be no question.'

He went on to describe what we'd seen, and what we surmised about how it had happened. Probably a passing star.

The writers kept him busy more than an hour. How long had the colony lasted before the catastrophe? How had he felt when he went inside the *Seeker*? How do you spell that? What did we estimate the population of Margolia had been when it was destroyed? Were we going back? What had led us there?

He was ready for that last one.

'I have to confess that Chase and I were not the persons really responsible for the discovery. Adam and Margaret Wescott found the *Seeker* almost forty years ago. It was a Survey mission, and when they returned they were still trying to figure out the significance of what they'd seen when both were killed in an earthquake.'

There was a flurry of questions at this point, but Alex overrode them. 'Fortunately, they'd brought back a cup from the *Seeker*, and that eventually led the way for us.'

When he described what we'd found on the derelict, the room became briefly quiet.

He never mentioned the three containers of priceless artifacts that had survived in the Tinicum region nine thousand years, only to get blown apart on the shuttle.

*   *   *

We weren't even out of the building before we'd heard that Casmir Kolchevsky had issued a statement describing our activities as 'desecration.' He was appalled, and suggested it was time some serious legislation was put on the books to 'stop the thieves and vandals who make a living looting the past.'

We got a call on the way back to the office from Jennifer Cabot, the host of *Jennifer in the Morning*. '*Alex*,' she said, '*I just wanted to alert you that Casmir will be on tomorrow. He'll be talking about Margolia. I thought you might like a chance to respond*.' Casmir. Her buddy, in case there was any doubt whose side she was on.

We'd just left the traffic stream and were heading in over the newly developed homes and malls that now covered what used to be old forest west of Andiquar. Alex made the kind of face he does when flying insects have gotten into the house. 'What time do you need me?' he asked.

When we got back to the office, I wondered whether he'd want me to help him prepare for his debate. 'It's okay,' he said. 'I'll be fine. Take the rest of the day off. You've earned it.'

It sounded like a good idea, but there was too much to do. We were in the center of the day's news, and calls were coming in from clients all over the world, each of whom seemed to think we had a pile of artifacts to make available. In fact, we had five, three cups, a plate, and the Abudai plaque.

We also had received more than twenty requests for interviews with Alex. This was an opportunity unlikely to come again, so I wanted to take advantage of it.

That evening, I set aside a few minutes to talk to Harry and update him on what was happening. You're supposed to do that with avatars, so they can be more responsive to the next person who needs them. But generally people don't bother much.

Usually, I wouldn't have gone to the trouble myself. But I couldn't *not* do it.

I told him a fresh expedition was going out.

'*Chase*,' he said, '*do me a favor*.'

286

'Sure.'

'If anybody is able to figure out what happened to Samantha and my kids, let me know.'

Okay. It's silly. I knew he couldn't remember them, had never known them, didn't even know what they looked like. It was strictly his software functioning.

And maybe mine. I decided to see what I could find out.

I called Shepard Marquard at Barcross's department of terrestrial antiquity. 'I want to talk about Harry Williams, Shep.'

'Okay,' he said. *'Congratulations on what you did. I saw the press conference. You guys are something else.'*

'Thanks.'

'Wish I'd been with you. That's some score.' He cleared his throat. *'Information about Williams is fairly sparse. What did you need?'*

'His family. How much is known about his family?'

'Did he have a family?'

'Wife. Two kids. Boys.'

'Okay.' He glanced down at something off to his right. *'I'm looking now.'* He frowned, shook his head a few times, stared hard, laid his index finger against his lips, and finally looked up. *'Wife's name was Samantha,'* he said. *'And yes, there were two sons.'*

'Harry Jr. And—'

'Thomas. Thomas was the younger. About five when they left.'

'What else do you have?'

'That's it.'

'Can we check off-line?'

'Can you make yourself available for dinner? I'll be in town tomorrow. As it happens.'

'Of course, Shep,' I said. 'That would be nice.'

'I'll get back to you.'

23

. . . Granted in recognition of exemplary achievement in the service of mankind . . .

—From the inscription on Survey's
Person of the Year Award

Shep showed up at Rainbow looking handsome and very much the man of the evening. He brought a data chip and a couple of books. 'I have some information on Samantha,' he said. 'I also thought you'd enjoy watching the departure of the *Seeker*.'

'You have *that*?' I asked, delighted.

He held the chip in his palm. 'Hologram record,' he said. 'Reconstructed. From December 27, 2688.'

I was anxious to see it, but he shook his head. 'Dinner first,' he said.

'Why can't we take a quick look now?'

'Because this way you have to invite me up.'

'Shep,' I said, 'the facilities are better at the office.'

He grinned. It was a splendid, clean, hold-nothing-back smile. 'I doubt it,' he said.

So we ate at the Porch Light, and I took him back to my apartment.

* * *

We watched colonists trek through the narrow concourses of an antiquated space station. The *Seeker* had been too big to dock, so passengers were taken to it twenty at a time by shuttle. According to the narrator, it had required almost a week to lift nine hundred people into orbit and transfer them to the ship. They were all ages, not just young, as I'd expected. And there were lots of kids. Some trailed balloons and chased each other around; others were in tears. Reluctant to leave home, I guess.

A reporter conducted interviews. Everything had been translated into standard. They were headed for a new frontier, they were saying, and life was going to be better. I was surprised to hear that they expected relations between the colony and the home world eventually to be established. '*After we get things up and running.*' *Up and running* seemed to be the catchphrase.

I'd had the impression the colonists had all been well-off. That they were a moneyed class. But the people in the visual record looked ordinary.

There didn't seem to be any well-wishers present to see them off. I assumed that melancholy fact rose from the cost of riding up to the station, which must have been considerably more expensive than it is today. Good-byes would have been said on the ground. Still, there was something lonely and dispiriting in that final departure.

A white placard had been left on a seat. I couldn't read the ancient inscription, but the translator gave it to me: *Margolia or Bosom.*

It made no sense. Still doesn't.

The last few filed up a narrow ramp and boarded the shuttle. The hatches closed, and the shuttle slipped away, while a correspondent talked about new pioneers.

Then we were standing in a room with a fireplace where several people discussed 'the significance of it all.' The significance of it all seemed mostly to be gloom and doom. The colonists were malcontents. Their good sense was questionable, as were their patriotism, their motives, and even their morals. They were putting loved ones in danger. Failing to support a government to which all owed gratitude and allegiance. *'It's the kids I feel sorry for.'*

After a few minutes we were back on the space station, looking out a wall-sized viewport at the *Seeker*. It was tethered fore and aft to supply units. Fuel and electrical cables had been run out to it. The shuttle was pulling away from its airlock, starting back.

The correspondent returned: *'So the largest single group of off-world colonists ever to leave us at one time is embarked and ready to go. And this is only part of the first wave. The* Bremerhaven *will be leaving for the same destination, wherever that might be, at the end of next month.'*

Tethers and cables were being cast off. Auxiliary thrusters fired, and the giant ship began to move away.

'In four days,' the voice-over continued, *'the* Seeker *will enter the mysterious realm we call hyperspace. And ten months from now, God willing, they'll arrive at their new home. And in two years, the* Seeker *is scheduled to be back to pick up another contingent.'*

The correspondent was standing in the space station. He was gray, intense, pretentious, melodramatic. Behind him, the concourse was empty. *'Chairman Hoskin issued a statement this morning,'* he said, *'expressing his hope that the people departing today will find God's blessing in their enterprise. He has offered to send assistance, should the colonists request it. Although he admits the distances involved would present problems. Other sources within the administration, who declined to be named, commented that the Republic is better off without the travelers, that, and I'm quoting here, "these were people who would never have been satisfied until they were able to impose their godless ideology on the rest of us."*

'Tonight at nine, Howard Petrovna will be a guest on the Lucia Brent Show *to discuss whether the colonists will be able to make it on their own.'*

I could still see the *Seeker* through the viewport. It was turning away. Moving into the night.

'*Back to you, Sabrina,*' the correspondent said. '*This is Ernst Meindorf at the* Seeker *launch.*'

One of the books was a hostile biography of a singer named Amelia who was apparently well-known at the time of the departure. She threw in her lot with the Margolians and left with the first wave, had been among the people I'd been watching. She abandoned a lucrative career and apparently became a legend for doing so. But for years afterward, there were sightings of her around the world, as though she'd never gone.

Her biographer discounted that possibility, of course, and portrayed her as a darling of those persons who thought society had become repressive. 'The government provides everyone with comfortable circumstances and a decent income,' she is quoted as saying. 'And we have consequently abandoned ourselves to its dictates. We don't *live* anymore; we simply exist. We enjoy the entertainments, we pretend we are happy, and we take our satisfaction from our piety and our moral superiority over the rest of the world.' But, argues the biographer, instead of righting the good fight, she abandoned the cause and fled into the outer darkness 'with Harry Williams and his ilk.' It was cowardly, he argues, but it was understandable. I wondered how anxious *he* would have been to stand against Chairman Hoskin.

'Unlikely,' said Shep. 'People used to disappear. Sometimes, when you came back, you were somebody else. Sometimes you didn't come back. You raised a fuss, you took your chances.'

The singer had been taken into custody on several occasions, usually for something called 'inciting to dissatisfaction.' The author, who lived a hundred years later in better times, comments that she would have been subjected to personality reorganization 'to make her happier,' except that she was too well known, and there would have been a political price.

The account ends with Amelia's departure on the *Seeker*.

The other book was *The Great Emigration*, written early in the Fourth Millennium. It covered the movement over three centuries of disaffected groups to off-world sites. The author explained the motivation for each group, provided portraits of its leaders and histories of the resultant colonies, all of which eventually failed.

Several of the emigrations were larger than the Margolian effort, although they tended to be spread over longer periods of time. The factor that made the Margolians unique was their secrecy, their determination not to be ruled from, or even influenced by, terrestrial political forces.

The book had a picture of Samantha and Harry. She was on horseback while Harry, holding the reins, stood gazing up at her. The caption read: *Cult leader Harry Williams with girlfriend Samantha Alvarez at her parents' farm near Wilmington, Delaware. June 2679.* Nine years before the departure of the first wave. She was about twenty, laughing, standing on the stirrups. She was considerably smaller than Harry, with long auburn hair cut well below her shoulders. And not bad to look at. She could have had her pick of guys down at the club.

There wasn't much else, about her, or the Margolians. The book was sympathetic to government efforts to placate the people the author consistently referred to as disgruntled. There had been concern, he said, at the highest levels of government for the colonists, who would be 'far from home,' 'determined to proceed on their own,' and 'in the hands of well-meaning but irresponsible leaders.'

There had been 'government efforts to placate' the Margolians, he said, although these seemed to consist mostly of promises not to prosecute. The offenses that were laid at the door of Williams and his associates consisted generally of charges like 'disruption of the common welfare.' He'd been imprisoned twice.

'I couldn't find anything about the sons,' he said.

'Okay. At least we have a picture now to go with Samantha's name.'

'She was lovely.'

'Yes.'

'Like you, Chase.'

One of the problems guys always have in a strange apartment is that they don't know how to turn down the lights.

I showed him.

Alex and I met Windy, at her invitation and Survey's expense, next evening at Parkwood's, which is located at a posh country club on the river. I never really felt at home in these places. They're too formal and too proprietary. You always get the sense that people are too busy being impressed (and trying to *be* impressive) to enjoy themselves.

True to form, Windy had gotten there first. 'Good to see you guys,' she said, as we rolled in. 'I have to tell you that the people at Survey are absolutely knocked out by your work, Alex.'

'Thank you,' he said.

'I have some news for you.' He leaned forward. 'You're going to be named Survey's Person of the Year. At our annual ceremony.'

Alex beamed. 'Thank you for letting me know.'

'There'll be a gala. On the eleventh. Can you make it?'

'Sure. Wouldn't miss it.'

'Good. And of course I need not remind you that this is strictly not for publication. We'll make an announcement later this week.'

'Of course.'

The drinks came, and we toasted the Person of the Year. The table was relatively quiet, considering the things that had been happening. Maybe the news that Margolia was nothing but a jungle had dampened Windy's spirits. Or maybe she was planning to use the evening to negotiate Survey's rights to the find. We were still waiting for our food to arrive when the operations chief wandered in and pretended to be surprised we were there. 'Great show,' he told us. 'Magnificent job, Alex.' He was a little man who waved his arms a lot. 'When you go back,' he said, 'I'd like very much to go with you.'

I looked at Alex. Had he told someone he was going back? He read my expression and signaled *no*.

And then came Jean Webber, from the board of directors. 'They'll be putting your statue up in the Rock Garden,' she said. 'The way things are going, you'll be here to see it.'

The Rock Garden was Survey's Hall of Fame. Plaques and likenesses of the great explorers were installed there, among flowering trees and whispering fountains. But the honor had always been posthumous.

Alex liked to play the role of a man unaffected by external honors. The only thing that was important to him, he liked to say, was knowing he'd accomplished something worthwhile. But it wasn't true, of course. He liked accolades as much as the next guy. When the plaudits had poured in for his work during the Christopher Sim affair, he'd been delighted. Just as he was hurt by the reaction of some who claimed he had done more harm than good and should have left things alone.

I had no trouble picturing Alex, with his collar pulled up to hide his identity, slipping into the grotto at night to admire his statue, while claiming by day that it was all nonsense.

They brought our food, fish for him and Windy, fruit dish for me. The wine flowed, and I began to wonder if Windy was trying to lower our resistance. The evening began to take on a pleasant buzz.

Until Louis Ponzio wandered in. He was Survey's director, and a man whom Alex found hard to stomach. Alex was usually pretty good at masking his reactions, favorable and unfavorable, to other people. But he seemed to struggle with Ponzio, who was a self-important, squeaky, artificially cheerful type. The kind of guy, Alex once said, who, when he was in school, was probably routinely attacked by the other kids. But Ponzio never seemed to notice.

'Well done, Alex,' he said, clapping a hand on his shoulder. 'You really put on a show this time.'

'Thank you. We seem to have been very fortunate.'

Ponzio looked at me, tried to remember my name, gave up, and turned to Windy. She took her cue. 'Dr Ponzio,' she said, 'you remember Chase Kolpath. Alex's associate.'

'Of course,' he said. 'Who could forget one so lovely?'

Who, indeed?

He didn't stay. We hadn't yet worked out all the details of the rights transfer for the *Seeker* and for Margolia. And I suppose he was smart enough to realize that Survey had its best shot at an outright grant by his staying clear and letting Windy handle things.

He would have been right. During the course of the evening, Windy negotiated access and salvage rights to the *Seeker* and to Margolia. Alex retained the right to make a return voyage and bring back more artifacts, although he accepted limits.

Windy made notes, drank her wine, and put away the fish, pretty much in tandem. And she did it with a flourish. 'Very good,' she said, as we finished. 'One more thing: We're going to mount an expedition posthaste. We'll want you to sit down with the people running the mission and give them all the help you can.'

'Sure,' said Alex, 'I'll be happy to.'

'And, Alex—?'

'Yes.'

'I know this hasn't entirely turned out the way you would have preferred. But there's a bigger payoff. This is a monumental find. Whatever happens from here on, you're up there with Schliemann and Matsui and McMillan.'

24

The sciences have always missed the point. Theirs is a dream world filled with quantum fluctuations, rubber dimensions, and people who cannot decide whether they are dead or alive. Perception is the only reality.

—Leona Brachtberg,
Last Woman Standing, 1400

For almost two days Alex was the toast of Andiquar. He appeared on *Jennifer in the Morning* and *The Daytime Show* and *Joe Leonard & Co.* Academic heavyweights showed up everywhere to pay him compliments and explain to the public the significance of the discovery. Alex confronted Kolchevsky on *Jennifer* and later on *The Dumas Report*, pointing out the contributions he'd made over the years, while Kolchevsky called him a tomb robber.

On the second night, somebody on the south coast was charged with murdering his wife and throwing the body off a small boat, and the Margolia story was driven out of the headlines.

Alex enjoyed playing the conquering hero and was even willing to show generosity to Kolchevsky. 'He stands up for what he believes in,' he told me. 'It's hard to take issue with that.' He even sent a message to him, congratulating him on his performance. He insisted, with a straight face, that he was not rubbing it in.

There was only one uncomfortable moment, which occurred when Ollie Bolton came to our defense.

Speaking on *The Data Drill*, he announced that he was proud to be a colleague of Alex Benedict. *'Alex and I are close friends,'* he said. *'I know him well, and he has always been a credit to the community. If he has perpetrated an outrage, then so have I. If he has gone beyond what is permitted by law, and by a decent regard for the opinions of mankind, then I have gone even further.'*

'Sanctimonious creep,' said Alex.

'Alex Benedict is right,' Ollie continued. *'If it weren't for people like him, many of these remnants of our past would remain adrift for ages. Might, in fact, never be found at all.'*

On the day that the South Coast Murder, as it came to be called, took over the media, the weather finally turned, and spring showed up. Birds were warbling, everything was in bloom, and a fragrant breeze was moving the curtains.

Windy called Alex to add her voice to the compliments pouring in. *'You almost had me convinced that we need more antiquities dealers,'* she said. *'So you can take it as an honest, but reluctant, appraisal.'*

'Thanks.'

'Something else I've been wanting to mention. There's talk in the office of bringing you on as a consultant. Would you be interested?'

He thought about it. 'Windy,' he said finally, 'you know you can ask me anything at any time, and I'll do what I can. But I don't think I'd want to enter into a formal contract.'

Her expression registered disappointment. *'There's nothing I can do to persuade you?'*

'No. I'm sorry. But thanks.'

'That's pretty much what I thought you'd say. But hear me out. We'll take you both on. The compensation would be steady, wouldn't take much of your time, and you'd have the sense of satisfaction

that comes with knowing you're making a serious contribution. And we'd approve your sales. That would give you cover.'

'And give Survey control of the business.'

'Alex, it would work well for everyone.'

'I appreciate the offer,' he said.

Bolton also called. *'I've been meaning to get to you,'* he said. *'What a magnificent coup. Margolia. How can any of us ever top this?'* He looked genuinely pleased and not at all envious.

'Thank you, Ollie,' Alex said, his voice neutral.

'I wish I'd been with you.'

Alex wasn't entirely able to hide his contempt. 'Or maybe even a bit ahead of us.'

'Oh, yes. I won't deny that. Anyhow, I've ordered a case of the best Kornot wine sent over. Please accept it with my congratulations.'

'You know,' Alex said, when the line was cleared, 'I listen to him, and I think maybe Windy is right. Maybe we *are* all thieves.'

'Well, Alex, we can be pretty sure *he* is.'

'Yeah.' He tapped his fingers on the arm of his chair. 'You know, maybe it's time Dr Bolton paid a price for Gideon V.'

Three days later I was at Windy's office with a packet of documents. 'Do you know what the Blackmoor Medallions are?'

'Of course.' She took a deep breath. 'You don't mean to tell me he's found *them* now?'

'No,' I said. 'But we'd like Ollie Bolton to think so.' I laid the papers on her desk. The top one stipulated that Alex believed the Medallions were located on a three-centuries-old imperial warship, the *Baluster.*

She registered doubt at first, then began to smile. 'Which is where?'

'In orbit around the supergiant star Palea Bengatta. The ship was damaged in the fighting, and they just left it there. What we'd like you to do is pass this up the line to the director's office.

The woman you suspect of giving out information is still there, right?'

'Yes. We haven't said anything to her.'

'Good. Please keep it that way. For a while.'

She looked at the report. 'Palea Bengatta? Where's that located?'

'It's on the far side of the Confederacy. In the direction of the Perseus Arm.'

'Okay.'

'It's just a derelict. There are several of them out there. Left over from the Morindan civil wars.'

'So what's the point?'

'The *Baluster* was a *battle cruiser*. A search will take months. Maybe years.'

'Have you explained how the Medallions got there?'

'It's all in the footnotes,' I said. 'Madness in high places.'

'And you think Bolton will buy it?'

'We think he'll find it irresistible.'

Alex had included legitimate (where it could be found) and bogus documentation: the nature of the damage, copies of fleet memoranda, pieces of personal correspondence. 'There was, in fact, a story that a member of the administration escaped on a warship with the Medallions, when things started to come apart.' I shrugged. 'Who knows what the truth is?'

'You two are something else, you know that?'

There was also an account of Rainbow's own plans to make the flight. *Leaving in five weeks. As soon as we can get things together.* Sources were named, and it all looked very official.

'I'll take care of it,' she said.

'Thanks.'

'It's okay. It's nice to see a little poetic justice. I hope it works. By the way, our Margolia mission will be leaving in a week. We'd like to have you and Alex come by for the farewell ceremonies.'

'Absolutely,' I said.

'And maybe we could have Alex say a few words.'

* * *

The event was conducted at the newly erected Pierson Hall in the Survey complex. Ponzio was there, of course, and a clutch of politicians. And the exploration team. There were about a dozen of them, and they'd be riding in two ships. VR representations of the ships themselves, the *Exeter* and the *Gonzalez*, floated on either side of the room. I'd once piloted the *Exeter*, which had since been specially modified with state-of-the-art sensors. The *Gonzalez* was loaded with excavation equipment.

Alex wore his best for the occasion: navy jacket, white collar, silver links. Windy introduced us around. 'You wouldn't believe how things have been going here,' she said. 'It's been a circus.'

The hosts passed out snacks and drinks, and as soon as all the scientific people were present, we were moved into a conference room. A man who seemed to be in charge took the podium, everyone quieted, and he introduced Alex, 'the gentleman who made the discovery.'

Alex got an enthusiastic round of applause, pointed to me, and said how he couldn't have done it and so forth. The audience swung around in their seats, I got up, and they clapped heartily. He described how the mission had gone, outlined aspects of the discoveries they might want to pay particular attention to (like finding the ground station at Margolia, which very likely had been located along the equator), showed some pictures, and asked for questions. The first one was a navigational issue, which he passed to me.

When they finished, he wished them luck and sat down. The guy in charge returned to the lectern. He made a few brief comments, thanked everyone for coming, and adjourned the meeting. I learned later he was Emil Brankov, the senior scientist and team leader.

As we headed back toward the main room, Alex told me he wanted to find out when the *Seeker* blew up. 'I'd like to know if it matches 2745.'

'When the orbits came closest to each other.'

'Yes. Do you think it would be hard to determine? When the engines went?'

'If they've got somebody along who's familiar with the way they built ships during that period, they ought to be able to do something. Ships have all kinds of clocks and timers. Probably did even in those days. It's just a matter of figuring out when the engines shut down.' I was becoming aware one of the younger team members had been watching me with interest. 'Why do we care?' I asked.

'I don't know. Maybe I'm still on a fishing expedition.' A strange look came into his eyes. 'I don't know what it is. There's something that doesn't feel right. And I think we owe them that much. To get at the truth.'

'Alex, all this is thousands of years ago.'

We found out the mission was carrying an expert on early FTL technology. His name was Spike Numitsu. He was an older guy, white hair, long nose, sparkling sea-blue eyes. Alex cornered him and asked whether he could work out the date of destruction.

'Possibly,' he said. 'I'll keep you informed.'

'I can't see it could make any difference,' I said.

'I know.' His eyes were focused somewhere in the distance. 'But I'd like to know why the *Bremerhaven* was released from its tether. And why its orbit doesn't match up.'

25

The would-be murderer was especially pernicious, having planned to do the deed before the victim had finished dinner.
—*Barrington's Ethics,*
third edition, 1411

Survey's field mission got off on time, and a few days later we were receiving reports from both ships. Spike and his team seemed less rattled than Alex and I had been. They talked about the presence of mummified remains as if they were simply one more result to be noted and filed.

Meantime, the *Gonzalez* went into orbit around the jungle world, completed a survey, and announced that the scanners had located ruins. Everything was buried beneath the jungle, but it was there. It was confirmed: We had found Margolia. That night, we called in friends and celebrated till dawn.

Windy informed us that the Medallion Report, as she called it, had been forwarded to the director. (He was, of course, in on the plot.) The suspect staff member had handled it, so now it was just a matter of sitting back and waiting for Ollie Bolton to pack his bags and take off for the far side of the Confederacy.

Meantime, there were no more attempts on our lives.

Alex, pleading he was exhausted, decided on a vacation and headed for the Guajalla Islands. 'Hold the fort,' he said. 'And don't call me.'

Which is how it happened that I was alone in the building when Bolton called. I almost told him I was disappointed to hear he was still in town. *'I need to speak with Alex,'* he said. There had always been an aura of both sincerity and vulnerability about him. I had to work to dislike the guy.

'He's not here, Dr Bolton,' I said.

He was seated behind a desk, collar open, looking tired. Looking disappointed. *'Chase, don't get formal with me. Where is he?'*

'He's on vacation.'

'Where?'

'He left instructions not to divulge the information.'

'Can you reach him?'

'No.'

He let me see he knew I was lying. *'When do you expect him back? Do you think you can tell me that much?'*

'In a week.'

'Chase—'

'Did you want to leave him a message, Doctor?'

'I guess the two of you left one for me.' He picked up a sheet of paper, studied it, dropped it back on the desktop.

'I'm sorry, but I'm not following you.'

'Palea Bengatta.'

'Oh.'

'I guess the secret's out.'

'What secret's that?'

'I'm not going to apologize.'

'I didn't expect you to.'

'It's competition. All's fair.'

'Sure it is. Was it you who destroyed the shuttle?'

He looked genuinely shocked. *'Was that aimed at you?'* His eyes got very large, and I got the sense he had to catch his breath. *'Chase, do you honestly think I'm capable of something like that?'*

Actually, I didn't. 'Are you?'

'*No! I've never harmed anyone. Never would.*'

'Is there anything else, Doctor?'

'*Maybe I should have realized. When it happened the same day you got back. And now this.*' He hesitated. '*Are you there alone?*'

'Yes,' I said. 'Why would you care?'

The lines in his face were sharply defined. Maybe it was the lighting. Or maybe he was scared. '*Be careful,*' he said.

It didn't sound like a threat.

I called Windy. 'Have you heard anything from Bolton?'

'*No,*' she said. '*Why?*'

'I just talked to him. He didn't bite.'

'*I thought you guys were underestimating him.*'

'Yeah. Looks like.'

'*Have I your permission now to get rid of the contact? The director isn't happy walking on eggshells.*'

'Yes. Of course. Do what you have to.' She looked annoyed. 'You okay?'

'*Yes. I'm sorry the creep is going to get away with it.*'

'I know. Me, too.'

I debated letting Alex know about the call from Bolton, but decided to let it go. I could tell him when he got home. I didn't want him reminded of it when he was supposed to be taking time off.

Two days later, Windy told me Brankov had landed on Margolia and begun excavations. '*They're into one of the sites,*' she said. '*It's down about thirty, forty meters under the jungle floor.*'

'How's the weather?'

'*Wet and hot.*'

'Not good conditions.' Anything left by the settlers would have turned to mush.

An hour later she released the first statement on the findings. It included a picture of Brankov holding a rock that was reasonably smooth on one side and that he said had once been part of a wall.

That evening, speaking at a dinner of corporate types, the director described his reactions to the news and added how pleased he was with the contributions made by Alex Benedict, noting that he'd been 'exemplary in his efforts' to protect the sites.

That was too much for Kolchevsky, who erupted again that evening. But he'd become old news, so he didn't get much play. But he'd drummed up some allies, and there was evidence a new push was on to criminalize artifact retrieval unless it was done under license from an authoritative source. Alex had always insisted that such a law could not be passed, that it was essentially unenforceable. When I mentioned it to Windy, she surprised me. *'You'll find out eventually,'* she said, *'so I might as well tell you. I'm one of the backers. I think we have a good chance to get it through.'*

I don't know why it took me off guard. She reminded me that Survey had always been willing to help Rainbow, but *'you guys never seem to have enough.'* She caught herself. Shook her head. Smiled. *'Sorry.'*

Next day, she patched through a call from Spike Numitsu. He was speaking from what appeared to be an operations center. *'Alex,'* he said, *'the explosion on the* Seeker *took place in 2742. Early in the year. We're going to take a look at the engine room tomorrow. I'll let you know what we find.'*

I relayed it to Alex, who was relaxed in beach clothes with a glass of wine in his hand. He was on a veranda, and I could see the ocean in the background.

'How about that?' he said, obviously pleased. *'Chase, what do you think?'*

'About what?'

'Twenty-seven forty-two.'

'I'm not following.'

'Do you recall when it happened?' He was talking about the near intersection of the orbits of the dock, the moon, and Margolia. The date of the disaster.

'Yes. It was 2745.'

'*Three years after the* Seeker *died.*'

'So what's your point?'

'*Chase, they had at least* three years' *warning. Think about that. Three years to save themselves.*'

'They tried,' I said. 'They rebuilt the *Seeker*. It didn't work.'

'You think they'd have given up that easily?'

'*Given up?* Come on, Alex. They were in an impossible situation. Once the *Seeker* exploded they had no interstellar capability. FTL communications didn't exist. What do you think they might have done?'

'*Chase, they had some bright people with them. They had technicians, physicists, engineers. They knew how FTL drives worked.*'

'Doesn't do them any good if they can't build one.'

'*But they had* three *years.*'

'You keep saying that. I don't see how it matters. It takes a highly advanced industrial base to produce the kind of energy they'd need. You can't do it out in the woods, no matter how smart your people are.' I'd talked with Harry Williams often enough that the whole thing frustrated me. If these people were so smart, why didn't they check the neighborhood before they moved out there? And took their kids with them?

'*No.*' Alex shook his head. Something off to the side caught his attention. '*I've got to go, Chase. But we're still missing something.*'

I forgot to tell him about Bolton's call.

Less than an hour later, as I was closing up for the day, Bolton was back on the circuit. 'He's not back yet,' I told him. 'Two or three more days.'

'*This can't wait.*'

'What's wrong, Ollie?' He looked so unsettled I forgot my resentment.

'*I don't want to talk over an open circuit. Will you meet me someplace?*'

'Come on, Ollie. I'm busy.'

'Please. It's important.'

I let him see I was unhappy. 'When and where?'

'Brockbee's okay? At eight?'

'Make it seven.'

I keep fresh clothes at the country house, so I didn't have to bother going home. I showered and changed and even though I didn't think Ollie could be a physical threat, I slipped a scrambler into my jacket. I took the company skimmer and, just as the sun was touching the horizon, I headed for town.

Brockbee's is a private club. It's located behind a high wall, and, because it's a favorite hangout of political and corporate heavyweights and celebrities of various stripes, security is serious. They queried me on approach. I gave them my name and explained I was meeting Dr Bolton.

'One moment, please.' I went into a slow circle over the rooftop landing pad. *'Very good, Ms Kolpath. Welcome to Brockbee's. Please turn control over to us. We'll bring you in.'*

Minutes later I strolled into the dining room. The host informed me Dr Bolton hadn't arrived yet, but he showed me to my table. It was precisely seven o'clock.

Twenty minutes later I was still sitting there. A house avatar came by and asked whether I would like something to drink while I waited. Or perhaps an appetizer. *'We have some excellent hors d'oeuvres this evening.'*

I passed.

At the half hour I debated calling him, but decided the hell with it. On my way out I told the host to give Bolton my compliments if he showed up.

Carmen's voice woke me out of a sound sleep. *'You have a call, Chase. It sounds important.'*

My first thought was that it was Bolton.

'Inspector Redfield,' she said.

It was still dark out. What on earth did *he* want? Then I got a premonition that something had happened to Alex. I grabbed my robe and hurried out into the living room. 'Put him on, Carmen.'

He appeared from the front seat of a police cruiser. Looking a bit frazzled. '*Chase,*' he said. '*Sorry to bother you at this ungodly hour.*'

'It's okay, Fenn. What is it?'

He made a face. Bad news coming. '*Ollie Bolton's dead,*' he said. '*Somebody cut a fuel line in his skimmer.*'

I needed a moment to digest what he'd said. Bolton dead? It seemed impossible. 'When?' I asked.

'*We're still putting it together. But it looks like a few hours ago. Apparently he lifted off, got up a little bit, and the thing shut down. Crashed on his own property. Neighbor coming home around midnight saw the wreckage.*'

'Okay. You're sure it was murder?'

'*No question.*'

'Why'd you call me?'

'*His AI says he had a dinner engagement with you last night.*'

26

In the morning of the world,
When earth was nigher Heaven than now.

—Robert Browning,
Pippa Passes, 1841 C.E.

The media interviewed Kolchevsky in the morning. '*I won't pretend I was a friend,*' he said. '*I won't even pretend the world is not better off with him gone. But I would have preferred that he had seen the error of his ways. I'm, sure the police will spare no effort to bring the perpetrator of this heinous act to justice.*'

I let Alex know, and he announced he'd break off his vacation, which was in its last day anyhow, and come directly home. '*Until we know who did this,*' he said, '*it's possible you and I are still in somebody's sights. Be careful.*'

Fenn summoned me to his office. It appeared, he said, the victim had been on his way to meet me when his vehicle went down. 'I take it you have no idea what he wanted to tell you?'

'No,' I said. 'None whatever.' I'd suspected it might have been an attempt to pry me loose from Alex. But that sounded too much like my ego working overtime. And even if it were true, I could see no way it would help the investigation along.

311

He asked about Alex's relations with him. Had the animosity become overt?

'No,' I said. 'You don't think Alex had anything to do with this?'

He shook his head. 'No. I know him too well to believe anything like that. Still, Alex had reason if anybody did. Where is he, precisely?'

He told me he'd want to talk to Alex as soon as he showed up.

The perpetrator remained hidden as spring passed into summer. We became more cautious than ever. Nobody could get near either the Rainbow skimmer or our personal vehicles without setting off alarms. We both carried weapons all the time, and I learned to keep a close watch on my surroundings. It wasn't the way I wanted to live. But the weeks passed, and nothing more happened.

Reports continued to come in from the mission. Four greenhouse globes were found on the Margolia orbiter. They had earth in them and accommodated watering and heating systems. All were defective; cracked shields, broken pumps, one that wasn't airtight. The mission was baffled. What purpose could a greenhouse have served?

Alex sent a question: Was the *Bremerhaven's* lander still on board the ship?

'What's that have to do with anything?' I asked.

'Patience,' he said. 'We have a greenhouse. Now everything depends on the lander.'

Fenn let us know that the trail had gone cold. Alex asked whether there were no suspects at all. 'None,' he said. 'Bolton had lots of friends and admirers. Hard to find anybody who wanted him dead. Other than his ex-wife. And maybe a few competitors.' He gave Alex a significant look.

After a while I felt the need for some time off and took a weekend to get away with my current love interest. With both of them, in fact, but that's another story. I turned everything off so I was out of touch with the office. I've already admitted I wasn't as committed to the Margolians as Alex was. Whatever else we could say about them, they were a long time dead, and it was just hard to get excited. But I spent an undue amount of time worrying about Alex, who'd become fixated.

I wasn't surprised when I got back to my apartment and found a boatload of messages from him waiting for me. *'Chase, call me when you get in.'*

'Chase, call when you can.'

'Chase, we were right.'

'They've started finding human remains.'

'It looks as if there were thousands of them at the south pole. People who survived the event.'

Spike reported back. There was no lander on the *Bremerhaven*. 'Excellent,' said Alex.

'Apparently they tried migrating,' Windy told us one morning in late summer. *'They headed toward the poles in summer, and back to the equator in winter. The winters were long; the summer was short. But Emil thinks they were able to survive for a while.'*

'How long?' Alex asked.

'They're still putting the evidence together. But it looks like a few generations.' She took a deep breath. *'Hard to imagine the courage of those people. You wonder what kept them going.'*

Waiting for help to come, I thought. Hoping someone would find them.

'They built some aircraft. And Emil says he found evidence of pretty ingenious food production facilities.'

The living conditions began to emerge. The polar retreat became a large, sprawling base, much of it underground to facilitate cooling during the summer. Living quarters were necessarily spartan, but functional. Anything that got you away from the sun during solar passage must have looked pretty good.

I tried to imagine what it had been like when the planet rolled in close. How big had the sun appeared in the afternoon sky? Had it been possible even to stick your head outdoors?

The answer, according to the estimates we were getting, was a surprise. The experts were saying yes. The amount of heat in the polar regions during the hottest part of the summer was on a par with temperatures at Rimway's equator. Hot, yes. But downright pleasant in contrast with the rest of the planet.

By the end of the year, the mission had found the remnants of a library. Several thousand volumes. *'But unfortunately beyond recovery,'* Brankov said. We had been to lunch with Windy and returned with her to her office to find that piece of news waiting.

Beyond recovery.

Brankov let us see the library. An interior room, no windows, walls lined with shelves, shelves filled with mush.

'Books just won't survive long under the best of conditions,' he said. *'These are the worst.'* I vividly remembered the jungle and the damp humid air.

Eventually the estimate came in: *'We think they managed to hang on for almost six hundred years.'*

Brankov looked like a military guy. About fifty. Blond hair cut short, jumpsuit absolutely correct, diction perfect. *'They couldn't maintain their technology. Not indefinitely under these conditions. Eventually they must have simply worn out.'* He looked away and shook his head. *'You'd have to be here to understand what they faced.'* He was in a modular hut, one of those traveling shelters. Through a window, we could see a heavy snowstorm raging.

'Six hundred years,' said Alex. Back and forth, equator to pole, every twenty-one months, while the world alternately boiled and froze.

I looked out at the balmy weather that passes for summer in Andiquar. Windy said, 'I wonder if anybody ever even looked for them.'

I was thinking how they'd wanted to be left alone.

We got more news as we slid into autumn. Some of the original towns were found, the ones built by the first arrivals on Margolia. I wondered whether any part of the house we'd seen in the holograms had survived. And what had happened to the little girl posing so happily with her mother.

Alex became engrossed in Margolian research. He traveled to libraries on the continent and in the islands. He brought home extracts on the movement, which he read religiously. They were mostly from books that had appeared originally in the twenty-eighth century. A number of them had been privately printed, family histories, church records, journals. He commented that such things survive because they tend to get thrown into trunks or attics, and when they show up a couple centuries later, there's historical interest. 'So people take care of them. Reproduce them. Get through the first two hundred years,' he said, 'and you have it made.'

When I asked what he was looking for, he laughed and pushed a sheaf of documents away. 'The *Bremerhaven*,' he said. 'I'm trying to figure out what happened to the *Bremerhaven*.'

Jacob's call light began blinking. Transmission for Alex. *'Dr Yashevik, sir. She wants you to call when you have a moment.'*

He told Jacob to connect, and moments later Windy appeared. *'Thought you'd like to know. They found this at about twenty degrees south latitude.'* The light changed and we were in an excavation, during a blizzard, looking at part of a building. A cornerstone, in fact, with symbols we couldn't read. Except the number. *'It says* Paul DeRenne School. 55. *We have no idea who Paul DeRenne is.'*

'What's the number?' asked Alex. 'The year it was built?'

'That's what they think.'

Fifty-five. 'That would have to be the fifty-fifth year from the foundation of the colony,' he said.

'Probably.'

'Has anybody been willing to make a guess how long a year was out there, prior to the event?'

'They think it would have been about ten percent shorter than a standard year.'

'So the school was built about forty-nine years after the landing, terrestrial time.'

'Somewhere in there.'

'Assuming the colony was founded 2690, that would have been about 2739 by the terrestrial calendar.'

'Yes.'

'The thing hit in 2745.'

'Yeah. I wonder if they even knew it was coming when they built the school.'

Alex rubbed his forehead. 'Probably not. Would the building have been tenable afterward? After the event?'

'I don't know. He didn't say.' Windy sighed. *'If it was, you wouldn't want to be there during summer or winter.'*

'No,' said Alex. 'I guess not.'

'It would have meant a lot of running around,' I said.

'They might not have had much choice,' said Alex. 'It's not as if they could have stayed a few months at the pole, and the rest of the year on the equator. They would have needed bases between. Places to stay. Maybe this became one. Spring City. I can't imagine they were able to stay very long in any one place.'

'I'm surprised they just didn't give up,' said Windy. She seemed saddened by the news. I think we'd all hoped the end had come quickly.

Alex smiled. 'Six centuries.' He told Jacob to enlarge the cornerstone. 'Incredible.' It had begun to get dark outside. *Our* outside. Rain clouds building. 'Anything else?' he asked.

'They found a monument. Maybe the place where the colonists first set foot on the ground. Hard to say for sure. Everything's so broken up.'

'What's it look like?'

The lights flickered and we were standing beside pieces of stone that were being painstakingly reassembled into a wall. There were fragments of an inscription that read, when translated, *On this site,* and – *in the name of—,* and *foot.* And a zero. There'd been another figure in front of the zero, possibly a nine, or an eight. Followed by c.e. *'Common Era,'* said Windy.

'It's *Earth-related,*' said Alex, for my benefit.

'We *think*,' she continued, '*the colonists arrived in January 2690. More or less. Emil says they wouldn't be likely to refer to terrestrial dates, in concrete, except for terrestrial-related events. They can only think of one.*'

She was back on the circuit again just before we closed up for the day. '*Got something else. Emil says he thinks they found the ground terminal for the flights down from orbit. It's in the southern temperate zone.*'

'Jacob,' said Alex, 'let's see the map.'

I didn't realize we had one. A globe of Margolia appeared. It showed the now-familiar island-continents, rivers, mountain chains. The location of the south polar base was marked and the various sites that the mission had uncovered.

Windy told us where the terminal was, and Jacob duly marked it. '*It was located just outside a major city.*'

Okay. No surprise there. 'Any sign of a lander?'

'*No,*' she said. '*They've scanned the area pretty closely. Emil says the jungle probably ate it. Was there a lander on board the* Seeker?'

'Yes,' said Alex. 'It was there.' He signed off and looked at me, waiting for me to say something.

What did he want from me? 'Why are you smiling like that?' I asked. 'What's all this about the lander?'

'Where is it?'

'Dissolved,' I said. 'Part of the jungle.'

'How'd they get down from the orbiter?'

'How'd *who* get down from the orbiter?'

'Whoever released the *Bremerhaven* from its tethers?'

'I don't know. Maybe they *didn't* come down. Maybe they—'

'Right,' he said. 'Maybe they boarded the ship.'

'No. The ship wouldn't function.'

'Then where's the lander?'

'It's on the ground somewhere. They'll find it. It's buried.'

'There's another possibility,' he said.

'Which is what?'

'Chase, I want you to do a favor for me.'

I sighed. Loudly. 'Okay.'

'I've been talking to every historian, librarian, and archivist I can think of.'

'About what?'

'Anything that might help us. I want you to check something out.'

'Okay.'

'You've been to Earth, right? No? Historic place. It's about time you paid a visit.'

27

The home world exercises its siren call over us all. No matter how far we wander, or how long we are gone, it waits patiently. And when we return to it, as we must, it sings to us. We came out of its forests, waded ashore from its seas. It is in our blood, for good or ill.

—Ali Barana,
Go Left at Arcturus, 1411

Earth.

It was an odd feeling, seeing Sol up close. The planet floated in the void, with its big scarred moon, and the continents, their outlines familiar, as though I'd been there before. As if I were coming home.

Harmony, the giant orbiting station, glittered in the night. Harmony was the most recent in a long series of orbiters. It began as a simple terminal and maintenance station a few centuries ago, but they kept adding to it, hotels here and rec areas there and a research facility out back. The original structure was hardly visible anymore, concealed within an array of pods and domes and spheres. There was a long argument raging at the time over whether to upgrade or replace it altogether.

A liner was leaving as I approached. It passed me, outward bound, light radiating off the bridge and through rows of view-ports. It was a big ship, though not in the same league with the *Seeker*, and certainly not as romantic. As it passed me, it fired its main engines and accelerated away until all I could see was a fading star.

I turned the *Belle-Marie* over to the controllers, and they brought us into a docking area crowded with small vessels. Mostly corporate vehicles. A boarding tube attached itself to the hatch, and I climbed out.

Three hours later I was on the ground, on the original *terra firma*, asleep in a compartment on a glide train headed west across the North American continent. In the morning I got my first look up close at the Pacific, and caught a commuter flight for the Destiny Islands, the Queen Charlottes in ancient times, about eighty klicks up the coast. I could see traffic moving below, and people on beaches. Flotillas of sailboats dotted the ocean.

The Destinies consist of more than 150 islands in an area still preserved in a predominantly natural state. There were tall trees, morning mists, and eagles on the wing. I'd never seen an eagle, and I understood immediately why it was an appropriate symbol for an interstellar. I looked down on snowcapped mountains, blue lakes, winding streams. Two days later, on the flight out, I'd see a dozen or so gray whales gliding through the quiet waters.

I'd made reservations at the White Dove Hotel, at Rennell Sound, overlooking the ocean. They provided a pleasant room, with wide windows and billowing curtains. The Pacific, at least at those latitudes, was more serene than the Eastern Sea at home. Looking west from the hotel, I could see nothing but water.

It was late morning when I finally got moving. I looked up the name Alex had given me, Jules Lochlear, and asked the AI to connect me with the University of the Americas. Lochlear, I was informed, would be happy to see me in the early afternoon. *'At one o'clock sharp.'*

He was located in the upper reaches of the campus library. It was one of those old-style buildings, designed by someone with a penchant for geometry run amok. There were multiple roofs and doors in unusual places. The corners of the various structures were rarely parallel with each other, and even the walkways through the upper tiers rose and fell seemingly at random, and at angles that suggested only an athlete might navigate them safely. It's a style that somebody once described as an explosion rather than a design.

I had some trouble finding Lochlear's office, but I suppose that's part of the game. He was alone when I got there, working at a table piled high with books and pads. It was spacious, its walls decorated with assorted academic accolades and awards. A large sliding door opened onto a veranda, providing a view of the campus. When I appeared, he didn't look up, but kept writing in a green folder while using his other hand to wave me toward a divan.

He was well past his prime years. In fact, I suspected I'd arrived none too soon. He was thin, and his shoulders were bent. A few strands of white hair complemented bushy eyebrows. His eyes were watery, and he seemed frail beyond endurance. 'You must be Ms Kolpath,' he said, in a surprisingly steady voice, still without taking his eyes off the paperwork.

'That's correct, Professor.'

'Very good, young lady. I'll be with you in just a moment.'

It took a bit longer than that, but finally he expressed his satisfaction with the task at hand, put the pen down, and favored me with a glance. 'Forgive me,' he said. 'Stop in the middle of one of these things, and sometimes it takes an hour to get back to where I was.'

'It's okay. It's good to meet you.' Alex had described him as a historian and an archivist. 'What is it you're working on, Professor?' I asked, by way of launching the conversation.

'Oh, nothing, really.' He pushed back from the table. 'It's just something I've been toying with.' He tried a dismissive smile, but he didn't mean it.

'What is it?' I persisted.

'It's *The Investigators*.'

'The Investigators?' I asked.

'It's a play. I expect they'll be performing it at the Theater by the Sea next season.'

'I didn't know you were a playwright,' I said.

'Oh, I'm not. Not really. I've done a few. But they never get beyond the local group. You know how it is.'

I had no idea. But I said yes, of course.

'I do murder-mystery comedies,' he said. 'Eventually, I'd like to see one of them go all the way to Brentham.'

I pretended I understood the significance. 'That would be nice,' I said. 'Good luck, Professor.'

'Thank you. I'm not optimistic.'

'What do you teach?' I asked.

'Not a thing,' he said. 'I taught history at one time, but that's long ago. I got tired trying to persuade reluctant students, so I gave it up.'

'And now you—?'

'I'm seated firmly in the Capani Chair. Which means I work with occasional doctoral candidates. God help them.' He laughed and got up, tottered momentarily, but hung on and laughed. 'The floor's not as steady as it used to be. Now, I believe you're here to—' His voice trailed off, and he rummaged through another pile of papers, gave up, and opened a cabinet. More searching, then his features brightened. 'Yes,' he said, 'here it is. Ms Kolpath, why don't you come with me?' He headed for the veranda. The door slid open, and he led the way outside. 'Be careful,' he said.

He immediately gained strength. His frailty slipped away, and he moved almost with the ease of a young man. When I stepped out behind him, and my weight melted off, I understood why. 'Antigrav units,' I said.

'Of course. You're about thirty percent normal weight at the moment, Chase. May I call you *Chase*? Good. Please watch your step. Sometimes the effect induces a sense of too much well-being. We've had people fall off.'

We were on one of the ramps I'd seen from the ground. Its

handrails consisted of ornately carved metal, and it angled sharply up to one of the rooftops. Lochlear started to climb, moving with practiced ease.

We went to the top and strode out onto the roof. He walked with a casual inattention that, combined with his frailty and reduced weight, left me worried that the wind – which was steady and coming in off the ocean – might blow him off. He saw my concern and laughed. 'Have no fear,' he said, 'I come this way all the time.'

I gazed across the rooftop at the sea. 'It's lovely,' I said.

'This is where I get to be young again. For a few minutes.' We hurried past chairs and tables, and reentered the building through a double door. I couldn't figure out what all the rush was about, until I realized that Lochlear did everything on the run.

We pushed through a set of curtains and entered a long, narrow room, crowded with shelves and files and chips and books and display cases. The cases held individual volumes. 'They're here somewhere,' he said. 'I thought I'd set them aside after the messages from your Mr Benedict.' The books on display were old, the covers discolored and worn, and in some cases missing. He opened a cabinet door, peered inside, and brightened. 'Here it is,' he said. He removed a box, set it down on a table, and began to go through it. 'Yes.' He pulled out several labeled containers. 'Good.' He dusted them off, sorted them, put a couple back, and placed the rest in front of me. There were four of them. Each held eight disks. The labels read Collier Array, uncollated, and were marked with catalog numbers.

'Tarim?' he said.

An AI's voice replied, gently, *'Good afternoon, Dr Lochlear.'*

He turned to me. 'Chase, Tarim will be happy to assist you.'

'Thank you.'

'One more thing: These are quite valuable. Please be careful. The scanner is over here by the wall if you wish to make copies. You won't be able to take the originals out of the room, of course. If you need to speak with me, just tell Tarim, and he'll put you through. When you're finished, please leave everything on the table. It's been a pleasure to meet you, Chase.' Then he was gone. The door closed behind him with an audible click.

At the time it became operational, the Collier Array had been the largest telescope of all time. It was based off Castleman's World, which supported and maintained it for the better part of seven centuries. With units scattered across the planetary system, it had possessed a virtual diameter of 400 million kilometers. It was a product of the Fifth Millennium, and it remained in operation until it fell victim to one of the incessant wars of the period. Its destruction had been a deliberate act of malice. By then, however, it had become obsolete.

The Array had drawn Alex's interest because Castleman's was four thousand light-years from Tinicum 2116. Four thousand years for light to arrive at the system's multiple lenses. So he realized that, if it had any record at all of that star, it would be of a time preceding the event that had disrupted life for the Margolians.

Much of the data gathered by the Collier was lost with the general collapse on Castleman's at the end of the Fifth Millennium. But in the early decades of the last century, investigators uncovered a trove of stored raw data in hard copy from the Array. No one had sorted it out, because much of it had since become available elsewhere.

The disks were marked with the dates they were thought to cover, but even about that there was uncertainty. Not that it mattered.

I sat down in front of a reader, took Belle's record of our flight to Tinicum, and inserted it. Then I removed the first disk from box #1 and put it in also. 'Tarim,' I said, 'please activate.'

Status lamps came on.

'Tarim, I'm trying to find Tinicum 2116 in the Collier raw data. I've provided you with a spectrographic analysis and images of surrounding star patterns. Please commence search.'

'*Working,*' he said.

I opened a novel and sat back to wait.

* * *

Sometimes you get lucky. Tinicum 2116 had been inspected, and the entry turned up thirty minutes later, on the second disk.

Tarim posted a picture of the star, as seen through the Collier. Beneath were the results of the analysis, spelling out quantities of hydrogen, helium, iron, lithium, and whatnot. And a final line: *Planets: 4.*

Four.

We knew of three.

The fourth was another terrestrial.

No wonder the orbits hadn't matched.

Two gas giants. And *two* terrestrials.

Bingo.

Lochlear called to ask whether I'd like to have dinner with him. Some of the faculty members got together most evenings. I'd stayed in the archives, going over the other disks to see whether there was more on Tinicum. There wasn't. But I was bored and stiff when the invitation came, so I was more than willing to find something else to do.

He picked me up and escorted me to the faculty dining room, which was in an adjoining building. There were five or six others gathered when we walked in. Lochlear did the introductions, everybody made room, and I was surprised to discover they'd heard of me. Kolpath? Furrowed brows all around. You were with Benedict when he found Margolia, weren't you?

I allowed as how that was so.

They wanted to shake my hand. All of them. 'Superb piece of work, Chase,' said an energetic young guy who looked as if he lifted barbells when he wasn't in the classroom. They asked me to pass my congratulations to Alex, and to tell him they were all in his debt. It was a nice moment. A couple of them asked light-heartedly whether Rainbow was taking on help. And they wondered what I was doing at the university.

When I told them it was just basic research, they laughed, and a middle-aged woman with honey-colored hair said she'd keep it quiet, too, if she were out to bag the kind of game I usually went after. They all laughed again. And I sat there feeling like the queen of the walk.

The guy with the muscles wondered if we were positive about what we'd found. Was it really Margolia?

'Yes,' I said. 'There's no question.'

They raised their coffee cups in a toast to Rainbow. 'The University of the Americas appreciates you, Chase,' said a heavyset man in a red sweater. Galan Something-or-other. His specialty was modern theater. I wondered what he thought of Lochlear's plays.

They didn't seem to feel any of the disappointment Alex and I had experienced. Exhilaration was the order of the day. The middle-aged woman excused herself and left, returning a few minutes later with a copy of Christopher Sim's *Man and Olympian*. 'I was wondering if you'd sign it,' she said.

My connection with the Sim business was a long time ago, and I hesitated. It was a leather-bound edition, gilt edge, black ribbons. Not the sort of book you want casually to mark up. 'Please,' she said.

I complied, feeling a bit foolish.

'What's next?' asked Lochlear.

'Home,' I said.

'I mean, what's the next project? McCarthy?'

Golis McCarthy was an archeologist who'd returned from a frontier world a century earlier, claiming to have brought back alien artifacts. Not Mute. Something else. He wouldn't go into details, but during the next three months the artifacts went missing, supposedly weighted and dropped in the ocean by McCarthy. McCarthy and his people – seven of them altogether – refused to comment and, within seven months, all were dead, the victims of assorted accidents. It was a conspiracy theorist's dream. 'No,' I said, 'I think we're just going to take it easy for a while.'

Lochlear leaned close. 'Did you find what you came for?'

'Oh, yes,' I said.

He beamed. 'I'm glad we were able to help.'

The guy with the muscles, whose name was Albert, told me if we had anything more like Margolia up our sleeves, he'd appreciate an invitation to go along. I told him next time I'd be in touch.

When it was over, and we were on our way back to the library, Lochlear commented that I'd been a big hit. I was sorry Alex hadn't been there.

I couldn't resist taking a day to go sight-seeing. I went rafting, tried my hand at a canoe, rode a tour ship through the islands, and allowed Albert to take me to dinner. There was a glorious late-summer sunset, and I decided that, if I ever found reason to relocate, the Destinies would be high on my list.

28

Sophocles, Dostoevski, al Imra, Bertolt, are all engaged, first and foremost, in mythmaking. They depict the best, and sometimes the worst, that is in us. They reveal how we wish to think of ourselves, how we would like to be, if only we had the courage.

—Muriel Jean Capaliana,
Introduction to *The Complete Benoir*, 2216 C.E.

I was becoming famous. Shortly after I entered the home system, the guys in ops told me there was a new sim I'd be interested in seeing. About Margolia. (There were, they said, two or three more in the works. Everybody was rushing to take advantage of the discovery.) Did I want them to relay it to me? It was called *Margolia, Farewell*.

I pretended to think it over. The truth was I thought, from the way they were talking, it was a dramatization of the flight Alex and I had made. So I put on a casual front and said sure, if they had a minute, they could send it.

To my disappointment, it turned out to be a historical epic about the last days of the colony. In this version it was a rogue planet that brought everything to grief.

A lone scientist arrives in the capital and seeks an audience with Harry Williams. The approach of the newly discovered world, he says, will be catastrophic. There'll be quakes, tidal waves, volcanoes.

'*It's going to alter our orbit*,' he adds.

'*Will we survive?*'

The scientist is tall, thin, gray, intense. Right out of Central Casting. '*Mr Director, I do not see reason for hope.*'

'*How long do we have?*' asks Williams.

'*Fourteen months.*'

(The writers either didn't know or didn't care that the colonists had had at least three years' warning.)

His colleagues react angrily, insisting such a thing could not happen. The world on which they stand is six billion years old. What are the odds that something like this would occur only a few decades after they'd arrived?

When the period of denial passes, there's an effort to determine whose fault it is. Williams takes to the airwaves, announces the finding, and accepts responsibility. '*We are working on a solution*,' he tells his listeners.

There isn't time to get help. So they decide to put as many people as they can on both ships and send them back to Earth. The watchword becomes *Save the children!* Then, catastrophic news from the engineers: Neither the *Seeker* nor the *Bremerhaven* is capable of making the long flight home.

That produces a second round of recrimination. Again, Harry accepts the blame. '*It was my responsibility*,' he tells the Council. And I thought, *Damn right.*

Ah, yes. Noble Harry. Played by a character actor who specialized in such parts.

We watch the fury when the word gets out. Angry crowds surround government buildings. Williams is driven from his position of leadership.

After a series of loud debates, the decision is taken to strip the *Bremerhaven*, and use its parts to fill in on the *Seeker*, which is the more reliable of the two ships. '*God help us*,' says a technician,

'*I'm still not sure it will get home.*' *Home* has once again become Earth.

At that point, I shut it down. I've no taste for downbeat sims, and I knew how this one was going to end.

Alex was waiting at the terminal outside Andiquar when the shuttle set down. 'Glad to have you back,' he said. 'The work's been piling up.' Then he laughed as if the comment had been raucously funny. 'I take it we were right.'

It was good of him to use the plural. In fact, I'd had no part in it. 'Yes,' I said, 'there *was* another terrestrial world.'

'Excellent. Were you able to get its orbit?'

'No. There were no details.'

'Nothing at all?'

'No.'

We took the elevator to the roof. It was quiet, the place nearly deserted. 'Another terrestrial world,' he said. 'That means it was in the biozone.'

'That's not clear. They didn't use the standard categories. But they list the makeup of the atmosphere. Nitrogen and oxygen look like the standard mix for a class-K. So I'd say yes, it was in the biozone. Had to be.'

'Good.'

'I still don't see why it matters. I know what you're thinking, but they wouldn't have been dumb enough to retreat to a world that was going to get ripped out of orbit. Surely they would have known what was going to happen.'

We arrived topside, and the doors opened onto a rainy afternoon. We walked out into the dispatch area, flagged a taxi, and headed west.

'Nevertheless, Chase,' he said, 'that's precisely what they did.'

'But it was suicide.'

'So it would seem.' He looked out at the storm as we rose over the city.

*   *   *

Twenty minutes later we walked into the country house. Jacob had coffee and jelly donuts waiting.

'So.' I sat down and treated myself. 'What's next?'

'We need to find the missing world.'

I had known it was coming. 'You're kidding.'

'From a business standpoint, it would bring us a bonanza. Its atmosphere would have frozen when it left the vicinity of its sun. So the surface would have gone void, and artifacts would have been preserved. Mint condition, Chase. And the story of that last group of colonists, if we can establish they actually existed, is going to approach mythic proportions.'

'How do you suggest we find the missing world? I doubt it can be done.'

'That's your area of expertise, Chase,' he said. 'Find a way.'

How do you search for a dark body lost among the stars?

I reviewed what I knew about the state of sensing technology. Not very much, I discovered. So I made some calls and eventually came up with Avol DesPlaine's name. He was described to me as the best we had on the subject.

I told Jacob to try to get through to him. We left a message, and he returned the call in the morning. He could, he informed me, spare a minute.

He had the darkest skin I'd ever seen. Unless you lived on Earth, skin color hasn't been a distinguishing feature for thousands of years. There'd been too much intermarriage among those who had headed out from the home world. And the result had been a moderate olive texture for almost everybody. Some were lighter, some darker. But not by much.

DesPlaine was the exception to the rule. I wondered whether he was the product of a few genes that had hung on, or whether he was a recent arrival from Earth. He was a small man, or he sat in the biggest armchair on the planet. It was hard to tell which. *What may I do for you, Ms Kolpath?* he asked.

I explained what I wanted to know. Nine thousand years ago,

a planet had been expelled from its solar system during a close pass by an extraneous body. We don't know which direction it went. 'Is there a technology that would help us find it?'

'*Sure,*' he said, warming to the subject. '*Of course. But you're talking about a substantial volume of space. Do you have anything other than what you've told me? Anything at all?*' He had a wide skull, a few strands of white hair, and deep-set eyes that never left me.

'No,' I said. 'We know which system it got blown out of. That's about it.'

'*I see.*' He scribbled a note. And he didn't crack a smile, although I sensed that he wanted to. '*How large will the search fleet be?*'

'I beg your pardon?'

'*How many ships would be engaged in the operation?*'

'One. It's not a fleet.'

'*One.*' Another near smile. Another scribble. '*Very good.*'

'I assume that creates a problem.'

He cleared his throat. 'Does the ejected world have a name?'

I scrambled for one. I'd once had a cat named for a character in an old novel. 'Yes,' I said. 'It's called Balfour.'

'*Balfour.*' He tasted it, ran it around on his lips. '*If people can give it a name, surely somebody would have an idea which way it went. If not, if you're just going out into the dark to search, you'd be as likely to find it as to find a coin in a sizable patch of woods. At night.*'

'Even with the best technology?'

He laughed. There was something of a rumble in it. Had we been audio only I would have thought him much bigger than he was. '*Consider the sensor gear a flashlight. With a narrow beam.*'

'Situation's that bad, huh?'

'*I always try to take an optimistic view.*'

29

There are persons who pass through our lives but briefly. And we are never afterward the same.

—Chile Yarimoto,
Travels, 1421

Alex doesn't believe anything's impossible. If you can travel faster than light, he liked to say, everything's on the table. The corollary is that you don't go to him and tell him an assignment can't be managed.

I needed help, so I went back to Shara. She was engrossed in a conversation with – I think – her AI when I walked in the door. She signaled me she needed a minute, asked a couple questions about stellar populations in a region I'd never heard of, got her answers, made notes, and turned my way with a big smile. 'Chase,' she said. 'How's it feel to be a celebrity?'

'I'm looking for a way to cash in.'

'I understand they're trying to get you to come work for Survey.'

'There's been some talk.'

'Don't do it. There's not much money, and I don't think anybody ever got famous.' She got serious. 'What can I do for you?'

'Shara, there was another world in the Tinicum system. A class-K. We suspect whatever scrambled the orbit of Margolia ejected it.'

'And you were wondering if there might be a way to track it down?'

'Yes.'

'Why on earth would you care? You think there might have been a base there?'

'Something like that.'

'Okay,' she said.

'So do you think it might be possible to find it?'

'This all happened, what, nine thousand years ago?'

'That's correct.'

'Good. That's relatively recent. But you don't know the nature of the intruder? Of whatever broke up the system?'

'No. We think it might have been a black hole.'

'Why?'

'Because there aren't any stars near enough to have done the job.'

She looked skeptical. 'Well, actually, it might have been any of a number of things.'

'Whatever. We don't care what the object was. All we're interested in is finding the missing world.'

'It might be possible. Tell me about the system again.'

'Okay,' I said. 'Right now, it has two gas giants in normal orbits. It also has Margolia, which is running in a seriously exaggerated ellipse, and a dislodged moon.'

'Does the class-K have a name?'

'Balfour.' It was starting to sound good.

'And you've got a couple of ancient spacecraft out there, too, right?'

'Yes. And a dock that went adrift at the time of the event. The *Seeker* was apparently trying to jump into hyper when it blew.'

'Okay. As I understand it, the *Seeker* set out with those kids three years before the event.'

'That's correct.'

'That means it probably won't be much help. What about the other ship? The Whatzis?'

'The *Bremerhaven*. Its orbit doesn't place it anywhere near Margolia when the intruder came through.'

'That's interesting.'

'Maybe it was orbiting Balfour.'

'Any reason to think that? Or is it guesswork?'

'It's guesswork.'

'What about the dock?'

'It would have been at Margolia when the object hit.'

'And they're both currently in solar orbit?'

'Yes.'

'Get me the details. Everything you've got. The first thing we need to do is establish when it happened.'

'We already know.'

'All right. Good. That might make it possible. Send me the data. I'll look everything over and get back to you.'

'Thanks, Shara.'

'My pleasure. I'm glad to help. It'll be a break from my routine. Is there a deadline on this?'

'No,' I said. 'It's waited this long; I assume it can wait a bit longer.'

She laughed. 'Get it to me tonight, and I'll try to have something for you tomorrow.'

'You were right about the time of the event,' she said next evening, as we sat at the Longtree, sipping cocktails. 'It happened March 1, 2745, on the terrestrial calendar.'

'That's only a couple days away from what we figured.'

'We're talking calendars rather than time itself,' she said. 'It's hard to deal with this sort of thing because of the odd things that happen with time when the objects are hundreds of light-years apart.'

'All right,' I said. 'We know *when* it happened. Where do we go from there?'

A singer was doing 'Fire and Ice.' It was cold and wet outside. But the Longtree was filled to capacity. A wedding party had taken over one wing, and another large group was celebrating something. Couldn't tell what. There were occasional bursts of laughter around the room. In the center of the dining area, several couples were dancing.

'Chase,' she said, 'we know where the gas giants were at the time of the event.'

'Okay.'

'They were undisturbed by the passage. That probably lets out your black hole. Had the intruder been massive, really massive, they would have been disrupted, too. But in this case, their orbits don't seem to have been influenced at all.'

'That tells us what?'

'That the intruder was less than a tenth of a solar mass.'

'Okay.' I didn't see how that could help. But she seemed to know where she was headed.

She finished her cocktail and ordered another round. 'Might as well,' she said, 'as long as Alex is feeling generous.' Rainbow, of course, was paying for the evening.

'Absolutely. Help yourself.'

'All right. So Margolia's orbit gets stretched, and its moon goes south. The other terrestrial world, Balfour, is tossed out of the system altogether. That suggests an intruder mass at least a hundred times greater than Margolia.'

'Okay.'

'My best guess,' she said, 'is a mass equivalent somewhere between a Jovian and an M-class dwarf star.'

'Shara,' I said, 'I know you're interested for academic reasons. But is any of this going to help us find Balfour?'

'Ah, you don't have the patience you used to, Chase. If we split the difference between the Jovian and the class-M, we're in brown dwarf territory.'

'Brown dwarf.'

'Yes. It's a star that never quite got off the ground. Not enough mass. So it didn't ignite.'

'It's a dark object, then.'

'No. Not necessarily. They have enough energy to glow. They stay warm for a long time.'

'What generates the energy?'

'It's left over from their formation. What I'm saying is that this thing won't look at all like a star. It wouldn't be a bright light in the sky. But if you got close enough, you'd be able to see it.'

'What would it look like?'

She thought about it. 'It might resemble a gas giant illuminated from within. It would have clouds. Probably a muddy brown.'

'That seems an odd color.'

Shara had a tendency sometimes to go into lecture mode. She did it now. 'Younger dwarfs are usually blood red. They're just radiating the heat generated during formation. As they age, they cool off. More and more molecules form in their atmospheres, and they acquire clouds.'

'What kind of clouds?'

'Ferrous and silicon compounds, mostly. With some curious weather patterns. Eventually they become dark red. In time, they'll fade to reddish brown, and finally to brown.'

'Okay. And if one of these things came through a planetary system, it could raise hell?'

'You bet. Look, Chase, it's massive. Probably one percent of standard solar mass. That sounds small, but it's a tight little package. If it gets anywhere near you, look out.'

'Can you tell what its path might have been through the system?'

'More or less. Mostly less.'

'Explain?'

'I tried a trillion combinations of intruder inclination, periastron distance, mass, and velocity.'

'Wait a minute,' I said. 'Try it in the mother tongue. What's periastron distance?'

'When it's closest to the sun.'

'Okay.'

'So I tried all that to see if I could track it. Something that would produce the results we see. I'd say it entered and exited the system on a path that was mildly inclined to the plane of the planets, with periastron occurring between the orbits of Margolia and Balfour. Margolia, by the way, was the inner of the two class-K worlds.'

'That doesn't sound like a guess.'

'It isn't. There are limitations on what Margolia's orbit could have been. If Balfour was also in the biozone, as you're saying, it would have had to be more remote. Anyway, with Balfour in the equation, it becomes possible to fit the orbits of the dock, the moon, and Margolia together.'

'That's why we weren't able to make the orbits intersect,' I said.

'Correct. You needed the fourth planet.' Her eyes were alight. She loved talking about astrophysics. 'This thing would have been massive. If it had gotten really close to the central star, it would have taken it out. Like the one at Delta Karpis in the last century.'

'Okay.'

Our drinks arrived. She tried hers and set it down without reacting to it. 'All right,' she said, 'we also know the two gas giants were on the far side of the system when the dwarf crossed their orbits. So far, so good. But the two terrestrials weren't so lucky. It passed close to them.'

'Shara,' I said, 'why do we care so much about the dwarf?'

She pointed at my drink. Have some. I complied. 'Because the dwarf can tell us where Balfour is.'

'Wonderful.'

'Not so fast. That brings us to the bad news. I can't give you even a rough estimate where Balfour might be unless we can find the brown dwarf.'

'Why?' I asked.

'Find the brown dwarf and that gives us its mass, current position, and velocity. From that we can work out its path through the Tinicum system. *Then* we can put together a decent estimate where we might find your missing world.'

'Shara, haven't we just moved the problem around? How do we find the brown dwarf?'

She was looking at something over my shoulder. 'Don't turn around,' she said.

I waited a few seconds, and saw a waiter leading a tall male in a dark jacket past us to a corner table. He looked pretty good, and his gaze swept across Shara, and held. There was an exchange of nonverbals and he moved on. Shara grinned at me as he passed out of her field of vision. 'Target of opportunity.'

Maybe she hadn't changed as much as I'd thought. 'The brown dwarf,' I said.

'Yeah.' She was still distracted. 'Well, the good thing about all this is that it can't have gone very far in nine thousand years. Certainly less than a light-year. It'll be quite bright in the near infrared, say tenth or at worst fifteenth magnitude.'

A young woman cruised past, headed for the guy. Shara shook her head. 'Pity,' she said.

'So we can find it?'

'It'll cost.'

'What do we have to do?'

'Go hunting for it. First you'll need to persuade Survey to let you have a ship.'

'Why?' I asked. 'We have the *Belle-Marie*.'

'It can't do the job. You're going to need to deliver a couple of wide-field telescopes to the search area. A private yacht wouldn't be able to handle that. Anyhow, Survey has ships already equipped to do this kind of thing.'

'I'll talk to Windy.'

'They'll want somebody from Survey to go along. It's in the rules.'

'What actually would we need to do? How do wide-field telescopes work?'

'They come in pairs. We set them well apart and let them do a simultaneous survey of the sky. The brown dwarf will stand out.'

'You're sure?'

'Trust me.'

341

'All right. Will the onboard AI be able to take care of things without my getting too much involved?'

'No,' she said. 'You'll have to provide some guidance. The ship will have the equipment, but this operation's a bit different from what the AIs normally do.'

She explained the procedures. Dinner arrived. Vegetables with salads, and sliced chicken. We were both hungry. She dived in, but I was still trying to write down everything I was hearing. 'I'll never get all this straight,' I said.

'Sure you will. I tell you what, before you leave, I'll give you a crash course.'

'Okay.'

'You'll be fine, Chase.'

'Is there anybody out there with the mission? Somebody I could ask, in case we have a problem? Who knows how these things work?'

'One or two, maybe,' she said. 'I'm not sure. But don't worry. The person Windy sends with you will know how to operate the gear.'

I wasn't comfortable with the arrangement. It felt like one of those situations where we'd get out there and discover I didn't know what I was doing. And the guy they'd sent along would look puzzled and comment how it had been a long time. So I took a plunge. 'Listen, you said that Survey would want to send a rep with us.'

'I'm busy, Chase.'

'I'd appreciate it. I'd consider it a personal favor.'

She lifted a piece of tomato on her fork and stole a glance over her shoulder at the corner table. The guy was absorbed in his companion.

'I'll never ask for anything again,' I said.

'I'm sure.' She tapped her fingernails on the side of the wineglass while she thought about it. 'It's not that hard, Chase.'

'This is a piece of history. Wouldn't you like to be there?'

'I think the history's already been made, Champ. I should have gone on the earlier flight.'

'Shara, Alex's instincts are usually pretty good. There might be something more. Something pretty big.'

She was already well along on the meal. I knew she'd be reaching for the dessert menu next. Shara was one of those irritating people who eats what she likes and never seems to pay a price. 'We're talking some serious time here, Chase. What about my social life?'

'We'll party on the way.'

Getting a ship turned out to be complicated.

Shara was correct as far as it went when she said official policy required someone from Survey to be on the flight. But the someone had to be the pilot. *'There are no pilots available,'* Windy told me. *'I can check to see whether anyone would volunteer to go. But it would be overtime. And I doubt we could find anybody anyhow.'* She went on to tell me who was currently on free time and why they would not be responsive to come back to work.

'How about me?' I said. 'I'm licensed.'

'For Arcturus-*class?'*

I'd been piloting yachts and small commercial. 'Not exactly,' I said. 'But how complicated can it be?'

'It's the rules, Chase. Sorry. I have no choice.'

Windy made some calls and, as predicted, both available people said no. Survey pilots are pretty well paid, and they don't get a lot of free time at home. Had we been at one of the outposts, or on a station somewhere, we'd have had no problem. But in Andiquar, it was no go.

So Alex signed me up for an accelerated program. And that's how I became qualified for the next level of superluminal. I have a *Longstar* license now, which is a level beyond *Arcturus*. I didn't really want to get that one either, but that's another story.

Three weeks after my conversation with Windy, I had my license, and she took me on as a temporary, thereby allowing her to classify me as an employee.

Shara in the meantime wondered what the fuss was about. 'I'll

343

never figure out why anybody would pay large sums of money for antiques. I understand their archeological value. But in this case, even that seems problematical. All you can hope to do is find out how a few diehards spent their last days. To be honest, I think you'd pay them more respect by letting them be.'

I'd been empowered to offer her a third of any profits we might realize if the discovery were made and after Survey got its share. That got her attention. 'How much are we talking?' she asked.

I provided a modest estimate, based on what the handful of *Seeker* trophies had brought. She was impressed. 'The business pays enough to get by on,' I said.

'I guess. Well, okay, Chase. I can't very well turn that down. But I still can't imagine why the Margolians would try to get over to a world that's going into the deep freeze. I think this is wrongheaded all around. But all right. What's to lose?'

Windy showed up a few minutes later, and Shara told her she was going with us. Windy's color changed. 'I'd thought better of you,' she said.

So on a cool, windy day in late summer, in the year 1430 since the Foundation of Rimway's Associated States, Alex, Shara, and I caught the shuttle to Skydeck, and boarded VHY 111. The *Spirit*. Within an hour we were on our way back to Margolia.

30

Hitch your wagon to a star.

—Ralph Waldo Emerson,
Society and Solitude, 1870 C.E.

The *Spirit* was twice the size of the *Belle-Marie,* with accommodations for eleven passengers. The life-support section consisted of the bridge, twelve compartments (one for the pilot), two washrooms, a compact storage area, an operations center, a workout center the size of a large closet, and a common room. The latter was considerably more spacious than the one Alex and I were accustomed to. That said, the *Belle-Marie* nevertheless made for easier living. The *Spirit* was strictly a vehicle to transport people from one place to another. There were no amenities.

The rest of the ship, launch bay, main storage, and engine access, all below, was normally maintained in vacuum to preserve resources. There was also a parts locker and systems access area immediately beneath the bridge. 'Control units are there,' I explained to Shara, 'in case anything needs tweaking. And the black boxes for the AI are there.'

I went through my preflight checklist and set our jump for nine hours post departure. Then I strolled back to the ops center, where I found Shara seated in front of a display. 'Good,' she said. 'I was just coming to get you.'

'You want to talk about our target?'

'Yes.' She showed me a star and a lesser light. 'Tinicum 2116,' she said. 'And Margolia.'

'Okay.'

'Let's back Tinicum up nine thousand years.' Coordinates rippled along the lower right-hand corner, slowed, and stopped. The star moved halfway across the room. 'During the period since the event, it traveled somewhat more than a half light-year. This is where it was when impact occurred.

'We know from the effects of the disruption that the intruder came through on an angle close to the plane of the planetary system. We also know that, by now, it will have gone about the same distance that Tinicum did. A half light-year, more or less.'

'Okay.'

'Keep in mind that's an estimate. But it should be reasonably accurate. What we *don't* know is which way it was traveling.'

'Okay. So we can draw a ring around the point of impact, a half-light-year radius—'

'—And the intruder is somewhere along the circumference. Yes.' She drew the ring. 'That's our search area. The target might be on the far side, or on the interior, probably a bit above or below the plane. But it's there.'

'That looks like a big neighborhood,' said Alex. I hadn't seen him come in.

'It is,' she admitted. 'But it's small enough that it makes a search feasible.'

'How fast is the dwarf likely to be moving?'

'About the same velocity as Tinicum. Roughly twenty kilometers per second.'

'So,' said Alex, 'it's possible the thing might still be close to the system? Traveling with it?'

'*Close* is a relative term. It *passed through* the system, so we know there's some deviation.'

'All right. Where do we start?'

'We make for the point of impact. Once there we deploy our telescopes on opposite sides of it. At a range of' – she hesitated, considering it – 'let's make it five AUs. We want the telescopes ten AUs apart.'

I spent the next few hours boning up on brown dwarfs. Shara was right when she said there are a lot of them. According to Survey there were hundreds in the immediate vicinity of Rimway's sun. That didn't make me comfortable. But then it's a vicinity that incorporates a lot of empty space. Modern technology makes travel virtually instantaneous, and it causes you to forget just how big everything is. As I think I remarked somewhere else.

Brown dwarfs are not massive enough to burn hydrogen, so they don't ignite, the way a full-fledged star does. But they still give off considerable heat, more or less from tidal effects. They can be observed through infrared telescopes, in which they will appear as a faint glow.

Get close enough to the average brown dwarf and it'll look like a dim star. It's only .00004 times as bright as the sun, either ours or Earth's. Still, according to the book, they're pretty hot. Temperatures on the surface range up to 3,200 degrees C. At that level, substances like iron and rock occur as gases.

During the cooling process, they generate methane. The gases condense into liquids and form clouds, which contain some of the heat. But continued cooling results in storms, which in turn clear off the clouds. When that happens, infrared light from the heated atmosphere escapes, causing the dwarf to brighten.

Shara wasn't kidding that there were weather patterns. Some dwarfs, the hotter ones, have iron rain. Others, which have cooled sufficiently, may produce rain that is ordinary water.

They come in a variety of classifications based on spectral features. 'But any of them,' I asked Shara, 'would be visible to our telescopes?'

She nodded. 'Actually,' she said, 'this whole exercise should be pretty easy. At least I hope so.'

'Why?' I asked. 'You got a hot date?'

'Chase,' she said. 'I'm an astrophysicist. But it doesn't mean I want to spend my weekends out here.'

We made the jump on schedule, but emerged several days away from our target area. She wasn't unduly happy about that. 'Seems as if we could use some improvements in the technology,' she told me.

I checked in with the *Gonzalez,* the mission command ship, to let them know we'd arrived in the area. Alex took advantage of the link to talk to Emil Brankov about the latest findings at the excavation sites. There were, Brankov said, *'a lot of artifacts. And some human remains. Not much left of them, but they're there.'*

While we cruised into position, we spent time talking, watching sims, working out. Shara enjoyed role-playing games that involved blowing things up. I wasn't sure whether she was trying to send me a message or whether it reflected a naturally combative spirit. I became more aware how much she had changed since our days together at college. When I mentioned that sometimes I felt as if I barely knew her, she asked if I was aware how different *I'd* become.

'In what way?' I asked.

'You were shy. Unsure of yourself. And, as I recall, you took authority figures pretty seriously.'

'I'm still shy,' I said.

She laughed. 'I have no doubt.'

We also enjoyed *Conversations with Caesar.* If you haven't tried it, it gives you a chance to sit and talk with avatars of historical personages. Shara had a taste for the ancients, so we spent the better part of two days discussing religion with Cleopatra, women's rights with Thomas Aquinas, and public relations with Henry VIII. Marinda Harbach explained why we have such a bloody history. *'Serious predators,'* she said, *'do not kill one another. Never have. A tiger understands, for example, it's*

348

dangerous to attack another tiger. It's not at all certain who will end up dead.' But humans had never been serious predators. On the contrary, they'd been innocuous creatures, had eaten whatever came to hand, and never developed the instinct to avoid quarrels. *'After all,'* she said, *'when a fight breaks out between two monkeys, somebody gets a few lumps, but that's about all. They actually enjoy it. Brain scans make the point beyond question. By the time the monkeys discovered advanced weaponry, it was too late.'*

We talked about war and peace with Winston Churchill, and bumping universes with Taio Myshko. Kalu, the AI, did impressions of each character. Nobody knew, of course, how Churchill had actually sounded, but Kalu had Myshko down cold.

He also did impersonations of us. He seemed to enjoy himself commenting in Alex's deliberate and studied manner on the advantage of antiquities as an investment. He did Shara talking about how stars go bump in the night. And he was forever ordering snacks using my voice.

'I don't eat that much,' I told Alex. But he just laughed.

When we got close to the impact point, Shara decided it was time to inspect the telescope packages. Rather than pressurize the cargo deck, we put on suits.

Cargo was divided into three sections, the middle being the largest. It was our launch area, and it contained the packages. The lander, which was a bilious yellow color with Department of Planetary Survey and Astronomical Research stenciled on its hull, was secure in the lone bay.

The two telescopes were cubes with rounded edges, not much taller than I was. Plastene sheets protected them. Working in zero gee, we moved them onto the launch track.

We stripped the plastene from one of the packages to get a good look. The unit was a shoulder-high black metal dish, with several minithrusters attached.

'It's a two-meter scope,' Shara said. 'Equipped with a thirty-two thousand times thirty-two thousand infrared-sensitive imaging array. It can cover three by three degrees of sky.' She circled the thing and clicked a remote. Lamps blinked back. She compared them with a checklist.

'Okay?' I asked.

'Yes, indeed.' We walked back to the second package, pulled off the wrapping, and repeated the process. When she was done, we inspected the launcher. 'I guess we're all set,' she said at last.

We went back up an ascent tube, passed through the airlock onto the bridge, and climbed out of our suits. Shara commented it was good to feel some gravity again. Kalu announced we were one hour from the impact point.

We sat down and, for whatever reason, began reminiscing. We discovered we'd both dated the same guy, and both had the same reaction. We talked about instructors I hadn't thought of for fifteen years. And ambitions, some fulfilled, some abandoned. 'You became a pilot,' Shara said. 'When I first met you, when you were still a kid, you told me that was what you wanted to do.'

That was true. I also wanted to be a sculptor at one time, but that didn't go very far. 'Yeah,' I said. 'I always liked the idea of coming out here. Thought it was romantic.'

'And it wasn't.'

'It wears off.'

She laughed. 'I remember when that guy Jerry Whatzisname was going to be the father of your children.'

'That's a long time back.'

'Whatever happened to him?'

'He became a banker,' I said. 'Or a financial advisor. Something like that.'

'You ever see him?'

'No. Not for more than ten years.' And, after a moment: 'He's married. Two kids, last I heard.'

'I can't imagine you married to a banker.'

'Me, neither.' Still, I thought of him on occasion. I wouldn't have minded running into him some evening. By accident, of course.

* * *

When Kalu announced we were within seven minutes of our destination, we retreated to the ops center, where Alex was waiting. Shara sat down in the operator's chair. 'Kalu?'

'*Yes, Shara. I am here.*'

'Prepare to launch the Alpha package.'

'*On your direction.*' There was a bank of monitors. One provided an outside view of the launch doors. We watched them open.

'Who the hell is Kalu?' asked Alex.

'The AI,' I said.

'I know that. But who *was* he?'

'When the government wanted to shut interstellar exploration down two centuries ago,' Shara said, 'he was the guy who dissuaded them. It cost him politically because people didn't want to pay for it. One opponent asked him where does it stop?'

'What was his answer?' asked Alex.

'"You stop, you die." He was the first secretary of the Department of Planetary Survey and Astronomical Research.'

'The first *secretary*?'

'This is a while back. They didn't have directors then.'

'Okay.'

A stellar cloud was coming into focus on one of the monitors. 'Up there,' she said. 'That's Virginium. Lots of hot, young stars. Come back in a few billion years and it might be a nursery for new civilizations.' She smiled at Alex. I was getting the impression he was taken by her. 'Time to launch. You want to do the honors?'

'You go ahead,' he said. And that generosity of spirit convinced me. Alex loved drama and ceremony.

'Kalu,' she said. 'Launch Alpha.'

The package went out through the hatch, its thrusters fired once, twice.

'*Alpha away,*' said Kalu.

The package dwindled and vanished in the night.

My turn. 'Everybody strap down. Kalu, prepare to depart.'

Kalu acknowledged. Shara talked with the Alpha telescope's onboard AI, giving it final instructions.

Moments later, Brankov's image blinked on in the ops room. He looked tired. '*We found some inscriptions on stone,*' he said. One of them appeared, a large marble block with English symbols. We couldn't read them, but he translated: McCorby Health Labs. Beneath it, a date. The name of the month was March. It was the fourteenth day, and the year was 11.

'*We've got a city hall down the street. And what was once the Chalkoski Botanical Gardens a half klick away.*' I could see the intensity in Brankov's eyes. This was the mission of a lifetime.

A few hours later we jumped one and a half billion kilometers to the far side of the impact point and deployed Beta.

'What we're going to do,' said Shara, 'is to run a full survey of the sky, three hundred sixty to latitudes twenty degrees above and below the orbital plane.'

I was tempted to ask what orbital plane because we were in the middle of nowhere. But of course we were working with the plane of the planetary system as it had been nine thousand years earlier. 'The units will run in parallel,' she continued. 'We need to look at a total of fourteen thousand four hundred square degrees. That means we need sixteen hundred image pairs. Each image will require five minutes of exposure plus dither time.'

Alex was glazing again.

Shara understood. 'It means,' she told him, 'we should be able to do the complete survey in about six days.'

'Excellent,' he said. 'And at some point during all this, we'll spot the brown dwarf.'

'We should. Yes. We'll overlay the images from the telescopes on the screen.' She tapped the central monitor. 'Everything's framed against the stars. The stars won't show any appreciable movement from one image to the other because they're too far. But anything close by will appear to jump. And that, Mr Benedict, should be our dwarf.'

'How much of a jump?' I asked.

'I'd say thirty to sixty arcseconds.'

Alex grinned. How much was that?

'It's okay,' Shara said. 'Just look for a separation. Now, when it happens, we'll want to measure the radial velocity. That'll allow us to figure out approximately where it was when the impact happened.'

'But we already know that.'

'Confirmation data. And the more exact our information is, the easier it'll be to locate Balfour.'

'Okay,' said Alex. 'Good.'

'The hitch is that we don't know the temperature of the dwarf, so we'll run the survey at wavelengths of two to ten microns. That'll allow for fairly hot or very cool dwarfs, and everything between.' She held up a remote. 'Are we ready to start?'

'By all means,' said Alex.

They exchanged glances. 'Thanks,' he said. 'I will.' Without another word he took the remote and started the operation.

31

There are worlds enough out there for all. Go, and you will see canyons to make your head spin, and solitary beaches, and rings of light, and iron rivers. But wear a topcoat.

—Tavron Hamm,
There and Back, sixth millennium

Once the survey started, *Conversations with Caesar* stopped. Alex never left the ops center except from necessity. He watched relentlessly as the images shifted every few minutes, showing a new patch of sky. If one of the points of light seemed a trifle blurred, he leaned forward expectantly, hoping Shara would react, or that Kalu would declare a hit.

Occasionally, he talked with Brankov, who said he was fascinated by what we were trying to do. *'I wish you all success,'* he said. *'Let us hope you find it. And that your speculations prove correct.'*

Shara stuck it out with Alex the first day. Until she couldn't stand it anymore. Alex was simply too intense. On the second morning, she told him to let her know if they found something and retreated to the common room. I stuck my head in once in a while to see how she was doing, but for the most part I stayed with Alex. Out of a misplaced sense of loyalty, I suppose.

'Why does he care so much?' Shara asked. 'He's already made the big finds. So what if a few of them retreated to a base somewhere else? Right? Or am I missing something here?'

'No,' I said. 'You're right. I've never seen him like this before. I think it has to do with the *Seeker*. Full of kids. That really shook him up. I don't think he buys the idea that they would have known what was going to happen to one world but not to the other. Of the two, they must have known Margolia was safer. He wants to know why they jumped into the lion's mouth. He thinks he owes it to them to find out.'

'If in fact that's what they did,' said Shara. 'I'm not convinced.'

'Neither am I. But his instincts for things like this are pretty good.'

'Chase,' she said, 'instincts are for things like food and sex. They don't have much to do with logic.' She shook her head. 'If they actually landed people on Balfour, the explanation will turn out to be that they screwed up the calculations.'

'But they should have been able to figure it out, right?'

'Sure.' She sighed. 'But it's not my call.'

We needed a change of subject. 'Shara,' I said, 'I was surprised to find out how common these things are. Brown dwarfs. Do we have the local ones mapped?'

'Surely you joke.' She smiled again. That mischievous, let's-not-be-naïve grin. 'There's no reputation to be made looking for local brown dwarfs, so it doesn't happen.'

'Maybe the Council should get on the stick.'

'Yeah, I'm sure it's at the top of their agenda. I mentioned it to one of their reps one time, and he asked how much warning we'd have if one blundered into the system.'

'How much warning would we have?'

'Probably twenty or thirty years.'

'And what did he say?'

'Told me twenty or thirty years would be plenty of time to deal with it.'

'Is he serious? What would we do if it happened?'

356

'Wouldn't be much you *could* do. Except evacuate the planet.'

'Evacuate the *planet*? We don't have the facilities, do we? For that kind of effort?'

'Billions of people? I doubt it.' She was sitting with a book in her lap. 'I don't think math was his strong suit.'

I was asleep the second night when Alex knocked on my door. 'We got a hit,' he said.

I woke Shara. She came out in a robe and sat down to look at the images on the screen. There appeared to be two dim stars, side by side.

'That it?' I asked.

'There's a decent chance. Kalu, what's the range?'

'Point six-four,' he said. Fraction of a light-year.

'Recessional velocity?'

'Twenty-two kilometers per second.'

She scribbled numbers on a pad. 'It's a pretty good match. That's probably it.'

'Probably?' said Alex.

'No way to be positive yet. We should reconfigure the telescopes' optical trains to a higher magnification.'

'Why?'

'That'll give us the transverse velocity. Allow us to get a 3-D picture, and pin it down for certain.'

'How long will it take?'

'About fourteen hours.'

'Okay.' Alex rubbed his hands. 'Then you can figure out where the planet is, right?'

'If the sighting is confirmed.'

'That's good. Shara, you're a treasure.'

She smiled modestly. 'I do what I can.'

I was standing around, pretty much irrelevant. 'Anything I can do to help?'

'No. Thanks. I can take care of it. You might as well go back to bed.'

357

'Yeah. Okay, I'll see you guys in the morning.'

I started for the door. Shara turned suddenly toward Alex. 'But there's something *you* can do for me.'

'Name it.'

'I've never seen a brown dwarf. From nearby. Instead of just sitting here, waiting for the numbers to come in, why don't we go take a look?'

'All right,' said Alex. He hid it well, but he wasn't excited at the prospect of going off on a side trip. Not at this point. But he figured he owed Shara. He looked my way. 'Chase?'

'Consider it done, boss.'

'I mean,' said Shara, 'as long as we've come this far, it would be nice to see one.'

That surprised me. 'You've never seen a dwarf star?'

'Actually,' she said, 'no. I never really had the opportunity.'

'Well, we'll rectify that.'

She looked delighted, a kid at a birthday party. 'I mean, we pretty much take them for granted. There are a lot of them, and they don't actually do anything.'

'Except barge around.'

'Yeah,' she said. 'Except that.'

Shortly before we made the jump, we got a transmission from Brankov. They'd found what appeared to have been a museum set up to honor the original settlers. Not much was distinguishable. The objects that had been exhibited, as well as the cases in which they'd been placed, had all but dissolved. *'We can make out some of the inscriptions. And that's about it. Some terrestrial dates. Some names we don't recognize.'*

During the course of the conversation, we told him we might have found the brown dwarf.

'Glad to hear it. So you can figure out where Balfour is? Are you headed there now?'

'We're going to take a look at the dwarf first. We have a lady on board with a special interest in compact objects.'

'*Okay. Good luck. Keep me informed.*'

We sent a message to Windy, letting her know what was happening. It seemed like smart policy to keep Survey's public relations officer in the loop.

We made a good jump and came out within a day's travel time. The brown dwarf looked like a gas giant, except there was no sun nearby, so the glow it was putting out wasn't reflected light. It packed about 5 percent of a solar mass beneath all-encompassing clouds. 'It's a little bit light,' said Shara. 'It needs about *eight* percent solar mass to ignite.' To become a legitimate star. There was a collection of moons, eleven of them altogether, and a wispy ring that wasn't immediately visible.

The dwarf itself – a curious term for so monstrous an object – seemed to be simply a sphere of eerily lit mud-colored clouds, with a few reddish streaks and spots. Surface temperature checked in at 800° K. 'The spots are storms,' Shara said. She was luminous that day. I had never seen her so filled with sheer joy. She was face-to-face with, as she put it, one of the objects that formed the gravitational center of her life.

She stood by a viewport, bathed in its autumn light. 'Isn't it gorgeous?'

'Yes,' I said.

'It's a class-T,' she said. 'Lot of methane. And it's got water.'

'Water?'

She nodded. 'Yep.'

I went over and stood beside her and she embraced me. 'Chase,' she said, 'I take it all back. I'm glad I came.'

'Good,' I said.

We were still there, exchanging pleasantries, when Kalu's baritone got our attention. '*We have the transverse velocity,*' he said.

Shara nodded and started back for the ops center. 'Let's see what it looks like.'

Kalu gave us a 3-D projection. Here was the brown dwarf. This was its track back to the time of impact, and over there, well toward the monitor bank, was Margolia and its sun. At the *point* of impact.

'They don't intersect,' I said. 'Something's wrong.'

'Kalu, run a check, please.' She looked at me and shrugged. These things happen.

'The display is accurate, Shara.'

'Can't be,' I said.

'Yeah. It's nowhere near the system.' She checked the ranges. 'This is not the one. Closest it got was a decent fraction of a light-year. A twentieth.'

I became aware of Alex, standing silently at the hatch, listening.

'Does this mean we got things wrong?' I asked. 'Are there *two* brown dwarfs in the area?'

'Could be.' She sat down at one of the ops consoles and the 3-D images vanished. 'Actually, sixty percent of brown dwarfs travel in pairs.'

'Really?'

'Yes. The companion is usually within a tenth of a light-year.' She put the scope images on the monitors. Views forward and aft, and off both beams. 'It's not very likely that this thing missed Margolia just as another, unrelated, dwarf took the system apart. So there's probably—'

Against the cosmic backdrop off the starboard side, a blood-red star appeared. First magnitude.

'That it?'

'I'll get back to you,' said Shara.

It was just under a half light-year from our position, and its radial and transverse velocities were almost identical to the brown dwarf.

'It's one of your bloodred jobs,' I said.

'Looks like.' She was tapping keys and watching numbers roll down the screen. Finally, she froze them. We were looking at a set of coordinates. Shara ran the dwarf backward until it intersected with Tinicum. At the point of impact. 'That's your intruder,' she said. 'No question.'

'Okay.' Alex took the chair beside her. 'Now we can figure out what happened to Balfour.'

'Give me a little time,' she said.

I sent off a report to Windy, then went back to my cabin and tried to read. I was tired, but I just lay there listening to the assorted sounds of the ship. The *Spirit* was noisier than the *Belle Marie*. The quarters were more cramped. And it felt more impersonal. I can't explain that, exactly. Maybe it was the AI. Kalu wasn't exactly charismatic.

Eventually I gave up, got a shower, and put on a clean set of clothes. Outside, Shara was in the middle of an explanation. And she looked solemn. Alex was pale. Shara waved in my direction. '—Doesn't mean it necessarily got swallowed,' she said.

Alex took a deep breath. 'Shara thinks,' he said, 'there might have been a collision.'

'*Might*,' she said.

'A direct hit?' I asked. 'Balfour?'

'It's possible.'

Nobody said anything.

'Look.' Shara leveled her voice. Let's all keep calm. 'We need to check this out more carefully. I need time to put the numbers together. Then we can get a better idea what actually happened.'

Alex looked at me. 'Chase,' he said, 'bring Emil up to date. And get us over there.'

'Over where?'

'To the intruder.'

We swung to starboard. The intruder was a distant red glow. We lined up on it, fed the range into Kalu, and belted down.

'Don't jump in too close,' Shara cautioned. 'We want to give ourselves plenty of space with that thing.'

I've always been a safety-first kind of person. Because of that, and the inaccuracy of the quantum drive, we came out almost three days away. Close enough.

Again, I was struck by the dwarf's resemblance to a gas giant.

Except that this one was red, with no visible moons and no ring. Its surface churned with tornadoes and cyclones. 'That'll be iron,' Shara said.

'What will?'

'The clouds. And silicates and corundum.' Occasionally, when the clouds parted, hot spots that were even brighter became visible. Shara spent time on the instruments while Alex watched anxiously.

'What are you looking for?' he asked.

'Maybe a surprise. Good news: It did not swallow Balfour. But it *did* have lunch recently.'

'How do you mean?' asked Alex.

'Probably Balfour's moon. This thing passed within a few hundred thousand kilometers of Balfour. And I'd bet it took the moon. Do we know whether Balfour *had* one?'

'No.'

'Okay. I'd bet it did.'

'How do you know?'

She pointed at lines on the central screen. 'Its atmosphere is saturated with silicates.'

'Which tells us what?'

'It swallowed a moon. And it happened at about the time of the intersection.'

Alex took a deep breath. 'How can you be sure it wasn't Balfour?'

'It wasn't a planet.' She spun around to face him. 'Terrestrial moons are made of the surface scum skimmed off terrestrial worlds by major impacts. Think of Rimway's structure. An iron core and a silicate mantle. The moon at home is pretty much nothing but iron-poor mantle material.' She indicated the screen. 'Take a look at the lines. You can see there's no iron.'

I couldn't see that, and I had no doubt Alex couldn't. But that was irrelevant. Shara could, and that was all that mattered.

'So where's Balfour?'

She was smiling broadly. 'It got close enough to lose its satellite. So at the very least, it's trailing behind the dwarf.'

'Can we get pictures?'

'I've been trying to. I haven't seen it yet.'

'Okay. It's still early.'

'Right. And there's another possibility.'

'Which is what?'

Bare minutes later, the second possibility materialized when a blue star appeared from behind the dwarf. 'Chase,' Shara said, 'Alex. Enjoy the moment. Unless I've completely blown it, you're looking at Balfour.'

32

Use your eyes instead of your brain, and you'll come to grief every time.

—Delis Tolbert,
The Adventures of Omar Paisley, 1417

'I don't think there's any question about it,' said Shara. 'That's your missing planet.'

We were getting a decent picture on the scope. And we saw immediately that it had oceans! And it was *green*.

Alex looked overwhelmed. 'It's a living world,' he said.

Shara nodded. 'Looks like.' And to me: 'How close is it to the dwarf?'

I passed the question to Kalu. *'It's about a million kilometers. Maybe a bit more.'*

She clapped her hands. 'Close enough. Who would've thought?'

It was a glorious moment. We danced and yipped and embraced. I got a huge hug from Alex.

'It's in tidal lock,' said Kalu. *'Orbital period looks like approximately two point six days.'*

It took a few minutes for us to come back to reality. We broke into the stock cabinet and passed out drinks. We lifted our glasses to Balfour.

'Brilliant,' said Alex.

'How do you mean?' I asked. 'Who's brilliant?'

'The Margolians. Now we know why they moved people to Balfour.'

'You think they knew in advance this would happen?'

'Yes.' Shara looked puzzled. 'They figured it out. Maybe they weren't sure. I don't know what kind of equipment they had with them. But they understood Balfour might come out of it okay.'

'Why the frown?' asked Alex.

'Well,' she said, 'living conditions on the surface, during the event, and for a considerable time afterward, would have been difficult.'

'In what way?'

'During the first few decades after capture by the dwarf, rotational energy would have had to be dissipated.' She ran through a few equations on a notepad. 'There would have been lots of earthquakes, tidal waves, typhoons, volcanoes going up. Global warming during the first century. Substantial evaporation. I'm thinking jungle pretty much everywhere.'

'Again?' I asked.

'Yes. Warm, wet catastrophes breed jungle.' She shook her head. 'They would have had to be desperate to cross to Balfour, and it's hard to see how they could have survived.'

I wondered whether I wouldn't have preferred going down with the original world rather than getting hauled off into the night by a rogue dwarf.

One side of Balfour, of course, was permanently dark. We trained the scopes on it anyhow and held our breath. I don't know what we expected, or what Alex was hoping for. But nobody said anything. And, as we expected, no flicker of light appeared anywhere.

'If there were survivors,' said Shara, 'if they'd actually succeeded in establishing a base and keeping it alive, it wouldn't have been on the back side anyhow. It'll be too cold there.'

She turned to the data coming in from the sensors, which were still examining the brown dwarf, noting its mass and gravitation, its rotational period, the distribution of elements in its clouds. Surface temperature was 1500°K. 'It's young,' she said. 'Much younger than the other one. They cool off as they age.' She grinned. 'Like guys.' The party girl survives in the astrophysicist.

'How old *is* it?' I asked.

'About a hundred million years.'

'That's *young*?'

'Relatively. Sure.'

I love the way these people talk.

Alex had been looking at the pictures of Balfour, paying no attention to the conversation. 'We'll want to go down to the surface and see what we have. What are conditions like on the ground, do you think?'

Shara started to answer. She said something about picking our spot and it would be comfortable enough, but then we got a blinker and she stopped dead. I switched over to the auxiliary display.

'What's wrong?' asked Alex.

'We're getting a code white.' I ran a confirmation, to be sure.

'Out *here*?' asked Shara. 'Who'd be in distress *here*?'

'Kalu,' I said, 'do we have a visual?'

'Negative, Chase. I am trying to get a lock now.'

'Is there a voice signal?' asked Shara.

'No,' I said. 'All we're getting is the beep.'

'Ridiculous,' said Alex. 'There can't be anybody in *this* area.'

'Somebody's here,' I said.

'Chase, I have the coordinates.'

We were all looking at one another. Everybody had a bad feeling. 'Kalu,' I said, 'do we have a visual yet?'

'On-screen.'

It was a Y-pod. An emergency unit. Something to keep you going until help came. *But the hatch was open.*

We enhanced the image.

'There's someone in the pilot's seat,' said Shara.

Wearing a pressure suit. I opened a channel. 'Hello, Lifeboat. What is your condition?'

I switched over and we listened to a carrier wave.

Alex leaned close to the mike. 'Hello.' He sounded hostile. 'Are you able to respond?'

'Kalu,' I said 'where is the thing?'

'Bearing zero-three-four mark two-seven. Range four hundred twenty-five klicks.'

'Any sign of a ship?'

'Yes. I'm getting data now.'

'Details, please?'

'Looks like a private yacht. KY designator on the hull. Rest not visible. It appears to be adrift. There's a power signature, but it's low.'

'Okay,' I said. 'Take us to the pod, quickest possible route. Everybody belt down.'

'Wait a minute,' said Alex. 'This is a setup. Has to be.'

'I think you're right,' I said. 'It's too much of a coincidence. But it doesn't matter. We can't take a chance and leave him. And we've got to get moving. We don't know how long he's been out here.'

Alex nodded. 'First we need to take some precautions.'

'Kalu,' I said, 'what's our ETA?'

'How much fuel are you willing to expend?'

'Whatever it takes. Quickest time.'

'Very good, Chase. I make it thirteen minutes.'

'What kind of precautions?' asked Shara.

The man in the pilot's seat wasn't moving. It was dark inside and hard to get a good look.

'We better hustle,' I said, as we slipped alongside. I climbed out of my seat, but Alex asked sharply where I thought I was going.

'To collect him.'

368

'No. Let's do this the way we decided.'

'I wasn't aware *you* would be the one to go after him.'

'Sorry I didn't make myself clear. But this isn't a job for a woman.'

Oh, Lord. Here we go again. 'Alex, I have more experience in zero gee.'

'What's it take to cross ten meters, pull him out, and bring him back?'

Well, truth was, Alex wouldn't have to go outside at all. And sure, I could have insisted. I was, after all, the captain. But I couldn't see that it made much difference. And when his testosterone was flowing, I'd always found it best to indulge him.

'Good,' he said. 'Now let's move on.' He glanced over at Shara.

A few minutes later, in a pressure suit, he was hurrying through the launch bay, which, you will recall, was maintained in vacuum. I turned the lights on for him and, as he approached the cargo doors, I opened them.

Kalu managed the attitude thrusters and angled us toward the pod until it floated in through the cargo doors. Then we raised the *Spirit* slightly, and the vehicle settled into a cradle.

'*Good,*' said Alex. '*Touchdown.*'

I activated magnetic locks to secure it and gave him a little gravity. Alex walked cautiously around to the open hatch, looked in, and found himself confronted by a laser. I saw the moment he did. '*Back off.*' A familiar voice crackled out of the speakers. A male. '*Don't make any sudden moves.*'

Alex froze.

'*Kolpath, I assume you can hear me. If you try anything at all, do anything except follow my instructions completely, I will kill him. Do you understand?*'

It took me a minute to remember. *Charlie Everson.* The young man with the shuttle reservations.

'Okay,' I said. 'Don't hurt him. I won't give you any trouble.'

'*Good. That's smart.*'

Alex found his voice. *'What's this about?'* he demanded. *'What do you want, Everson?'*

Charlie got out of the pod. *'I'm sure you know, Mr Benedict.'* His voice was laced with contempt. *'Now turn around and walk straight ahead and don't reach for anything.'*

Alex started to walk. Charlie kept his laser leveled at Alex's back. *'What's this all about anyhow?'* Alex asked.

'Just keep going.'

Alex started to turn, and Charlie fired his weapon at the deck. Alex froze. Charlie waited a few seconds and turned the beam off. *'I scare easily,'* he said. *'Don't do anything unless I tell you to first.'*

'Chase,' said Kalu. *'Lower deck is punctured.'*

'It's okay, though,' Charlie continued. *'You do what I say, and nobody's going to get hurt.'* He was in a bright yellow pressure suit with no markings, Alex in Survey's standard forest green. They reached the zero-gee tube, got in together, and came up to the main deck. I heard them enter the airlock and close the hatch. The compression cycle started.

The inner hatch opened directly out onto the bridge. I turned to face it.

'Who do you work for?' Alex asked.

'No need for you to know,' he said.

'You planted the bomb, didn't you? You took down the shuttle and killed twenty-two people.'

'Yeah. I guess I did. Don't remember the exact number.' His voice was deadly calm. Full of menace. *'Kolpath.'*

'What do you want, Charlie?'

'I want to remind you. No surprises when the door opens. I want you and the other woman standing directly in front of the airlock. With your hands in the air. If you're not there, I'll kill him. Do you understand?'

'What other woman?'

'Don't play games with me. You know who I'm talking about. Michaels.'

'She's not on board. There's nobody here but Alex and me.'

'*You're lying.*'

'Suit yourself.'

'*What happened to her?*'

The lamp on the hatch was amber. Still pressurizing.

'She—'

Alex broke in: '*She switched over to the* Gonzalez *when we stopped at Margolia.*'

'*Why'd she do that?*' He wasn't going to buy it.

'*Boyfriend on board,*' Alex said. '*Dumb bitch. It's the only reason she came with us.*'

Well, it was better than my story. I was going to claim she got sick at the last minute.

'*You're lying,*' said Charlie.

'*I wouldn't do that. Not when you're carrying a laser.*'

He hesitated, unsure what to do next. '*Anything happens, anything at all I don't like, somebody's dead. You understand, Benedict?*'

'I understand.'

'*And you out there, Kolpath?*'

'Nobody'll give you any trouble, Charlie.'

'*If I see anybody else, anywhere, he's gone.*'

'Stop it,' said Alex. '*You're frightening her.*'

'*That's a good thing, Benedict. A little fear at the moment makes for a healthy attitude.*'

'*Do what he says, Chase. He's a nutcase.*'

'*Watch your tongue,*' said Charlie.

'*Why? What are you going to do? Kill me?*'

'*I can if you like.*'

'Please let him be. We'll give you whatever you want.' The status lamp turned green. I took my place a few paces in front of the airlock and raised my hands. 'Kalu,' I said, 'open the hatch.'

It swung wide. Charlie ordered Alex forward and stuck his head out and looked around. When he saw nobody, he pointed to a bulkhead. '*Both of you over there. Keep your hands over your heads.'* We did as we were told while he removed his helmet. He took a deep breath. 'Damned stale air,' he said. I didn't know whether he meant the air from his suit, or the air on the bridge.

Alex pulled off his own helmet. 'How'd you know?' he asked. 'How did you know we were here?'

He shrugged. No problem. 'Anything you do, I know about.'

'You lunatic,' I said. 'What the hell's this about?'

He didn't care much for criticism. The laser swung in my direction. I threw myself to one side and he fired a short burst. Only a second or so. It seared into my leg, just below the knee. I screamed and tried to roll away from it. Alex started forward. But Charlie turned the weapon back on him. 'Don't,' he said.

Alex stopped dead.

'I don't want to hear any more mouthing off from either of you.' He glared at me, offended. 'Do it again, and I'll shut you up permanently.' Alex came over to help me while Charlie looked around the bridge. He spotted a couple of air tanks. 'I hope you don't mind if I borrow these on the way out.'

'When are you leaving?' I asked. I wasn't bleeding, but my leg hurt like hell. Alex tried to get ointment from the first-aid locker, but Charlie told him no. 'Don't go near anything unless I tell you to,' he said.

The airlock door was still open. 'Kalu,' I said. 'Close the hatch.'

It swung shut.

'No need to do that, Chase,' Charlie said. There was something obscene in the way he pronounced my name. 'I wasn't planning on staying long.'

I stared up at him. 'Force of habit.'

He glanced through the door, down the passageway. 'Let's just go make sure we're really alone.' He backed off, keeping as much distance from us as he could. 'You go first, Benedict. Any trouble, I shoot *her.'*

'Be careful with that thing,' Alex snapped.

'Just do what I tell you.'

I got to my feet. It wasn't as painful as it would have been at full gravity, but I still tried to keep my weight off the injured leg.

I limped along behind Alex into the passageway, and Charlie brought up the rear. All the doors were closed. 'We're going to open them one at a time,' Charlie said. 'And Chase, you stay back here near me.'

One hand closed on my shoulder.

'Anybody we see,' he said, 'is dead. No questions asked.'

'There's nobody back here, Charlie,' Alex said. His cabin was immediately off the bridge. The first room. 'Kalu,' I said, 'open room one.'

The door rolled up into the overhead. 'Inside,' Charlie told Alex. I followed. He stayed at the doorway, where he could watch the passage. There was a single closet in the cabin. 'Open it,' he said.

Alex pushed the manual and the door slid into the bulkhead. A few shirts, a pair of slacks, and a jacket hung inside. Otherwise, it was empty.

We crossed the passageway. 'Your cabin?' Charlie asked, looking at me. Clothes were everywhere.

'Yes.'

'Pretty sloppy.' We opened the closet for him. More clothes. 'You always travel like this, Chase?' he asked, allowing himself a grin.

'I like to be prepared,' I said. I was seriously hurting at that point, leaning against a bulkhead, trying to stay upright.

Shara's quarters were next. Alex opened the door and showed him an unused room. Nothing in the closet. Nothing in the cabinets. Charlie had already seen all her stuff in my place. When he was satisfied we closed it and moved on.

One by one we went through the remaining compartments, same routine each time. We inspected the operations center, the common room, the washrooms, and the storage area at the far end of the passage.

Charlie looked puzzled. He'd been sure we would find Shara

Michaels. 'How have you been managing the search without having a technician on board who knew what she was doing?' he asked.

'I know what I'm doing,' I said, trying to sound insulted.

'I'm sure.' He used the laser to start us walking back toward the bridge. His eyes were hard and cold. Pure ice. He kept looking around. When we got to the bridge, he noticed the deck hatch – the one that led down into the parts locker. 'What's that?'

'A hatch,' I said.

That earned me a slap that drove me to my knees. Alex glared at me. Stop provoking him.

'What's down there?' Charlie demanded. 'And forget the smart mouth.'

'Supplies,' I said. 'Equipment.'

'Open it up.'

I told Kalu, and the door slid back into the deck. Charlie moved us away, looked down, and growled something. 'Okay. You can close it.' He opened one of our comm links and pulled on a pair of earphones. 'All set,' he said to someone at the other end of the circuit.

We couldn't hear the reply.

Charlie nodded. 'Everything's under control.'

Something more from the yacht.

'Okay.' Charlie kept a careful eye on us. 'We'll be changing course in a minute,' he told his confederate. 'Once we're lined up, I need you to bring the yacht alongside. Off to starboard. Just tell her and she'll take care of it. I'll be coming back in a few minutes.' He listened and nodded. 'I'll let you know when it's done.'

I wondered about the course change but said nothing. Alex's eyes caught mine, and I couldn't miss the message. Bad things coming.

Charlie was still listening. 'Okay,' he said finally. He was nodding at whatever was being said. Then he switched on the speaker and signaled to Alex: 'The boss wants to talk to you.'

Alex nodded. 'Hello, Windy.'

'*Oh,*' she said. It was her voice, whispery and sad and filled with regret. If I'd been sitting in a chair, I'd have fallen out of it. '*So you knew.*'

'Sure. Who else knew we were out here?'

'*Very good.*' She paused. '*I wanted you to know I'm sorry things are turning out the way they are.*'

'It was you all the time,' I said.

'*I tried to talk sense to you, Chase. But you wouldn't listen. Neither you nor your sanctimonious partner was willing to back off. You were going to keep defiling sites, keep stealing artifacts, and keep selling them off for your own damned profit. I'm sorry for you, Chase.*' Her voice shook. '*You have so much potential. And you've made me do things I'll always regret. But somebody had to stop you.*'

'Why'd you kill Ollie?' Alex asked.

'*He ransacked the Gideon V site. I thought he deserved it. I assumed you'd agree. He bought one of the director's people. What I told you was true. I wouldn't lie to you.*'

'Not in so many words,' I said.

'*That's hardly fair. I don't know how many times I warned you about what you and your partner were doing.*'

'So you arranged to bomb a shuttle.'

'*No. I didn't intend that.*'

'That was *my* idea,' said Charlie. There was something surreal about that moment. Charlie was standing, grinning, proud of himself. 'It seemed foolproof. Most people don't screw around the way you two do.'

'*You and Chase had to be stopped. I told him to take care of it, but to find a way to make it look like an accident. I never imagined—*'

'It's too late to worry about it now,' said Charlie. 'Can't put the wasps back in the nest.'

Alex tried to lower his hands, but Charlie signaled him to keep them high. 'You didn't really kill Ollie,' he said, 'because of Gideon

V, did you? You killed him because he'd begun to suspect the truth about you.'

'*I killed him because of Gideon V. But it's true he'd begun to put things together. He was, in fact, foolish enough to ask me the same question you just did, whether I'd been responsible for the shuttle. I was offended.*'

'I'm sure,' said Alex.

'*I mean it. I didn't want those people to die. If I'd had any idea—*'

'How'd you know?' I asked Alex.

'What else could Ollie have wanted to tell you?' he said. 'Look out for Windy.'

'*I had no sympathy for him. I mean, we're talking about a guy who robbed tombs. Who bribed one of our staff to get access to information. That was what outraged me. People like him and you have no morals at all. I'm sorry to say it, but it's true. Even you, Chase. You've corrupted Shara. By the way, I haven't heard her voice. Hello, Shara. I'm sorry you had to get involved in this.*'

'She's not here,' said Charlie. 'There's just the two of them.'

'*Of course she's there, Blink. Look around. And be careful. She's hiding somewhere. Call me when the job's done.*' She broke the connection, and I shut down our end. We did not want to take a chance on Windy's overhearing the next few minutes.

'*Blink?*' said Alex. 'Is that *you*?'

'Yeah.' He looked nervously around to reassure himself there was no one coming up behind him. 'Okay, where is she?'

'Windy's mistaken,' Alex said. 'Shara's with the *Gonzalez*.'

I moved a couple of paces to my right. Away from Alex. Alex gave me a moment and inched in my direction. Charlie responded by moving to his right. He wanted to keep some distance between us. But we wanted to inch him around where he'd be standing with his back to the cargo airlock.

'What's your full name, Blink?' asked Alex.

'What do you care? Where's the bitch?'

'She's not here.'

He aimed the weapon at a point between Alex's eyes. Alex flinched a bit, but he didn't back away. 'I'll say it again,' he said. 'She's not here. You know she's not here.'

'Okay. It doesn't matter.' He pointed the weapon at the pilot's chair. 'Sit down, Chase. You, too, Benedict.'

We complied.

'Chase, put this thing on a collision course.' He nodded toward the brown dwarf.

I started to turn around, but he held the laser where I could see it. The torch end of the thing, which was big, black, and lethal.

'Kalu. New course. Make for the brown dwarf.'

'Orbital?'

'No.' I hesitated.

Charlie pushed the laser against the back of my neck. The metal felt cold. 'Tell him,' he said.

'Make it collision.'

'Are you sure, Captain?'

'Yes.'

'Very good. It will require only a moderate adjustment to our present course.'

'Do it.'

'And we will be accelerating for a few seconds.'

Alex was watching me. 'You know, Charlie, Blink, whatever your name is,' he said, 'you're going to get caught.'

'It's possible. But I doubt it.'

'Two minutes to start of maneuver,' said Kalu.

'Very good,' said Charlie. 'Buckle yourselves in, people.'

He braced himself against a bulkhead. 'I hope neither of you will try anything foolish during this.'

The *Spirit* slipped into its turn and began to accelerate. Something went bump in the airlock.

'What was that?' he demanded.

'Storage,' said Alex. 'We probably dislodged something while you were turning the place upside down.'

Charlie stole a look down the passageway. It was still empty.

377

He hung on to a monitor while gee forces pushed us into our seats as we simultaneously accelerated and turned to port. Then it all went away. *'Maneuver complete,'* said Kalu. *'We are on collision course with the dwarf. Impact in four hours, eleven minutes.'*

'Thanks, Kalu.' I started to release the harness, but Charlie told me to sit still. He came up behind me and I caught a glimpse of the laser. I thought he was going to use it on me. But instead he fired at the controls. Didn't aim; just cranked it up and swept the beam along the panel. It cut through modules and monitors. Wires popped and burned. I said something unkind and released the harness, but he shook his head no and swung the laser, still firing, in my direction. He aimed low. I got my feet out of the way, and the beam sliced into the base of the chair and cut it off its mount. It collapsed and spilled me onto the deck.

'Don't get up,' he said. 'Just stay where you are.' The air filled with the acrid smell of burning cables. He smiled at me. 'Believe me, I'm sorry about this but I don't really have any choice here, love.' My heart stopped. He laid an index finger alongside his jaw. 'It can be a hard world,' he said. His back, finally, was to the airlock.

'You know,' Alex said, 'it's painful to have this happen when we're so close.'

'Yeah.'

'I mean, this would be a good time. To be out here on a mission like this.'

That was intended to signal Shara. Charlie, not paying strict attention, missed the line. *This would be a good time* . . . Now or never.

Behind him, the airlock began to open.

'I'd like to leave you both alive for these last few hours,' he said. 'But I can't. I'm sorry about that but I'm not sure what my chances would be to get out with you two loose up here. For example, I'm pretty sure you could seal me in the airlock. Couldn't you?'

'We can't do that,' I said. 'There's no way.'

'Good. But I can't be certain. Sometimes you just don't get a break, you know?'

I was straining to keep my eyes off the hatch.

'Ladies first, I suppose. I'm really not sure of the protocol in this sort of arrangement.' He leveled the weapon at me. 'Goodbye, Chase. It'll be—'

Shara charged out of the airlock with a wrench.

Charlie heard her, started to turn, and I grabbed the laser. Shara swung for his head. He got one arm up, and the wrench nailed him on the shoulder. Good enough. He screamed and went down. Alex jumped on and we all wrestled for the weapon.

Charlie pushed me aside and hit Shara in the jaw, sending her tumbling. Alex and Charlie were both holding the laser when it went off again. Metal crackled and smoked. Charlie screamed and tried to wrestle it away. It popped into the air and bounced under the auxiliary seat. They flailed away at one another, trying to get to it. But Shara got there first, grabbed it, spun around, and came up firing. The bolt hit Charlie in the head. He grunted, staggered back, and crumpled, slowly, as people will in low gravity.

Shara, who is not given to messing around, held the beam on him as he went down.

'That's enough,' Alex said. He took the weapon from her. Charlie lay flat on the deck with his face gone and a wisp of smoke rising from his skull.

The controls were a disaster area, charred and cut.

Shara looked at Alex, assured herself he was okay, and turned to me. My leg wasn't so good, and my neck hurt. 'I was beginning to think you'd forgotten me,' she said.

'I wish we could have gotten you out of there a bit sooner,' I said. 'I'd hoped you'd get him when he first came aboard.'

She gazed at Alex. 'There was never enough separation between you. He kept the laser aimed at your neck.'

'Well,' said Alex, 'he's out of business. That's all that matters.'

I wasn't so sure. 'Kalu,' I said, 'status report, please.'

'Hello, Chase. I no longer have control over the flight path. Control systems for main engines and attitude thrusters on both beams are inoperative. Quantum engines are down. I have no specifics on them at the moment. Life support is okay.' He started reading off a laundry list of problems, but I interrupted. 'Details later, Kalu. Are we losing air?'

'Hull integrity is intact, except hole punched through lower deck.'

'Can we maneuver at all?'

'I can turn us around the central axis. That's about it.'

'How about we use the lander to get clear?' said Shara.

'It doesn't have enough thrust. We'd just follow the Spirit down.'

'Go to manual,' suggested Alex.

'The problem's not the AI,' I said. 'It's the controls. They don't exist anymore. Kalu, send a code white to the Gonzalez. Tell them they have four hours to get to us.'

'No,' said Alex. 'Wait.'

'What's wrong?'

'Is the comm link off?' Alex asked.

'I shut it down a few minutes ago.'

'Then Windy doesn't know what happened?'

'No.'

'You send that code white and Windy'll know quickly enough.'

'It doesn't matter, Chase,' said Kalu. 'The long-range transmission system is inoperative. We do have radio available.'

'That would get them here in maybe six months,' said Shara.

Alex was opening the deck hatch. 'We'll have to make repairs,' he said. 'We have spare parts.'

I took a long look at the bridge. 'I hope we have a lot of them.'

33

The future is no more uncertain than the present.
—Walt Whitman,
'Song of the Broad-Axe,' 1856 C.E.

'Can you make repairs?' asked Alex.

I looked at the wreckage. 'I'm not optimistic,' I said.

Outside the viewport, the vast red clouds blocked off half the sky. 'I'm not asking you to be optimistic. Just jury-rig something.'

They watched hopefully while I did a quick survey. 'I could get it up and running again,' I said, 'if we have the parts, and if we had time. I've got Kalu to help. But the relays are gone, the wiring's up in smoke, some of this stuff is fused. Give me a week, and I might be able to put something together.'

'It's that bad,' said Alex.

'That's about it,' I said. 'The answer's *no*.'

'*You have three hours, fifty-seven minutes,*' said Kalu, '*before reaching a point from which we will not be able to extract the ship.*' I guess he was trying to be helpful.

I looked at Shara. 'Why don't you call it a *red* dwarf?'

'They've always called this kind of object a brown dwarf.'

'The yacht's our only way out,' said Alex.

'I don't think Windy's going to invite us over.'

'I love riding with you guys,' said Shara. 'Does this kind of thing happen all the time?' Despite the bravado, she looked frightened. 'Anybody have any ideas?' She'd gotten the burn ointment and was rubbing it into my leg while I sat with my head back and my eyes closed.

'Does Windy know,' asked Alex, 'that we've lost thrust?'

'Yes,' I said. 'No way she could miss that. What she's waiting for now is for Charlie to tell her our communications are also down, that we can't contact anyone. Then it's just a matter of picking up her guy and clearing out.'

Alex looked down at the body. 'If she figures out Charlie's gone to his reward, she's just going to take off and leave us.'

'Look.' I pointed at the viewports. Windy's yacht was pulling into position off our starboard beam. Getting ready to extract Charlie.

I did a quick scan of the vehicle. 'It's a *Lotus*,' I said. 'Carrying capacity is *three*. Pilot plus two passengers.'

'My God,' said Shara. 'We've got to do better than that.'

Alex was staring at the approaching yacht. 'Only if we're worried about Windy. I think I'm past that point.'

'Well,' I continued, 'there's always a safety margin. You can get one or two more on board. Considering the size of that thing, I'd say *one*. But if we could take the damned thing, we could alert Brankov; and then it would just be a matter of hanging on until he got here.'

'You figure there's anybody else over there?' asked Shara.

'I doubt it,' said Alex. 'This isn't the kind of flight where you take friends along.'

Shara was standing with her back pressed against the bulkhead. 'Okay, how do we manage it? She's not going to open up for us.'

'She might,' Alex said. 'After all, she's expecting Charlie.'

'So we give her Charlie?' I said.

'Exactly. Kalu, can you impersonate Charlie's voice?'

'*I believe so.*' I jumped. It sounded as if Charlie was up and around again. '*I want to remind you. No surprises. I want you standing directly in front of the airlock when it opens. With your hands in the air. If you're not there, I'll kill him. Do you understand?'* Tone and inflection were perfect.

'Good,' said Alex. 'Beautiful. Now let's call Windy and have Kalu do his Charlie impression and tell her everybody's dead and he's coming home. Tell her to open the airlock. If I put on his pressure suit, I should be able to cross and get inside without her being aware it's me.'

'You?' I said.

'Who would you suggest?' He knew what was coming and sent me a warning glance. 'The sooner we get this going, Chase, the better.' He checked to make sure he had the laser.

'I should go,' I said.

'Why?'

'Same as before. I have more experience working in vacuum. And this time all our lives depend on getting it right.'

'Chase, it's too dangerous.'

'You think it's not dangerous sitting here waiting to see how things turn out?'

He took a deep breath and let it out slowly. 'Look, it's not that I don't think you can handle it. But you're right: All our lives are on the line here. We have to give ourselves the best possible chance. She may have to be killed.' His eyes bored into me. 'Are you prepared to do that?'

'If I have to.'

Shara had been watching the sparring. 'You know,' she said, 'I don't want to create more problems, but this babe is a psycho. She might be thinking this is a golden opportunity to get rid of the one person who ties her to it.'

'You think?' I asked.

'Why not? If I were in her place and operated the way she does, the minute Charlie checked in and told me everything here was taken care of, I'd say good-bye, Charlie, *hasta la vista*, and be on my way.'

Alex and I traded unsettled glances. 'She's got a point,' he said.

'So what do we do?'

'We better think about it before we call and tell her *anything*.'

'We need a better idea,' Shara said. 'And by the way, since my life is hanging here, too, if somebody's going to make a jump across to the *Lotus*, I want the most experienced person doing it.' She looked at me.

'Okay,' Alex said. 'Chase, I guess you've got it.'

'Good.'

Alex was standing back, away from the viewport, trying to look out without being visible to the other ship. 'You say the *Lotus* is small. Does it have any interior airlocks?'

'No. Just a cockpit, three small cabins, and a maintenance area.'

'So once you're inside, that's it. No obstacles?'

'None.'

'Okay. I have an idea.'

'Which is?'

'We have one thing going for us.'

'What's that?'

'Our main airlock's on our port side.'

'How's that an advantage?'

'The *Lotus* is off to starboard. She can't see it.'

'Okay,' said Alex, 'are we ready?' He was wearing Charlie's yellow pressure suit. Shara and I were in the *Spirit* suits.

'I think so,' I said.

'One question,' said Alex. 'When you talk to Kalu, is there any chance Windy will be able to listen in?'

'No. The hull should provide adequate shielding.'

'Don't forget that the launch doors will be open,' said Shara.

'That's right. I forgot.'

'Then she *will* be able to hear us.'

'Maybe we better assume she will.'

'Okay,' he said. 'Everybody keep it in mind. Are we ready?'

Nods all around.

'Let's move.'

Shara and Alex cycled through the cargo airlock onto the lower deck. I waited five minutes, spending most of my time watching the dwarf get closer. A storm was floating in its upper atmosphere, a circular smear, darker than the bloodred clouds around it.

I had Charlie's laser. I checked its power levels and tied it to my belt. Then I strapped on my air tanks and a thruster pack.

When the five minutes had elapsed, I told Kalu to get ready and opened a channel to the Lotus. '*Windy,*' said Kalu, in Charlie's voice, '*we have a problem.*'

'*What is it, Blink? What's taking so long?*'

I fed Kalu the reply. '*I took out the main boards. But they have a backup bridge on this thing. In the launch bay. In case of emergency.*'

'*Knock it out, too.*'

'*I'm working on it.*'

'*What do you mean, you're working on it, Blink? Just demolish it. Where's Benedict?*'

'*He's loose. He got clear.*'

'*Say again.*'

'*He got clear. Windy, the laser failed. That's why there's a problem.*'

'*Goddamn it, Blink. I told you to check everything.*'

'*It was charged. But the damned thing blew up in my hand.*'

'*Where are you now?*'

'*On the auxiliary bridge.*'

'*Okay. Do what you have to. Take the goddam thing apart physically. How about communications?*'

'*They've got a long-range capability.*'

'*Then don't let it happen. Kill them.*'

'*The two women are already dead.*'

'*At least you got that part of it right.*'

'*Benedict got down through the airlock when the laser went out.*'

'*You can't find him?*'

'*He's down here somewhere.*'

'All right. Don't worry about him. Just destroy the controls and make sure you get their communications. Let me know when it's done.'

I opened a circuit to Alex. Because of the possibility that Windy might overhear, we couldn't talk to one another. So I simply left it open for six seconds and shut it down. Alex would hear the carrier wave, and the six seconds told him phase one had gone according to schedule. Initiate phase two in five minutes.

I disconnected Kalu and put the chips that constituted his memory and programs into a pocket. Then I put on my helmet and went into the main airlock. Two minutes later I was outside, bathed in dark red light.

If Windy wasn't watching the *Spirit*, we had no problem. But we knew she would be. Probably, her attention would be riveted on the cargo airlock, where Charlie had made his entry and which was still open.

Precisely five minutes after I'd sent Alex the carrier wave, I sent a prerecorded message in Charlie's voice. '*Windy, I got the son of a bitch*.' Moments later, if our timing was right, two space-suited figures, one in Lotus yellow, the other in Survey green, fought their way past the open doors. The struggle went silent as, presumably, Charlie's radio was shattered. (There was no way we could realistically coordinate the sounds of combat with whatever Windy might be seeing.)

But it worked. '*Blink!*' she said. '*Kill him. Don't let him near the other bridge.*'

I climbed atop the *Spirit*, and launched myself toward the *Lotus*. '*Blink! Answer up! You got him. Finish him off!*'

The cargo airlock came into view as I cleared the hull and began to approach the yacht. I caught movement but couldn't quite make out what was happening.

For the minute or so it took me to get across I was horribly exposed. In full view. All she needed do was look away from the theatrics.

The *Lotus*'s airlock was shut. I landed beside it as gently as I could and touched the manual control. The lock opened, and I slipped inside.

The outer hatch closed and air pressure began to build. If Windy was paying any attention at all, she knew by then someone had invaded the airlock. And it shouldn't be hard to guess what was going on.

Her voice broke out of the link. '*Who's in there?*'

What a dip.

'*I know you're there, Alex. It won't do you any good.*'

I could hear her, tinkering with the hatch. Probably trying to figure out a way to seal it so I couldn't use it. But airlocks aren't designed that way. It's a safety feature. You can always open the inside hatch as long as the air pressure matches whatever's outside.

'*You might as well go back where you came from, Alex. You come through that door, you're dead.*' Her voice was pitched high.

Air pressure reached normal and I shut it off. I thought about what would be waiting when I opened the hatch. Nutcase with another laser. Or a scrambler.

A shoot-out could go either way, and there was too much at stake to take any chances. I thought about the question Alex had put to me. If it came to it, could I take Windy's life? And I realized the only certain way to save the situation was to do so.

I reversed the lock controls, putting it back on the decompression cycle. She saw immediately what I was doing.

'*That's smart,*' she said. '*Get out while you can, Alex.*'

I knew the makeup of the yacht. Beyond the bulkhead on my right was a cabin. A storage compartment lay to my left.

'*I assume you killed Blink,*' she said. '*And this has all been an elaborate charade. But no matter. He wasn't very competent anyhow, was he? How did you manage it?*'

The air pressure hit zero. I opened the outer hatch and looked across at the *Spirit*. Shara and Alex were standing near the cargo doors, watching. We'd agreed they were to stay clear until the thing got settled. Nothing they could do, in any case.

'*You don't want to talk to me, that's okay. It doesn't matter, Alex. I won't take offense. I understand you're upset. I'm sorry things are turning out this way. It's nothing personal. I just can't continue allowing you to rape the sites. You're too good at it.*'

'Hello, Windy,' I said. 'How's it going?'

'*Chase!*' She sounded horrified. '*He sent you? That coward sent you?*'

'It was my idea.'

'*He's even a bigger lout than I thought.*'

I wondered if Alex was getting this. 'He hasn't killed anybody.'

'*You're a cool one, aren't you, Chase? Lecturing me about morals. What a joke.*'

'I'm sorry you think so.'

I picked the right-hand side, the side that bordered the cabin. I released the laser from my belt, aimed it at the bulkhead, and pushed the firing stud.

'*Stay away, Chase. Go back where you came from.*'

The red beam snicked on and touched metal, about head high. The metal started to scorch. Black drops bubbled and ran down the bulkhead. I watched it with a sense of satisfaction. Pictured her standing on the other side. My longtime friend. God help me.

'*All right. Get out of the lock. I'm leaving. If you're still there, you're going to get bounced around pretty good.*'

I can't say I felt any sympathy for her.

'*Go, Chase. Get clear.*'

I lengthened the cut, drawing a line about a half meter long.

'*Are you out, Chase? Last chance.*'

I did a parallel cut an arm's length lower. More bubbles; more air.

'*Chase?*'

'I'm still here.'

Air pressure inside the yacht was thirty-two pounds per square inch. It began to push through into the lock.

A white lamp flashed on, started to blink. It signaled a maneuver coming up. Danger. Belt down.

'*What are you doing?*' she screamed. '*Chase, stop!*'

She was up front now, probably climbing into her seat, and suddenly getting warning lights. The deck trembled. The engines were coming on-line.

I made a vertical cut at one end of the parallel lines, connecting them.

'*Whatever you're doing, Chase, please stop. Please. I'll open up.*'

Good-bye, Windy, I thought. And started the fourth cut, to complete the rectangle.

The bulkhead blew open as we began to accelerate. I was thrown backward. A hurricane of clothing, plastic, and towels blasted into the airlock and were spewed out through the open hatch.

34

You may have your quantum-powered marvels, darting into the deepest vaults of the sky. You may jump between the galaxies, leaving light in your wake. As for me, I like to see what's out the window. Give me a brisk wind and a schooner under a full head of sail.

—Kasha Thilby,
Signs of Life, 1428

The acceleration pinned me to a bulkhead in the airlock, and I had to wait it out. After a few minutes, it shut down and I was able to get out of the lock and up to the cockpit. Windy was dead, tangled in the harness, frozen, asphyxiated, bloated. It didn't look like her anymore.

I pulled her clear and set her on the deck. The AI wasn't going to accept direction from a stranger, so I went off-line and started the long turn that would take me back to the *Spirit.* Then I used the *Lotus*'s comm system to contact the *Gonzalez,* and told them we needed assistance. Not an emergency, I added, because by that time we had things under control. They acknowledged and said they'd be on their way in about an hour.

I put Windy in one of the compartments and closed the door.

Needless to say, Shara and Alex were relieved when I pulled alongside the *Spirit* and took them off.

We closed the outer airlock hatch and repressurized. They listened to my account of what had happened, and Alex became solicitous. Was I okay? You did the right thing. No choice.

We debated going back to the *Spirit* to recover Charlie's body. But it entailed too much risk. We were getting deep into the dwarf's gravity well. So we took a pass and lifted away, while the *Spirit* continued its long plunge toward the bright red clouds.

Alex got on the circuit with Brankov and guaranteed he'd find the flight worthwhile. He refused to divulge details, but Brankov had no trouble guessing we'd found Balfour.

We welded a patch over the section I'd burned out of the airlock, restoring it to working order.

'I think it's time,' Alex said, 'that we take a look at Balfour.'

The optical equipment on board the *Lotus* was minimal. The yacht had a single telescope, intended for navigation only, which meant no serious long-range capability and no fine-tuning. We couldn't make out much planetary detail until we were virtually on top of the place. The atmosphere, a gauzy cloud-filled envelope, looked terrestrial enough. Gradually two island-continents and a vast globe-encircling ocean came into view. We could see a few storms. Polar ice caps appeared. And mountain chains and rivers.

'I guess they knew what they were doing,' said Alex.

Shara looked thoughtful. 'I don't see how it could have made any difference. They couldn't have survived the transition phase. But it would have been a nice try.'

Alex asked again about ground conditions while the world was being hauled out of orbit.

'It's unlikely any of the larger land animals could have survived,' Shara said. 'After the initial shock, planetary rotation would have been disrupted while it went into tidal lock. That triggers every-thing. They'd have had turbulent oceans, supersonic hurricanes, volcanic eruptions, you name it.'

'And this would last—?'

'Forty years. Maybe fifty. Maybe longer. It's not my specialty, but I'd guess it would continue well beyond any capability a colony would have for survival.'

'It looks placid now,' I said.

Blue water, clouds, river valleys. Even the jungles looked inviting. 'It's exactly the right distance from the dwarf,' said Shara.

'For reasonable ground temperatures?'

'Yes. On the facing side, of course. The back side of the world will be pretty cold.'

'Would the ocean freeze?'

'Don't know.'

Clouds were, for the most part, white cumulus, but colored by the crimson glow of the pseudosun. The storms we'd seen through the scope drifted across the broad expanse of the ocean. Snow lay on some of the higher peaks. 'You were right about the jungle,' said Alex. It appeared to be spread across both landmasses.

The *Lotus* burned an exorbitant amount of fuel. Alex had been anxious to get to Balfour, so we came in at a pretty good clip. 'I'm going to use the planet to slow us down,' I said. 'We'll go around, about three-quarters of an orbit. A lot of it over the cold side. I'm sorry about that, but there's not much I can do.'

'Okay,' said Alex. 'What then?'

'We'll come out with an angle that'll allow us to go into orbit around the dwarf. When we've shed enough velocity we'll come back here. Less stress on everybody and a lot easier on the fuel.'

Alex looked wistfully at the arc of the world. 'Wish we had a lander,' he said.

'The *Gonzalez* will have one.'

Shara laughed. 'I'm sure Emil will be happy to accompany you down.'

We were in orbit around the dwarf when the *Gonzalez* contacted us and announced it was in the neighborhood. '*What* is *that*

393

thing?' asked Brankov, referring to the dwarf. '*Is that the surprise you promised us?*'

'Yes,' said Alex. 'That's it. Or part of it, anyhow.'

'*What's the rest of it?*'

'I'm not sure where you are just now, Emil. But can you see the blue planet in orbit around it?'

'*Negative.*' His response took more than a minute. So the *Gonzalez* was still at a considerable distance. He was wearing a Beron jacket, one of those stiff models with pockets everywhere. '*Is there a blue planet here somewhere?*' I wasn't sure whether he was asking us or his pilot.

'In orbit around the dwarf,' said Alex. 'A living world.'

'*Are you serious?*'

'Absolutely.'

'*Okay. That's interesting. What's it have to do with us?*'

'It used to be in the Tinicum system.'

Brankov grinned. It was a big, what-time-does-the-celebration-start expression.

A few hours later we slipped into an equatorial orbit around Balfour. We were over the dark side during those early minutes, and could see nothing below, except land and water.

We watched the sun rise, and crossed the terminator into the daylight. It was our first leisurely look at the world. Alex was glued to the viewport, and Shara was watching the monitor. They both reacted at the same time, Alex pumping a fist while Shara told me in an excited voice to look.

I saw an inland area on one of the island continents. Other than that—?

Shara tried to enhance. Alex waved me closer to the viewport. Get a better angle, look, down there.

The jungle seemed to have been cleared away and there was a cluster of straight lines. Near a large lake.

'A city?' I said.

'And there,' said Alex. More lines, farther north. Embracing a river.

I'm not sure what I saw in his eyes at that moment. Usually, when we find a new site, he assumes his modest genius appearance. Sometimes, if it's been a long hunt, he doesn't bother, and there's simply a sense of triumph. But I don't know what it was that time. Delight. Sadness. Wistfulness. Exhilaration. All wrapped together.

'More,' Shara said. Along the southern coastline, but still in the terminator. We counted five clusters.

'Nothing on the other big island,' said Alex.

'That's because it's in direct sunlight,' said Shara. 'It's too warm. Everything we've seen is in the twilight zone. That's where the weather would be most comfortable.'

We passed over and lost them. The *Lotus* didn't have a telescope that could look down to the rear. Alex confronted Shara with a huge smile. 'So much for the tidal waves and tornadoes,' he said.

She was frowning. 'Shouldn't have been possible.'

'Sure it was. They rode it out in orbit. They built modules on Margolia, hauled everything over here, and assembled an orbiter. They stayed in it until things calmed down.'

'For *forty* years?' Shara and I both blurted it out. Nobody was buying that story.

'Yes. That's why they needed the greenhouses. Look, they needed to get the *Seeker* under way as quickly as possible, so it could get to Earth and, they hoped, trigger a rescue effort. They expected there'd be some survivors on Margolia. But they probably didn't trust the *Seeker*. It was their best shot, but they weren't sure. They knew Balfour would eventually become livable and that conditions on Margolia would be extreme. So, before cannibalizing the *Bremerhaven*, they used it to bring some people here. *Then* they stripped it and sent the *Seeker* on its way.

'The Balfour group stayed on board. In orbit. Forty, fifty years. Whatever it took. When conditions settled down on the ground, they were able to go down and establish themselves.'

'That's why there was no lander,' I said.

'Right. It's below us, somewhere.'

'How many you figure there were?' I asked.

'Don't know. Not many, I'd think. As few as they could get away with. Only a few hundred, probably. Maybe not that many. The fewer they had, the better their chances. What's the minimum number you'd have to have to allow safe reproduction?'

Nobody knew.

Shara stared at the blue world. 'Pity,' she said.

'Why? What do you mean?' I asked.

'The cavalry's a little late.'

Suddenly there was ocean before us again. Behind us, the dwarf-sun sank toward the rim of the planet. The sea was blue and polished and quiet. We rushed toward the darkness.

'That one area,' said Shara, 'is probably the only piece of real estate on the planet that has comfortable temperatures. I'll tell you what I think—'

We never found out because she broke off and *squealed* and pointed at the screen.

Something in the ocean.

'Can you enhance it?' she asked. 'It looks—'

Like a *ship*.

It wasn't much more than a wake. The object leaving it was too small to make out.

'Might be a large fish,' said Alex. I tried to get a better picture but it went fuzzy. 'Damn this thing,' he said.

Confirmation came from the *Gonzalez*, which was, as it approached, able to use its telescopes. I'll never forget Brankov's first words: *'My God, Alex, they're alive down there.'*

35

Human existence is girt round with mystery: the narrow region of our experience is a small island in the midst of a boundless sea. To add to the mystery, the domain of our earthly existence is not only an island in infinite space, but also in infinite time. The past and the future are alike shrouded from us: we neither know the origin of anything which is, nor its final destination.

—John Stuart Mill,
Three Essays on Religion, 1874 C.E.

Who would have thought?

The *Gonzalez*'s sensors and telescopes keyed on the planetary surface and they picked up images that were relayed to the *Lotus.* Cities. Bridge and highways. Harbors and parks. Something that looked like a trail arced across a canyon. And I thought I caught a glimpse of an aircraft.

Brankov called again: *'There's an electronic cloud. They're talking to each other!'* We heard cheering in the background.

I don't know how to describe the exhilaration of those moments. I almost wiped out my discomfort over the events of the preceding hours. It was a good time. I took a moment to congratulate Alex, to kiss him and hang on to him in the way sometimes we try to hang on to a special moment, hoping it will never end.

A tidal wave of news broke over us. The *Gonzalez* picked up video signals, music, voices. I tried to get some of it directly using the yacht's equipment. The sky was filled with traffic.

Alex was ecstatic. Shara pronounced herself dumbfounded. 'They've been isolated out here more than half of recorded history,' she said. 'These people could not have survived.' She literally *glowed*.

A few hours later, the *Gonzalez* came alongside, and we crossed over to handshakes and claps on the back. Have a drink. How'd you guys ever figure this out? They've got satellites! Look at this over here: A ball game. With three teams on the field. How long did you say they've been out here?

They were throwing the incoming images across banks of monitors and relaying some of it back to Survey.

Alex looked happier than I'd ever seen him. He accepted congratulations from everybody. Shara and I got smooched by every guy on the ship. They weren't fooling anybody. But what the hell, how often did something like that happen?

Shara's eyes were bright with emotion. When things calmed down a bit she came over. 'You did good, Chase,' she said.

'It was Alex,' I told her. 'I'd have let it go a long time ago.'

'Yeah. But I think you deserve a large piece of the credit.' She grinned. 'My buddy.'

Those first minutes were filled with images: a tower that had to be part of a radio transmission network, a beach loaded with people, a park with fountains and broad lawns and children. 'I guess the lesson,' one of the researchers said, 'is that we're tough little monkeys. We don't go down easily.'

Brankov stood erect and beaming like a conquering hero. 'Biggest discovery in human history,' he said. They raised their cups to Alex, the Margolians, Shara, and finally to me. As I write these words, I've a picture of that glorious moment on the wall at my right hand.

We found additional cities. They were all located along the terminator, where weather would be most accommodating. Some had tall needle towers like the City on the Crag, some had vast parks, a couple seemed simply to have spread out haphazardly. One resembled a vast wheel. In each of these places, the inhabitants had beaten back the jungle, literally walled it off.

We saw more aircraft.

And listened to radio broadcasts. 'Can't understand any of it,' said a frustrated Brankov. 'I wonder if they know we're here.'

The AI was assigned to acquire a translation capability.

Brankov had undergone a transformation. The formality and reserve were gone. He stood revealed as a collection of enthusiasms. Loved his work. Loved being out in the field. Loved being on hand when things were happening. Loved his lunch. I'm not sure I ever knew anyone maintain so high a level of exhilaration through so prolonged a period. That first night he tried to talk Shara into his bed. She ducked, and he tried his luck with me. 'It would be a way to celebrate,' he told me. 'A way to make the event unforgettable.' As if it weren't already. While he waited for a response, he added, 'This seems like a moment when anything is possible.'

All in all, it was a magnificent time.

A debate started over whether it would be prudent to pay our groundside cousins a visit. 'They're an *alien* culture,' one of Brankov's specialists argued. 'Doesn't matter that they're human. We should let them be, to develop as they wish. They should be let alone.'

I wasn't really invited to comment, but I did anyhow. I pointed out that I didn't know anything about impeding development, but going down to say hello to people who'd have no clue who we were or what we wanted, could be dangerous. 'We might get a missile up our rear end,' I said. 'They've been alone a long time. Strangers dropping out of the sky might make them nervous.'

It was Alex who made the decisive observation: 'They're not supposed to be out here. Leave them here, and they'll remain isolated. They can't see any other worlds. They probably do not know where they came from. Probably think they're native to Balfour. Let them be, and they're stuck here.'

There was a tall, angular woman who looked as if she worked out a lot. She was an archeologist, whose name I've forgotten, determined that we would go down. And that she would accompany the effort. What were we afraid of? For God's sake, all you had to do, she said, was look at the images. Kids in parks, people walking the streets. These were clearly not barbarians.

I wondered if the various bloodthirsty governments down the ages had made it a point to keep everyone out of the parks and off the streets, but I let it ride.

She succeeded in making all the males feel as if they were cowardly, so they decided that sure, it was their clear duty to make our presence known. We'd take our chances, what the hell.

Even Alex, who's usually shrewder than that, bought in to direct contact.

So we organized a mission. Brankov was literally drooling at the prospect of descending onto a capital lawn somewhere, getting out, and saying hello. The female archeologist talked as if there'd be a band and a cheering crowd.

The lander could accommodate seven, plus a pilot. Alex, of course, automatically could claim a seat. Did I wish to go?

I preferred to hear what they were talking about on the surface before I got into anything. I had this image of savages rushing Captain Cook. 'No, thanks,' I said. 'I'll wait here. Let me know how it turns out.'

Shara said she'd be happy to take my place.

Brankov and four other archeologists, including the female, would fill out the mission. They were anxious to get started. There was even some talk of not waiting for the translation capability. But Alex took a stand on that. Let's hear what they're saying before we do anything rash, he insisted.

We estimated a population of about 20 million. The inhabitants didn't have an extensive land surface at their disposal, of course.

The night side of the planet was too cold, the side facing the dwarf, too hot. That wasn't to say no one could live out there. But it took a pioneer.

We loaded the lander with supplies and settled back to wait for the AI.

I know this is inconsistent, but I was annoyed that they'd leave me behind. I'd expected Alex to put up an argument when I backed off. If he had, maybe I'd have caved. But I'd have liked to see the effort.

While they waited for the AI to get a handle on the language – '*I don't have translation software*,' he'd explained, '*so I have to improvise*' – I went back to the *Lotus*, tied Kalu into the yacht's base system, and said hello. He thanked me for the rescue and, at my request, produced Harry.

Harry wore an all-weather jacket and looked resigned. 'I've got good news,' I told him.

Something very much like suspicion crept into his eyes. '*What?*' he asked.

'They're here,' I said. 'The colony survived.'

The relays from the *Gonzalez*'s telescopes were flickering across the monitor. Kids. Boats. Farms. Aircraft. Cities. Roadways.

'*I've prayed for this, but did not dare hope.*' I wondered if the prayers of an avatar counted for anything. '*I would not have believed it possible.*'

I described how they'd done it, and he nodded as if he'd known all the time they'd survive.

'*Do they know who they are? Where they came from?*'

'We don't know yet. That may be expecting too much.'

'*Okay. I don't suppose you know anything about Samantha and the boys?*'

'No,' I said. 'Harry, it's been so long.'

'*Of course.*'

'Maybe there'll be a record somewhere.'

* * *

Alex called from the *Gonzalez*. '*We've got the translator*,' he said. '*We're going down.*'

'Be careful,' I told him. 'Tell them I said hello.'

I crossed back to the other ship because I didn't want to be alone while it was happening. I got there a few minutes before launch and just in time to hear the AI stop the proceedings dead in their tracks.

'*We are receiving a transmission from the ground,*' he said. '*It is directed at us and addressed to "Unidentified Vehicle."*'

'From whom?' asked Alex, who was struggling into a pressure suit.

'*Do you wish me to ask?*' said the AI.

Brankov and Alex looked at each other, and simultaneous grins appeared. 'Put him through,' said Brankov.

It was a woman. Gray hair, stern features, intense green eyes. She stood beside a cabinet with glass doors. The cabinet was filled with plates and goblets. She looked across the short space of the common room at Brankov and then at two or three of the others. She finally settled on Brankov. She asked a question in an unfamiliar language, and the AI, translating in a female voice, said, '*Who are you?*'

Brankov signaled for Alex to reply. He took a deep breath. 'My name is Alex Benedict,' he said.

'*No. I mean, who are you?*'

'*I'm sorry,*' said the AI. '*I do not think I'm getting the translation quite right.*'

Alex laughed. It was okay. He kept his eyes on the woman. 'We've come looking for you,' he said. 'It's a long story.'

Epilog

Harry's colonials had no idea who they were. The world on which they lived was simply *The World*. There was no other. The great migration across the stars had been lost, but the episode of the brown dwarf and their own descent onto Balfour was dimly remembered as part of a sacred text. The ancient writings maintained they had been brought into the world by a company of divine beings, across a shining bridge. That an earlier attempt had failed when the recipients proved ungrateful and proud. And that the divinities would return one day to lead a select few onward to paradise.

Only a few still believed any of that. Margolian science, thousands of years ago, discovered there were two mutually exclusive biosystems in the world, one embracing humans, a wide variety of edible fruits and vegetables, and certain animals and fish. Everything else was of a different order altogether. Food from one system did not nourish creatures from the other, nor could diseases generally strike across the boundary. Biologists explained it by concluding life had gotten started twice. But a few true believers maintained that the dual stream of life, as it was known, showed the original second-creation story to be valid.

Alex had told the woman at the other end of the comm link the entire story. She'd listened, gone pale and looked skeptical by turns. She'd brought in someone else, a tall, glowering man who behaved as if we were trying to push real estate, and Alex had told the story again.

And still again, to an even taller man in a blue robe.

Emil – we were by then on first-name terms – took over, and talked to someone else, short, dumpy, red-haired, dressed in white. The offices kept getting bigger, so we knew we were moving up the chain.

Between the redheaded guy and whatever was going to come next, we intercepted a video broadcast. And there was Alex's conversation with the woman, explaining how everybody on the planet had come from a place called Earth, that they'd been missing for hundreds of generations, and that the visitors were delighted to have found their long-lost brothers and sisters.

Smile, Alex. You're on Universal TV.

Despite the fears of some on board that there'd be rioting in the streets, the Margolians accepted the assertions with equanimity. Within the next hour we picked up televised debates and commentary on whether the story of the visitors was credible or preposterous. Within thirty hours we'd received an invitation to visit the community leaders.

The landing party were received as friends. The Margolians had a good laugh at our speech patterns and the way we dressed. We found their food impossible to get down. Prominent men and women were invited to say hello, and they had questions for us designed to elicit the truth. They also took tissue samples and, later that day, announced that we were indeed kin.

It never got dark along the terminator. The trees whispered in the westerly wind, the sun remained permanently affixed just over the horizon. It always felt like early evening.

The Margolians had sent ships into the icy waters of the dark side. They'd established bases, sometimes for military reasons, but usually for scientific purposes, at various points on the globe. They'd developed different languages, different religions, different political systems. That had resulted in wars during their early years, but they'd long since banished armed conflict. There were too few habitable places in the world. Common sense dictated peaceful societies. They'd developed manufacturing capabilities so early there was no record when it had happened.

Because there were no seasons, and no day-night cycle, they acquired some curious ideas about time. It existed only as a measurement of duration between events. It was purely a human contrivance. There had never been a second Einstein.

On the whole, they've done well for themselves. (None among them, I understand, would recognize the name *Margolian*.) They've prospered with limited natural resources. They've established democratic governments throughout the *Bakara*, the terminator, that happy zone where sunlight is indirect and it is always early evening.

Today, of course, you can see replicas of Margolian statuary and other art forms, and even a few originals, at major museums throughout the Confederacy. Some of their architectural designs have been adopted in places as far away as Toxicon and the Spinners. Last year's number one best-selling novel was by a native of the Bakara. And I should add that their average life span is almost twelve years longer than ours.

They never got off-world. There was no moon, and they could see no targets for exploration. Knowledge of the outside universe appears to have been lost early, and the conviction that theirs was the only world remains hard even now for many of them to shake. To this day, there are Margolians who insist that the Visitation, as they call our arrival, never really happened. That it's all a conspiracy of some sort.

Despite their advances in so many fields, astronomy remained in a dark age. The nature of the lights in the night sky (which were, of course, visible only to those who ventured out onto the dark side) was for them an enduring mystery, one whose solution defied generations of scientists.

The first translations of Margolian histories began to appear within a few months after we got home. They have a decent record of events going back almost five thousand years. Before that, their history becomes spotty and eventually vanishes into a welter of myth. The earliest city of which they know, Argol, was destroyed in the wars and is now the subject of a major archeological effort.

Their history, in its general outline, is not unlike that of humanity at home. There were invasions and massacres, dictators and dark ages and rebellions. And an occasional renaissance. Philosophies, some rational, others destructive, had their day. Religions seem to have been there from the beginning. They were tolerant of each other during their early years, oppressive and exclusive as the years passed and, I suppose, as memories of Earth faded.

There's a fair amount of talk now that we'll be able to learn a great deal about human nature by comparing the experience on Balfour with that of society at large.

As I write this, Alex is there. He got interested in some of their myths, which refer to a lost city. Sakata is said to have been an advanced civilization built, for reasons no one can imagine, on the night side. Alex thinks it might have been the original base, established before the catastrophe. He says he knows where to look.

I haven't said anything to him about Harry because he would accuse me of being sentimental. But I hope he succeeds and that he finds evidence that Samantha, Harry Jr., and Tommy made the flight to Balfour. I know Harry himself wouldn't have gone. Not if he's the man he seems to be.

I'm happy to report that the Wescotts' reputation has prospered. Their achievement in finding the *Seeker* has more than overshadowed any question of their using the discovery for selfish purposes.

Blink had several names. He turned out to be a renegade navy pilot who had already been convicted of murder for hire. He'd undergone personality reconstruction, but obviously his old tendencies resurfaced, and he sold his services to Windy. He remains the best known case during modern times of recidivism after a mind wipe.

Amy Kolmer got a lot of money out of the cup, but I understand she is broke again.

Hap Plotzky was convicted of two more assaults after my experience with him. After our return from Margolia, he asked me to be a character witness at his trial, one of the more brazen acts I've seen in my life. Currently, he does hedge trimming and general yard work in Kappamong, in the Kawalla Mountains. He has no memory of his years as a burglar and a thug, and he thinks his name is Jasperson. Last year, the townspeople named him one of their one hundred model citizens.

Next time you're in Mute territory you might enjoy visiting the Museum of Alien Life-forms on Provno. They have an entire wing devoted to Margolia. And avatars of Alex and me. Counting the Neandertal, that makes three of us.

The Devil's Eye
Jack McDevitt

Alex Benedict receives a cryptic message asking for help from celebrated writer Vicki Greene, who then voluntarily has her memory erased. She has no memory of her past life, or even of her plea for assistance. But she has transferred an enormous sum of money to Alex, also without explanation.

The answers to this mystery lie on the most remote of human worlds. There Alex and his pilot companion, Chase Kolpath, will uncover a secret connected to a decades-old political upheaval, a secret that somebody desperately wants hidden, though the price of that silence is unimaginable.

Praise for Jack McDevitt:

'The logical heir to Isaac Asimov and Arthur C. Clarke'
Stephen King

'Another highly intelligent, absorbing portrayal of the far future from a leading creator of such tales'
Booklist

'Combines hard science fiction with mystery and adventure in a wild tour of the distant future. Stellar plotting, engaging characters, and a mastery of storytelling'
Library Journal (starred review)

978 1 4722 0313 7

headline